WE
HEAR
VOICES

WE HEAR VOICES

EVIE GREEN

BERKLEY
NEW YORK

BERKLEY
An imprint of Penguin Random House LLC
penguinrandomhouse.com

Copyright © 2020 by Emily Barr
Penguin Random House supports copyright. Copyright fuels creativity, encourages diverse voices,
promotes free speech, and creates a vibrant culture. Thank you for buying an authorized edition
of this book and for complying with copyright laws by not reproducing, scanning, or distributing
any part of it in any form without permission. You are supporting writers and allowing
Penguin Random House to continue to publish books for every reader.

BERKLEY and the BERKLEY & B colophon
are registered trademarks of Penguin Random House LLC.

Library of Congress Cataloging-in-Publication Data

Names: Green, Evie, author.
Title: We hear voices / Evie Green.
Description: First edition. | New York : Berkley, 2020.
Identifiers: LCCN 2020002363 (print) | LCCN 2020002364 (ebook) |
ISBN 9780593098301 (hardcover) | ISBN 9780593098325 (ebook)
Subjects: GSAFD: Horror fiction.
Classification: LCC PR6102.A77 W4 2020 (print) | LCC PR6102.A77 (ebook) |
DDC 823/.92—dc23
LC record available at https://lccn.loc.gov/2020002363
LC ebook record available at https://lccn.loc.gov/2020002364

Printed in the United States of America
1   3   5   7   9   10   8   6   4   2

Jacket image of child by Cat Simpson / Shutterstock
Jacket design by Katie Anderson
Book design by Laura K. Corless

For Craig, my husband

AUTHOR'S NOTE

This book is arriving in a very different world from the one in which it was written. When I finished writing, late in 2019, the novel coronavirus was just beginning to appear on the horizon, and we had no idea about what was to come. So I find this post-pandemic novel being sent out into a pandemic-altered world. As I write, the world has just passed one million cases of COVID-19 and life has changed dramatically for all of us.

This book is not a response to any of that. It was already written. It's just a piece of fanciful fiction inspired by a John Wyndham novel I read when I was nine.

To all the health workers, all the scientists working on a response to the virus, and particularly to my friend Kevin Fong, who talked space travel through with me in that different era and who is currently working flat-out in London fighting the virus: thank you more than words can say.

Evie Green
April 2020

WE
HEAR
VOICES

ONE

Rachel threw the medical mask on the floor, climbed out of the quarantine suit, and took her son in her arms. He was so light and bony that it was like picking up a stray cat. She buried her face in his hair. He smelled like sickness and plague.

Billy had been sick for a month. For almost all of that time she had believed he would get better, but tonight she knew he wouldn't. Rachel was living in a single moment: she felt it had lasted a thousand years, and she wanted to stretch it to infinity, because she couldn't bear to step into the moment that would come next. She bargained with the universe. She would take any future it could throw at her as long as it involved Billy staying alive.

She was supposed to wear her full mask and quarantine suit, and she had done it until now. She had followed the rules to the letter, trusted the government, done everything she was supposed to do to take care of her boy, and none of it had worked.

She sat on his bed and shuffled back so she was leaning on the wall with Billy lying in her arms. Downstairs, she could hear Al talking to Beth, and Henry talking to Nina. She loosened her grip a little, because she didn't want to hurt Billy, and she kissed him all over his face, but he didn't respond. He was breathing, though. Those sickly breaths were still coming.

Billy's bedroom was tiny, with a single bed, a bedside table, a chair, and a chest of drawers. The walls were a dirty white (the landlord wouldn't let her paint them, and when she tried to clean them, the paint rubbed off), but she and Billy had covered them with drawings, posters, things he liked. All that was gone now. Rachel had taken it all down and put it into a box, then washed the walls with disinfectant, like the rules said. Once, a million years ago, the room had been a giant mess, with Legos and dirty clothes and drawings and books all over the floor. Now it was sterile, pristine. The government guide to dealing with the pandemic was on the bedside table, along with a glass of the powdered drink that had come in sachets with the guidelines, with a metal straw and a pile of medication that was mainly placebo.

She had done everything by the book. She had sent Nina to live with her dad, even though that had almost killed her. This room was separated from the rest of the house with two sets of the plastic sheets the government had sent out, and the only person who ever walked through them was Rachel, and then (until now) only in her quarantine suit and mask. It had been logistically difficult, with baby Beth, but she had done it.

Tonight, though, they had taken turns using the suit. She had lent it to her ex-husband so that he could say good-bye to Billy, their son. She had sat downstairs with a cup of tea while Henry spent an hour with him. Then Al, and then Nina had gone in, one by one, and now there were only Rachel and Billy in the world. She was glad she had ditched the suit and the mask. She was just herself now, wearing her baggy sweater and pajama trousers, holding her child. Billy needed to see his mother as he died, rather than a figure in a space suit, and he was hardly going to be infectious now. She picked up his toy rabbit from the pillow and put it on his chest.

He took in a breath. Nothing happened. He breathed out. Still alive. *Billy is alive,* she thought. *Still Billy right now.*

She would carry on living after this, because she had to. She had to do it for Beth and for Nina. She thought of the times she had shouted at Billy for being slow, or had been cross with him for being cheeky or for his table manners. What, she wondered, had been the point? What had been the fucking point? If she could go back, she would let him spend all six years climbing trees and watching telly and eating cake. She would grant him six years of perfect happiness, even though she supposed that might mean staying with Henry for longer than she would have liked.

Billy was so pale that his face was a bluish green color. His hair was slicked back with sweat. His temperature soared while he shivered. She waited for the next breath. When it didn't come, she pulled him tighter against her chest, trying to use her heart to jump-start his.

"Billy," she whispered into his hair. "Billy, it's Mum. Stay. Stay with me." She looked up, her child in her arms. "Universe," she muttered. "God," she added, hedging her bets. "Allah. Whoever you are. Give me Billy back. Give me my Billy, and I promise I will do anything. I'll sell my soul to anyone. Let me keep him."

Nothing changed.

Millions of people had died. Billy would add one to the number of casualties. Children under ten were particularly at risk. *Plus one* for the children-under-ten statistics.

"Please," she said. She kissed his head one more time. One more. One more. "I love you, Billy." She pushed her face into his and rubbed her warm cheek on his cooling one and tried to imagine her life without him.

He wasn't moving. He wasn't breathing. He had . . .

"Let me keep him," she said. "I don't care what else. Let me have Billy."

His body jerked in her arms, and he opened his eyes, just a fraction. She felt his lungs expand. She heard him exhale, felt the sour breath on her face. He inhaled again with a rattling noise, a vibration. He was breathing.

"Mumma," he said, his eyes still closed.

Downstairs, the baby started to cry.

· · ·

Nina was downstairs, waiting. Her father and stepfather were waiting. Their stilted conversation had long since dried up. Dad had never been in this house before, and he would, she knew, have raised an eyebrow at its shabbiness under normal circumstances. But these circumstances were not normal. Right now Al was getting Beth ready for bed, and Dad and Nina were staring at their phones because it was easier to sit in silence if you had something to look at.

"Cup of tea?" she said.

"Sure," said Dad, forcing a smile. "Thanks."

Billy was going to die. She knew (because how could you not?) that the trajectory he had taken would end that way. That was how it went. The pandemic had arrived, and the people were dying, and somehow she, Nina Stevens, was waiting for her mother or her stepfather to walk into the room and tell her that her brother was dead.

Everyone knew people who had died. From her observations, about one in five people who caught the J5X virus died from it. That was what had happened at school, and as the illness was no respecter of money or class, it was about the same at her boyfriend's very much more exclusive school. Even Princess Louisa, the heir to the throne, had disappeared from view a few months ago; she had been only a little older than Billy and had obviously died, although it had been kept secret because of public morale, et cetera. People got ill, with a soaring fever, and quite a lot of them died. Schools had closed, opened again, closed, and then opened. Nothing really seemed to change the way the virus traveled.

Nina had been reading about the bubonic plague. If you'd caught the plague in this same city, nearly seven hundred years earlier, your chances of dying would have been more than half. There had been other pandemics since then over the years, some more severe than others. No one seemed to know quite why this one was called J5X, and most people ignored that name. As it became more familiar, it had become almost universally known as "flu."

She had seen her brother tonight for the first time since the beginning of December, last year. But it had not been Billy. He had been a husk, barely there at all. In a sense, to Nina, he was already dead. It had been the worst Christmas ever.

Mum had called her yesterday. "Come over," she'd said, her voice husky. "And . . . I think you need to bring Dad. Billy won't last the night. You need to see Billy to say . . ." She hadn't been able to say the word. Nina had tried to be strong, but as soon as the call ended, she had cried and cried and cried. She went to Dad for comfort because he was all she had, and he hugged her and pretended that Billy would be fine. Then he agreed that they should both go to Mum's house to see him, and now here they were, in the rented house with its drafts and its peeling paint, letting their tea go cold.

But Mum stayed upstairs until after midnight, and then when she did come down, the news was different.

On that same night, in a different part of London, a man was sitting at his wife's bedside. Her face was waxy, her skin white, with blotches that sometimes looked pink, sometimes almost blue. She was sixty-seven years old and she, too, was dying of the flu. He pushed the hair back from her face and talked without stopping.

"Imogen," he said. "Immy, I've been an idiot. You are the most wonderful person in the world. I love you. Please, don't go. Please. Please. Please, don't, darling. Please, stay and let me look after you. I'll make it up to you, I swear. Please, stay with me."

He said it all, and he meant every word of it.

TWO

Two days later, Al came home furious. He walked straight into the living room, switched the television on, and flicked around with the remote until he found the news.

"Sorry," he said to Rachel. He was still standing up, and he paused and kissed her. "So rude. I'm really sorry. How's Billy? Where's Beth?"

Al and Billy had lived in the same house for all these weeks, but they had barely seen each other since the terrible night when they'd realized Billy was sick. Billy had lived in his tiny sterile zone, and until they had taken turns to go in and say good-bye two nights ago, it was always just Rachel who put on the suit to go in.

"Billy's sitting up in bed," she said, smiling. "He's watching cartoons. Beth's in the kitchen playing with bricks. What's the matter?"

"I saw a news flash on a screen," Al said, sitting down to watch. "He got off! The bastard got away with it! That's what it said."

"No."

She went to fetch Beth, who shouted in delight at the sight of her father. Al set her on his lap, and they watched the news report together.

They had been following this trial through Billy's illness; it had been a landmark case. This man, Ben Alford, was probably not much older than Rachel was, but he had the red face and the air of entitlement of a powerful man from any era. He could have been a Victorian mill owner, a medieval baron, a disaster capitalist from the more recent past. The gist of the case had been that he employed many thousands of people in this city and had invented a new scheme whereby he was gleefully paying them nothing at all.

For the past few years, Starcom had been buying up housing all over London. They would aggressively step in and make impossible-to-refuse offers for whole terraces, blocks of flats, anything at all. Then they would rebuild the property as "workers' accommodation." They gave their workers a place to live and paid them in vouchers and free things. "Cash-free living," he called it, as if that were a positive. A group of citizens had crowdfunded to challenge the legality of the "worklifeplus" scheme, and now, it seemed, they had lost.

Al, who worked with the homeless and saw exactly what happened when you bought up all the affordable housing from a city that was already struggling, had been desperate for Alford to lose.

"Mr. Alford is delighted to be vindicated," said a spokeswoman with shiny hair and a steely smile. "He looks forward to expanding the worklifeplus program across the city and beyond."

"Our landlord is going to sell to Alford," said Al. "I know he is. That's why he's letting the place fall apart around our ears."

M umma!" Billy was shouting down the stairs. She ran up, leaving Al swearing at the television, and Beth, who was eight months old, attempting to join in, yelling at the screen. Beth seemed to be as angry as her father about this.

"How are you doing, darling?" Rachel said, then kissed Billy's head and straightened his duvet. He was not, in fact, watching cartoons on the old iPad his father had brought over for him, but was watching the same news report about Ben Alford. He looked pale, with blue bags under his eyes, but he was bright eyed and interested in everything.

"Doing OK. Thank you," he said. "This man is boring. I want to see the proper news." Billy considered "proper news" to be anything about the J5X virus or the space program. He wanted to know everything there was to know about the thing that had happened to him. He studied the reporters who stood outside government departments talking about the epidemic. He nodded along to what they were saying, writing down numbers and random words, with no context, on a piece of paper by his bed.

She would have preferred him to be watching cartoons, sleeping, or drawing meaningless pictures, but she wasn't going to complain. She still couldn't believe the miracle.

"How are you doing?" she said, taking the iPad out of his hand and putting it on the table. "Warm enough? Hungry? You know it's nearly sleep time."

"I think we would like a drink, please," said Billy. "Can we have some hot lemon?"

Rachel smiled. "Of course you can!" She didn't pick up on his use of the royal "we."

"Do you know what astronauts drink on the space station? They drink their own wee," Billy said. "It did say so on the telly. And their sweat. Next year's mission will be to the Rock. It's an asteroid and a launchpad."

Rachel wrinkled up her face. "You're very well-informed. Seriously? They drink wee and sweat? That doesn't sound very nice. They must filter it."

"Nina will have to drink her wee when she is an astronaut," he said, and he giggled. "Wee! For a drink! For Nina! Yuck!" He laughed and laughed.

Rachel sat on his bed and laughed along with him. "They *must* filter it. And treat it before they drink it."

"Yes, but it is still wee."

"Well, that applies to all our water, doesn't it? Sewage gets recycled back into tap water." She didn't like this idea, so she stopped talking. Billy needed lots of fluids, and she shouldn't be putting him off. "Anyway, I'll get your drink. Any food? You could have a banana, you know." She could smell their jacket potatoes cooking in the oven. Billy hadn't eaten anything solid yet.

"No food. Thank you. Not today."

The next day Billy said: "You know you said there was a banana?"

It wasn't easy to get them anymore, but Al had found some brownish ones in the supermarket months ago and had brought them home in triumph. Rachel remembered her own mother feeding her mashed bananas when she was recuperating from anything, and to her they were the taste of convalescence. She had kept them in the freezer for ages, waiting for Billy to be able to eat again.

"Yes!" said Rachel. "Yes. Would you like one?"

"Bananas have good things in them, and Delfy says I need to eat food so she can see how my digestions works and so I can get strong again."

Rachel laughed. "*Who* says that?"

"Delfy."

"Who's Delfy?"

"Delfy is my friend." He paused. "Delfy says hello to you, Mummy."

"Does he live in your head?"

"Not he! She! Yes, at the moment, she does."

Rachel sat on the edge of the bed. "Oh, good! Tell Delfy hello back from me. I'll get you a banana, and you can give some to Delfy, too. Shall I mash it up?"

"Yes. I will have it all myself because Delfy is watching in me. She doesn't eat food. She wants to see *me* eat food."

"Well," said Rachel, "that's perfect. You can eat enough to make both of you strong."

. . .

A s the days went by, Billy spoke about Delfy more and more, delighted with his invention. Rachel saw the imaginary friend as a way of coping with the boredom of being stuck in bed, and she thought it was a godsend. Delfy, according to Billy, lived inside his head and wanted to find out about the world exactly as Billy rediscovered it. Delfy and Billy read books, drew pictures, and watched TV indiscriminately. As time went by, they tried standing up on Billy's wobbly legs and fell back onto the bed, giggling. They laughed at things that weren't objectively funny. They watched the news and wrote down more and more numbers on the pieces of paper beside the bed. They dozed as Rachel read them stories. Delfy was the personification of recovery, and with her voice in his head, Billy got better.

THREE

When she woke in the night, though, she knew something was wrong. She had the same old feeling in the pit of her stomach.

She knew it had been a nightmare but couldn't remember any details. Just the feeling lingered on. She seemed to be sitting bolt upright, and even when she was wide-awake, she couldn't shake the feeling that something was catastrophically wrong.

She crept out of bed and made her way to the door, hoping not to wake Al, who was breathing heavy, sleepy breaths beside the rumpled space where she had been, or Beth, whose cot was right beside her. She tiptoed across the landing in the dim light of the streetlamps that shone through the frosted glass pane in the door downstairs. That glass had a crack in it. Everything was falling apart.

She passed through the strips of plastic sheeting into what had once been the sterile zone and stood on the threshold of Billy's bedroom. It was still gratingly tidy, as he had barely got out of bed except to go to the loo. Still, there was no longer a flu handbook on the bedside table; now there was a pile of picture books and a piece of paper with the number 633,910,111 written on it.

She gazed at him. His breathing was even, and his face was untroubled. She put a hand on his forehead and knew that his temperature was normal. There was no fever anymore.

"All right, Mummy," he said, three-quarters asleep, and she kissed his hair. His curtains were not quite closed, and as she pulled them together, she saw the unusually starry night outside and wondered whether it could be true that people, including, perhaps, her daughter, were going to go and live up there. Could the human race really abandon the perfect home it had trashed? Privately, she thought the talk of space colonization was a distraction from the awful things going on down here, but she wouldn't say that in front of Nina, who had started going to some space classes that were, at least, free.

It was when she came back into her own room, relieved and sleepy, that she saw that her instinct had been right, but that its focus had been wrong. It was Beth. Baby Beth, the unexpected joy of Rachel's early forties, was panting. She was burning with a fever, and Rachel grabbed her from her cot and held her close. That woke her properly, and her chubby face crumpled as she started to wail. Al sat up.

Their eyes met. She saw her own dread reflected.

"She's . . . sick," said Rachel. It hurt her to say the word, and for a moment, all her strength was gone, and she sat on the edge of the bed.

She could not go through this again. She couldn't. Everything was supposed to be better, and if Beth had the flu, then it would begin all over again. It couldn't. She couldn't. She couldn't lose Beth. No.

Al put a solid arm around her, and she collapsed onto his shoulder. He took the baby from her arms. Everything about him calmed her, and when he said: "Go to sleep. I'll do the night shift. We'll need you in the morning. Sleep. I've got her," she rolled over and closed her eyes.

D aylight was coming around and through the flimsy curtains. The room smelled normal. It didn't have the sick scent that was lingering, just a tiny bit, in Billy's room.

She shuffled down the landing to look in on Billy, who was asleep, and then walked slowly down the stairs, following the smell of toast and coffee to the kitchen. She dreaded what she would find, picturing the baby limp on Al's shoulder, gearing herself up to sterilize Nina's room and put Beth in there, behind plastic sheets, for weeks and weeks. She would have to get back into the quarantine suit, and Nina would stay away for even longer: it would be weeks and weeks, all over again, and at the end of that, they would need another miracle.

Beth, however, was sitting in the high chair, throwing toast crusts onto the floor and giggling.

Rachel tried to compute what she was seeing. "Did that happen?" she said. She checked the wall clock: seven a.m. Al passed her a coffee and half his piece of toast and peanut butter. "Was it real? Last night? Thank you."

He kissed her and then put a hand on top of Beth's black curls. Both of them smiled at Rachel, with their matching dimples.

"It was," he said. "I don't know what happened, but she fought it off. Or it was something else. Who knows? She fussed a bit. We walked around the house, and I gave her some medicine. And then she settled and fell asleep on me. I didn't want to sleep. I wanted to be alert around her, so I just sat right here, drinking coffee and listening to the radio, with Beth sleeping on my shoulder until the sun came up. There was a World Service program about the anniversary of the plane crash. I could tell you anything you wanted to know about that. Apart from what really happened, I guess."

She shook her head. "I don't want to know anything the government has to say about anything. Thanks. Do you think my milk made her better?"

Al stroked Beth's hair again. "Probably."

Rachel had, until last night, attributed the fact that Beth hadn't got sick to the fact that she was breastfeeding her. And now, if Beth had been attacked by the virus, she had overcome it instantly. Rachel had peered back into the abyss, then woken up and found it wasn't an abyss at all. It was just a pothole, and it was already filled in.

Poor Al had to go to work, and she walked to the door with him, as she did sometimes, and waited while he wheeled his bike out of the hallway. It was cold outside. Icy. The blast came into the house, and she knew it would linger because they couldn't afford to use the heating very often. However, that didn't matter because Beth and Billy were well. They were all well. The things that had bothered her before the epidemic were negligible trivia, because she was looking at them differently.

"You stayed up all night," she said. "And now you're going to work. Will you be OK?"

Al reached out and hugged her, and she pressed herself into his chest, holding him as tightly as he held her.

"Of course I will," he said into her hair.

Al was her world. She had never expected to meet someone new when she was forty-one, and yet here he was, living with her, hugging her tightly to him, father of her baby, stepfather to her older children. They made an unusual couple, she white and forty-three, he black and thirty-five; she a divorced and stressed mother, he an eligible bachelor when they met. Yet it worked. It actually worked. Everything about it worked. She adored him, and somehow he loved her, too, and their baby was perfect, and she was healthy.

Later that morning, Rachel was sitting on the floor with Beth, admiring the baby's effortless good health. They were pushing toy cars around, Rachel saying, "Brmm-brmm," and Beth giggling and blowing raspberries. Eight months, Rachel thought, was a wonderful age to be.

"Here are Mummy and Beth," said Billy, and Rachel stifled a scream. He was right there, standing in the kitchen doorway. Billy, who still needed her to support him to the bathroom, who had not walked more than a step on his own for weeks, had come downstairs.

"Billy!" she said.

"Delfy said I must come down."

Rachel looked up. He was thin and wobbly, but he was there, upright, in his pajamas. He had walked all the way down the stairs alone. She had not expected him to get out of bed for another four days. That was what it said online. Now she would be able to tear that plastic right down. It could be properly over.

She was on her feet in a second, and a moment after that, he was in her arms, warm and sleepy and, at last, smelling more of little boy than of illness. Beth clapped her hands, delighted at the sight of him. If she could, she would have been yelling his name.

"You got up!" Rachel said when she could. "How did you even *do* that?"

"I did get up because Delfy said. I just told you."

"Oh, my darling. That's amazing. Clever Delfy! How do you feel? You made it all the way down the stairs on your own. You should be resting."

"Resting is boring, though, Mum."

Beth shouted and waved both arms. Billy wriggled off Rachel's lap and sat carefully next to her.

"Red car, Beth," he said, picking one up and holding it out to her with a trembling hand. He was making an enormous effort. Rachel could see what hard work this was for him.

The kitchen was tatty, the house rented and neglected by the landlord. The cold found its way around the edges of the windows. The oven worked at twenty degrees cooler than it said it did and often didn't work at all. Everything needed replacing, and they couldn't afford to do any of it. Most of their technology was thirty years out of date. Rachel looked at the children playing together and wondered what their future would hold.

Beth had stayed with Rachel and Billy throughout the illness. They had wondered whether to send her away to live with Rachel's mother, but Rachel couldn't do it, and not just because her mother would probably have baptized her into her weird church. She wanted to carry on feeding Beth and decided that she would trust in the immunities that the milk gave her. Until last night's scare, it had worked, and she supposed that it was probably her own breaching of the sterile zone, on the night when Billy hadn't died, that had brought the virus to Beth. Well, no harm seemed to have been done. They were lucky.

And now that Billy had come downstairs, the quarantine was over. Those were the rules. Nina could come home, too. Rachel looked for a phone. She needed to let her know right away.

A t four o'clock the front door opened, and Nina said: "Hey! I'm back!" Rachel was standing at the stove, cooking. She turned to Nina and pushed her long hair back from her face (her hair was half gray now, she had noticed, and she didn't care) and said, fake casual: "Oh, hi! How was school?"

They laughed as Rachel opened her arms and Nina flew into them. Rachel held her tightly. She buried her face in her daughter's hair and smelled the Nina smell mixed with Henry's house, Henry's shampoo, Henry's washing powder. She pulled Nina's skinny body close and savored everything about her darling child. They hadn't seen each other properly over the past six weeks (Rachel had only half-noticed her on the night when Billy didn't die), just talking on the phone while looking at each other through the front window, Nina standing outside the house, both of them pressing their hands to the glass. They had texted every day. But still, apart from that one night, Nina had been absent, outside the cordon.

And now here she was. She was back, and the nightmare receded a little further.

"Are you hungry?" said Rachel.

Nina threw her schoolbag down in the corner. "Starving," she said, and she picked up Beth. "Bethie Bethie Bethie. Look how you've grown! Oh, I like what you've done with the paintings."

Rachel looked around. She hadn't noticed, but Billy's paintings, which she had always stuck up around the kitchen (sometimes to cover patches of mold), were now arranged in rainbow order, starting with red ones by the door and going through the spectrum to purple by the cooker, and they were in a perfect straight line.

"I didn't do that," she said.

"We did do it just now," said Billy, who had, indeed, been padding around the room.

Nina put Beth down and pulled Billy onto her lap.

"It looks nice," she said. "Good to see you, mister." She ruffled his hair, and Rachel could see she was trying not to cry.

"This is my sister, Nina," Billy said. He was sitting up straight, with wide blank eyes. "She has been staying with our dad because she needed to not get ill. Now I am better, she has come home."

"Erm, yes, I have," said Nina. "Who are you introducing me to, Bill?"

"To Delfy."

"Remember Delfy?" Rachel said. "The imaginary friend. I told you about her on the phone. We are all in favor of Delfy." She got out the biscuits. Rachel and Al were so poor at the moment that a budget packet of store-brand custard creams was a treat. She shook them onto a plate to make it feel like more of an occasion.

"Sure." Nina took two. "Thanks. Well, nice to meet you, Delfy."

Billy was silent for a moment. Then he said: "Delfy says it is nice to meet you, too, Nina. She says you're good."

"Thanks. Tell her she is, too?"

Again, Billy was silent, and then he said: "She says thanks."

Nina turned to Rachel. "So, Mum? So much has happened. Can I bring Louis over to meet you?"

Nina, who was sixteen, had never brought a boy home. She had sounded elated talking about Louis on the phone. Rachel knew that she had not shown enough interest in her daughter's first boyfriend, when her son had been dying. Now she was going to make up for it.

"Of course!" she said. "We'd *love* to meet him. You know that. Bring him over anytime. I can't wait."

"I will. You'll really like him. His family is quite posh, but you'd never know it. Mum, I've got to do some homework for tomorrow. Can I clear a space on the table and do it here? I don't want to go away from you all. It's too nice to be back."

"Of course," Rachel said, and she was perfectly content. When Al came home from work, she would have her whole family right here. Billy was getting better fast, and she knew that the old banal worries would start to creep back in soon. She was supposed to be going back to work, after her extended, unpaid maternity leave. They had no money, so she had to go back full-time, however much she didn't want to. Her mother was going to look after Beth while Rachel was at work, and that in itself was a minor worry.

And if Nina's boyfriend was "quite posh," she supposed that when he came round, she would have to make a big effort. She would clear all the junk from the kitchen table and cook something that would somehow be impressive and yet cheap.

She savored these worries. These were the ordinary things she had thought she was going to lose forever. These were the things that made life real. She relished them.

FOUR

On Saturday Nina woke up thinking about Beth; her brain seemed to have made a plan while her body slept. She had a quick shower, dressed in jeans and a jumper, and went down the stairs two at a time.

"Hi!" She stood in the kitchen doorway and looked at the clutter, the homeyness of it all. Mum was drinking coffee and looking exhausted. Beth was sitting on the floor, bashing a saucepan with a wooden spoon. Al was frowning at a piece of paper on which he seemed to be making a shopping list. Next to everything on it was a number, and Nina could see that they were budgeting hard.

Mum beamed at her, and Al said: "Oh, Nina. I can't tell you how great it is to have you back."

Beth looked up and clapped her hands.

"Can I take Beth out?" Nina said. "I've missed her. And Billy, too, but I know he can't go out yet. I want to take Bethie to a coffee shop or something and let her get some fresh air. Would you like that, Bethie? And would it be OK with you?"

"Suits me," said Al. "I was about to take her to the SupaSava to try to do history's most frugal family shop. She'd have much more fun with you. She missed you, too, and she didn't get out much over the past six weeks. Your mum didn't get out at all."

Mum laughed. "I stood in the backyard sometimes. I didn't want to go farther than that."

"Are you sure?" Nina was talking to Al. "I know you don't see her so much in the week."

"Very sure. Take her out and have fun."

Nina had money in her pocket from Dad, and although she knew he paid Mum maintenance for her and Billy, she also knew it wasn't much. She decided she would use her allowance from Dad to get some extra bits for the household while she was out.

"Yes," said Mum. "You girls have a nice walk. Wrap her up as warm as you can, and get some fresh air into her. Well. Not exactly fresh. But outdoor air anyway. Air. Stay away from . . . Oh, you know. Just stay away from bad stuff."

Nina enjoyed guiding the pushchair through the streets of South London. She felt like a young mother and tried to imagine herself in a completely different life. Girls at school got pregnant sometimes. Imagine getting pregnant at fifteen and having your very own baby in a pushchair at sixteen, like this. Not just to play with Beth, but to be responsible for keeping her alive, day and night. Nina was sure she would never be ready for such a thing. She was training to go to space, and that would be impossible to combine with motherhood. Besides, she didn't think the world (or the galaxy) needed any more people.

Although she had been born at a bad time for the world in general, Nina felt she was here at exactly the right moment for herself. There was no other point in history when a sixteen-year-old girl could have had a real chance of spending her adult life in a different part of the universe. Her mission was to play a part in moving the human race across galaxies. There was the technology for it now (though its details were a closely guarded secret), and there was also a huge need to escape from this place, to try again, to do it better.

Meanwhile, there was human shit on the pavement, and the wind was blowing so hard that she had to stop and unwind a burger wrapper from Beth's feet. They passed an apartment block that was boarded up and cordoned off, ready for demolition. A couple of streets later, a terrace of little houses had bright purple ACQUIRED BY STARCOM boards on them, and Nina wanted to rip the signs down. That was what she wanted to escape. The Starcom case had been on in the background for ages, and she hadn't taken much notice of it until Ben Alford won. She hated it when the bad guys won. *Why,* she wondered, *would this man, who no doubt lives in luxury in a castle somewhere, want to buy up normal people's houses and say they can only live in them if they work for him for vouchers?* The injustice of it burned inside her.

This was why she had set her sights on creating a new world. She stopped for a second and looked up. There were patches of blue in the cloudy sky, and somewhere up there in the blue was the International Space Station, and beyond that there was an asteroid called the Rock. The Rock would be captured by rockets and towed to a stable point between the Earth and the moon very soon. It was going to become the base.

Somewhere else, unimaginably far away, there was another planet. A planet that was a bit like this one but pristine. They had already identified it. They would go there. If she worked hard, she could move there herself.

Nina imagined how it would feel to walk on the surface of a different planet, one with similar-enough gravity and a close-enough atmosphere. How would it feel to know that you were millions of miles from home? It made her dizzy.

She had to be a part of it because if they were colonizing space, she could not let it be the same all over again. She could not let the greedy men shape the new world, too, and she knew that Starcom, for example, was heavily invested in the New Earth project. Humanity had to look after their second planet, wherever it was, and the best way for her to make that happen would be to go there and do it herself.

Nina had already been on the fast-track science program at school when she saw that poster stuck up on a science noticeboard: HAVE YOU GOT WHAT IT TAKES TO BE A SPACE PIONEER? When she looked into it, it turned out to be offering the chance to apply for top-level training for traveling to and living in space, co-run by the British Space Agency and NASA. It was open to anyone aged between fifteen and eighteen, and you had to be able to get to the South Bank of the Thames every Sunday after-noon, with no exceptions.

She had spent weeks finessing her application. It was a ruthlessly com-petitive thing, but she knew, in her heart, that she could do it, and she did. She had been short-listed and interviewed several times, and she had un-dergone a full, invasive medical examination and a series of blood and urine tests. Then she, Nina Stevens, had beaten out thousands of others and got a place in the space pioneers course. Now she went to the South Bank every weekend and learned rocket science, which was, it turned out, exactly as difficult as you'd think.

And that was where she met Louis Ricci.

She skirted around the dodgy areas, the places everyone knew you should avoid unless you were into drugs or guns, and she and Beth ended up on the high street, with its mixture of charity shops, coffee shops, and generic chain stores. There were advertising hoardings every-where, some of them with photographs, others with moving images. As she pushed Beth past a bus stop, a picture of Guy Clement appeared, holding a bar of the overpriced Rockolate he advertised. "Hey there!" he said. "Fancy one of these? It's out of this world."

"Fuck off, Guy," she said. Guy Clement was the superstar British astronaut, but he advertised everything relentlessly, and his name had be-come shorthand for selling out. That, for Nina, had almost overshadowed everything he had achieved. Here he was, trying to sell her chocolate that she couldn't afford and that would part-fund the space mission. "Fuck off," she said again.

An elderly man in a kurta turned and frowned at her language.

From time to time, she looked down at Beth, who was wearing lots of clothes (all of them from the charity shops on this very street) and was wrapped in a blanket, her springy hair tucked into a big woolen hat with a bobble on top. Beth was resolutely awake, gazing at everything around her with polite interest and the air of a minor royal looking around a factory.

Nina's phone chimed with a message, and she was pleased to see that it was from Louis.

I miss you! he wrote. What are you up to? xxxxx

Nina did appreciate a boy who used proper words in his texts. And lots of kisses. She had to stop and put the pushchair brakes on to write a good enough reply.

Out with Beth, she wrote. The baby. Walking the streets of London, pretending to be a teen mom. We're about to go to UnionBeanz. Come join us? Then she remembered she hadn't put kisses and followed it up with a text that just said xxxxxxx.

Ten seconds later he replied.

On my way! I'm ditching my friends for you girls xox

Nina arranged her hair and slightly wished she'd put on some makeup and better clothes. She found a table at the back of the coffee shop and parked Beth's buggy, then dragged a grimy high chair from a stash of them by the toilets and transferred the baby into it. Beth wriggled and made it clear that she actually planned to sit on the floor, but the floor was sticky with all kinds of spills, and there were crumbs and bits of paper napkins and coffee stirrers and something that Nina thought might be a piece of bacon fat, so she enticed Beth into the high chair by whispering, "Cake," into her ear.

She folded the pushchair. Being a teen mother was harder work than she had thought it would be. Mum did all this stuff without even thinking about it, although Mum never went to coffee shops because she didn't have any money.

She settled Beth in, turned the high chair to face the queue, and went to wait at the counter, watching Beth the whole time, waving at her, desperate to keep her happy, while keeping a close eye on anyone who walked anywhere near her. When she got to the counter she ordered two Bigwhitebeanz (this chain was ridiculous) and a BaybeeBeeneeCheenee, which was a cup of milk froth with a marshmallow on top, and then she pointed to a plate of chocolate brownies and asked for two of them. She would never be able to tell Mum or Al how much it cost her.

"I'll give you a shout when they're ready," said the barista, who was young and androgynous and wore big-framed glasses that they probably didn't need.

Beth was happy and mercifully unkidnapped when Nina got back to the table, and two minutes after that, Louis arrived. Somehow he didn't have to push his way through the people as Nina had. The room cleared a path for him, and then he was there, all cheekbones, bright blue eyes, and floppy dark hair, right in front of her. He looked like a hero from a movie. He was gorgeous. Nina was still amazed that he had been single when they met, and she was even more amazed at the fact that he had been so nervous when he approached her. She would always remember him tripping over his words as he put a hand on her upper arm as they were leaving the class and asked whether she would like to go for a coffee with him sometime.

"I mean," he'd said, "you might not even like coffee. It doesn't have to be coffee. What I mean is . . . Oh, you know what I mean."

"I do know," she had said. "And yes, I would like to."

"My favorite girls," he said now, kissing Nina on the lips and patting Beth's head.

"She can't really be your favorite girl," Nina said. "You haven't actually met her."

Louis sat down. "Hello, Beth." He held his hand out, and she patted it and giggled. "Pleased to meet you. I'm Louis." Beth smiled her dimply smile at him, and Louis said: "Oh, my God, she *is* adorable. There you go. My two favorite girls. Done."

"Accepted. Thank you. Oh, look, that's our coffee. I got some brownies to share. I'll give Beth some of mine because she really shouldn't have one. She shouldn't have sugar at all, I don't think. Oh, well, we won't tell Mum."

Louis stood up. "I'll grab it."

They sat there, the three of them, drinking mediocre coffee and eating gloopy brownies, and Nina thought of Billy, healthy at home with his imaginary friend, and she decided she might never have been this happy in all her life.

FIVE

A week later Rachel realized she hadn't seen any of her friends for two months. She messaged Sami and invited herself, Billy, and Beth over.

Amazing! Sami replied. Of course! Is he OK?

Yes, Rachel wrote. She stopped and looked at the word and was pleased with its straightforwardness. Yes. He is.

She sent the text.

The imaginary friend was still there. Billy explained his day-to-day life to her, and because Delfy seemed to like things orderly, his room was still tidy. He read books to her and giggled at things she said. He told her about every part of his life, and sometimes he frowned and listened to whatever she was saying in reply. Rachel was charmed by her. She had always wished she had been the kind of child who'd had an imaginary friend. She could have done with one; her childhood had been stressful and lonely, and she'd never have had the imagination to conjure up a companion. She was oddly proud of Billy for his invention of Delfy and a little bit jealous.

. . .

They sat in Sami's kitchen. Billy had defied everything, all predictions, and he was well again. She could say it out loud: "Billy is well." It was too much for her, and whenever there was an excuse to laugh, like now, she would take it. She knew she was laughing too much (she was on the brink of tears much of the time), and she knew her friends didn't mind. She was supposedly laughing about an impression Sami had just done of the children's school principal trying to stop a class revolt, but really she was letting the emotion out.

Billy was better, and soon he would be going back to school. He was a normal boy again. Beth hadn't become ill, in spite of the midnight scare, and neither had Nina or Rachel or Al. She was certain of that now. The flu was in the past tense for them. It had been a near miss. Hundreds of thousands had died, maybe more. It was hard to tell because no one believed the official figures, and the guesses online were wildly different, ranging from (conspiracy!) no one actually died at all to (conspiracy!) the population of the world was now less than half of what it was. But it was better for *them*, for Rachel and her family, and that was a thing to hold on to. It was a solid fact. It had been scary, and now it was over, and she was laughing because she could. Also, Billy's principal was truly crap, and it turned out she wasn't the only one to think so.

She adjusted the baby on her lap and buried her face in Beth's hair for a second, to hide the fact that she was somehow crying now, and managed to say: "Was it literally that bad?"

Sami sat down. "Yep. I was helping with reading, and Miss Lu nipped out to smoke or to cry in the toilets or whatever she does, and they just went fucking feral. Excuse my language, Beth. So along comes the head to calm them down, but it turns out she can't do a thing. I sorted them out myself in the end. Anyway, do you guys fancy a drink? I've got some wine. We have to celebrate Billy."

Emma nodded. "Oh, my God. I'd love that. Thanks."

Rachel hesitated. She was happy. She was with friends. Billy was playing upstairs. She allowed herself the luxury of considering a glass of wine for a few seconds. She would be like everyone else, and it would be fine. Everyone else could drink and be all right.

"No, thanks," she said, because she wasn't really going to start drinking now. Beth wriggled on her lap, and Rachel put her on the floor, patting the top of her head as the baby scanned the room for interesting things at ground level. Beth was always staring at things, assessing them.

"Oh, yeah. Sorry. I forgot. You don't mind if we do?"

"Of course I don't!"

Sami's house was small and chaotic, with every surface covered in pieces of paper and with all sorts of strange pictures pinned to the walls. Sami was a graphic designer, Sri Lankan by ancestry and a Londoner through and through. She was boyish and brisk, and she seemed just able to scrape together enough work to support herself and Lola. She stuck her projects up around the house so she could think about them no matter what she was doing. Right now the three of them were sitting around the kitchen table, a tower of paperwork in the middle of it like a campfire. It was like the table at home, and that comforted Rachel.

Sami put a glass of white wine in front of Emma and another in her own place, and she handed Rachel a wineglass with juice in it.

"Here you go," she said. "Cheers."

They clinked glasses.

"Lovely," said Emma. "It's so brilliant to see Billy up and running again." Emma was blond and glamorous, an accountant who had taken a year off work because she was sick of never seeing her children. Rachel didn't know her as well as she knew Sami. She couldn't begin to imagine a life in which you could choose not to work. Her own maternity leave had brought them to the brink of destitution.

"I know." Her words fell over one another. She hadn't told her friends about that night yet. "He was so ill. I felt it. I knew he was going to go, to die, in my arms. I haven't even got the words. That *care for them at home* thing is really just a way of saying either you'll die or you won't and there's nothing we can do about it, so deal with it. All the medication is pain-killers or placebos. Even Henry came over to say . . . to say good-bye to him. I invited Henry into my house. But Billy didn't die."

She knew she was barely coherent. Her words were all slurring into one another.

"I keep thinking, is this really happening?" Sami said. "I mean, to us? Here, now, in our lifetime, to us and our children? This plague that kills the children and the old people and some of the people in between?"

"Yes," said Emma. "And meanwhile the superrich are getting ready to fuck off into space and start all over again. Twats."

"I know!" said Rachel. "I hope they fire Ben Alford into the sun." Al's passion on this subject had infected her.

"If they did get to the new Earth," said Emma, "they'd trash that, too. You know they would."

"They won't go anywhere," said Sami. "It's a load of bollocks."

They sat in silence for a while. Eventually Sami lifted her glass again.

"Anyway. No point being morose," she said. "You made it. Billy made it. Cheers to that. To our microcosm. The whole world is better for Billy, at least."

"Cheers," said Rachel. "I think about the people who didn't make it all the time." She did. She knew his school had lost seven students. Seven. Not eight.

The other two nodded.

"You know Shana in their class?" said Emma. "She's got it. No idea how ill she is. Other than that, people are coming back. Or not."

Everyone talked about the pandemic all the time. They had for months. People would talk about it, Rachel thought, forever. She wondered whether this was how it had been during the Black Death. Three women sitting together in a kitchen, swapping stories.

The children dashed into the room. The sight of the six-year-olds, Billy, Lola, and Seth, made Rachel catch her breath. It was so precious, so unlikely. Billy looked strong and bright, with long limbs and boundless energy. His hair was falling into his face, and his eyes shone. Lola stood in front of a clear patch of wall and did a handstand, her feet on the wall and her black ponytail brushing the floor. Seth, who was cuddly and rosy cheeked, snuggled up to Emma. They were like a litter of puppies, tumbling in play.

Beth shrieked and pointed at Lola upside down. Billy knelt on the floor next to his sister and said: "I know, Bethie. Lola is upside down because she's good at gymnastics. She keeps her center of mass above her wrists, but the wall is there for balance, so it doesn't matter if she does get it a bit wrong."

"What?" said Emma. She looked at Rachel and back at Billy. "That's a bit scientific, Billy."

"Billy's been spending a lot of time on the iPad," said Rachel, "researching things for Delfy's benefit."

"Do you guys want a biscuit?" said Sami.

"Oh, yeah!" said Lola, dropping back down. The children followed Sami to the cupboard and stood around her while she opened a tin and held it out.

"One each," she said. "Homemade, for better or worse."

Billy ignored the tin and looked behind Sami. "There is a spiderweb in your cupboard," he told her. "There are lots. Lots of spiders live there. Up at the top. They like it there."

Everyone looked. Billy was right: there was a silky tangle of web at the very top of the cupboard. Sami laughed. "Jesus, Billy! Don't tell everyone. Do you want a cookie or not?"

"Billy!" said Rachel, who hated spiders. "Don't be so rude!" She decided not to eat anything that came out of that particular cupboard. Sami was already standing on a chair and sweeping the cobwebs away.

"Delfy likes spiders," said Billy. "She says they're interestin'. They like her, too."

Rachel held out her arms and pulled him onto her lap. "Don't talk about spiders," she whispered. "And don't be rude about people's houses. OK?"

"OK, Mummy," he replied. "Sorry. It was true, though."

She snuggled his hair, smelled him. She was going to appreciate every atom of him forever, even if he was a bit too forthright sometimes. Rachel loved Delfy because she was part of the recovery. Rachel supposed Delfy would go now that Billy was back with his real friends. She would miss her, but soon Billy wouldn't need her anymore.

After a while Sami said: "Do you want me to make some tea for the kids? If my hygiene standards are acceptable, that is."

Rachel winced; Sami was offended. Of course she was. Anyone would be.

She looked at the clock and realized they couldn't stay anyway.

"I wish. I have to take Billy over to Henry's. He's barely seen him for eight weeks and this is the first time Billy's staying over. He'll be getting home from work now."

Henry had, of course, wanted to have Billy to stay as soon as he was well enough to leave the house. Rachel had clung to him for as long as she could, had restricted it to weekend outings, messaging extracts from the government convalescence instructions as backup, but today she knew she had to let him go. He had recovered enough to stay at his dad's house, and that was a fact.

"Oh, right," said Sami. "Well, fair enough. Good luck."

"Thanks." Rachel closed her eyes for a moment. "I know I have to do it. It's going to be horrible. But I have to. Billy, what do you say?"

"Sorry I said about the spiders," said Billy.

"I meant, 'Thanks for having us to play,'" said Rachel. "But yes, that, too."

It was cold and dark outside, and Rachel didn't like it. She hated being out in the dark. That was one of her *things*. She particularly hated it when she was with children, because she could never make the dark night in the city feel safe. She hated spiders because they were creepy and evil. She hated shower curtains in people's bathrooms in case they had murderous clowns waiting behind them. She hated seeing homeless people because they made her acknowledge how close she and Al were to having nothing. She had a history of spiraling anxiety, and she clung to sanity as tightly as she could.

"It'll be nice for you to see Dad," she said carefully as she pushed Beth along, with Billy walking beside her.

"Delfy hasn't seen Dad's house yet," Billy said. "She didn't like Dad when we saw him before. She said he was a silly man. I wonder if she will like him today. Nina says it doesn't matter if she thinks he's silly."

"I'm sure she'll like him," said Rachel, even though she kind of hoped Delfy would be as rude to Henry as she had been to Sami.

"Delfy likes you and Al and Nina and Beth."

"And we like Delfy, because she helped you get better."

They walked quickly round the corner, across the road, and up a few more streets until they got to the far smarter road on which Henry still lived. Here there were trees, neatly pruned, and security lights that snapped on outside most houses as they passed. The houses themselves were spacious, and a few of them even had cars in their drives.

When Billy saw his dad's house, Rachel expected him to run toward it, but he didn't. He dropped back, and she saw in the light from the flickering streetlamp that he was frowning, deep in thought.

Rachel was happy to take the last bit slowly. She hated her visits to this house because she had lived in it for ten years and it had not been a happy time. Henry had kept the house because Rachel was the one who wanted to leave. Now she scraped by in their rented place, which was held together with Scotch tape and willpower, while Henry had probably paid off his mortgage. Nonetheless, she didn't regret a thing.

The security light snapped on as they walked up the crunchy path. Billy pressed the bell on the blue front door, which had been repainted since Rachel last visited. Henry opened it at once and looked her up and down very quickly, as he always did. She felt exposed in the bright light and was glad of the pushchair as a shield, though Henry, as ever, acted as if Beth didn't exist, and Beth ignored him right back.

Rachel wished he hadn't been in her house that night. Now that the crisis had passed, it felt too exposing. At the time she hadn't cared at all.

Her ex-husband was wearing a lumberjack shirt that was tucked precisely into jeans, with a pair of deck shoes on his feet. His hair was almost completely gray, and it was as short as though he were in the military—a look he cultivated even though he had never been anywhere near a barracks. When Henry and Rachel first met, he had been doing legal aid work, helping refugees, trying to use his training to make the world a better place. Now he worked for a corporate legal firm and had started talking about sending Nina to a boarding school for sixth form. Nina refused and wanted him to save that money for her university fees, because she was sensible even when the world around her was not.

She watched his face change as he looked at Billy, and she knew that, in spite of everything, she and Henry were bonded forever. Henry loved Billy, too, and the emotion on his face, before he controlled it, matched hers in a primal way.

"Come here, son," he said, and he picked Billy up and hugged him, hiding his face from Rachel. Billy wriggled down and ran into the house, and Henry took a deep breath, did a fake sneeze so he could wipe his eyes, and snapped back under control.

"Rach," he said. No one but Henry had ever called her *Rach*; she had never thought of it as her name.

"Henry."

"Good . . . good to see him up and at it. Excellent job looking after him, BTW." He actually said "*bee tee double you.*" She smiled. That was Henry's way of saying that he didn't hold the state of her house against her.

"Thanks."

"See you Sunday."

"I'll text about timings."

"Sure."

She wanted to give Billy a last hug, but he had gone. Instead she shouted good-bye through the door to him and set off home, talking non-sense to Beth as they went to stop herself from crying.

There was a man on the opposite side of the road watching her, an older man standing in the shadows. That was unnerving. There was an uncountable number of homeless men in this city, and it could be terrify-ing, particularly if you were out in the dark. She knew, from Al's work, how many people there were out there with nothing to lose.

She pretended not to see this man as she stopped to fix the rain cover over her baby and the first drops of rain began to fall. He didn't approach, though she thought she felt him following her at a distance all the way home.

He probably wasn't following her. She was just paranoid. She hated being out in the dark with Beth. That was all.

SIX

Across London, Professor Graham Watson had found a way of getting through the days without his wife. Unfortunately it involved working all the time. As it happened, his professional life had never been busier, and what had started as a desperate attempt to fill every hour was, he thought, turning into something different.

He had almost stopped going home altogether because (although he couldn't say this out loud) the Marylebone flat was haunted. It was properly, objectively haunted; Graham had never believed in such things, but now he had to. He would walk into a room absently, expecting to find Imogen there, and there she would be. She would be in the kitchen, standing at the counter making a pot of tea. In the bathroom, stretched out in the bath, a glass of sherry beside her, her perfect little pink-nailed feet emerging from the bubbles. He would freeze and stare, willing her to be real, smelling her perfume, wishing that she was his actual wife and not this mocking, malevolent ghost.

Then it always went the same. Someone would scream (him), and sometime later he would come back to consciousness crouched in a corner, pulling his hair out strand by strand, with no idea of how long he'd been there. Every time there was a pile of white hairs and scalp flakes next to him, and his face was wet with tears, his heart beating much faster than was healthy.

When he was at work it didn't happen. The ghost didn't go to his office; Imogen had hated it there. He was focusing on one particular part of his work, the part that had fascinated Imogen. He had off-loaded all the patients he could, apart from these ones. He was immersed and obsessed.

His boys had come over for the funeral, from Australia, Dubai, and New York, and as soon as it was over, they left. One of his daughters-in-law, Michelle, called occasionally to ask how he was doing, but his sons had no interest.

They had adored Imogen to the point of donning quarantine masks and gloves and braving international air travel during a pandemic to get to her funeral. They wouldn't do the same for him; he had overheard them saying how much they wished it had been him who had died, not her. He had been a distant father, aloof, sending them to boarding school at thirteen because that was what you did, leaving every tearful phone call to his wife to deal with, every difficult thing to Imogen to sort out. His payback was this: they didn't care about him, and that was fair enough.

It was dark outside, and it was nearly six, and that meant that he and Lauren had to go downstairs to receive their new patient. Graham wasn't sure he was doing the right thing with this particular admission, but it turned out that when you were a distinguished professor in your seventies (and when the only forthright person in your life had just died), there was no one above you to tell you that you were wrong. He was managing all of this as scientifically as he could, but things were about to go up a gear, and a part of him was far more nervous than he could possibly have admitted.

Lauren was maybe thirty-two, and currently, although he would never have told her this, she was the most stable presence in his life. When he stood in the doorway of her office, she beamed up at him.

"This is exciting," she said, and hastily added: "Don't worry. I haven't told anyone." He watched her tap on the keyboard of her computer until the screen went blank, and then she tidied the papers, dropped the post down the chute, and said: "Harmony, do we have enough tea, coffee, milk, and cookies for tomorrow?"

"We do, Lauren," said the female voice from the speaker. Lauren had made a point of setting Harmony to be a woman.

"Great," she said. "Thanks."

"You're welcome, Lauren."

"Right!" She grinned at Graham, shaking back her shiny hair and picking up her bag.

"Shall we?" he said, and they went out onto the landing, where Lauren called the small lift, the one that was camouflaged to look like a bookcase, and they squeezed in together, which always felt slightly awkward. Both of them pressed their thumbs to the track pad, and Lauren told lift Harmony to take them to floor minus seven.

G raham's consulting rooms were on the second floor of what looked, from the outside, like a normal town house. If you didn't know, you would never have imagined that, beneath it all, an underground hospital stretched down fifteen floors, across the whole terrace. Most of it had nothing to do with him (it was part cosmetic surgery, part real medicine for people who wanted to skip waiting lists and recover in five-star luxury), but level minus seven? That was his.

It was the psycho-pediatric department, and it didn't exist. There was one long-term patient now: Kitty had grown up here. She was technically too old for a pediatric hospital, but her parents had offered more and more money for Graham to keep her, and he was bound by a complex set of obligations. Graham was sure that right now it was the best place for her, so she was staying. Her symptoms had been bizarre when he first saw them, but now they looked premonitory. They were the forerunner of a thing he was seeing now all the time. He needed Kitty in place as his patient zero.

Although Graham knew it was dark outside, down here it was daylight in such a way that he felt there was a sunny sky just around the next corner. They went through thumb and retina scans, as well as a chat with a human to check that no one had cut off their thumbs and pulled out their eyes to get in.

"Perfect," said the receptionist. She checked the time. "Well, we're all set down here. We're very excited to meet our new patient. Do you have the forms?"

Graham and Lauren had each signed a watertight confidentiality agreement and had it witnessed by a lawyer. Lauren handed the documents over and Graham led the way into Giraffe ward.

It was a bright space, with beds at one end separated by curtains, and an entertainment area at the other. Graham had modeled the space's look on the pictures in the brochures his patients' parents would sometimes show him, when they said, with guilty eyes, that "boarding schools are different these days." (Often they were talking about five-year-olds.) He had styled it to look like those photographs and tried to make it as appealing as he could, because telling a child they were going to be detained indefinitely seven floors underground was a pill that needed some heavy sugarcoating. He always emphasized the security, making sure everyone knew that no stranger could get in there, but he never spelled out that it worked in reverse, too.

Now three of the four children who were currently resident were sitting on beanbags, playing on an Xbox and laughing. The fourth, Anita, was alone with a book, muttering to herself.

"Hey, Graham," said Majid. "We've got another controller. You playing?"

Graham saw that the game was a complicated one involving role-play and dragons. He looked at the three children on the beanbags: they were Majid, Peter, and Suki. He knew them all well, and had some serious doubts about Peter, though this wasn't the moment for them. Majid, the eldest, was twelve. Peter was only seven, and Suki was nine.

"I'm too old for that," he said, though he did sometimes join their games. He would always join a driving one. Those ones were great. These ones? He would never keep up. Similarly, there was a gym down here, and they often invited him to visit it with them, but he only sat in a corner and supervised.

"Can I play?" said Lauren.

"Yes, you can, Lolly," said Suki.

It was Peter who had started calling Lauren Lolly, and they'd all picked it up. Lauren loved it. She pulled up a beanbag and grabbed the controller that Majid held out to her. Soon she was laughing and chatting as if she, too, were twelve years old. These kids loved Lauren.

"Is Kitty around?" Graham said to the nearest nurse.

"She's out for her walk," he said. "Angela's going to keep her out all afternoon under the circumstances."

Twenty minutes later, the doors opened again. Two security people, both men, both in black, walked around the ward, checking it in silence. Then a woman came in, leading a very cross little girl who had long dark hair and a scowling face. Graham thought she was looking worse than the last time he'd seen her, and he was glad, in spite of his misgivings, that he had managed to arrange this. Her family had accepted his offer with alacrity, subject to all the security provisions. They could have continued to hide her away themselves easily enough, but, like Kitty's family, they seemed to have decided that she was better off where no one at all could see her.

"Here you are," the nanny said. She was a very thin woman in her fifties, wearing a knee-length skirt and a high-necked blouse. "See? It's lovely! And you can talk to the other children. See how happy you'll be. Look! Here's Mr. Watson!"

"*Professor* Watson," he said reflexively. "But actually Graham. You always call me Graham, don't you, Louisa?"

Louisa looked at him and narrowed her eyes. "How long do I have to stay here?" she said. "I don't like it, Graham. I'm better now. It's not fair. How long?"

"I don't know," he answered. "It depends on various things. A couple of days, to start with. I promise we'll look after you, and I promise you'll have fun. And you can talk to the others. That's what you wanted, isn't it? To meet other children who know what it's like."

He watched her look at the other patients, sizing them up. The three who were playing with Lauren hadn't stopped their game, but Anita was suddenly standing beside them. Graham jumped. He hadn't seen her move.

"Look," Graham added, putting a hand on each girl's shoulder. He saw a security guy step forward but ignored him. No one was telling him he couldn't touch his patient's shoulder. "This is Anita. You have a lot to talk about. Anita, this is Louisa."

He saw the girls looking at each other and saw the thing that passed between them.

"Hi," said Anita.

"Hello," said Louisa with a tiny smile. "A new child."

"Welcome to the house of weirdos," said Anita. "Did you do something bad?"

Louisa's eye flicked to the nanny and then away again. "Mmm," she said.

"All of us have a . . ." Anita tapped her head. Her voice was cut glass, like that of a character from a British film from the nineteen fifties. "You're here, so you do, too."

"Yeah. What's yours called?"

"Jesse."

"Mine's Blob."

"Did you nearly die with flu?"

"Yeah. You?"

The girls walked off, deep in conversation. This was exactly what Graham wanted. Lauren showed the nanny into her private side room, and one of the security people left. Louisa came with two attendants at all times, and that was nonnegotiable.

G raham said good-bye to Lauren, had a look in Kitty's room (she was back from her walk, sitting on her bed wearing headphones and singing loudly; she signaled to him with a finger to go away), and went back to the office. He didn't want to move onto level minus seven because he needed to maintain professional distance, but he couldn't go home either, so he usually slept at work. It no longer felt odd letting himself back into a silent consulting suite.

Graham could have retired years ago. He and Imogen had been married for nearly forty years; they had both known that, at some point, it was likely that one of them would die and the other would be left alone. He didn't know why it had devastated him to the point of hallucination and psychosis. He longed to die, too, and he considered it often. It was the children who stopped him. Not his own kids (they would be fine with it) but his patients.

He was looking at an epidemic within a pandemic. A rash of children with increasingly difficult voices in their heads. The children changed slowly and then dramatically, and people around them got scared, and then, if they could afford it, they tucked them away for residential treatment on level minus seven along with Kitty, the first of them all, who had been here for thirteen years.

Nothing he did made it better. He kept them safe and kept the world safe from them. Some of the kids who were here now had done terrible things. Now their behavior was largely contained, controlled with medication, and he was running a very exclusive version of a young offenders' institution.

He walked around the desk and tried not to look in the mirror. The mirror was grand, because everything here was grand. It was what people expected.

He spun back, thinking that he'd seen a different reflection, a woman, a ghost.

"Are you here?" he said, feeling his heart pounding, his sanity slipping, but she wasn't. There was just a haggard man, a man who seemed to have grown a beard by mistake. He thought he might as well keep it. It made him look a bit like Santa Claus. If he squinted, he could almost become Steve Jobs. Men who looked like that were respected. The man in the mirror nodded. They were in agreement.

He turned back to his desk and took the sleeping bag out of its drawer. Years ago, when he used to cycle to work, Graham had had a tiny shower room installed here. Now it was his main bathroom. Early each morning, he would shower, dress in clean clothes from his cupboard, and take himself out for breakfast and lots of coffee before the cleaners arrived, timing his return to ensure he strode back into the office when Lauren was at her desk so he could present it as his arrival for the day. It was ridiculous, but it was better than going home and losing his mind in something that he didn't want to look at with a professional eye.

He thought sometimes about the space program. If it happened (and he supposed it would, because the money was all headed that way), then hundreds of people would get used to sleeping in little pods, a bit like the space under his desk. Thousands. By the time they got to the supposed second Earth, they would populate it with millions, though it felt unlikely that that would actually happen. Graham felt the whole idea was stupid hubris. He was glad he was going to die and miss it.

He was hungry, and even if he'd been at home, he wouldn't have bothered to cook. He had been lazy—he knew that—and left that side of their life to Imogen. Throughout their marriage, he had made a show, from time to time, of producing scrambled eggs for breakfast or making a basic pasta dish for supper and expected (and received) plaudits for it like an indulged child.

He reached for the receiver of his desk phone and punched in a number he knew well.

"Hello, Domino's," said the voice at the other end.

"Hello," he said. "I'd like to order the meal deal, please."

SEVEN

Rachel stood in the doorway and watched her son by the light of the streetlamps outside. It was two in the morning, and Billy was kneeling in front of a kitchen cupboard, pans all around him, muttering as he sorted them out, matching them with their lids and putting them in a circle on the floor. The muted clatter of lids on pans cut through the silence of the night. Outside a motorbike went past.

He was muttering, almost crooning, to something he was cupping in his hands. Rachel had no idea what it was or if it was anything at all. When she got close, he put his hands to the floor, and she thought she saw something scuttling away.

She wished she knew how to stop him from sleepwalking. She took him by the shoulders and steered him upstairs, and he didn't resist. When they got to his room, she saw that he had opened his curtains. She closed them, and immediately Billy leaned over and opened them again.

"Come on, darling," she said. "You're going back to school tomorrow. Today." She tucked him up in bed, kissed him, and decided not to bother to close the curtains again. She went and lay awake in her own bed, hooking a leg round one of Al's for comfort. She didn't sleep again, and then it was six thirty and the alarm was going off. She heard Al making coffee downstairs, including some swearing as he kicked the pans she had forgotten to put away.

Billy's recovery, she told herself, was a journey. Of course no one could slip straight back into their old life. His body was better, but his mind had been affected by going to the brink of death and back, and that was natural. It would just take a bit of time, and then he would settle down.

She had arranged to take him back to school today. The sooner he got back to his old life, the easier he would find it.

At half past seven, she went to wake him. He was sound asleep, his cheek pressed to the pillow. It broke her heart, having to get him up, but he needed to go to school because that was what children did.

"Billy," she said, and she kissed his cheek. "Wake up. School."

"No," he said, and she decided to leave him for a bit. Ten minutes later he came downstairs, bright eyed and cheerful in his pajamas, and sat at the table, writing an alphabetical list of mammals while he ate his cereal.

"Can you think of one beginning with 'f'?" he said, yawning.

"Fish?" said Nina, who was packing files into her bag.

"That's not a mammal! Silly Nina!"

"OK, then. Fox."

"Thank you. Yes. Fox. And 'g' is for giraffe. Are giraffes real or pretend like unicorns?"

"They're both," said Nina. "They used to be real. Then they all died, so now they're pretend."

"Oh," said Billy. "Poor giraffes. Why did they die?"

But Nina was halfway up the stairs, and Rachel decided to pretend she hadn't been listening because she didn't have the energy. Not now.

R achel busied herself with Beth, and then it was time to go and Billy wasn't there.

"Billy!" Rachel shouted up the stairs. "Come on!"

Even from down here, she could hear him thudding in his bedroom; the walls were so thin, and the house so small, that it was hard not to hear what everyone was doing. Billy, however, was apparently unable to hear her shouting. That meant they would be late for his first morning back at school, but she couldn't make herself care. She was still astonished at the thought that he was going back into the world. Now that he would be at school, she was going to spend her days pushing Beth on a baby swing or meeting friends or (more sensibly) planning for her return to work. The flu had eaten weeks of her maternity leave, and there were only a couple of weeks left. She would make the most of it by taking Beth out on tiny, free adventures.

Billy had never been late for school when he went from Henry's house, because Henry dropped him at the ill-named Healthy Startz Breakfast Club, where he got to eat a cardboardy cereal bar and scribble on coloring sheets until the other children arrived. That was deemed by the school to be "better" than Rachel dropping him off just after the bell. She didn't care that the office ladies would give her a look on Billy's first day; she would give them one right back.

"Good luck with that," said Nina, swinging her bag onto her shoulder. "It all looked so promising when he was doing the mammals."

"*Billy!*"

Nina was sliding her feet into her shoes, treading down the backs and then wriggling into place. Rachel handed Beth to her and took the stairs two at a time.

"Two seconds," she said. She noticed as she went up that there was a new patch of mold on the wall. She hoped it wouldn't affect Beth's breathing or give her asthma.

Billy was jumping on his bed, stretching an arm at the top of each bounce in an attempt to touch the ceiling. His hair was all over the place, and strikingly, he was entirely naked. He was laughing helplessly as he leaped higher and higher.

"Oh, Billy," said Rachel. "You've taken your clothes off."

"Because we're jumping."

"*I'm* jumping."

"You is not."

"There's one of you. So you should say, 'I'm jumping,' not '*we're* jumping.'"

"We're jumping. Both of us is jumping." He stopped jumping and turned his freckled face on her.

She sighed. "You and Delfy are jumping."

"She wanted to see if I can reach the ceiling."

"Naked?"

"Delfy says, who cares? She said clothes is strange and silly."

Rachel sighed.

"Tell Delfy," she said, "that you can't be naked at school because lots of people *would* care, believe me. You need a school uniform to show you belong there, and it's freezing outside because it's February, so your clothes will keep you warm, and it's . . ." She checked herself; there was no need for this when Billy knew perfectly well that he had to get dressed. "And anyway we need to leave because we're going to be late, and you haven't even gone back yet."

"Mum, I'm off!" Nina's voice came from the bottom of the stairs. "Literally have to dash right now. Beth's in the high chair. I gave her spoons to play with."

"Thanks, darling! Have a good day."

She heard the front door close and went to Billy's window to watch Nina leave. As she stood at the window, something touched her face, and when she raised a hand to brush it away, she found her hand covered in a spiderweb.

"Argh," she said, trying to shake it off. "Horrible! So gross. Go away! Where's the spider? I'm going to kill it!" She thought she had kept Billy's room clean, but clearly not, if spiders were moving in. She remembered the webs in Sami's cupboard and shuddered.

Nina turned on the pavement, looked up at her mother, and raised an arm. She tossed her hair back, hitched on her backpack, and strode away toward the Tube, into the teenage school world that Rachel could no longer actually know and that she found scary, though Nina seemed to navigate it just fine. She navigated everything brilliantly. Rachel dreaded the moment when Nina would get through all the training and actually set off into space. It might happen in ten years, and that was no time at all. Her heart pounded at the very idea of it. They could not strap her baby into a rocket and blast her into space. She wouldn't allow it.

For now, though, it was just school. Nina's skirt was shorter than regulation would have it, and she was wearing thick black tights and no coat even though there was frost on all the cars and the pavement was shiny with ice.

Rachel had Nina and she had Billy. She had Beth. She had Al. She was lucky. Delfy showed no signs of leaving, but Rachel was happy to think of her as an imaginary sixth member of the family. She thought of Delfy as the spirit of recovery, the last traces of the conquered flu, staying on for comfort and entertainment. It was always Delfy who wanted to jump on the bed or stay longer at the park or eat half a packet of biscuits. So what if she made him sleepwalk or say annoying things on purpose? It was harmless.

Rachel watched Nina until she was out of sight, besotted as ever with Nina's mass of frizzy hair and her awkward walk and the perfection of every single bit of her. She knew she must have been a bit like that herself once. She had been a teenage girl with wild hair and slender legs and no idea how beautiful she actually was. Now she was a haggard mother of three with a naked son who was going to be late for school, and there was a spiderweb on her hand and that was gross.

"You must not kill the spider, Mummy," Billy said. "It wants to be your friend."

"It does not," she said. "It's a horrible thing." As she watched, the spider ran up the window frame and disappeared. She looked at Billy and saw that he was rigid, his face blank. "OK, not that one. But if it was up to me, I'd exterminate all of them. Creepy little things. I know they're good at catching flies, but honestly I'd rather have the flies."

Billy spoke in a calm voice. "Spiders are good," he said. "Spiders have three sets of spinners that are filled with liquid silk. Their silk is stronger than steel. Do you know what a baby spider is called?"

"No, and I don't think I need to. Here." She grabbed him and pulled the white polo shirt with the school logo over his head, taking care not to squash his nose.

"Spiderling," he said. "I'm your spiderling."

"OK. You're half done. Now, put your pants on."

While he was pulling his school trousers carefully up, Beth started to shout, and Rachel ran downstairs to find her wailing with her arms up, demanding the spoons that she had hurled to the floor. Rachel picked her up and snuggled her. The baby took a big handful of Rachel's hair and pulled. Sometimes Rachel didn't feel there was enough of her to go round.

They left the house in the end, and it felt like a triumph. Billy's school was a ten-minute walk away, and she told him to stand on the back of the buggy, even though he was too big to do that, so she could jog through the streets, trying not to slip on patches of ice. Against the odds they arrived just as the bell was ringing without falling over, and she hugged him, kissed his head, and gave him a push and said: "Run!"

All the classrooms opened out onto the playground, but the parents weren't allowed past the fence. She stood and watched as Billy sauntered over to his class, turning to give her a double thumbs-up as he took his place in the line and entered the building with the other children as if he had never been away. He was happy to be at school. She could see that from his face.

Miss Lu, his teacher, looked at Billy and smiled. She came striding over to Rachel. She was so young. Impossibly young.

"Hi there!" she said. "Amazing to have Billy back! I'm so, so pleased."

She touched Rachel's arm to emphasize this fact. "We'll take good care of him, I promise. How is he?"

"Fine," said Rachel, and out of nowhere, she started to cry. She mopped her eye with her sleeve, pleased that she wasn't wearing makeup. "He's absolutely fine."

She was composing herself to tell Miss Lu about the imaginary friend, but she missed her moment, and the teacher rubbed her arm again, said, "Wonderful!" and walked briskly away.

Rachel flashed a watery smile at the other parents and spun around. Sami wasn't here and neither was Emma, and there wasn't anyone she wanted to stop to chat to, because she would cry again.

She noticed the absences, the parents who weren't here because they were at home with their sick children. Yesterday she had been one of them, and today she was not.

"We did it, baby," she said to Beth, and Beth looked up and grinned, her cheeks dimpling. Although Rachel was longing to take her for coffee and feed her froth from the teaspoon and look into her beautiful little face, they had other plans. (Also she knew that she could not even remotely afford frothy coffee.) They were going to do a practice commute. They were going to catch the Tube to Orla's flat, and Rachel would leave Beth there for a bit so she could get used to it.

Going back to work was going to be difficult. However, the money would start to get them back on track, and it would have been worse if she were going back to her old professional job. She had trained as a lawyer, and she still believed the anxiety had almost killed her. When she had given it up and started working as a receptionist instead, life had become immeasurably better.

They wandered home, pausing to look at icy puddles and to smell the wintry air. Rachel pointed out three different delivery drones and swore at a cyclist who came past them with no warning, riding on the pavement even though there was plenty of space on the road. He swore back enthusiastically, without slowing.

"What a dick," Rachel said to Beth, and Beth laughed.

When they were home, she called Al, and unusually, he was able to answer.

"All done," she said. "I ran, but I got him there. And he went in happily. So that's good."

She could hear things going on in the background. Al worked at one of the biggest homeless shelters in London, and Rachel knew that his days were frantic, that this cold winter had been almost unbearable. There was a flu-quarantine zone within the shelter, and policing it was all but impossible, but Al and his colleagues tried. Al wasn't allowed into the zone: it was staffed only by people who had come through the flu and so were immune to it, and even then they all wore the suits. There was apparently going to be a vaccine, but so far nothing had happened.

Rachel felt guilty about stopping him from doing his work. She always felt guilty when she called during the day. But she needed to hear his voice.

"How's my Betty?" he said, raising his voice above the clatter of whatever was going on around him.

Rachel looked at Beth sitting on the kitchen floor, sucking her fingers, looking equably around at everything. Al liked to call her Betty and told her she could call him Al, though Rachel thought that he wouldn't like it if, one day, she actually did.

"She's blissful," she said. "Perfect. Wonderful. Oh, God, I'm going to miss her. Stupid work."

"I know," he said. "But, darling—everyone will be fine. I hate being away from her and you, too. It's shit, but that's the world we live in. We're lucky to have jobs. You know that, my darling. Maybe one day Nina'll make a fortune, and we'll all give up work. Or she'll create a new utopian society in space and invite us to live in it. And meanwhile your mum will dote on Beth. You know that."

She smiled at the phone. "Of course. We're heading off now. I'll leave her there for a bit and see how they get on without me. I love you."

"I love you, too! Shit! Stop that, mate! Got to go." The line went dead.

. . .

After a coffee and a shower, they set off again. Rachel had wet hair because she couldn't be bothered to dry it even though it was freezing outside; the fact that she knew she was going to have to be attentive to that sort of detail when she went back to work made her keener to neglect it now. She just pulled a warm hat over her hair. She had Beth in a sling because it was easier for the Tube, and it hurt her back because the baby was eight months old with chubby thighs and round cheeks and she was gloriously bulky.

It still amazed Rachel that she and Al had created Beth. They had *made* a *person*, and right now she was untainted by the world. She had been subjected to a deadly virus, and the worst it had been able to inflict on her was a few hours of fever in the night, a distracted mother, a brother with an imaginary friend, and too much television.

It was impossible, though, to imagine Beth's future. While Rachel felt that everyone who saw her should love her, she knew that they wouldn't. There were racists and misogynists everywhere, and they were emboldened enough now to say all sorts of things. It broke Rachel's heart to think it, but it was true. Beth was innocent and perfect, but the world was harsh. She had something about her, something a little bit magical. But, Rachel thought, it was easy for her to see it because she was Beth's mother. Other people might not.

When she thought about the future, she became so anxious that she wanted to curl up and scream. (One day she would die! And all her children would be motherless! And meanwhile they were a hairbreadth away from homelessness, which would involve them all piling into her mother's single spare bedroom!) All she could really do was concentrate on the next thing she had to do and look after the people around her as far as she could, in the moment.

There were security cameras everywhere, and in places that seemed not to have them, they were, Rachel felt, just better hidden. She knew someone was watching her, wherever she went and whatever she did.

There probably wasn't an actual human behind the lens, because who would care about Rachel? But the idea that some kind of AI was filtering her movements out as uninteresting was just as bad.

She pulled face masks onto herself and Beth as they arrived at the station. No one was allowed on the Tube without one, and that was a rule that was enforced by actual human beings who had boxes of them that they handed out to anyone who turned up at the barriers without one.

Beth pulled hers off at once, as she always did, and lobbed it onto the ground. Rachel picked it up and brushed off the dirt, holding it over the baby's face as they walked past the guard and down the broken escalator.

The train came as soon as they stepped onto the platform. Rachel loved it when that happened. The train was relatively empty, as rush hour was over, and she sat down and arranged Beth on her lap. She put the face mask on her again, and Beth took it off and hurled it to the floor once more.

In front of them was an advert for Rockolate, which was a stupid-expensive chocolate bar that was a fund-raiser for the space mission. It was going to take more than that, she thought. Farther down the carriage, Guy Clement was advertising mattresses, with the slogan "The most comfortable night's sleep in the galaxy," which didn't even make sense. That man was shameless. He had a funny face, she always thought. His chin tipped upward, and his nose plunged toward it, so his face looked as if it wanted to join up.

He annoyed her disproportionately, so she focused on a government warning instead.

FLU WANTS YOU. Cough and sneeze into your sleeve. J5X has bad effects. Rest is best. Quarantine is what we mean. Wash your hands whenever you can. Stop the flu before it gets you. IF SOMEONE IN YOUR HOME IS SICK, CALL THE HEALTHY HOTLINE QUICK. WE WILL SEND YOU ALL YOU NEED. TOGETHER WE WILL ALL SUCCEED.

Did people take more notice of slogans that rhymed? she wondered. Or did they just sound horribly condescending? Horribly condescending, obviously. She shuddered at the memory of her own call to the "healthy hotline." A bored man had taken her details, and the plastic sheeting, space suit, and a selection of powdered drinks and energy bars had been dropped into the garden by a drone a few days later. That was all the help they had had.

The conspiracy theories had spread faster than the J5X virus itself. Rachel had spent an immense amount of time online during their quarantine, and she had read everything she could find. The flu had been engineered in a lab and released into the population to kill off the poor. It had come from rats, from monkeys, as a result of immigration, on the direct orders of the prime minister, from God. Whatever it was, it had happened fast.

She guided Beth's chubby little finger to the buzzer. Beth pushed it, giggling.

"Hello?" said Orla's voice. "Is that my darling little Bethiepie?"

Beth shouted: "Gah!"

"Yes, it is," said Rachel for clarity. She pushed the door as the buzzer sounded, and they were in the stinking concrete hallway. The lift was working, which was good, and it didn't jolt to a halt between floors: also good. When the doors opened on the fifteenth floor, Beth shouted again at the sight of her grandmother standing in her doorway, right opposite the lift doors, and Orla practically wrenched her out of the sling and ran back into the apartment, saying: "Are you Grandma's lovely girl? Yes, you are!"

Rachel wandered over to the window and looked across London. This block had issues, but it offered a spectacular view of the city. It was breathtaking. Her mother took no notice of it anymore, but Rachel thought that if she lived here, she would never get used to it. She stared out. There were fires dotted all around the place, sending spirals of dark smoke into the sky—probably, she thought, coming from the various encampments that Al had said were springing up on patches of grass across the city, as the cheap housing was bought up and the homeless shelters overflowed. She watched a low-flying helicopter buzzing around, noticed a new cluster of cranes and building work over to the right, and saw the beacon of Crystal Palace in the distance. To the left, although she couldn't see it, she knew that the new, strengthened flood barrier was keeping the sea away, that the water it held back would have drowned the city long ago if it hadn't been there. In the foreground, the gap where the old apartment block had been was still there. She looked directly down, to the paved area. There were just an old man loitering down there and two kids on bikes. Three drones crossed above their heads like flies.

Rachel took a deep breath and followed Orla and Beth into the flat. Her baby, she conceded, was going to be spending five days a week with someone who adored her.

The flat smelled of incense and perfume. There were plastic flowers and fairy lights everywhere, and the Beatles were singing "Your Mother Should Know" on the little record player. Since she had been widowed, Orla had never looked back. She wore what she wanted, lived how she liked, and had thrown in her lot with an eccentric local church rather than the hard-line Catholicism of her youth. Rachel had imagined that her mother might have stopped going to church completely once the shackles were off, but that, it seemed, would have been a step too far.

Orla was dressed in a pair of orange flared trousers and a red T-shirt with a huge spider brooch on it; Rachel knew she was wearing the spider only to annoy her. She looked ten years younger than she had a decade ago. Her hair was dyed raven black.

"You should try going blond, Grandma," Nina had said last year. "Black is a bit . . . witchy."

"I like being witchy," Orla had said. "That's why I do it."

Orla was happy as a widow. Rachel was happy as a divorcée. Maybe the Jackman women just weren't cut out for marriage. Rachel had certainly never felt any need to marry Al. She didn't think they needed a piece of paper, and they didn't have enough money for a party. She barely had enough to buy a bag of lentils for dinner. She really did need to start earning again.

"Off you go," said Orla. "Me and the baby will be just fine. Go to the shops near your office. And then come back again. Try it out."

"No baptizing her into your church," Rachel said, heading back toward the door. "No taking her to church at all. No Jesus. No indoctrinations."

"Oh, fine. I'm still waiting for Jesus to visit. It will happen."

Rachel opened her mouth to reply to this but couldn't think what to say, so she didn't say anything. Last year, when there had been that explosion over London, Orla had been convinced that it marked the Second Coming. She had been waiting for her special visitor ever since.

"Bye, then." Rachel went straight back down in the lift and caught a bus to Canary Wharf, where she wandered into the shopping mall at the base of the tallest tower and looked around with no particular purpose.

The atmosphere in the shopping mall was odd. The cameras were obvious and intimidating. The same rhyming signs about the flu were everywhere, and there weren't nearly as many people around as there would once have been. Although this was a private space that officially had no tolerance of rough sleepers, there were people tucked away, sitting in the crevices of fire doors, darting away as security staff approached. Rachel hoped they had found a way into some of the empty offices because empty office space, coupled with thousands of people sleeping on the streets, was a grotesque thing. As grotesque as spending all the money on space exploration when people were starving to death at home.

She walked past another advert for that stupid chocolate ("Hey there!" Guy called as she approached), put her head down, and carried on.

When Rachel had worked here, before she'd had Beth, the place had always been busy with corporate drones and busy shoppers. Today it was like the aftermath of a zombie invasion. Rachel could hear her own footsteps as she walked across the shiny floors. They weren't the clip-clopping sort she would have made in her work shoes, but a kind of squeaky peeling of the charity shop trainers.

She forced herself to stroll around a bit, looking in the windows of shops she couldn't afford to go into. In the shops were meticulously folded jumpers on shelves and dresses that cost much more than Al's monthly salary. She knew she was going to have to dye the gray out of her hair and learn to walk in heels again before she could come back to work, and even then she would barely fit in. They had employed her here because, as the office manager (half her age) had said at the interview: "We find clients respond well to someone a bit mumsy." She had laughed out loud at that and taken the job.

In fact her work here had been almost entirely enjoyable. It was a million times more fun than her legal work had ever been; she just had to turn up at the tower and use her fingerprint to get the lift to the seventh floor. She remembered the day, a year earlier, when she had sat at her desk and watched a plane exploding in the winter sky. That had been odd, because it hadn't felt like a plane while she was watching it. It had felt like the apocalypse. It had turned out, however, to have been a cargo airplane, and the only casualties were a handful of staff, and no one on the ground. Not nuclear war and (almost certainly) not the Second Coming.

She stretched her walk out as long as she could bear to and then found the bus stop and headed back to Orla's, terrified that in her seventy-five-minute absence something terrible might have happened, but in fact Beth was sitting on the floor, laughing and clapping, while her grandmother danced around her singing "Yellow Submarine."

It would be all right.

"This will be all right," Rachel said to Orla, putting the kettle on and taking out the teapot.

"It'll be a blessing and a joy," said her mother.

EIGHT

Billy came out of school looking happy and told her about his day all the way home. When they came into the house, Rachel patted his head and said: "Why don't you hop upstairs and change out of your uniform?"

Billy hung on to the banister and laboriously hopped all the way up. Rachel heard him muttering: "Because she said 'hop,' but she didn't mean really hop. She just meant go, but this is hopping."

Rachel cooked a curry that was made mainly from tinned tomatoes and textured protein, using enough spices to hide the grimness of it all, and tried to help Nina review for a history exam. In fact, they were talking primarily about Louis. Rachel had seen photos of him and concurred with her daughter that he was a gorgeous-looking boy; he was half Italian apparently. But was he *nice?* Nina said he was. She said he made her laugh, and he made her happy, and she adored everything about him. Also that his family was rich and he went to some private school in another section of London.

The last part of this worried Rachel. She knew she could become obsessed with the idea that the power balance between this boy and Nina was too big. This privileged boy might be abusive and horrible to Nina, who thought she was worldly-wise but probably wasn't.

Beth was in the high chair sucking on a crust and smashing some toys around, without taking her eyes off her sister.

"Anytime at all," Rachel said. "Please, darling. Bring him for dinner or just a cup of tea or, you know, anything you want. You did say."

"Yeah, I know." Nina twiddled her hair, noticed herself twiddling her hair, and then stopped doing it.

Rachel knew this was a mannerism her daughter was trying to lose. If she had wonderful long hair like that, then she, too, would fiddle with it. Rachel had had that hair once, before she'd had it cut to look like a sensible mother's. She had twiddled it all the time.

"So . . . ?"

"Oh, I do want to. It's just a bit strange. I mean, it's the first time I've had a proper boyfriend and it's all a bit . . ." She put on an affected voice. " 'This is my *boyfriend*. These people are my *family*.' I mean, I'm the only one who knows all of you, and that's weird."

"So introduce us, and then we'll know one another. I promise we won't be embarrassing. Unless this house is, you know, too horrible."

"It's not that!" Nina said, though Rachel knew that it was, a bit. "You and Al are OK, Mum, as long as you promise not to grill Louis about whether he's a psychopath. Beth's no problem. Are you? No, you're not. I know!"

"And Billy's better."

"He's not himself, though, is he? He was a normal six-year-old before, and now he's not. It would feel a bit weird going, *This is my brother, and you also need to say hello to Delfy, the creature who lives in his head.*"

"It's not *that* weird!" said Rachel. "He's six. He nearly died. He went to somewhere we've never been and then came back. No wonder he's using whatever coping mechanism helps him."

"I know," said Nina. "I do know that, Mum. Louis' aunt died from the flu, and he really loved her, and I'm sure he'd give anything to have her alive with an imaginary friend rather than dead. I just don't think Delfy's necessarily good for Billy. I hope he shakes it off."

Rachel thought of Billy. He asked questions on Delfy's behalf often. She thought he wasn't sleeping well, because he still appeared in odd places in the middle of the night, doing odd things. He was currently taking things people said literally because it was funny, but she was pretty sure that was all Billy and not Delfy. The hopping up the stairs was cute, as long as he didn't fall, and he hadn't fallen, so that was fine.

"Billy nearly died," she said. "But he didn't die. I felt his heart stop. And it started again, and here he is. It was a miracle. And you know what? I think he's doing brilliantly. Just tell Louis that Billy has an imaginary friend. Loads of kids do. It's not a thing to be ashamed of. I could have done with one myself as a kid."

Nina sighed. "I know. I just worry about Bill. I have a bad feeling about Delfy. But also, I'm just so nervous about bringing Louis round. It makes me cringe, imagining it. I haven't been to his house, and that would be just as bad. How do people do . . . like, social things? It's so *awkward*."

Rachel measured two teaspoons of cumin into a bowl, then added a bit more for extra flavor. "It'll be great," she said. "And once we've met him, then we'll know him and there won't be any more awkwardness." She hoped that was true. It might be, or it might not. "I'll get Billy to behave. So."

She watched Nina open her mouth, start to say something, and then think better of it.

"Yes," Nina said. "Thanks. Maybe I'll bring him home after school one day. Kind of informally. He knows I've got a little brother. He's got a brother himself, and he says he's a twat. And he has a sister from his dad's first marriage, but he doesn't see her. So families *are* complicated, and maybe it would be all right. And he already met Beth and that was lovely and he said he wished he had a little sister, too." She smiled. "It was incredibly lovely, actually."

Rachel froze. "Louis has met Beth?"

"When I took her out once the quarantine ended. We went for coffee, and Louis came and joined us."

"Oh! Lucky Beth, I guess."

"Lucky Louis."

"Exactly. Darling. Just . . . don't try to be the way you think your boyfriend wants you to be." She tipped the spices into the tomato sauce, turned the heat right down so it wouldn't stick to the bottom of the pan, and walked over to Nina. She hugged her and sniffed her hair, because, she thought, you never stopped wanting to sniff your baby's hair. It smelled of perfume and hair product, but the smell of Nina was still the scent of Rachel's first baby, and it was there, underneath all that. "Because you're perfect. Don't go changing for anyone."

"You're my mum, so you have to think I'm perfect. And of course I won't change. I don't know how to be anyone else."

"Good. So, are you going to tell me about the causes of World War One or not?" Rachel patted Beth on her curly head and went to rescue the sauce. "Tell Beth, if you like. She was asking the other day."

"Were you, Bethie? Well, as you probably know, the catalyst was the assassination of Franz Ferdinand, in Sarajevo on June twenty-eighth, nineteen fourteen. Imagine if someone shot me, Beth, and I died and that meant World War Three started. That would be weird, wouldn't it?"

Beth replied with some babble, and Nina kissed her.

"World War Three is going to begin with something small, I'm sure," Rachel said. "But I hope it won't involve anyone shooting *you*. So, why did one person being shot lead to a world war?"

"I know this." She counted on her fingers. "Nationalism. Militarism. Imperialism. Alliances."

"Can you expand on those? Can you chop some garlic?"

"Yep. Both."

Rachel passed her the garlic, a knife, and a broken chopping board. Beth tried to grab them. Nina tickled her cheek, and Beth laughed and flung a plastic cup onto the floor, laughing even more when the lid came off and diluted orange juice went everywhere.

Nina told them about the causes of the war while she mopped it up. Rachel partly listened, but Nina was mainly addressing it to Beth, and anyway Rachel wouldn't have known whether she was right or wrong because she had only a hazy memory of the Tudors and the Nazis from history classes at school. She tended to worry more about the future than the past. She knew that her anxiety had started up again: with Billy better, she was edging back to free-floating worry rather than the laser focus she'd had when he was sick. She worried about people without anywhere to sleep while some bad guy bought all the housing. She worried about Al, trying so hard to help them when he couldn't make everything better. She worried about the families of the people who had died in that plane crash, because going back to her office building had made her remember the shock of that sudden blast of light in a cloudy sky. She worried about Guy Clement getting ready to go to the asteroid while his image tried to sell them things indiscriminately. He had monetized everything; he couldn't be happy, even though he must be rich.

She imagined Nina in space. She looked out of the window and pretended her daughter was up on some asteroid close to the moon. It was easy to do. She tried to analyze how it made her feel.

It did not make her feel that her future was calm.

R achel wondered whether she should go and see what Billy was up to. As soon as she put the rice on to cook, she nipped up to his tiny room and stood in the doorway.

Her little Billy was lying on his bed, reading a book. He didn't look up. He turned a page. His hair was falling across his face. Rachel was not sure whether he knew she was in the doorway or not, because he was completely absorbed. She looked at his little brow, furrowed in concentration. She didn't know what he was reading, but she could see that it had pictures in it and that meant it was probably more or less appropriate for his age.

She didn't even know he could read well enough to be absorbed by a book like this. She took a half step closer and looked over his shoulder. He was reading a children's encyclopedia that Henry had given him, and the page was all about spiders. There was an illustration of a giant tarantula with hairy legs, and it made her shudder.

Still, she thought, whatever Nina said, Delfy was a positive thing. Billy's imaginary friend was encouraging his education. That had to be all right. It was the one thing she refused to worry about.

She tiptoed away. As she was at the top of the stairs, she heard his voice saying something.

"What was that?" she said.

"I said, 'Bye, Mum,'" he said, but for some reason she did not think he was telling the truth.

She could not think what to say, though, and so she left it.

NINE

Nina closed the bedroom door and bolted it before she opened the laptop. The bolt was a recent thing; she had attached it herself last week after she woke in the night to find Billy standing beside her bed, staring at her. When she opened her eyes, he put a hand on her forehead, and his hand had been freakishly warm. Then he had said, "Nina, you are good," and she closed her eyes, and when she opened them again, it was morning.

She wasn't completely sure it had happened, but she wasn't taking any chances. She really wanted a lock with a key so she could leave it locked when she was out, but Mum said they didn't have any keys to these doors and that she didn't want to ask the landlord because she didn't want to draw his attention to them, as that might remind him to put up their rent or sell the house to Alford.

There were postcards of the covers of old sci-fi novels on her wall and a framed photograph of a patch of space taken through the Hubble Telescope many years ago, bright with planets and stars. Her schoolbooks were on the desk. Nina liked things organized. Her mum's chaos, which was made of baby stuff and laundry and bits of paper from school, was all right. It was the bigger chaos, the tide she could feel at the heart of everything, that made her worry. At least she could keep her patch of the universe in order.

She checked the hiding spaces behind her hanging clothes and in the square of floor at the end of the bed, because Billy could have been there doing something weird on Delfy's instructions. It turned out that he wasn't, but he might have been.

Nina wasn't sure that Delfy was as harmless as Mum thought she was. She didn't really know what to make of it, but it made her uneasy. It was strange to have her little brother, who had always been straightforward, talking to a part of his brain he'd sectioned off and given a name. As Mum had said, Billy had been to the point of death, and then he had come back. It wasn't surprising that it had changed him.

She got out the laptop and started applying herself to some homework. First up was computer science, because she should have started it last week. She went to the template page she needed to use and wrote a tentative heading:

Delfy.

Like many of us, she wrote, **Billy was sick with the flu this year. Unlike many kids he got better.**

She stopped and looked at the words, wishing that she found writing easier. Would this be all right? Could she make her coursework project a website about Billy?

She went back and changed the word "Billy" to "Josh."

This was an ongoing project that would make up forty percent of her exam grade. It was important to do it well. The aim was to set up a site and use every tool available to make it as secure as possible. The content barely mattered. It would be good, though, for her to have an outlet for this. She really wanted to get her feelings down.

She would change details. And she knew that no one in the outside world would ever read it. She had tried to keep an old-fashioned diary once, but it hadn't worked. This felt better. She carried on writing.

His mum, Fiona, was pleased. She had looked after him, and now he was well again. He had an imaginary friend, and that was good because it gave him someone to talk to.

She stopped, looked at what she'd typed again, and changed the words so they were in the present tense. His mum is pleased. Now he is better. He has an imaginary friend.

She wrote about Billy and about Delfy, but it didn't feel right. She tried adding the words:

I am Josh's sister, and this is my family's story.

That was better. Now she could do it. She wrote about having to lock her door because otherwise Billy would come and stare at her in the night. She wrote about the way Mum said it was fine because he was sleep-walking.

Josh's illness is the most scary thing that has ever happened to me, she wrote. I know I should be proud of him because he's a survivor. And everyone calls it the flu, but it's not. I hate the word "flu." It sounds cozy, the name of an old-fashioned illness that has been around forever. This is an uncontrollable fever, above all else. It's J5X.

When she had a block of text, she set about doing the technical side of it all. That was a relief. She set up the security and the plug-ins in the way they'd learned in class, and chose a theme.

Mum, like everyone else, had never taken on board the basic fact that this wasn't flu. No one in the mainstream had. In fact this virus, according to stuff Nina had read online, was unlike anything that had been seen before. There were so many ideas about its origins that she had stopped reading about it because it made her feel too weird. She didn't like things that resisted explanation or control. So she didn't put any of that on her homework site. As she got to work on the technical stuff, she felt calmer.

Nina had, of course, known Billy for all of his life, and sometimes he annoyed her absolutely fucking massively, but his recovery felt to her, as it did to Mum, like a miracle. She had been nine when he was born, and she had adored the baby, then found him irritating when he started destroying her things and getting all the attention. Soon after that, though, she was just glad that she had a sibling to hang on to during their parents' divorce. Even though Billy was too young to understand, Nina had been relieved to be able to take him along with her to whichever house they were going to. He had stopped her feeling awkward because there was always something to do for Billy, and then things began to be normal. When Beth arrived, everything was properly lovely.

Now Nina was old enough to be pleased that her parents weren't together, to notice that Mum was able to be herself with Al, that Dad was better off on his own because he loved to be in control. Dad would rather do his own cleaning than entrust it to anyone else, be it a cleaner or a girlfriend. Nina could see that trait in herself, and even though she didn't like it much in Dad, she was doing her best to harness it for good. It would be useful, she thought, in space.

However, Delfy wouldn't stop niggling at her, and when she looked at the words she had written, it was clear. Billy needed help. This was still a part of his illness, and there might be an easy treatment. The imaginary friend might be a known aftereffect of the virus and would, perhaps, be banished with extra vitamins or something. Nina didn't want to worry Mum more than she was already worrying ceaselessly about everything, but she thought she could, perhaps, have a word with Al. She would set her alarm for a bit earlier than usual and go to talk to him when he was making his and Mum's coffee when Beth woke up. Al would be able to suggest a doctor's appointment in a way that Mum wouldn't interpret as criticism. Nina wouldn't.

Nina closed her work and switched on the camera so she could make sure she had her best angle showing. She pulled her hair over one shoulder and decided not to touch up her eye makeup because that might look desperate.

She clicked the icon with the phone on it. He answered at once.

"Hey, space girl," he said. She grinned. Louis was her boyfriend, and she arranged her hair and got excited about talking to him and all of those things, but he was also her best friend, and she loved to hear his voice. That had begun as soon as they started going out.

Nina vividly remembered the first time she had gone to Space Skills, which was also the first day she had seen Louis. She had hung around the house too scared to leave. Al was the only one who had realized what a big deal it was. He had looked up the course and said: "Bloody hell, Nina—it says here there were five hundred applicants per place! That is incredible!" However, Mum had been busy with Billy and Beth, and then Billy got ill, and so a couple of days later, Nina had to pack her stuff and move to Dad's.

That first time, though. She had arrived a few minutes early and stood in the big hall, certain she was going to be exposed as the person whose name had been written down by accident. Maybe there was another Nina Stevens, a much cleverer one, whose place she had taken.

Then she saw a boy across the room, and something had clicked instantly. She hadn't spoken to him, but at one point had got close enough to read the name on his jumpsuit: Louis Ricci. The following week he asked her about coffee, and that was that.

The more time they spent together, the more she liked him. (Loved him? They hadn't said that.) Maybe, she thought, this was what having a boyfriend was like. She didn't know because she hadn't properly had one before, but she had always assumed that if you *had a boyfriend*, you had to be rigorously in control of how you did your hair and whether you were wearing a dress he'd seen you in before and what you let him do and what you didn't. That was the approach many of the girls at school seemed to take, as if it was the nineteen fucking fifties. There was still this idea even now that boys were ruled by their urges, and a girl's role was to defer and to allow and to restrain.

Nina had never fancied any of that, but now she had Louis, and it wasn't like that at all. He made her laugh, and she made him laugh. Nina and Louis. Louis and Nina. She was surprised to find herself so conventional, even if they were, less conventionally, training to colonize the universe.

"Hello, gorgeous," she said, wishing she could reach through the screen and touch his cheekbones. "Y'all right?"

"Now I've seen you, I am," he said, and she laughed.

They discussed their days. She looked at the room behind him, but all she could see were blue walls.

"How's Beth?" said Louis.

"She's brilliant. She wants to see you again."

"Same! I can't wait to see her. Can we take her out for coffee after school or something?"

"Of course. Or . . ."

"Mm?"

"Or you could come over here. Sorry. My mum *really* wants to meet you."

He exhaled and ran his fingers through his hair, and Nina watched it fall back down across his face. "Mine wants to meet you, too."

"Shall we do it?"

"Meet the families?" he said. "That's somehow scarier than moving to a spaceport on an asteroid."

"I know."

"So yes, let's do it."

Nina knew no one really spent their life with the person they were going out with at sixteen, but she hoped that, in her case, she would. She never wanted to break up with Louis, to have to cry and miss him and hate him. She imagined breaking up with him and then being strapped into a rocket with him anyway. That would be fun.

Louis went to private school, like most of the other space cadets, but he was embarrassed about his family and liked to gloss over it and say they were wankers. Nina's dad sometimes said he wanted to send her to a posh school for sixth form, but she wasn't going. She went to the closest secondary school to her house, and it was fine. It was what she knew, and she liked it: she knew she was going to do well in her exams because she was working hard. Her focus was beyond that.

Class sizes were smaller now that people were missing. Three students in her year had died. Everything was strange.

"Better go," Nina said after a while, when she realized it was late and she still had a lot of homework and a plan to get up early in the morning.

"Yeah," said Louis. "Same. You look beautiful."

For a couple of seconds, she wanted to say, "I love you," but she held it back. Thank God. It would have been terrible to blurt that out, even if it was true.

In the morning she stumbled, yawning, down the stairs, her dressing gown wrapped tightly around herself. Al was standing by the kettle, singing to himself as he fiddled with mugs. The kitchen looked different, and she realized that it was because everything was lined up. The things that they kept on the sideboards were arranged in height order, from tiny spice jars to the huge china pots that were filled with lentils and pasta from the refill shop.

"Morning," she said. "This looks neat."

He turned and smiled at her. "Wasn't me." Nina and Al were uncomplicatedly friends. She thought he was the best thing that could have happened to Mum. "You're up early."

"I wanted to talk to you." She looked up at the ceiling to signify *away from Mum and Billy.*

"Gotcha." He lowered his voice. "Delfy, right? You're worried?"

She sat down, and he sat opposite her. "Yes," she said. "Do you think it's OK? I mean, it probably is, but I don't know. He must have done this. I wish he'd stop." She gestured at the tidy kitchen.

Al looked at her and sighed. "Yeah. Your mum's always finding him in the night and taking him back to bed."

"He came into my room the other night! I woke up, and he was staring at me."

"He does that to us *all the time.*"

"Could we get Mum to take him to the doctor? I mean, I was thinking, maybe it's a post-viral thing. There might be a tablet or something. It could be easy."

Al nodded. "Good point. I'll suggest it right now. You know, I've seen guys at work, rough sleepers, with this same thing—a voice in their head that starts to control them. And for what it's worth, they seem to shake it off in the end. Billy probably just needs a bit of help. It's been worrying me, too. But your mum's had such a hell of a time, it's hard to say anything."

"Hasn't she! You've had a hell of a time, too."

Al nodded. "Who hasn't?" He stood up. "Coffee?"

"Yes, please."

He grinned at her as he got a third mug out. "Your mum really wants to meet your boyfriend, you know. She really, *really* wants to meet the mythical Louis."

Nina put her face in her hands. "Oh, God. Yes, I know she does. She will. One of these days, she will."

TEN

Rachel was sitting in bed, feeding Beth, and the smell of the coffee was making her happy. All the little things were miraculous. The sun was shining through the tatty curtains and making everything glow. For a moment, she let herself believe that the world was as it should be. Beth was dozing as she fed. Billy hadn't stirred, which meant that Rachel was filled with blissful tranquillity. Nina, in weekend mode, would probably not be up for hours.

Al came in with a waft of coffee, a mug in each hand, and she tried to freeze that moment. Since he had been in her life, she had finally managed to exhale; she had never known before that she had been holding her breath, waiting for him. Now he was here, and something was complete.

"I'll put it here." He set on the table within easy reach a mug that had THE HOLY GRAIL printed on it, and she managed to take a sip of coffee without spilling any on the baby's head.

Quiet moments together were rare for them. She looked into his eyes and grinned.

"If she goes back to sleep . . . ," she said, nodding to the baby. She smiled at him in what she hoped was a flirtatious way, though she knew it might actually look a bit deranged.

"Oh, yes," he said. "Nina's up, though."

"Nina? Are you sure?"

"I met her in the kitchen. We had a chat. I made her a coffee."

He climbed into bed beside her, kissed her, and tickled Beth's toes. Rachel breathed in the smell of him.

When she had left Henry, Rachel hadn't planned to need anybody except Nina and Billy. She would be self-sufficient, and they would live by their own rules, and no one would complain about the way she did the housework or try to make her wear the clothes he thought would suit her, which, in Henry's case, happened to be the dull, boxy things his own mother would have worn.

When Nina and Billy were at Henry's, she had done the classic post-breakup things. She went out with friends. She went to the gym. She lost weight and got her hair cut and then dyed it as blond as she could manage without looking scary. She had self-conscious sex with a much younger man once.

And then Sami had invited her to someone's house party, and she met Al, eight years younger and gorgeous, with something in his eyes that made her feel she had always known him. They just hadn't met before.

They went on dates and then spent whole weekends together when the children were with Henry. Then he met them, tentatively at first, then slotting into the family and somehow becoming its backbone. Last year they'd had Beth; Al had desperately wanted a child with her even though they couldn't afford one. She had not expected to get pregnant at her age, but it had happened. They never had enough money, and things often got difficult with Henry. For the past few months, Billy had been the overwhelming worry, but in themselves, they were happier than Rachel had ever dared to imagine possible.

Al made her feel desirable. He made her feel alive. She knew she was prone to panicking, and Al talked her down. She had no idea what was in this for him, but she knew that she was the luckiest woman in the world.

Beth finished her feed, and Rachel sat her up on her lap and rubbed her back. Beth looked at them both in turn and giggled. She was wide-awake.

"Another time," said Al, and he stroked Rachel's face.

"Another time," she said.

He covered his face and uncovered it again, and the baby giggled. Beth was the sweetest baby ever. She needed to stay this way, Rachel thought, and never become a difficult six-year-old and never, never, never get ill ever again.

"Meanwhile," she said, "lunch with my mother?"

"Next best thing."

She saw that Al wanted to say something. He kept starting to talk and then stopping.

"Say it," she told him. "Whatever it is. Say it. It's fine."

He hesitated, then spoke. "OK. In a way this is none of my business. But Nina was asking, and I wonder if she's got a point. Do you think we should take Billy to the GP? Now that he's better? Just for a checkup? You know?"

As soon as he said it, she could see they were right. She couldn't believe she hadn't thought of it.

"Sure," she said. "Good idea. I'll call in the morning."

At nine o'clock, Billy still wasn't up. Rachel pushed his door. His floor was still clear, even though he was well, and all his toys were stacked in their box. Billy was fast asleep, his hair on his creamy cheeks, one arm flung out. She paused, watching and listening.

He was breathing. It was OK.

Rachel picked up the laptop that was beside him, surprised that Nina had let him take it. (It was officially a "family" computer but was used almost exclusively by Nina.) Billy had the iPad Henry had got him, but

Rachel took it away at six every evening and generally used it, if she had a spare moment, to search for "imaginary friend" on parenting forums.

She brushed the hair from his face. He mumbled, and she crept out of the room, almost closing the door behind her.

An hour later Billy shuffled into the kitchen, looking confused.

"What does 'organism' mean?" he said.

"It's anything that's alive, I think," said Al, who had just strapped Beth into the pushchair. "Right, I'm taking Betty out for a walk. Those drones are not going to point at themselves. Have a nice breakfast, Bill. We'll be back in time to go to lunch."

As soon as the door clicked shut behind them, Billy looked up from his cereal and said: "Grandma didn't like Al because he's got brown skin, but now she does."

"Billy!" Rachel said. "Grandma loves Al. Please, don't say that to her. Or to Al. Grandma votes for some dodgy people, unfortunately, but she loves all of us. God only knows what she's thinking."

Billy nodded.

"She loves Beth," he said, "because Beth is cute. Babies make everyone think they're cute so people will want to look after them because they is too little to look after themselves. Beth would die if you didn't look after her. If you and Al died, Nina would look after her. If Nina died, too, then some other parents would have her because I would be too small to look after Beth."

Rachel stared. "Billy?"

"Beth is in Grandma's family, and that makes her not be racist to her. Lots of people hate people who are different from them. Humans do actually *want* to fight because otherwise they wouldn't care about skins and things. People always want to fight other people."

"Billy? Where's this coming from?"

"Delfy wants to know if it's true. She thinks it's 'diculous."

"Oh, for God's sake, stop saying things like that."

"Sorry, Rachel."

"My name is *Mum*."

"Sorry, Mum."

He ate his cereal in silence after that, frowning and mouthing things as if conducting an internal dialogue. Nina stumbled in after a while, her hair huge around her head, and made herself a coffee. If she had been up early, Rachel thought, she had certainly gone back to sleep.

"Where's the laptop?" she said as she waited for the kettle.

"Billy had it."

"Christ's sake! Billy, you *never* take that laptop without asking, OK?"

"Sorry." Billy didn't look sorry.

"Let me guess: the voice in your head told you to do it."

"She did want to know things."

"What things?"

Rachel saw his eyes flick to her, then to Nina, then back down to his bowl. "She wants me to start to find out things for her. Even if I don't want to, she makes me. She is practicing using my body to do her own things. She shares it with me. She wanted to know about racist people, and she wanted to know about organisms."

"What kind of organisms?"

He looked miserable. "I don't know. I don't understand."

"How did you even get into my room? I swear the door was bolted."

Billy shrugged. "It did open."

Nina always said she didn't want breakfast because it might make her fat, but when Rachel put a piece of toast and peanut butter in front of her, she ate it. Rachel had known she would. She understood Nina. Even though she was not always easy (Nina liked to be right about everything, all the time), Rachel knew her better than she knew anyone. Nina made herself another piece of toast and left the room in a cloud of frizzy hair and sleep.

Rachel didn't know how Billy's mind worked anymore.

. . .

When Billy finished his breakfast, Rachel picked him up and held him as if he were a toddler, walking around the room, snuggling her face into his neck while he squirmed and then relaxed.

"We might take you to the doctor next week," she said. "Just for a checkup. Now that you're well."

Billy laughed. "Silly Mummy! Doctors is for when you are *not* well."

"I know. Just to check you over. The doctor might, you know. She might like to talk to you about Delfy."

"OK," said Billy. "Yes. Delfy would like to see a doctor." He paused. "She would like that lots."

"Then that's settled," she said. "Right. What else? Oh, could you grab your lunch box from your bag? We forgot to do it on Friday, didn't we? I'll wash it up now, and you can have it nice and clean for school to-morrow."

She put him down and watched his face change.

"No," he said, his voice tight. "I'll sort it out on my own. I don't think you need to do my lunch box, Mum. You have enough to do of the other things."

Rachel stared at him, and then they both moved at once, racing to his schoolbag. Billy got it first and held it to his chest. His breathing was jagged and panicky. She didn't want to prize his bag out of his hands, but if she had to, then she would.

"Please." He was crying now. "Please, Mum. I maked a mistake. I'll put my whole lunch box in the bin and buy a new one with my own money. You mustn't see it."

"Billy?" she said. "Billy—what the hell is it? What's happened?"

"You did say it," he said through his tears. He paused to collect himself. "Delfy doesn't get it right. She did want to give you a present. We called them, and they did come. Delfy said this was what you wanted. This is what *you did say* you wanted. You wanted them all to be dead, but they weren't, but they will be soon." He stopped. Sniffed noisily. Wiped his eyes on his sleeve. "You *won't* think it's a nice present, Mummy. You will hate it. Delfy doesn't understand. We must put the box in the bin, and you must not look. Please. Sometimes Delfy does make me do things, and I can't . . ."

Rachel knew she had to calm him down, so she held open the lid of the bin and let him drop the lunch box into it. She hugged him. Billy sniffed and hiccuped for a minute or two, then perked up and went into the living room to watch TV.

When she could hear the cheery tones of generic children's television, Rachel took the lunch box out of the bin and opened it.

Spiders ran up her arm. Some of them went into her hair. She screamed and dropped the box, and they dispersed across her kitchen floor and into every crack and crevice. They went everywhere, and then there was just an empty box on the kitchen floor, and her hair was alive with crawling creatures.

ELEVEN

G raham was walking in Regent's Park at lunchtime. It was sunny but cold, his favorite weather, and he was making the most of it because the sky seemed to be throwing icy rain on the city almost every day. He was marching around, getting his steps in, listening to Shostakovich's *Gadfly Suite* on his earphones (it made the world dramatic and meaningful) and wondering how to move forward with his research.

He was carrying a paper bag of lunch that he had bought from a chain café. In an attempt to be healthier and more ethical, he had picked up a vegan wrap, a pot of fruit, and a bag of kale chips. He was already regretting it: he had bought it mainly so he could show Lauren that he listened to her advice. He would almost certainly get a pizza later.

Last week he had asked Lauren to do an experiment. She had called a random selection of GPs' surgeries. "About one in five," she reported back. One in every five surgeries had been able to report that they had a patient who fitted Graham's niche criteria: they must have had J5X flu, and they must have used an imaginary friend to pull back from the brink and recover, and they must now be troubled by that friend. He had put no age parameters in place, but all the results were prepubescent children.

This was enormous. He needed to cast his net wider, and wider, and wider. He needed to work out what the hell was going on, because his sample of five very rich children (only four of whom really had post-flu psychosis), plus Kitty the outlier, wasn't enough. He had more children he saw weekly, but again, he saw the tip and he wanted the iceberg, because nothing made sense. You didn't get psychosis from flu. It could be triggered by various conditions (Alzheimer's, lupus, a brain tumor) or by drugs or alcohol, or it could be part of schizophrenia. But it didn't come on the heels of an illness that wasn't really flu at all. It did seem, however, to be an effect of the mysterious J5X.

The sun was shining, and he was curiously energized, and so he walked down to Oxford Circus, where the old Topshop site was still rubble (smoke from several small fires rising straight up into the sky), and he stood and surveyed the scene. It scared him. There were so many homeless men, and . . . He looked into the fire exit of a bank and took a step closer. There was a woman. She had long, straggly hair and a black eye. He took his earphones out and shoved them into his pocket.

He couldn't remember seeing a homeless street woman for years, and he had always hoped that it was because they were prioritized for help. Yet here was a woman on the street. She could have been any age from thirty to sixty.

She looked up. "Man looking at me," she said with glazed eyes. "I don't know. I don't think so."

Graham fumbled in his bag. This woman looked very much like someone with a voice in her head. What would Imogen have done? He tried to channel her voice. He screwed up his eyes and concentrated.

Then heard it loud and clear, coming from somewhere to his right. *Give the woman food and money! Honestly, Graham. Do I really have to tell you?*

He looked around, and there she was. Imogen was standing beside him, in one of her vintage coats, with impeccable bright red lipstick and her hair done exactly the way she had liked it, cut at her jaw in a straight line. She rolled her eyes and started to walk away.

"Wait!" he shouted.

He felt his knees wobbling, and the world tipped over. This was the first time she had appeared to him outside the flat. He screwed his face up and willed himself to stay in control. The thing that happened when he met Imogen's ghost must not happen here. He felt the blackness coming for him. He felt it above his head, ready to drop down.

"No," he said, though he didn't know whether he had spoken aloud.

It kept coming.

"No!" he shouted, definitely aloud.

Everything disappeared.

H e was sitting, leaning on a fragment of a wall, and smoke was acrid in his nostrils. In fact the smell of everything was intense. It was the smoke of random things being burned, and it was unwashed clothes, sweat, piss, and who knew what else. He stayed like that for a moment, eyes closed, and began to orientate himself.

"Because he looks after the children," said the woman.

He opened his eyes just a slit, then closed them. He was sitting somewhere in the rubble, in a place a person like him would never have ventured, and four pairs of eyes were fixed on him.

"You OK, mate?" said a male voice. Graham nodded, eyes still closed.

"You had a FUNNY TURN." That person shouted the last two words.

"He's awake, but he's pretending he's not," said the woman. "Doesn't want to see us. But we take care of him because he takes care of the kiddies. He's the man with the place under the ground."

He opened his eyes properly. The people were staring at him, and beyond them there were more people, also staring at him. The street was perhaps fifteen meters, and a different life, away. There, people walked past in their warm clothes, eyes firmly ahead.

"Oh," he said. "Sorry." He started to stand up, but his faculties were half gone and his head was dizzy. Imogen had been here, and then she'd walked off. If she was going to follow him around town, he would be done for. He wouldn't be able to function at all.

He fell back and sat down hard. The four people around him laughed. When he looked, he saw that they were three men and that woman.

He looked at the woman. "What did you say about the place under the ground?" he said.

"The place," she said. "You know, mate. Your place." She looked at him, and he looked back at her. Of course she didn't know about the ward. She couldn't possibly. He shook himself. Pulled himself together.

"Here you go, mate," said one of the men. Graham reached out and took whatever he was being offered without thinking, then looked at his hand, which was holding a squashed sausage roll. "Eat it," said the man. "Get your strength back."

Graham handed it back. "You're very kind," he managed to say. "But really, you have it. I don't . . ." How to be tactful? "I don't think I could eat anything right now. You should have this, too." He handed over the paper bag with his lunch in it, which was still, oddly, in his hand. At least that got rid of the vegan wrap. A tiny bright side. He looked around at the campfire, the pile of dirty sleeping bags, the clusters of people around different fires, and he saw that, since the site had been abandoned for so long, it had become a home for people who had no home. It was a community.

They all spoke at once, but he couldn't focus. A young man (very young) helped him to his feet, and another took his other hand for balance, and so he managed to stand upright. He looked around. No one was there. Actually plenty of people were there—it was teeming with life— but Imogen wasn't.

"He's standing up," said the woman, who, he was sure, was talking to a voice in her head. "He's going to fuck off now."

Graham smiled at everyone, embarrassed, and took out his wallet. "I am going to fuck off," he agreed. "Thank you so much for helping me. It's extremely kind of you all." He handed them all his cash. "Thank you. You're very kind."

"Look after them," said the woman, almost to herself, as he picked his way through the rubble and left.

H is strength came back as he walked. In five minutes, he was back at the office, and no one would know what had just happened. They could, he realized, have taken his wallet when he collapsed. Instead they'd given him a sausage roll.

The woman could not have known about this place. She just couldn't.

He decided to go down to the ward before he went up to the office. He had to wipe his hands on the back of his trousers before he could get the lift to recognize his thumbprint, and when the doors opened at the bottom, he was excited about seeing his young patients.

There was one spare bed in Giraffe ward. He would very much like to find a patient to put in it.

TWELVE

Rachel washed her hair three times and scrubbed her whole body in the shower again and again and again, but even then she couldn't get the feel of all those tiny legs off her hands, her arms, her neck, her head. She brushed her teeth and carried on brushing them even though she had not, of course, eaten any spiders. There had been a few dead ones left in the box, and she had tipped them into the bin, but all the spiders that hadn't fallen out of her hair under the shower were in the house, alive and hiding. If Delfy was trying to give her a present, as Billy had said, then she could not have picked anything worse.

She remembered the conversation: she had said she wanted all the spiders to die. Billy had checked whether she meant it. She had said that yes, she did. Spiders were evil. She had been emphatic about it because they had always been one of her *things*, and she had exaggerated it for effect, because she thought it might make Billy smile.

This was her fault. Somehow, most of the spiders had survived two days in a box with Billy's lunch crumbs. Billy had known—of course he had known—that she didn't want a box of mostly alive spiders brought home. How could he have done this?

Billy had brought her a present from Delfy. A grotesque present that was very definitely not from Billy himself.

She was out of her depth.

Last time Orla saw Billy, she had thought Delfy was hilarious, a sign of Billy's innate brilliance. Orla always thought everything about Billy was a sign of innate brilliance because he was a boy. She had wailed down the phone to Rachel when he was ill. Her whole church had prayed for him, and it was, according to Orla, thanks to them and to God that he had pulled through.

Maybe it was, Rachel thought. Something had saved him. God seemed as likely as anything.

As Orla often said, she had always been disappointed that Rachel, her only child, was a girl, and then Nina came along to be a disappointment, too. Now there was Beth. Billy stood alone, a brilliant brave boy among a sea of boring girls. That, at least, was sometimes Orla's view of the situation. Other times it was more nuanced; it depended on her mood.

Rachel stepped out of the shower and wrapped a towel around herself. Lunch at her mother's was a difficult thing at the best of times, and this was not the best of times. Rachel's father had been a violent alcoholic; she had been relieved when he died, but Orla was beyond that. She had been cautiously, then wildly, delighted. She came back to life on the day she realized he was gone for good, and she had grown into her real self since then.

Orla liked Al because she had seen him "take on another man's children and treat them like his own," which made him a saint. Also he was a man. Still, she had been suspicious at first and had questioned him for a long time on his parentage and where he was *really* from. It had been mortifying, and Al had been incredibly gracious about it, as she refused to accept Liverpool as a valid answer. Orla had, however, adored Beth from the start. She had been desperate for Rachel to have another boy, but she never mentioned that again once she saw the baby. Beth was magical. Rachel truly believed that. She calmed everything around her.

As Rachel got dressed, she tried to scrub the spiders from her mind and also attempted not to think about work, though making an effort not to think about it made her dwell on it by mistake. This journey to Mum's flat was going to be a part of her life from next month. Making herself look like a receptionist, and dropping Billy at the school breakfast club, then commuting first to Orla's flat and then on to Canary Wharf, was going to be a monumental challenge; actually welcoming people into the company and telling them to sit down while she phoned through to the person they were visiting was the easy part. She liked sitting there, working the phones, never responsible for anything but the internal mechanics of the company and the coffee run. She liked smiling and helping people out or else producing a steelier smile and making them go away.

The struggle would be the part where she did her hair, eyebrows, and nails and buffed and polished and straightened everything when all she really wanted was to hang out in the park with Beth.

Rachel put on a red flower-patterned dress that she had just managed to squeeze back into and a warm cardigan, and she thought she looked nice enough. She had to add thick tights because she could see how cold it was outside: everything was glittering, and people were wrapped in scarves and hats, with their heads down and their hands in their pockets.

She dried her hair and tied it up, then put on some lipstick and plucked her eyebrows in a cursory fashion. Nina, of course, had eyebrows that were "on point" at all times. Rachel secretly thought they looked a bit silly, but she knew that was because she was old. When she had been a teenager, she, too, had had stylized eyebrows.

She looked at herself. So much effort, just to stop her mother from announcing that she had "let herself go." Mum was going to say that anyway. She knew she was, because Rachel's hair was grayer than Orla's and she couldn't afford, or be bothered, to do anything about it. And why would she? Hair lost its pigment as you got older. So what? She was hoping they wouldn't mind that at work, that they would see it as part of her "mumsy" charm.

When Al and Beth came back from their walk, Rachel ran upstairs to fetch Beth a pink jumper that Orla had knitted and found three spiders in the cot. She killed them, scooped up their little bodies with a piece of paper, and threw them out of the window.

Billy did not speak during the Tube journey to Upton Park. It was hard to talk with the masks on, but he didn't even try. He was silent during the walk to Orla's building. Al was quiet, too. Nina was still furious because of Billy stealing the laptop from her room. Rachel's head was full of spiders, but she chatted to no one in particular as they walked, to make sure they weren't the kind of family who walked in silence.

"I hope Grandma's cooked something nice," she said. "I wonder if she's got any biscuits for you, Billy." No one really answered. She kept talking instead, right up to the foot of Orla's tower block. "Here we are, then."

Rachel looked at Billy. Normally he rushed to press the buzzer and announce them over the intercom, but he barely seemed to have noticed that they were there, and so she nodded to Nina, who did it instead.

"Is that my Billyboy?" Orla's voice crackled.

"It's Nina," said Nina. "We're all here, though. Billy's here."

Orla buzzed them in, and they went up fifteen floors in the stinking lift. Rachel continued to say inane things to plug the silence. She thought of spiders and spoke faster and faster, about anything at all, weaving her own web of distraction.

The doors opened, and they were on Orla's corridor. Billy ran to the landing window and stared out, frowning.

"What's that?" he said, pointing across the city to a metallic shine on the horizon. These were the first words he had spoken since they left.

"That's the flood barrier, mate," said Al.

"Will you take me there, Al? It's int'resting."

"Sure. It keeps all the water out. If it wasn't there, the river would be too big for London."

"Would we drown?"

"No. We'd go and live somewhere else."

Orla was waiting in her doorway. "Here you are, then," she said. "Come in, all of you. Hello, little Bethie. Aren't you quite the little darling today? Did I knit that?"

"You did," said Nina.

Orla fingered the cardigan. "Clever me."

She looked Rachel up and down, nodded, and kissed her cheek. Her face was soft, and she smelled very strongly of perfume. Today she was wearing a purple dress with lilac flowers all over it.

"You look nice," Rachel said.

Orla nodded. "Thank you, my dear. You, too. Are you going to dye that gray away? Where's my Billy?"

Billy was still at the window.

"Billy!" said Rachel. Nina and Al were already inside. Rachel could smell roasting chicken, but all she could think of was spiders. A roasted chicken with spiders climbing out of it. Spiders roasting in the oven. She shivered.

Billy came over slowly, looking back over his shoulder at the view from the window. Orla had her arms out, and when Billy came close to her, she took his shoulders, looked into his eyes, and gasped very quietly.

"Oh, yes," she said. "Oh, there it is. What is it you're calling it, Billy? Dolby, was it?"

"Delfy," he said.

U nder the circumstances, everything was going all right. Al was drinking the beer that Orla always bought for him, a grateful glint in his eye. Nina was checking the time, because Space Skills started at three. It was only one o'clock. Rachel kept signaling to her with her eyes that she had plenty of time to eat lunch, that she shouldn't worry.

The food was all on the table: chicken, potatoes, and heavily boiled broccoli and carrots. It was bland, old-style food. The air was thick with lunch smells. Rachel felt sick. She stared at her broccoli: the ends of the florets looked like little legs.

They were picking up their cutlery when Orla held up a hand.

"Grace!" she said. Rachel caught Al's eye and looked away, half-smiling. Orla's grace didn't come from church, or from the Bible, or from anywhere, as far as Rachel could tell. It was just something she enjoyed inflicting on them.

"Dear Lord," said Orla, "we thank you for the food that is before us today. We thank you for your boundless grace. May we be worthy of your infinite love and wisdom. May we repent of our sins."

Rachel tuned out because she thought she saw a spider running across the floor—could it have come from her own hair? Or from Billy?—and tuned back in when Orla stood up and raised her arms to heaven.

"May I be smitten down if I steal!" she shouted. "Struck down if I blaspheme! Smite me if I tell a lie!"

"Mum," she said, "he gets the message. Can we eat?"

Orla sat down again. "Go on, then. Dig in."

Billy ate only potatoes, though he did, Rachel noticed, manage eight of them. Nina handed Beth bits of food, and Beth ate them from her little fist. They talked about the safest topics Rachel could manage: going back to work, how Nina and Billy were doing at school, when Beth might manage to crawl. Rachel enjoyed the chicken. They only ever ate meat when they came here.

Billy came to life when he'd eaten his potatoes and gravy. "Have you got any chocolate, Grandma?"

Orla looked at his untouched chicken, carrots, and broccoli and laughed. "No," she said. "No. I most certainly have not. Not a single piece."

Billy pouted. Rachel was pleased that, for once, Orla hadn't sent him straight to the cookie tin. She knew that it would be filled with chocolate and that her mother would let Billy take everything he wanted later.

"But, Grandma," Billy said, "you must not tell a lie. You said so."

He wriggled in his chair, scowled. Rachel watched his face contorting as he had some kind of internal argument. He picked up a fork and slammed it onto the table. He grabbed his knife and held it up. It glinted in a sudden ray of sunlight. Rachel looked at his eyes and recoiled, because it wasn't Billy looking out. For a moment, everything froze.

Billy stood up, the knife still in his hand. Even Orla was staring at him without speaking. He took a step back, and his chair fell over. His breathing was labored, almost asthmatic. He walked toward Orla, and it felt as if he were the only moving thing in the universe.

Beth broke the spell by shouting, "Gah!" Billy stopped and looked round. Rachel exhaled.

"Billy," said Nina, "stop it. You're being weird."

Rachel walked over to him and unpeeled his little fingers from the knife's handle. She looked into his eyes. He looked back, then away. He screwed his face up again, listening to his internal voice, and twitched.

"Leave the table," she said. "Go and do something else."

Billy ran away.

And how about you, Nina?" said Orla when the three of them were clearing the plates. "Will you be answering phones for the bankers like your mammy when your time comes?"

"No, Grandma! I'm training for space, remember? I'm going to do my bit making the new world. I want to be, like, a pioneer, but not like when the British used to go everywhere and oppress everyone. I want to be a pioneer of space, making empty places habitable. I wouldn't colonize or displace any actual beings, I hope. If there did turn out to be any, that would be amazing! I don't know what we'd do."

"Well," said Orla, "thank the Lord I'll be long gone by then, that's all. My nerves couldn't take it. Watching a rocket doing one of those blastoffs and knowing my Nina was on it!"

Nina laughed. "Gran, I could go to the Rock in, like, seven years! It's that close. You'll still be very much around. Sorry."

"Oh, I'll be gone by then." Orla was convinced and pleased about it. "And anyway, there's change coming. Jesus doesn't like the way things are going. You won't need to go to Mars, my girl. You'll get your salvation right here. In fact you shouldn't go to space because you might miss the Rapture."

"It won't be Mars," said Nina.

"Would the Rapture happen on Mars, too?" Orla mused. "If He knew you were there, and of course He *would* know . . ."

Billy walked into the kitchen, picked up the biscuit tin from the countertop, and took the lid off. He stared from the tin to Orla.

"You said there wasn't any," he said. "You did. You said *not a single piece*. Oh, Grandma, I wish you didn't say that."

"Well, you can have your chocolate now," said Orla. "Go on. Take two cookies if you want. Three."

"No, you don't," said Rachel, and she took the tin from his hand and put it back on the side. He glared at everyone.

"You said you should be *smited*," he shouted over his shoulder as he stomped away.

"We need to do something about that boy," Orla said, and Rachel felt herself collapse just a little.

"I know we do, Mum," she said. "He doesn't always feel in control of himself, which is awful. He's doing more and more weird things, and I don't think he even knows what he's doing. I'm taking him to the doctor tomorrow."

"Good," said Nina.

"Yes," said Orla. "The poor boy. I'll have a talk with him."

"Don't do anything weird," said Rachel, and she caught Nina's eye and saw her anxiety. "Nina needs to go in a second," she said, and Nina signaled her gratitude.

"I saw another child possessed once," said Orla, "in Ireland."

Rachel closed the door of the dishwasher and stared at it, waiting for the noise to start. Orla always said you had to point at it for it to work, and in spite of herself, she did, and it started immediately. Normally her mother would have crowed at this, but this time she didn't notice.

"A child *possessed*?" Nina said. "What by?"

"An evil spirit. It was years ago now."

"What happened?"

"Well, there was a priest. An exorcism. I don't know quite what happened, but the child was never the same again."

Rachel said: "Mum, tell me you do not think Billy is possessed by the devil."

"No! A demon. One that's come from hell. Now, will one of you put the kettle on and make us all a nice hot drink? Nina, you go if you have to, darling."

"It's an imaginary friend," Rachel said, but her words sounded lame, and anyway, no one was listening.

THIRTEEN

Billy was standing at the window, staring at London again.

"This is a good view of London," he was muttering. "It's the city where we live. Lots of other people, too. We can't see this from our house."

He turned and looked up at Rachel, and she made stupid faces until he smiled. She picked him up. He gripped her with his legs like a monkey and nuzzled into her hair.

She wanted to whisper, *Go away, Delfy,* into his ear, but instead she said, "I love you." *Don't think of spiders,* she reminded herself. *Do not. Think. Of spiders.*

"I love you, Mummy," Billy said back, and nothing else mattered. Rachel sat on the sofa and kept him on her lap, as if she could keep him safe that way.

"What do you wish for, Grandma?" Billy said. "If you could have one wish come true?"

"Jesus," said Orla at once.

"I wish for all of us to be healthy and happy," said Rachel.

"I wish for a chocolate cookie," Billy said.

Orla nodded, and Billy ran off to get the tin. He ate three biscuits.

Nina had two. Rachel sat on the sofa, next to Al, with a cup of milky tea, and ate two of them herself.

Beth and Al were restless. Rachel put the baby down on her tummy on the floor. Her inability to get around on her own was driving Beth crazy. She wriggled and struggled, then burst into tears. Her face went red, and she made a high-pitched, heartbroken noise.

"Take her home if you like," Rachel said to Al. "She needs a nap. That would be all right, wouldn't it, Mum?"

Al's eyes lit up; in fact, his whole face lit up. His relief was almost a presence in the room in itself.

"If it's all right with you, Orla?" he said. "Thank you for a lovely lunch."

Orla nodded as Al and Beth left. "Yes. Billy and I need to have a talk. Come on, Billy." When he didn't look at her, she stood up and held out her hands to pull him from Rachel's lap.

Rachel let him go reluctantly. "You haven't got anyone hidden there, have you?" she said, imagining an exorcist in the spare room.

"Don't be ridiculous," said Orla.

"I have to go, too," said Nina, and she started gathering her stuff. "Thanks, Gran. It was lovely."

Billy allowed Orla to lead him toward the door and out of it, toward the bedrooms. Rachel wondered whether she should go with them.

Nina sat on the edge of her chair and laced up her boots. She had tied her hair back from her face in a knot, twisting it around itself and sticking a pencil through; Rachel knew she would have only done that with close family, behind closed doors. Now she stood in front of a mirror and made herself presentable for the outside world, shaking her hair out and plaiting it back from her face. Her little face was beautiful. Rachel wished she would understand that. Nina was beautiful and clever, and her generation would do things better.

"I'll see you later," Nina said. "Mum—does Gran really think Delfy is a devil out of hell? That's completely mad."

"You know your grandmother."

It was nice to be alone with Nina; they didn't have much time together anymore. For the nine years before Billy was born, Nina and Rachel had been together, the two of them, almost all the time. Rachel hadn't gone back to work until Nina started school, so she had been with her daughter through her baby and toddler years, while Henry spent more and more time at work. They would go exploring together on the Tube and on the buses. Rachel took her to the National Gallery and the Portrait Gallery and to any exhibitions that took their fancy. They met up with friends. They would often stay out all day, playing in parks and reading in libraries. Nina had kept Rachel going while her marriage was falling to pieces.

The second child had been Rachel's idea: she had thought, nonsensically, that another baby would take the marriage back to the way it had been in the exciting days when Nina was tiny and everything had been an adventure. In fact Billy's arrival had blown what was left of it to pieces. However, it had propelled her out, and it meant that Billy existed, so the whole thing had, in a complicated way, been one of her better ideas.

She looked at Nina again. That first baby was all grown up, and she had a boyfriend. Rachel sipped her tea. "I know you have to go now. Don't worry. Just go to your thing and have fun."

"Thanks, Mum," said Nina. "I'll pop in and say bye to Gran."

When Nina left, there would be only Rachel, Billy, and Orla in the flat. She and Billy would walk to the Tube together. Perhaps they would stop at the park on their way home. As long as she had Billy, and he was breathing, things would be all right.

And in the morning, she really would phone the doctor. She pictured herself in the consulting room. "I just thought I'd get him checked over," she would say. "He was so ill."

"Of course," the doctor would say. Dr. Singh, she hoped. She was the nicest. "You're doing the right thing. The imaginary friend is nothing to worry about. These mild tablets with no side effects will sort it."

Rachel hugged Nina and reached up to give her a kiss. Nina had been taller than her mother for a couple of years: she accepted the kiss, as she always did, by inclining her head down and presenting the top of it.

"Bye, Gran," Nina called, and Rachel heard her knocking on the bed-room door. Then she heard her scream: "What the fuck? Billy, what are you doing?"

Rachel was in the doorway in a moment. She stood beside Nina and stared at the impossible sight of her tiny son with his face screwed up and his hands around the throat of her elderly mother.

FOURTEEN

Nina got out of the flat as quickly as she could. She leaned against the wall in the lift, willing it to get to the ground floor without stopping on the way. Her head was spinning.

Outside the block she stopped and breathed in. There was nothing fresh about this air, but breathing it was better than being in Gran's flat. There it smelled like boiled vegetables and meat, a scent that hung heavy over everything because she would never open a window before May. Nina hadn't eaten meat for years, so she'd had potatoes, broccoli, and carrots for lunch. Gran had never noticed because she cared about only what Billy was eating, and that suited Nina fine. Gran had always really had eyes only for Billy.

Billy would never have actually hurt Gran.

Would he?

Delfy would.

She shook her head to push that thought away. Delfy didn't exist. There was just Billy, and he wouldn't do it.

She would write about it on her secret website. Even though no one would read it, getting it all written down was helping her immensely. She would replace the text with something else before she submitted it at school.

Nina had left Gran's later than planned, and she was going to have to rush to get to her class. She ran to the station, nearly skidding on an icy puddle, waved her phone at the barrier, pulled a face mask on to get past the bored attendant, half-tumbled down an escalator, and managed to dash through some closing train doors.

The train was gloriously empty. She moved a chicken wrapper off a seat and sat down. The lights of the station disappeared, and the black of the tunnel appeared outside. She looked at the adverts, which were for new technology, worklifeplus jobs, and, as ever, that stupid Rockolate.

Guy Clement was her model of how not to be an astronaut. At first she had thought he was amazing. A space scientist in his forties, he had spent more time on the ISS than anyone else in history, and now he was at the forefront of the project to capture an asteroid and use it as a space-port.

Everyone in Britain had loved him, because he was the British figure-head of the project. Then he had started accepting the offers of money and had forgotten to stop. Guy was the face of Rockolate, a mattress ware-house, and a chain of estate agents. He had written a children's book, four guides to living in space (one of which Nina had read many times), and a series of coauthored sci-fi novels. He had recorded an album. Been photo-graphed laughing with the royals. His face with its squinty eyes and his bald head were everywhere. There were two women, one from the US and the other Japanese, who had done pretty much the same as him, but you never saw them trying to sell things.

Nina wondered what had happened to make him want to gather as much gold as he could and sit on it like a dragon in an old story. It was disappointing; she hoped that, if her time came to go to space, she would come back (if she did) with some kind of beatific calm.

A spider crawled out of her sleeve and scuttled away. She gasped and made an effort to calm down. That was weird and disturbing. As she watched, it ran along the row of seats and disappeared between them.

She leaned her head back against the window and screwed her eyes shut to block it all out.

"All right there, darling?"

She sighed and opened her eyes just enough to check the situation. There were three men opposite her. Great. They were scary men, men with no options, and they had taken off their masks. There were a lot of men like this in the city at the moment, and Nina, like all her friends, had evolved strategies. Now she avoided eye contact, stood up, and walked down the carriage. It was an old-style carriage, blocked at each end, so she couldn't just walk down the train until she found someone benign to sit with. She stood by the door, ignoring the things they were shouting, though hearing the words despite herself. "Think you're too good for us, you stuck-up bitch." That kind of thing.

It felt oddly symbolic, to be wearing her anti-infection face mask when they weren't. To be shouted at while having her own mouth covered by the state.

The train stopped at West Ham, and she got off quickly and walked as fast as she could to the Jubilee line platform. It was a bit busier there, and she found a group of women and stood next to them. The women looked as if they were on their way to an exercise class of some sort, and a couple of them nodded at Nina, seeing at once that she was using them for safety. The rats ran around on the tracks below.

A s she ran to the hall, she called Louis.

"See you in there," she said. "I'm running late. Family stuff."

There were protesters outside, as there usually were. She dodged past them, making an effort not to look at their placards. She knew what they said: EARTH FIRST, WE HAVE NO PLANET B; KIDS, PLEASE DON'T GO—WE NEED YOU. She knew they were right, but she also knew it wasn't her generation that had trashed the Earth. Things here had already been beyond repair for long-term human habitation when she was born. She knew that, and they did, too, really. She wasn't going to stop and discuss it, least of all today.

She ran into the ladies' loos to get changed. The room was stuffy, and all three cubicles were occupied, so Nina changed beside the basins. She took off her jeans and hoodie and pulled the uniform on over her leggings and T-shirt. The cadet uniform was a black zip-up suit, and it was Nina's favorite thing. She washed it every Monday, ironed it every Tuesday, and kept it on a hanger for the rest of the week. What she loved the most was the fact that it had a Space Program London logo on the front, which looked a bit like the NASA one, and her name, Nina Stevens, was embroidered below it. Someone had actually stitched her name onto this thing or at least programmed a machine to do it.

From the moment Nina had realized that there really was a plan to set up a spaceport on an asteroid and set off from there for a new, habitable planet, and that the project was already well under way, she had known it was her destiny. She burned inside when she thought about the way it would work if people like herself didn't step up. It would be the same again, with no lessons learned. Resources in space were precious, and they could not burn through them in the way they had burned through everything on Earth. Her generation needed to take charge and sort it out.

It was the first thing that had made her feel idealistic, and she loved it. She had worked so hard to get here.

One of the loos flushed, and Shelly came out. She was the only person Nina had half-known before they started the course.

"Nina!" she said as she washed her hands. "Brilliant. Going in?"

"Yes," said Nina. Shelly was a tall girl, ferociously clever, with an afro that Nina thought looked incredible. She put her arm through Nina's, and they walked to the hall together.

Space Skills were not an easy thing to learn. Nina loved the classes, but they were a million times harder than school, and once she and the others were in the room with their suits on, there was absolutely nothing glamorous about any of it. It wasn't about growing wheat in a space greenhouse and leaping around in zero gravity. It was the minutiae of engineering and astrophysics and astrodynamics. They needed to have the engineering skills to fix anything, and the lateral thinking to improvise solutions in life-and-death situations with no backup. It *was* rocket science. You couldn't do this unless you were incredibly studious and determined, and you also needed to get on with people.

She and Shelly passed through a security gate, tapping their fobs to get in.

The hall was huge, with windows high up in the walls. Today the tables were arranged in blocks as in primary school, and a screen had been pulled down on a wall. Nina looked around until she saw Louis, and she pulled Shelly over to his table.

"Oh, please," said Shelly. "Do we *have* to sit with your boyfriend?"

"Don't you want to?" Nina jerked to a halt as Shelly pulled her arm back.

"How well do you know him?" she said in a quiet voice.

Nina saw Louis looking over at them. She waved.

"Very well, thanks," Nina said. "We haven't had sex, if that's what you mean. No . . . opportunity." Also, though she didn't say it, she was scared of the idea. Getting pregnant would be beyond awful, and if she didn't have sex, she definitely wouldn't get pregnant. There was no place in her future for a baby.

"Have you been to his house?"

"No."

"You might be surprised," she said. She paused, then added: "Ask about his sister."

Nina ran over to Louis, because Dr. Fong was striding up to the whiteboard. She sat down, looking back to Shelly, who had taken a seat at a different table.

Nina put their conversation from her mind for the moment. She would, of course, ask Louis about his sister as soon as she could (she knew he had a brother, and he'd said he had a half sister from his dad's first marriage), but for now she needed to work out a bonus scenario Dr. Fong had put on the board about what you would do if your colleague was fixing something on the outside of your spaceship and the door stuck so they couldn't get back in.

"Good afternoon, space cadets!" said Dr. Fong, who was an enthusiastic man in his forties, one of the architects of the program. "Today, I'd like us all to give a massive welcome to the wonderful Natsuko Nakamura. We're very lucky to have her talking to us today. Natsuko has played a big part in designing the journey from the Rock to Earth Two. She can't tell us much about it, but she can tell you some things."

A small, intense woman in a NASA tracksuit came up and glared, then smiled at them all.

"Great," she said. "Let's dive straight in. You guys are, what? Sixteen? Seventeen? Still at school? Perfect. Young astronauts are the future. Kids are going to be born up there." She gestured to the sky. "They'll be training as engineers before they've cut their first teeth. So, who wants to go to the Rock?"

Every hand went up.

"Who wants to go beyond? It's obviously a journey the likes of which we've never attempted before. We need to get across an unimaginably large distance. Who would be a pioneer?"

Every hand went up again. Nina was excited beyond measure. Natsuko talked about life in a space colony, threw problems at them, and set them some fiendishly difficult work to complete. For a couple of hours, they all forgot about everything else.

FIFTEEN

A t a time like this," said Orla, reaching for the bottle that was on top of her fridge, "you have to have a drop of brandy."

"I'll get it," said Rachel, but the bottle was already in Orla's hand, and then the cap was off, and then Orla had put two glasses on the table.

"Oh, Mum, no," said Rachel. "Not for me."

She had only occasionally had an alcoholic drink; she was too terrified of her genetic inheritance, and while the memories of her father were never at the front of her mind, they were always somewhere, playing like a reel of old film, near the back. It was possible that a shot of brandy might have done her good, as Orla said. However, she felt quite certain that, for her, it would be bad, that one brandy might lead to ten and then to the loss of everything she had and a jump off a bridge in the manner of her father, and so she put the kettle on, made a cup of peppermint tea, and took it over to the sofa. She knew where she was with peppermint tea.

Billy was on the floor, trembling all over. He leaned back against Rachel's legs. He wasn't looking at the television.

Orla sat on the floor next to him, huffing and puffing as she got herself down there, and Rachel felt a bit silly to be the only one on an actual seat.

"Delfy," said Orla, looking across at Billy with sly eyes, "you leave my Billy alone." Orla was not shaken; in fact she seemed energized by the skirmish. She tossed back her witchy hair and pointed at Billy's head with all ten fingers, as if transmitting an electric current. "You *leave him alone*. Right now you let him watch the telly and give the poor boy a bit of peace. And stop trying to take control, because you get it wrong. I asked God to do the smiting, not you. Billy knew that. Listen to him."

Billy refused to look at either of them. He had tried to strangle his grandmother, and it sounded to Rachel as if she had come close to actually being hurt.

"They were struggling with each other." That was what Nina had said, and it was what Rachel had seen, too. "He had her by the neck. And he was crying."

Orla had asked, in her prayer, to be stricken down if she told a lie, and then, soon after, she had told a lie about whether or not she had chocolate in the house. Delfy had used Billy to do the striking down. Orla didn't blame him, and Rachel loved her mother for that. This was typical: her adored grandson had attacked her, and she managed to twist it into not being his fault. Poor Billy, sitting watching children's TV and sucking his thumb, was the victim of the nasty spirit that had come from hell.

It was preposterous. It was impossible. Yet Rachel didn't have a better explanation. She knew Delfy wasn't actually a spirit from hell, but it was feeling as likely as anything. Billy had done two things (the spiders and the smiting) that he hadn't wanted to do. He had been forced to do them by . . . something. Something that, he felt, was outside his control, even though it was inside him.

"I'll start by having a word with the priest," Orla said, twisting to look up at Rachel. "Come here, Billy. Give your grandma a hug." Billy, limp and disengaged, allowed her to shift up and put an arm around him.

"We're dealing with an *imaginary friend*," Rachel said. "Billy can stop this. Maybe he can make up a new friend. One that doesn't mess things up. Or he can take on board that he's better now, and he can fill his time with real friends. Billy can get rid of it. And he will."

She wanted this to be true so desperately that she almost made herself believe it. It didn't feel true, but it had to be.

"Oh, Rachel. No," said her mother. "This is far bigger than Billy. We can't expect him to do it on his own." Billy had shifted away from Orla. He was staring at a TV comedy about King Arthur, smiling slightly. "No. We'll need a qualified exorcist." Orla was frowning, her eyes narrowed as if she were flicking through a mental file of all the exorcists she knew (she probably was) to check who had the best qualifications. "We need to drive the spirit out. She'll be looking for somewhere else to go, so Al will need to be keeping little Bethie out of the way."

Rachel stood up. "Absolutely no way," she said. "No. Way. No. Fucking. Way. I am Billy's mother, and you don't get to do that. No crazed extremist is getting their hands on my little boy. I'll find a psychiatrist."

The two of them stared at each other, each convinced that the other's idea was madness.

S he managed to get a GP appointment the next morning by begging the receptionist and telling her it was an emergency, while assuring her that although Billy was on the flu list, he'd been better for ages, so he wouldn't spread the virus. In the end the woman sighed and said: "Fine. You can see Dr. Singh at nine if you *promise* it's a real emergency."

"I need you to refer Billy to a psychologist," she said at one minute past nine. "Psychiatrist. Therapist. I don't know. Whatever someone is who sorts out children's brains. Ever since he got better, Billy's been troubled by a voice in his head. It's getting worse. He's tormented."

Dr. Singh exhaled. "Do you happen to have private health insurance?" she said. "Through work, maybe?" Rachel shook her head. "Right. Well, waiting lists for child mental health interventions are years long. Children literally grow up before they reach the top of them. I'm sorry, but it doesn't really exist anymore as a state service. It's not a priority. They won't hesitate to throw kids in jail when they're still babies if their mental health . . . Anyway. I'm not meant to say things like that. But it's true."

Rachel put Beth on the floor. "So," she said, "what happens to children who need help?"

"All kinds of things," said Dr. Singh. "The parents find a way to pay for it. That's the best one. But tell me what's been going on, and I'll stick in a referral if you like. You never know."

Rachel told the details quickly, aware that she had only a five-minute appointment.

When she had finished, Dr. Singh tucked her hair behind her ear. "Sorry to hear all this," she said. "But realistically I'm afraid it's not enough to access emergency help. You can sit on a waiting list, and something might come up, or—more likely—you'll get bumped down the list by more urgent cases and nothing will happen. Realistically, if you want to see someone, you're going to need to go private. I could give you some names. There are several people who could work with Billy. It's not an uncommon thing, you know. The imaginary friend responsible for all the bad behavior."

"He tried to strangle her."

"But he didn't succeed, and frankly he was never going to, was he? I mean, he's a little boy, and he'll have been weakened by the illness, too. And it sounds like you didn't actually see it?"

"My daughter did."

The doctor looked at Beth, sitting on the floor and staring up at her with huge eyes.

"My other daughter. She's sixteen. And I saw the end of it. Billy says Delfy made him do it."

The doctor nodded. "It was a glorified tantrum. He wanted chocolate."

Rachel opened her mouth to protest but decided not to bother. Nothing she said was going to change anything.

Dr. Singh tapped at her keyboard. Beth was gazing intently at the scales, and Billy was at school. Rachel didn't want to talk about Delfy in front of him anymore. Partly, although she didn't want to articulate it, she didn't want Delfy to hear her talking and make Billy attack her. The box of spiders had been quite enough; and that was the kind of thing that happened if you were in Delfy's good books.

Rachel took the piece of paper when the doctor printed it and handed it to her. It was a list of names and e-mail addresses.

"How much do these people charge?" She and Al operated on no margin whatsoever. There was zero chance they would be able to find the money to pay for a single appointment, much less for anything regular. She would have to ask Henry. Meanwhile, she would never talk to her mother about Delfy again.

Rachel assumed that a real-life exorcist, in twenty-first-century London, would be a man from an extreme corner of the church, putting his hands on a writhing Billy, yelling at the spirit. She could not bear to imagine it. Children died from those things; she was sure she had read about it happening. She was going to keep Orla and Billy apart until Billy was cured.

"I'm afraid it won't be cheap," said Dr. Singh. "I'm sorry. If I were in charge, things would be different. Now, how are *you* doing? We're out of time but very quickly—do you want to talk about your anxiety? I can see from your notes that you've been prescribed some serious stuff in the past, and you could probably do with something to take the edge off it all again now. You've got a lot on your plate. Billy's flu was a huge strain. I'll give you a script if you like. Billy's issue might not feel so bad if you had a bit of help. It's very common in the parents of recovered flu children to flail around a little as things get back to normal."

She didn't wait for an answer but typed a couple of things, and then a prescription form appeared on the printer. Rachel took it from the doctor's hand, and told herself she must throw it away as soon as she left the surgery.

She remembered the glorious feeling of numbness that various medications had delivered in the past. She had been on different combinations of antidepressants for most of her twenties and thirties, and she didn't want to go back.

She did want to.

She didn't.

"I'm breastfeeding," she said.

"I know. These are fine."

Rachel hesitated. "Thanks," she said, and put the form in her bag. Maybe she would keep it as a talisman. A bit of protection just in case one day she might need it.

"Do come back if you need to. Oh, look at her!" For a moment Rachel and Dr. Singh both stopped and gazed at Beth, who was trying hard to crawl to the scales but just kept landing flat on her tummy. As she stooped to pick Beth up from the floor, Rachel caught sight of the words "anxious mum" appearing on the screen as the doctor typed on Billy's record. She opened her mouth to complain, then closed it. She could hardly contradict that.

SIXTEEN

The following afternoon Rachel went to her old house to ask Henry for money. This was one of her least favorite things to do, even though it was for their joint child. She sat awkwardly on a faux-leather sofa that had not been in the house when she lived there, and looked at the lack of clutter, the shiny neutrality of everything.

The floor was polished wood, and it looked expensive. (In her day it had been battered floorboards and charity shop rugs.) The walls were magnolia, with framed photographs of Billy and Nina hanging at intervals. Perhaps, Rachel thought, she should have framed photos of the kids on her walls, too. She had Billy's and Beth's art stuck up everywhere, but no photographs, and she imagined that framing things was expensive.

She could hear Billy walking around upstairs: he had run off as soon as Henry opened the door. She hated it that this house was Billy and Nina's home, too. It was their other home. She had got out of it, but they hadn't. They still lived here, and they seemed happy. It was a delicate balance, she thought; she needed them to be happy. However, she wanted her house to be their actual home. This one was grander and not rented, and she could no longer imagine having this much space, this little clutter.

"Like I said, it's Billy." She spoke quickly because she wanted the conversation to be over. "Delfy. The imaginary friend." She shifted to the edge of the sofa and leaned forward, elbows on knees. She waited for the smirk.

"The imaginary friend?" There it was: the smirk. Today her ex-husband was wearing a Stereophonics T-shirt tucked into his jeans, with a cardigan over the top. He looked, she thought, stupid.

"Yes."

"I haven't noticed any problems. All I've seen is Billy with his nose in a book. If this Delfy causes mischief—well, he knows not to do it here because that stuff won't be indulged."

"Delfy's a girl," Rachel said without thinking.

Henry did a comedy double take. "Er, right," he said. "I was talking about Billy."

"Oh. Sure. Well, I have no idea what to do with Billy. He tried to strangle my mother." She looked at Henry's face. "Don't say it! Please, don't. This is serious."

"Billy tried to strangle your mother?"

"Yes. He didn't succeed. Again, *don't say it.*"

"Consider it unsaid." Henry made a show of looking very serious.

"I went to the GP. The NHS won't do anything for years, if ever. Waiting lists that go on until he's grown-up and off the system. They just send kids to prison when their mental health gets too much."

"That's a bit dramatic. Billy's hardly going to *prison*. What did she do to provoke him?"

Rachel sighed. She couldn't bear to tell the whole story, so she just said, "She said she didn't have any chocolate."

"Fair enough."

"Before that, last week, I said I hoped all the spiders died because they made a huge disgusting web over the window, and I got it on my arm." She shuddered. "Billy brought me home about a thousand spiders in his lunch box. I think he thought they'd die in there, but most of them were still alive. I have no idea how he got them all. It was the most disgusting thing." She stopped and took some deep breaths, remembering, shivering. Remembering them running up her arm and into her hair. She relived it every night. "He's been . . . not himself for a while, but this week it's been beyond anything. I just . . . Well, I want to take him to a therapist. I can't afford to pay for it. Would you?"

She sat back. She had talked herself up to it and then done it. The house smelled aggressively clean, like pine and lemons and the other flavors chemical companies put into their products to make them seem natural.

"Rach," Henry said in the end, "he's six. He's been ill. He doesn't need a shrink. Christ's sake."

"A counselor, then. Something. I'm out of ideas. Mum wants to get an exorcist."

Henry sighed. "This is such a crock of shit. If Billy was 'possessed,' or if this was a problem in any way, I'd see it here. All I see is a harmless imaginary friend. In fact, better than harmless. A positive force that's made him get his act together with reading and schoolwork. Spiders— unpleasant, yes, but it's the kind of thing little boys do. Everyone knows you hate spiders. It's a practical joke. Your mother has been known to exaggerate. It's not rocket science to connect all of it to the new baby, is it?"

"It's not because of Beth!" Rachel said the words first and thought about them afterward. Could Delfy be a reaction to Beth? But Beth was nearly nine months old, and Billy hadn't had any problem adapting to her arrival. Had he? She had no idea. Delfy had never shown any interest in Beth. Billy thought Beth was brilliant. Didn't he? He had always seemed to adore her. Maybe, she thought, she hadn't looked deeply into it because she hadn't wanted to know.

The idea knocked her off-balance, and she tried not to show it.

"I know you never want to accept it when your actions have adverse consequences. But there's no question about it in my mind." Henry stood up and left the room; Rachel heard him shouting, "Billy!" up the stairs. Moments later, Billy crashed down them.

"What?" he said.

Rachel looked at his little face as he walked into the room. She stood up and walked across the room and took him in her arms, breathed in the smell of his hair and tried not to cry. She was so worried about him. It consumed her.

At home he would have hugged her back, but here he wriggled and giggled out of her grip. She sat back on the sofa and pulled him down beside her.

"Billy," said Henry before Rachel could speak, "what is this *Delfy* business? Straight answer. What is it?"

Billy looked from one parent to the other. "You know what it is. She talks in my head."

"You made it up when you were ill?"

"I did *not*!" said Billy. "Delfy is real. She did come after the flu. She does say . . ." He frowned, then spoke quickly. "Delfy says to tell you she is a thing without a body, and she is very real, and that if you don't stop it, she will make you sorry."

"Billy!" said Rachel.

"Enough of that. Thank you," said Henry.

"Is Delfy easier for you to manage here at Dad's house?" Rachel asked him.

"She likes me to look at Dad's 'puter," Billy said, not answering the question, "so we can look things up. She doesn't like Dad. She says he's bossy. She says she does not wish to *engage* with him."

Henry stood in the middle of the room, arms folded, wearing a closed *that's ridiculous* expression. Rachel looked out of the window at the patio garden, which was now home to a large barbecue set, a metal table, and an uncomfortable-looking collection of chairs. She used to have potted plants out there and an old sofa with a tarpaulin to cover it in the rain. Back then she and Henry had liked each other.

"Bossy?" said Henry. "Well. Stop saying and doing ridiculous things to get a reaction. It's stressing Mum out. You can see that. I know it's fun and it gets her attention away from the baby, but you don't need to do it.

All right, mate? And no strangling your grandmother either, however annoying she may be. Also cut out the spiders. Yep?"

No one said anything. Rachel didn't look at Henry because she didn't want to see his expression. She knew he would be making *humor her* faces at Billy, inclining his head toward her. Henry actually thought he was sorting this out. "And also," he said after a few seconds, "you may say I'm bossy, but I call it getting things done. Men can't be bossy anyway. They're strong-minded. *Women* are bossy." He gave a jovial laugh to signal *a joke*, and then side-eyed Rachel.

"Jesus Christ, Henry." That was enough. The downside to her leaving him was that now he had no one to tell him to shut up, unless Nina was doing it, and Rachel had no idea whether she did.

"On your 'puter," said Billy to his father, "we read that women are weak and men are strong, but Nina said that women is actually strong. Delfy says women is strong, too. Nina and Delfy thinks the white men are scared that they might not to be in charge all the time, and that is why they do bad stuff."

Henry inhaled sharply. "That's enough! Did Nina say that? About white men?"

"Yes."

"Nina!" He yelled it, making Rachel and Billy jump. There was silence.

"She isn't here," said Billy.

"Oh. Yes. Right. Well, then, I'll call her." He looked at Rachel. "If she's saying this, it's clear where she's got it from. Could you tell your new boyfriend to watch what he says in front of my children?"

"He is not my *new boyfriend*. He's the father of my child. And what the hell makes you think Al said that? Nina doesn't get her ideas from whatever the nearest man happens to be saying. Have you *met* Nina?"

"Hmm."

"Forget it. I'll find a way to get someone to treat Billy on my own. I cannot believe you've found a way of blaming Al and Beth for this. You absolute bastard." She could not be in the same room as this man. She had to get away, and she longed to take Billy with her, but she knew she had to leave him behind because it was what Henry always called "*my* night."

Billy shouted: "Yes! You do not blame Beth, Dad! *You do not blame Beth!*"

He drew in a long breath. It went in and in and in, deeper and deeper, until his lungs were inflated as far as they would go. He let it out in a scream and flew at Henry, fists pumping. Rachel couldn't move. She just stared as he screamed and fought and screamed and fought. It wasn't play fighting. He meant this. He hit his father in the face and kicked him between the legs. He pounded Henry as hard as he could.

When she unfroze, she ran to pull him off, and Henry grabbed one of Billy's wrists and half-incapacitated him. Together they overpowered him until he was screaming and crying, with his arms pinned to his sides by Henry and his face buried in Rachel's chest. She kissed the top of his head over and over again as his tears soaked through her jumper. She stroked him and hushed him as she had when he was a baby and then again when he was sick.

"Shhh." She held him as tightly as she could. His sobs subsided.

"For God's sake, Billy!" yelled Henry. "What the hell are you thinking?"

When Billy could speak, he said: "I am thinking that I hate you, I hate you, I hate you!" And then he started screaming again. Rachel didn't know whether he was talking to Henry or to Delfy.

Much later, Henry sent her a text reiterating his position that this was all her fault, but agreeing, in his most infuriating and magnanimous manner, to go halves with her on a psychiatrist. She replied to thank him and to say that, in fact, she needed him to pay for the whole thing.

SEVENTEEN

Good to meet you, Billy, Ms. Jackman, Mr. Stevens," said the man, looking from Billy to Rachel to Henry and making a point of getting all the names right. He was a serious man, with bushy eyebrows and a white beard, and he was surely far beyond retirement age. "Let's have a look at this, then. Good. I'm glad you've come to see me. Very glad."

Professor Watson was a spectacularly expensive child psychiatrist on Harley Street, the London road famous for its private doctors and hospitals, and he listed "imaginary friends" as one of his specialities on his website. In fact, in the small print he referenced "particular interest in the post-flu imaginary friend," and that was why they were here.

This appointment was costing so much that Rachel was struggling to think of anything else. She was the one with the voice in her head now, and it was reminding her constantly that talking to this man for a couple of hours was a more valuable thing, in the eyes of advanced capitalism, than living in her house for a month.

Billy was swinging his feet, sitting on the chair between Rachel and Henry. Professor Watson had asked to see them all together, so here she was again, trapped in a room with her ex-husband.

Henry was on his best behavior. He liked the professor because he was a Harley Street physician with a posh voice. Henry, she knew, would be trying very hard to make this old man like him back. Rachel could sense it in him already: he was sitting up straight and trying to look like a colonel or something. Whenever he met an older man with authority, Henry turned into a little boy seeking paternal approval. She had told him that once. It hadn't gone well.

Billy was staring at a picture on the wall. It was the *Pale Blue Dot* photograph of Earth taken from space. Space looked like stripes of color, and Earth was a tiny speck. Rachel wanted to talk to Billy about it, but she didn't because it wasn't appropriate. Not here, not now.

"So. Ms. Jackman," said the man, "could you begin by telling me how this all started and what the problem is with Billy as you see it?"

She looked down at Billy. He took his eyes off the photograph and gave her a real-Billy grin.

"Right," she said, energized by that. "Well, it started when Billy had flu. He got ill before Christmas. You know what the flu's like."

"I do." She saw his eyes flicker to a picture frame on his desk, but the photograph was angled away from her, so she couldn't see it.

She set Billy's story out, every bit of it, and he didn't interrupt. The more she spoke, the better she felt about it. Professor Watson wrote notes as she talked, and he didn't look skeptical or judgmental. She sensed Henry wanting to jump in and correct her, often, but the professor silenced him with the movement of a hand. At one point, Henry said, "No, that's—" and the professor said, "You'll get your turn, Mr. Stevens."

Billy did not respond to anything Rachel said, but at one point, his hand appeared on her lap, and she picked it up and held it as she carried on talking.

". . . and now," she said, "it's become a problem. Billy says he can't always control what he does. He's not happy. The spiders disturbed me a lot, and then with the strangling the same day . . . and the attack on his father a few days after that. He says Delfy was practicing using his body, which doesn't feel good at all. There are other things. Smaller things. Differences. He gets up in the night and changes things in the house, and watches people sleeping, and he doesn't want to do those things, but he's somehow compelled to."

"I've had a look at the school report you submitted with the paper-work," Watson said, "but it's a couple of months old and so presents the pre-flu Billy, which seems to mean a very typical, lively six-year-old boy. Have you spoken to his teachers?"

"Yes. Mixed," Rachel said. "Some positive changes—ridiculously so, in fact. His teacher says Billy's been interested in finding things out about the world around him. Particularly the J5X virus. Also space travel, which I suppose is to be expected. His sister is passionate about it. She goes to the Space Skills course at the Festival Hall, you know?"

"Impressive," said Watson politely. "I hear they were very over-subscribed."

"His reading level's jumped up. But I have a feeling his behavior might be more challenging. I mean, he gathered all those spiders at school."

Professor Watson was scribbling notes. Rachel tried to read them up-side down, but he had everything turned away from her. The bits she could see were illegible anyway.

"Why me, out of interest?" he said after a while.

She looked at Henry, but he mimed a zipped mouth, so she rolled her eyes and turned back to the doctor.

"Because it mentions post-flu imaginary friends on your website. It was the first time I'd seen that phrase, and I cried, just seeing it written down."

"Yes. You're in the right place. Mr. Stevens, I understand that, in the main, none of this has manifested at your home as strongly until the inci-dent that Rachel has just related?"

Rachel listened to Henry's version of events.

"I assume this is a result of the changes in Billy's life over the past couple of years," he said calmly, and Rachel knew that he was *telling on her* to an authority figure, hoping for agreement. "Billy's always been fine with me. Happy as anything. It wasn't my idea for the marriage to end, for the record. Rachel instigated everything."

The professor was writing again.

"Thank you. Now, if you two could wait outside while I talk things through with Billy? Lauren will get you a drink. For the record, there's CCTV on Lauren's desk, so she can constantly see the room"—he pointed at a camera in the corner—"in case you have safeguarding concerns."

Rachel gave Billy a hug, and Henry ruffled his hair. Rachel angled herself to get a look at the photograph in Professor Watson's frame, and she saw a stylish older woman with sharply cut gray hair and bright lipstick.

Watson saw her looking. "My wife," he said. "Imogen. My late wife. Flu. I miss her every moment of every day." He touched her face with his fingertip and shivered.

R achel tried to say the right things to Lauren, a slightly aloof young woman with glossy blond hair who showed them to a waiting room and made them each a coffee. The waiting room door was open, but Lauren closed the door to her office, so there was absolutely nothing for Rachel and Henry to do, once they had their coffee, but talk to each other or read the magazines. Rachel heard the phone ringing from time to time, but she couldn't hear Lauren talking.

This place had the ambience of a country house hotel, but with a steely undertone of medication.

"Harley Street, eh?" said Henry. "I hope he's going to send us away and tell us everything's fine, because I'm not fancying his hourly rate."

"No." Rachel couldn't contribute much to this line of discussion. "Let's just see what he says."

She took a magazine from the table. It turned out to be a plastic surgery brochure, and she flicked through the pages without reading.

"I'm glad Billy's taking an interest in space colonization," Henry said. "Quite fancy hitching a ride up when they're ready. Nina'll save me a spot. On the new planet, not that rock."

"We're too old for any of that," she said.

Time stretched on. Henry was playing on his phone. Rachel looked at an array of different chin options in the brochure and touched her own chin, which was something she had never thought to feel bad about.

The doctor smiled as they came in. He looked energized. When Billy turned, he, too, looked almost happy.

"OK, Billy?" said Henry, and she was annoyed because she had been about to ask Billy how he was, and now she couldn't.

"Yep," said Billy.

"Billy's done very well," Professor Watson said. "Extremely well. He's filled me in thoroughly on what this feels like from his perspective, and I'd like to start by saying that I work with many other children who are suffering like this. It's a very real syndrome." He tapped his pen on the desk. "Delfy is fascinating to me. As with my other patients, this voice arrived at the moment at which Billy started to recover from the flu. Billy fully believes in her as an entity that is separate from himself. To Billy, Delfy is as real as this table." He knocked on his huge desk. "He can remember the first conversation he had with her, when he was somewhere dark and painful and was ready to let go. She pulled him back to life, comforting him. He believes it is Delfy who saved him, and he cannot entertain the idea that he invented her or that she could be malign." Rachel grabbed Billy's hand. "I'd be delighted to work with him," the doctor said, "and indeed I'm extremely interested in his case. I'm researching the phenomenon as a matter of urgency."

"Right," said Henry. "Great. What do you suggest we do, bearing in mind that funds are . . . limited?"

The professor steepled his fingers and rested his chin on his two index fingers.

"Well," he said, "to start with, I'd like to see Billy weekly. I'd also like him to meet a group of similar children. This would be for my own research as well as for Billy's well-being, so . . ." He cleared his throat. "I fully understand that funds are limited. I know my rates are somewhat prohibitive if you don't already have private health insurance in place, so in this case, as long as we keep it absolutely confidential, I'm willing to waive my fee and see Billy free of charge. All I ask is that one of you bring him here for a regular weekly session, every single week without exception, and that you don't object to my potentially using his case, in the future, in an article in a medical journal or similar. Anonymously. Also I'd like him to meet with the other children at least once a month for a group session. You'd be amazed at the comfort they take from one another."

Rachel stared. She'd had no idea that private medicine could work like this.

"That's very kind," she managed to say. "Thank you. Thank you so much. Of course you can write about him."

"We appreciate it enormously," said Henry. "We really do."

"As I say, though, I wouldn't have a livelihood if I made a habit of this. It is purely because of . . . well, the specifics of this particular issue. I have been trying to assemble a wider range of patients. Now, I could prescribe him something if you wanted, but to be honest, these things are strong— they are never recommended for children, and I generally try to wait until they're at least eight—and they're also ineffective."

"OK," said Rachel. "Let's not, then."

"You need . . ." She watched him sigh and choose his words carefully. "You need to be aware that there might be an escalation in these incidents. It's not certain by any means, but it does happen. If there is any escalation at all, please, let me know as a matter of urgency. Call Lauren. There are options. It is a thing that moves swiftly once it gets going, and you will need to keep a very close eye on Billy indeed. Do promise you'll call when . . . if anything more concerning happens."

"Absolutely," said Rachel.

Henry grunted in agreement. Henry would have agreed to absolutely anything Graham Watson asked.

EIGHTEEN

Graham unlocked the door and pushed it. It was slowed down by the junk mail that was piled up on the other side, but he was through it in the end. Then he was in the flat.

He stood still. The air smelled of mustiness and emptiness, but with traces of the things that broke his heart. There was a hint of Imogen's Chanel perfume. There was a tiny trace of coffee, but more than anything, the flat still had the smell of sickness about it. The J5X fragments were floating in the air. Even though it was cold outside, he decided he should open some windows.

He closed the door behind him and walked to the middle of the sitting room and waited.

Nothing happened.

"Imogen?" he said. His voice sounded odd. He was so scared that his legs were trembling. He tried to be strong. Men were not supposed to fall apart. They were not meant to be felled by widowhood. Widowerhood. Whatever the word was.

Nothing happened. Maybe she wasn't here anymore.

The sitting room was exactly as it had always been, except that now it was unloved, untended. He'd canceled the cleaner when Imogen was ill, so no one had been in here at all. The cushions still had dents where he'd punched them on the night she died.

He walked into the kitchen and opened a window. There were coffee rings on the counter, and a few plates, with mold growing on them, were piled in the sink. Everything was suspended.

"Imogen?" he said again. He walked as quietly as he could to the bedroom and stood on the threshold, but she wasn't in there either.

She wasn't there, he thought, because she was dead. His rational brain told him that, but he didn't really believe it. She had been everywhere, since her body died. Imogen was not a quiet spirit, and her work on Earth was not done.

He stood in the bedroom doorway. He couldn't bring himself to go any farther. The duvet was rumpled on the bed from the last time Graham had tried to sleep there. Imogen's makeup was on her dressing table. A lipstick with the top off. A few bottles of things. That Chanel perfume he had always bought her (on her instructions). He walked over to the radiator, unfrozen by the sight of a piece of tissue paper that was sitting on top of it, vibrating in the heat, as he had forgotten to turn off the heating.

It was a little tissue covered in lipstick kisses. They were bright red, one of Imogen's favorite lip colors. She had blotted her lipstick on this piece of paper. Imogen's lips had touched it. He put the tip of a finger on the paper, and when he turned around, she was there.

"Oh, Graham," she said.

He felt his body doing the things it usually did. His legs started to sag, his head pounded, his vision blurred. He struggled to hang on.

"Immy," he managed to say. He wobbled, grabbed at her hand, but there was only air. He came to, sitting in the corner, like he always did, but this time she was next to him, and there was something on the floor beside him.

"Why?" he managed to say. He hoped she understood what he meant. He meant: why did she have this effect on him? Why, when he loved and missed her so much, did her ghost make him collapse, even in public? Why couldn't he just tell her how he felt?

"Oh, Graham," she said. "You always were a silly twat. Why do you think?"

She was smiling at him. He wanted to kiss her, but he couldn't. The tissue was still in his hand, so he kissed that instead. He held it to his face and put his lips where hers had once been.

"I don't know," he said through his tears. "I really don't know."

She leaned against him. It was a curious feeling, because there was nothing there, but at the same time, he was suffused with everything Imogen. He remembered her leaning her head on his shoulder before, at the theater or cinema, or on the way home in a late-night taxi.

"Graham," she said into his ear, and he shivered. Her voice in his ear had always made him feel all kinds of things. This was highly inappropriate. "Graham. It's the regret and the guilt."

"What regret? What guilt?"

"You tell me."

He sighed and looked into her face as he spoke. "I regret that I was a terrible husband. I didn't cheat on you, but I was rude and mean. You were the most wonderful woman in the world, and you worked ceaselessly to make the world better, and I took you for granted. You wanted to go back to work full-time, and I stopped you. You wanted to go away for weekends, and I never took you. You would turn up at work with a picnic, and I'd say picnics were for people who couldn't afford restaurants. I always said I had to work. I thought we'd have plenty of time to travel, but we didn't." He gasped. "We didn't."

"And the boys?"

"They hate me. You were wonderful with them. I wasn't. I didn't delight in everything they did. You did."

"It's not too late."

"It is, though! You're dead."

She nodded toward the phone. "They're not," she said. "And neither are your patients." She took his hand, and he almost, almost felt it.

"The guilt," he said, realizing all at once what she meant. "The guilt is about them. It's about Kitty."

"You have to bring Kitty home," she said. "You have to. Do it for me. When you need strength, just ask for it. I'll help. I want to help. I don't want to upset you, my love. I want to help you. And I can't believe you never found this."

He followed her gaze and saw that the thing she was pointing at was the thing on the floor. It was a piece of paper, folded over, with *Graham* written on it in Imogen's handwriting.

He stared at her. "How did you do that?"

But she had gone. He picked the paper up and opened it with a certain amount of dread.

Dear Graham,

I have the flu. I've called the hotline. I've been sitting in front of the television, watching old Christmas films, and I'm waiting for it to hit properly. I haven't told you yet. I'll tell you this evening.

There's every chance it won't end well. There are so many things I want to say, and I don't know how you'll react to my being out of action. If the worst, most likely thing does happen, then I hope you'll be able to cope, in your way.

Graham: something huge is going on in the ward. It's like Kitty but bigger. You know that. I've seen how in thrall you are to my brother (you would ultimately want to please him more than me), and I want to say this now:

DO NOT LISTEN TO HIM.

I hate seeing you caught up with him in the way you are. Look after those children, with their well-being in mind above all else. He doesn't matter. Kitty matters, and the smaller children, too. There's something murky going on, and you are one of the few people who might be able to work it out.

I love you. Our children do, too, if you'd give them a chance. I know it's been up and down, but marriage to you has been everything I could have asked for, and I have loved you unceasingly. If I do die, I will be looking out for you as best I can from whatever is beyond. Thank you for forty years of happiness.

Take care of those kids. Look after Kitty. That, plus fatherhood, is, as far as I'm concerned, your only obligation now.

I'm feeling a bit wobbly, so I'm going to stop writing.

Your loving wife,
Imogen xxxxxxx

With her words in front of him, he called Rachel Jackman's number. He knew Billy was about to do something terrible. He knew it, for certain. He had seen it happen time and time again, and this time he had the opportunity to step in before it happened. That was what Imogen was telling him to do. That sort of thing.

Rachel didn't answer her phone. Neither did Billy's dad answer his. He tried the third number they had given, for emergencies, and found himself speaking to Billy's older sister.

"Could you ask one of your parents to give me a ring?" he said. "It's about Billy's treatment. It's important."

"Oh, God, yes, of course," she said. She paused. "While you're here, is this something that happens? Does it happen to every kid who gets flu? What's going on? I'm really worried about him."

He hesitated. "It happens to a lot of them," he said. "And yes, it is worrying."

"Is there, like, a support site or something where we can find out more?"

He thought of the confidentiality of his patients and said: "This is at an early stage, and I don't think there's really anywhere to collate the information yet. I'm sure there will be in time. Someone could make a website. Gather together anecdotal experiences, set up a support group. You're young. You could do it."

He could hear the smile in her voice. "Maybe I will," she said. "Anyway, I'll get Mum to call you back."

Graham put the phone down and wondered whether he dared to call his sons.

NINETEEN

Al wheeled his bike out of the house, and Rachel and Beth stood on the threshold. It was the first of March, but there was no sign of spring in the air. In fact there was an Arctic blast, and she wondered whether they would ever feel warm again.

"I hope your day's OK," Rachel said. She knew that she didn't say that enough. His days at the shelter were busy and stressful. His home life was busy and stressful, too, and Rachel knew that she hadn't had enough time for him. He got in from work, and she handed him Beth and turned her attention to Billy.

Al was happy with that, of course. Beth was the light of his life, his most adored thing. All the same, Rachel knew she was taking him for granted. He spent all day every day working with homeless men, and tens of them had died in his shelter in the past few months. She'd barely had time to help him come to terms with that. She knew there was horror upon horror that he hadn't shared.

"Thank you," he said. "It's all right, you know. I manage. It was worse doing this job before I met you, because then I didn't get to come home to you."

"I love you," she said, standing at the flat's front door with Beth in her arms, and he turned and came back and kissed her, balancing his bike against the side of the house. He kissed Beth's head and said: "I love you, too. Everything will be all right."

She let herself believe it because Al was holding her and she was holding him and they both had Beth enclosed in their arms. She buried her face in his shoulder and smelled his smell and knew that, even though she felt alone, she wasn't.

She took a few seconds to savor the moment.

"Thank you," she said, and she knew she didn't need to say more than that, because he understood.

As soon as he had gone, she called Graham Watson back.

"Hear me out," he said. "I could offer Billy residential treatment in a secure location."

"Residential?" She was horrified. "You mean he'd have to sleep there? Like a hospital? Like a prison?"

"Not exactly like that," he said, but she declined the offer and got off the phone as quickly as she could. Billy was troubled, but he didn't need to go to a secure hospital. Nothing was that bad.

Oh, you poor thing," Emma said. They were walking to school together. "Poor Billy. He's just struggling to get back on his feet, isn't he? Seth said he's absolutely brilliant at math and reading, but that he's been spending some time in the 'calm room.'"

Emma made quotation marks in the air around the phrase and used a sarcastic voice to show that she didn't agree with the calm room. When Nina had been at that school, there had been an actual room with beanbags, a couple of tables, posters on the walls, music playing. It had been staffed, and any child who was having problems could go there and talk to someone and calm down. It had been used by children with additional needs who had to escape for a while as well as by anyone with behavioral or emotional problems. Rachel had thought it was a wonderful idea back then.

Now the former calm room was used as an office by the business manager, and the new calm room was a desk in a cupboard overseen by the office staff. A child sent to the calm room was given work to do and wasn't allowed to talk. It was a place to put someone to keep them out of the classroom when you weren't allowed to send them home.

Billy hadn't mentioned being sent there, but Rachel had suspected things weren't going well at school. All she wanted to do was to wrench him out of school and hold him so tightly that nothing would ever reach him without going through her first. She was right on the edge of panic. Graham Watson had offered Billy residential care, and now she was thinking about it every second of the day. She wondered what he knew that she didn't, felt she should have let him explain a bit more.

"Sorry," she said, and stopped walking. Emma put a hand on Rachel's back, and Rachel felt the tears welling up and tried to blink them back. They kept coming. She kept blinking. She took deep breaths and refused to succumb. She couldn't break down now.

Emma stroked her hair and said, "Hey, don't be sorry. It'll get better," and Rachel pulled herself together. Emma had lots of friends, and without intending to be mean, she would tell them what Rachel said because it was interesting. And then it would all be out of her control and not everyone was kind. Things warped and changed in the retelling. She hated the idea of people talking about her, about Billy, using them for entertainment.

"Thanks," she said, smiling what she hoped was a rueful kind of smile. She started walking again. "I'm glad he's doing well at his lessons. I was really delighted about that at first. But it's been a bit of a strain. First, he was so ill, and I know the only thing that matters is that he's better. But the imaginary friend is kind of . . . making him do things he doesn't want to do, and we can't work out how to get rid of it. Henry and I took him to a therapist, and he's going to be seeing him every week." That sounded good, she thought. "Therapist" didn't sound too medical. Not too gossip worthy. "The therapy is actually free," she said, because that downplayed it even more.

"Oh, good," said Emma, and Rachel was seized with a fierce envy of everything from her lovely clothes to her straightforward children. Emma's partner, Eric, had lived in Shanghai since his office transferred him there a few years earlier. They were still officially together, and even that strange circumstance seemed to make Emma happy. "Though if you could manage to *pay* for therapy, it would probably be better quality. Maybe get Henry to fund something?" Rachel nodded, because she couldn't be bothered to explain. Emma continued. "And yes," she said, "I'm sure if he concentrates he'll be able to get rid of . . . Is it Daffy? Sounds like a coping mechanism that's gone a bit too far. It will pass."

"It's Delfy." Rachel instantly regretted saying the word, as if to utter Delfy's name somehow legitimized her as separate from Billy. "The friend. Yes, you're right. Something in his brain hasn't settled back after the flu. Apparently he's not the only one this has happened to. There do seem to be treatment options, of a sort. We'll get there."

"You will." Emma visibly made a decision to change the subject. "Anyway—how's Nina?"

"She's fine," Rachel said. "She got to play in a flight simulator the other day on her space course. And she's working hard at school. She won't let us meet her boyfriend. Or to be accurate, she's only allowed Beth to meet him because *Beth* is not embarrassing."

Emma laughed. "She's on safe ground with you, Bethie." They walked around the corner, onto the road with the school on it. "I was like that," she said, clearly relieved to seize on the normal thing. "I would never take a boyfriend home. Never. I preferred keeping that side of things to myself."

"Well," said Rachel. "Yes. So does Nina."

"Unless he's imaginary, too?"

Rachel burst out laughing. She laughed and laughed far more than the joke warranted. She laughed until she cried. She laughed until they reached the school gates, and then she stopped.

. . .

The playground was filled with the three-twenty crowd. They were mostly mums, with some dads, grandparents, nannies and au pairs, and with a sprinkling of toddlers running around. Rachel stood close to Emma and noticed that a few of the parents from Billy's class were looking at her and muttering. Or maybe they weren't. She was expecting it so much that she was seeing it either way. Sami came over to join them, and Rachel was grateful for that. Sami was always chatty at the end of the day because she worked alone and was desperate for company.

"I have to tell you this," she said. "I was invited to quote for a local design project. It looked all *community* and lovely, but something about it didn't quite ring true. When I dug a bit deeper, it turned out to be a community initiative for the bad guys! For worklifeplus—you know, the ones that buy up all the houses. I can't tell you how much I hate them and that man. Moral dilemma! The money's shit, but it's money. And I am in no position to turn down—"

The bell rang, and the children started to come out.

Billy saw Rachel and bombed straight at her, and she crouched down to catch him.

"How are you, my darling?" She stared into his eyes, trying to work out what was going on in there.

He looked away. "OK."

"How was school?"

"Boring. Let's go home." He tugged at her, wanting to leave as quickly as possible. He pushed her away from the pushchair and took its handles himself, turning it clumsily to navigate Beth through the crowd toward the gate. Sami had walked off to intercept Lola, and Emma watched Billy until Seth tugged on her arm. Rachel smiled vaguely at a few people and was following Billy, who was almost at the school gate when she felt someone tap her on the shoulder.

It was Billy's teacher, Miss Lu.

"I'm so sorry," she said, slightly out of breath. "Do you have a moment? I'd like to have a word, if that's all right."

TWENTY

Miss Lu was the politest person in the world, and she looked about sixteen. She was mortified about whatever it was that she was about to say, and Rachel's insides shriveled in anticipation. Billy was sent to wait in another classroom with a trainee teacher because this was not a discussion that he was allowed to hear, even though only yesterday he had sat between his parents while a Harley Street therapist offered to treat him for free.

Beth sat on the floor, playing with wooden bricks. Beth was always sitting on the floor while things went on around her.

Rachel looked around the classroom. They lived in a world that had the technology to set up a city in space, in which adverts would shout at you as you walked past and, if you could afford it, your fridge would monitor your health and order a shopping delivery to restock itself accordingly. Yet this classroom was woeful. It was not so different, she thought, from the way it would have been in Victorian times. There was an old "interactive whiteboard" that was long broken. The old-style whiteboard had gone because the school couldn't afford to keep replacing the pens, and now things had come full circle with a blackboard, a tin of white chalk, and a fluffy eraser. Those things had been obsolete when Rachel was at school, and now they were back for the poor children.

The chair was too small. The room smelled of sweat and shoes. There were bad paintings of extinct animals on the wall, and Rachel imagined them coming to life, grotesquely misshapen, and running at her.

She turned her attention, reluctantly, to the teacher.

"I'm sorry," Miss Lu said. "Billy's dad e-mailed me this morning. I nearly called you then. I wish I had." She paused, fiddling with the two pens in front of her. They seemed to mark schoolwork in purple and green at the moment. One color meant you had done something good, and the other meant you had done something bad. Rachel had no idea which was which, but she liked the suffragette color scheme. "He brought me up to speed with Billy's issues."

"He's going to be fine," said Rachel. She had a bad feeling.

"Oh, of course he is! Yes! Absolutely. We're all very much on Team Billy. We want him better. This therapy Billy's having sounds like a *fab* idea. What I really wanted to say was that . . ." She paused for breath, more stressed than she was letting on. "Well, I should have said before now that I was concerned about his behavior. I kept making allowances because of his illness but it's been increasingly difficult to manage. Today, unfortunately, he's crossed a line, and we can't make those allowances any longer. It's been . . . disturbing." Rachel wanted to interrupt, but she could see that Miss Lu was desperate to get the words out, just as much as Rachel wanted to stop her. "He's been— Well, he's been asking . . . aggressive questions. About sex, and they are emphatically *not* age appropriate."

"Oh, shit," said Rachel.

"He stormed into the staff room and shouted questions at the teachers about their sexual histories and experiences. His main concern seemed to be why people would, well, have sex when they don't plan to have a baby, with very pointed questions about whether it was fun and why. He confused the words 'organism' and 'orgasm,' and we didn't correct that.

We got him under control and kept him in the calm room because I couldn't put him back with the class. Safeguarding, you know. The other children."

Rachel took a deep breath. "I can see that you had no choice," she managed to say. "But I wish you'd called. I would have come straight in. I hope that with his therapy these things will stop. He's seeing someone at the top of the profession, every week."

"Yes, so I understand. And that's good, but . . ."

"I'm sorry he said those things. I'll make sure he doesn't do it again."

"Of course. But it's the children. That's the issue, I'm afraid. Staff can deal with these things, but he said explicit things to the children, too. I'm sorry, Ms. Jackman, but when a child exhibits this kind of sexualized behavior, we have a legal duty to intervene."

"How?"

"By making a referral."

"A referral?"

"To social services."

"Social services?" Rachel wasn't able to do anything but parrot Miss Lu's words.

"This kind of thing is almost always indicative of something bigger having happened in the child's life, and our absolute priority has to be Billy's well-being."

"Nothing has happened to Billy."

The world closed in on Rachel. She couldn't hear. Black spots danced in front of her eyes. How did she know that? How could she know? Had she failed her child far more than she had ever realized?

She had no idea what had happened to Billy. Delfy had happened, but what was Delfy? What did *Delfy* mean? Billy had constructed Delfy, and the things she said were, in fact, things that Billy was saying.

Rachel wanted to defend her family, but even now she could see that the school had no choice. Delfy had come from somewhere, and though Professor Watson had not suggested abuse, she supposed she had been blanking out the possibility before she could even notice it. Billy was on the iPad and the laptop all the time, and Rachel didn't know what he was doing. He probably wasn't reading up on the J5X virus or the extinct animals or the space program all the time. Not really. His interest in those things had waned long ago.

This referral meant that social services, the people responsible for safeguarding children, were going to come to their house.

She had no idea what that would mean in real life. In her head, social services were the people who snatched children from loving homes. They were either overzealous (what if they took Billy and Beth?), or they were lax, leaving children in nightmarish misery. From all the stories she had heard, there was no sensible middle ground.

But that was because you heard only the sensational stories.

Was it? Was her family about to star in one of those stories?

She tried to speak, but no words came out. She held on to the edge of the table to steady herself.

Miss Lu filled the silence. "I'm sorry. I really am. I haven't known Billy long, but between September and December he was a lovely, happy, well-balanced boy. I know this behavior is out of character. I also know, as I said, that you and his dad are getting him help, and that really is the best thing you could do."

That was what her mouth said. However, Rachel watched her eyes saying something completely different. Miss Lu didn't know what to believe, and she was suspicious of Rachel.

"Can I keep him home tomorrow?" Rachel said. "I can't send him to school, can I? I'd like to keep him with me for a while."

Miss Lu looked relieved. "Yes. If you call in sick for him, that's probably the easiest. It saves a load of paperwork."

Rachel looked at Beth. She was hitting a wooden brick with another wooden brick while looking at Miss Lu. She hoped Beth was all right. She didn't know anything anymore.

B illy walked beside the pushchair, holding Beth's hand, and they chatted to each other in gibberish, Billy bending down so their heads were close together.

"What are you two talking about?" said Rachel.

"Oh, stuff," said Billy. "Not things for you to know."

"What was the calm room like, Billy?" she said as they turned the corner onto their road. She was trying to keep her voice casual. Social services were going to call. They were going to come over and look at her family and decide whether Billy was allowed to carry on living there. It made her cold all over.

She was going to have to tell Henry.

Before that, she would have to tell Al.

This was going to blow everything apart.

"Boring," said Billy. "I just drawed some pictures and writ some words."

"You *drew* some pictures and *wrote* some words. Did you do it with Delfy?"

"No. It was just me."

"Delfy wasn't there?"

"She wasn't talking to me. She was there, but she was talking to someone else."

"To someone else? You mean she was in another person's head?" Rachel would have been shamelessly delighted to off-load Delfy into anyone at all as long as she kept away from her family.

"No. One of her people. She was telling stuff to other people about me."

"But she was still in your head."

"Course. She lives here."

"Billy, how do you fancy a day off tomorrow? Stay at home with me and Beth?"

"Yeah, I do, please. Can we go to the park?"

She forced a smile. "Sure. If it's not raining."

As they got back to the house, she checked and saw that there was an old man standing across the road, watching, but it was a different man from before. She turned away, shepherding Billy in through the front door, pulling Beth in so fast that she almost tipped her out of the push-chair.

TWENTY-ONE

Nina and Louis were walking hand in hand. She held his hand more tightly than she needed to, and she was trying to pretend to be calm.

Going to meet his family was, she thought, the worst thing she had ever had to do. She knew they were rich, but as soon as they got off the bus, and she saw where they were (a part of London she had never visited before), she realized that he had underplayed his family's wealth to a spectacular degree.

Even though Nina didn't know the area, she had heard of this road. It was known as Trillionaires' Row, and the nine houses were new and lavish, built on the site of a riverside council estate that had housed thousands. It was notorious as a symbol of the city's raging inequality.

"Seriously?" She tried to say it in a light way, but it came out weird. "You live here?"

She had googled him, as Shelly had suggested. Louis Ricci had almost no Internet presence. The only thing that was unusual was how little had come up. She had not asked him about his sister, though Shelly had told her to, because it was a hard thing to say out of the blue to someone who had talked only about his brother. He had once mentioned a half sister he never saw, and that must have been the person Shelly meant, but would never talk about her.

It was a gray and windy day, and her hair was blowing around all over the place. Each time they walked toward a house, she thought it might be that one, but each time it wasn't. All she could see of each of them was a tall electronic gate and a row of massive trees that must have been planted ready grown, probably with a crane. It took several minutes to walk past each house. "Yeah, we live just along here. I wish I could say it's not as grand as the rest of them, but it actually is."

"What are you doing catching the bus? Shouldn't you have a driver or something?"

He looked at her and smiled the little smile that made her flutter. "I don't want a driver," he said. "I could get a lift to school if I asked, sure. My brother did. I don't want to. I choose not to be that guy."

"Do you just have a brother?" she managed to say.

"Harvey," he said. "He's a wanker. There's my half sister, too, but that's complicated."

"How's it complicated?"

They stopped beside an ornate set of wrought iron gates.

"I'll tell you about her later," he said. "Meanwhile, brace yourself." He leaned forward to let a box on the gatepost machine scan his eyeball. "They have all this security for the outside world. Inside, it's fine. It's not like there're cameras . . . I mean, my room is private. This top-of-the-range stuff is just to keep the world out. Sorry. I'm being a bit random. Babbling. I've been dreading this. Also." He stopped and put a hand on her shoulder, swinging her around to look at him. "We didn't meet at Space Skills because they don't know I do it. Don't say you do either."

"Why?" She was pretty sure she wasn't going to be able to say anything at all, so that would be all right. All the same, Space Skills was the one thing she was proud of. She wasn't going to disown it.

Louis sighed as he straightened up, and the gate rolled open. "Sorry. Of course you can say you do it. I've left this to the last minute, and I should have said it before, but I kept not being able to do it. So here goes.

I don't have to do Space Skills because my parents will just pay for us all to go if it comes to it. My dad's made sure he's right in there. He's deeply involved in all of it. But I don't want to be the idiot boy hitching a free ride when the new planet's ready. I want to know what I'm doing. So. That."

"Fucking hell. OK, then. So where did we meet?"

"Maybe at a party? A school one. If it's school sanctioned, it's good."

"I would never be allowed into your school."

"You would. If it was for a 'social.' If someone had invited you."

"I'd better not say where I go to school, then. My school is shit."

"It can't be shit, Nina, because it's got you in it."

She smiled, and they stopped in front of a camera by a second gate. This one took Nina's photo. A bit farther along, they both left their fingerprints, and only then was she allowed to approach the house her boyfriend lived in. It was enormous, and although she knew it was new, it had been built in the style of a Venetian palazzo. For all she knew it was a real Venetian palazzo dismantled before the flooding and reassembled.

"Wow." She didn't know what else to say.

"Yeah. I know. It's everything that's shit. A monument to excess, while people are dying in the streets. My dad is a wanker. Building us a house on a thousand demolished homes, just because he wanted a river view. I mean, how much of a fucker do you have to be?"

"Louis." She couldn't do it. She knew she couldn't. "I don't belong here. I can't."

He looked at her with huge eyes, and she could see that, somehow, he was as nervous as she was.

"Please, don't," he said. "I mean, do if you want. I can't tell you what to do. But please. Please, stay. Just come to my bedroom, and we can watch a movie, and then you can go home. Seriously, Neen. I know this is bullshit, but I want to be with you, and I can't hide it any longer. I hate it. My family are the bad guys. Nothing I say makes any difference; they just laugh and call me a communist. I don't want to be this guy. I love you because you're so brilliant. You don't do any of that bullshit."

His hand was warm in hers. It was reassuring. She knew that she couldn't really run away now, that it would be the end for them if she did.

Also, unless she was very much mistaken, he had just said that he loved her.

"Promise it'll be OK?" she said.

"Promise." She saw him hesitating and waited. "Also. Sorry, but there's one other thing. It's a . . . sizable one. I should have told you before. You know my surname?"

Nina had read the name on the front of Louis' space suit at their first meeting and every Sunday since. She had thought, even before she spoke to him, that Louis Ricci was a cool name. It was much less Anglo than Nina Stevens.

"Ricci," she said.

"Yeah. That's not my name. I told them I use the name Ricci, and they were fine with it. It's my mother's maiden name, and I like it better than my real one."

"Which is?"

Silence. She waited.

The whole of London was muffled by the row of conifers behind them. In front of them was the house, looking intimidating. They were standing in a kind of Japanese garden, with geometric shapes filled with little stones and a stream with a bridge over it. She listened to the water and waited some more.

"Alford," he said in the end.

"Alford?"

"Yes."

Nina couldn't speak.

"Alford" meant Ben Alford. It meant Starcom. It meant worklifeplus. It meant taking away the housing from the people who needed it. It meant everything she and Al, in particular, detested.

Ben Alford was one of the dragons sitting on a pile of gold.

She pictured the kind of house he would live in. She looked up at the house in front of her. They matched.

"Ben?" she managed to say. Ben Alford ("BA" as he liked to style himself) was a red-faced idiot who looked nothing like Louis. Dad was the only person she knew who liked him, who referred to him matily as BA as if they went out together to the cycling club and the pub.

"But you're here now." Louis pulled her onward.

"Is he your . . ."

"Dad. Yeah. Come on."

Nina's head was so full of the fact that Louis might as well just have told her that he was the heir to the throne that it didn't even seem weird that the front door swung open as they approached even though no one was there.

Louis stepped in and called out, "Home!" Then he kicked off his shoes and threw his schoolbag onto a shelf. Nina took her shoes off carefully and lined them up, looking at the scuffs on them and wishing she had polished them recently. She licked a finger and tried to make them look a bit better. Louis pushed his hair out of his eyes, and she pulled hers over one shoulder. She could hear rap music coming from upstairs and voices from somewhere nearby. The air smelled aggressively fresh, like jasmine and fresh laundry.

"Drink?" Louis said, setting off down a corridor. She nodded. She wanted to go to his room, but apparently they couldn't. Her feet (holes, she noticed, in her black school tights) dragged along the stone tiles as she followed him, with the greatest reluctance, to the kitchen.

She had no idea why Louis was secretly going to the space course. Getting into that program had been difficult, and he should have been proud of it. She supposed he was pretending to be normal, which meant she was part of that project. She felt sick. She had a new sense of herself as part of a social experiment, and she didn't like it. He had tricked her. Was he trying to have the best of all worlds? The money and the appearance of normality?

The kitchen was enormous, with double doors leading out to a conservatory that seemed to have a rain forest in it. There was a massive table, a pale blue AGA, a thousand pale blue cupboards, and lots of other things that were pale blue, too.

A woman came in from the conservatory. She was brightly blond and so thin she looked as if her arms and legs could snap. Although she was wearing exercise clothes, she didn't look as if she had done anything to make herself sweat lately.

"Darling," she said to Louis, her voice brisk. He inclined his head down to let her kiss the top of it, the way Nina did with her mum. It was odd to see Louis like this, as someone's child. "Now, you need to introduce us. Oh, never mind. Darling," she said to Nina. "I'm Elena. I'm this boy's mother, for my sins."

"This is Nina, Mum," said Louis, his mortification coming out in every syllable he spoke. "Nina, this is my mum, but you know that."

"Wonderful. Finally we get to meet you!" said Elena, holding out a hand. "The mysterious Nina." Nina tried not to squirm as Louis' mum sized her up during their handshake. This woman made Nina feel fat. Her hand was a bag of bones, and her thighs looked like those of a skeleton draped in Lycra. "Louis, get the girl a drink, for goodness' sake. There's some of that elderflower in the fridge or smoothie if you don't mind the fructose."

Nina smiled as big and fervent a smile as she could. "Thank you," she said. "I don't mind fructose, no."

A disembodied female voice said: "Louis, your blood sugar is low. I suggest the mango smoothie."

Nina gasped and tried to pretend she hadn't. She knew this technology existed, in theory, but had never met anyone who had used it. Louis had to be wearing a patch, with some remote thing connected to the fridge, that monitored his micronutrients.

Was he doing that while people in this very city were dying of starvation and flu and malnutrition? Yes, he was.

"Thanks, Harmony," said Louis. "Sounds good."

Nina nodded her agreement to a mango smoothie because she couldn't bring herself to speak to "Harmony." Mango was the kind of thing Mum would never, ever buy, because it was expensive, and because mangoes grew thousands of miles away and importing them was a terrible use of scarce resources and could really be done only if you didn't give a shit about the ecosystem.

"She's lovely," Elena said to Louis. "I love your hair, Nina. Lucky you. Anyway, you two want to head off upstairs, no doubt. Harvey's up there somewhere."

Louis had poured two glasses of juice, and he said, "Thanks, Mum."

"It's lovely to meet you, Mrs. Alford," Nina said, and she tried not to make it clear how delighted she was to leave the kitchen.

"Elena, may I suggest some iced water?" said the fridge.

"You may indeed," said Elena.

"Yeah," said Louis as they walked toward the stairs. "That's just my mum, talking to the furniture."

Nina had seen Elena before, she realized. She was often in magazine articles, looking thin and wearing expensive dresses at her husband's side. She had been at the last few royal weddings, singled out for her elaborate outfits, on the front pages of celebrity magazines.

And she was Nina's boyfriend's mum. It felt impossible. She let her mind travel, just for a moment, to her own wedding. If she were marrying Louis, Elena, in one of her expensive outfits, would sit next to Rachel in the front row of the ceremony. Nina tried to imagine them finding common ground for small talk. She failed.

And there was Dad, cozying up to BA. If she and Louis ever got married, they had better do it in space.

Louis' bedroom was enormous, and it smelled of wood fires. This was, Nina realized, because there was a wood-fire-scented gadget of some sort stuck to the radiator. The room was so big that Nina almost laughed, though she didn't really think it was funny.

"You could fit my mum's house in here," she said. "Almost. You *could* get Mum and Al's room and my room and Billy's room, all three of them, into yours with space left over."

"Oh, God," said Louis. "I didn't want things to feel weird, and now they do. Don't hate me."

"I don't hate you." She did feel wary, and she wanted time to think, but she would try to hide that for the moment. "Don't be stupid! I don't want you to think I'm some kind of feral slum dweller when you see where I live. We'd better start with my dad's house because it'll be less shocking. We can do it incrementally. I can't believe you're . . ." She didn't really know how to finish the sentence. He knew what she meant.

Louis' room was painted blue, and the ceiling was covered with luminous stars. He had a thick blue carpet, several rugs, and an enormous bed.

The huge bed was interesting. He saw her looking at it.

"Yeah," he said. "I wish my mum wasn't here. And Harvey."

Nina wished that, too. She looked at his television. "Maybe watch some telly, then?" she said. "Like you said?"

"Let's put on a movie." He took a huge bar of Rockolate, broke off a row of squares, and handed them to her.

"Oh, God," she said. "I've never had this stuff. I boycott it because of those stupid adverts. Also it's expensive." She realized, as she said that last bit, that this wouldn't matter to Louis.

He turned away. "Yeah," he said. "It's quite nice, though. Honestly. The adverts aren't so bad." He took some, too, and they sat on his bed, entwined together with the duvet on top of them. "Harmony—telly," said Louis, and the TV came to life. Once again, Nina had to work hard not to exclaim at the technology, like a peasant. She saw clearly that all the technology in her life, even at her dad's, was decades out of date. Stuff like this was inaccessible to almost everyone.

"What would you like to watch, Louis?" the TV said in a conversational tone.

"Show us the movies."

They flicked through the films that were available.

"As soon as we see one that looks OK," said Louis, "we have to watch it. Otherwise we'll just get paralyzed, and we'll spend two hours not deciding. I do that all the time. The telly suggests things, but it just adds to the pressure, really, when you feel the TV itself judging you for being indecisive."

"OK," she said. "Can we ask it? I've never done this before. Can I speak to it?"

"I don't think it'll recognize your voice. Let's set you up as a user."

They did that, and Nina found herself in dialogue with what was, effectively, a disembodied robot. A voice with no body. Maybe, she thought, the Harmonies had found a way of getting into bodies. Maybe that was Delfy; perhaps she was a rogue bit of AI.

"Delighted to meet you, Nina," it said. "What would you like to watch?"

"Something exciting, please, Harmony?" she said. "Maybe a thriller? Set in Asia. How about that?"

"Something that's won awards," added Louis.

"With a female detective."

"And a dog."

The television obliged, and a minute later, they were watching the opening credits of a film about a serial killer stalking the citizens of Hong Kong just after its flood defenses had gone up. There was a female detective, and she had a guard dog that kept her safe as she went out on the killer's trail.

The chocolate was nice enough. It must have been filled with caffeine and sugar because it made her feel very wide-awake; or maybe, she thought, that was just because she was next to Louis on a bed. When he offered more, she asked whether she could take a few squares for Billy, and he laughed and took a box of Rockolate Planets from the drawer and told her to give it to Billy as a present from him. The Planets were the more exclusive version of the chocolate bars. Nina had never expected to see any in real life, let alone to put a box of them into her bag.

She leaned her head on his shoulder. He kissed her and whispered lovely things into her ear. She kissed him back. She noticed he had a purple birthmark on his neck. He found the mole behind her ear. They didn't watch much of the film, but she didn't dare do anything too adventurous either, as she didn't trust the house not to be filming her, didn't trust the telly robot not to be telling the fridge robot, who would have reported straight to Elena.

As the end credits were going, Nina knew she had to get home. She wanted to be back in her own world, but without having to make her way through this house. If humans were about to live in space, if fridges could tell you what to drink, then surely something in this house should have been able to teleport her home.

She could not tell Dad that her boyfriend was an heir to Starcom. She couldn't tell Mum either: Mum would be nervous and disapproving, and when Louis came over, she would fall apart. She couldn't tell Al because he spent all his energy dealing with people who had been screwed over by Ben Alford and his policies. She certainly couldn't write it into her computer science project. It was best for everyone if Nina kept Louis' background a secret, she decided. Just as he had done. She could see now exactly why he had done it.

"How's Billy?" Louis said.

"Terrible. Properly bad." Nina was pleased to be able to talk about this, glad to stop thinking about Louis and his inheritance. "So, first, his imaginary friend was making him do things like giving my mum a box of spiders, when she hates spiders, and punishing Grandma for telling a lie. The shrink was so concerned that he's seeing Billy for free. Hopefully that will help. But Mr. Harley Street, working for nothing? That surely never happens. The guy called the other day and said Billy could stay at some private hospital. I mean, what?"

Louis shrugged. "Yeah. It wouldn't happen to my family."

"And not only that," she added, "but now Billy seems to be interested in sex. I had to explain it to him last night. He was interested in the details. Very. He wanted to know if I'd done it. I mean, fuck's sake. I told him it was a totally inappropriate conversation—and also that the answer was no—and he said in that case he'd ask at school."

"Jesus! What did you say to that?"

"I told him not to! I hope he didn't."

It felt daring, telling this to Louis. She was alone in his bedroom with him, and even though it was in the least enticing of conversations, she had just said the word "sex."

"You know, the thing with my sister—" Louis was saying when the door crashed open and a boy burst into the room. He looked a tiny bit like Louis, except that he was older and broader and quite fat. His face was acne scarred and red, and his hair was short. He was a version of Louis that didn't quite work.

Nina was shocked at the way he had just burst in, though she supposed siblings did that kind of thing, and that was exactly why she had the bolt on her door at home. She looked at this boy and thought he must hate his handsome younger brother.

"Hey. Oh, sorry! I didn't mean to interrupt anything. I didn't realize."

Louis sighed. "Nina," he said. "This fuckwit is my brother, Harvey. Harv, Nina. Sorry, Nina. We'll carry on our conversation afterward because it's impossible to say anything intelligent when this idiot is nearby."

"Enchanté," said Harvey, and he came forward as if to shake Nina's hand, so she held hers out awkwardly. She had never known anyone of her age to offer a handshake. However, he took her hand and kissed it, which made her laugh. His lips were a bit moist.

"Wanker," said Louis, and punched his shoulder.

"Anyway," said Harvey. "It's dinner. Mum said to tell you."

"I'd better go home," said Nina.

"I think," said Harvey, "that Mum thinks you're staying to eat, actually, Nina. She's got Mathilde to set you a place. And cook you a thing. You're veggie, right?"

"Oh, God," said Louis. "Dad's not here, is he?"

"He is! He came home because he saw on the security system that

Nina was visiting. He wants to meet your girlfriend. Our houseguest isn't having dinner with us tonight, and Nina is."

"So you did know Nina was here," said Louis. "*Oh, sorry! I didn't mean to interrupt*, indeed. You twat."

Harvey shrugged. "Whatever. Stay for din-dins, Nina."

She looked at Harvey and then back at Louis, who, she could see, was agonized. She wanted to make it OK for him, and apparently someone called Mathilde had cooked her a *thing*, so she said: "OK. Thanks. I'll just text my mum."

Her heart sank as she did it. What the hell had she got herself into?

"You have a houseguest?" she said to Louis as she combed her hair with her fingers, used her phone camera to check for love bites, and wished she was wearing a dress rather than a school uniform.

"Just a friend of the parents," said Louis. "There's always someone staying. Mum likes it to feel like a villa in Cannes or something, with all her rich friends dropping in. Don't worry: you won't meet him."

TWENTY-TWO

She didn't meet the houseguest, but she did have to meet Ben Alford. It was agonizing: she was torn between wanting to make a good impression on Louis' dad and hating him for everything he was and everything he did.

In real life he was taller than she had expected, and ruddy faced, and he had clearly had a hair transplant. Harvey looked exactly like him, Louis not much. It felt weird to see him in the flesh. He was too familiar. She had never known that he had any children, though. Louis, his brother, and his half sister seemed to be shielded from the media.

Ben Alford looked Nina up and down and seemed to find her acceptable. He introduced himself as BA and asked where she went to school. She told the truth because she was wearing a uniform that had the school's name on the jumper; he raised an eyebrow (badly) but didn't seem to hold it against her. Or perhaps he did, but his social skills were too polished to let it show. Perhaps when she left, he would instruct Louis to break up with the girl from the gutter.

"It's just a kitchen supper," said Elena. She had put a frilly apron over her exercise clothes, and it was white and spotless. "That's OK, isn't it,

Nina? Just a little weekday thing. It means you're part of the family. We haven't had a girl over for supper since Harvey broke up with Charli."

"Mum!" Harvey was annoyed. "She broke up with me. Also, you hated her."

Louis laughed. "Mum didn't hate Charli. She just didn't *like* her."

"Charli was a nice girl," said Elena, but her tone told a different story. "And anyway, it's nice to have Nina here."

Nina saw herself as a future anecdote being told to a new girlfriend (*"the girl who went to state school"*), and she wanted to run away, through all the security and the Japanese garden and all the way home. She was conscious of everything she did, everything she said, and that meant that she couldn't really say or do anything.

She sat where she was told, which luckily was next to Louis, and accepted a glass of wine because wine was alcohol and alcohol was a drug and drugs felt like a good idea right now. A woman in a black-and-white uniform brought in two lasagnas and a huge bowl of salad, and put a warm plate in front of each of them. Elena's apron had been for show. She was like a little girl playing dress-up, Nina thought, though she knew she was being mean because she didn't know this woman at all. There was nothing about Elena she could relate to.

"Louis said you don't eat meat," said Elena. "I'm the same, though I don't eat dairy either, or gluten, so I'm just having the super salad. Anyway I got Mathilde to make you a veggie lasagna. I hope it's OK."

"Wow," said Nina, and she told herself to stop saying "wow" at once. "Thank you so much. It looks perfect."

"So, Nina," said Louis' dad. BA. The very famous man who was sitting opposite her. "You live somewhere south of here—is that right? Met our Louis at a party?"

"Yes," she said. "Yes, that's right. My dad lives in Streatham. My mum and my stepdad are in that area, too. We met at a school party a few months ago."

"Ahhh. Good."

She hazarded a question back. "Are you from London originally?"

She wasn't sure if it was an all right thing to ask, but no one seemed offended.

"Oh, yes," said Ben cheerfully. "Londoner through and through. I love London, and I love its people. My company employs thousands of them, and I'm incredibly proud to be doing my bit. In fact I'm running a newish project. Worklifeplus. Do you know it? Bit of a pioneering thing. I had to fight to get it up and running, but we got there in the end."

"I've heard of it." Nina stared at her plate. There were unfamiliar vegetables in the lasagna. Artichokes perhaps?

"We provide accommodation for our workers. Totally take the burden off. We know how hard it can be in this market, so we give them a place to live, satellite TV, a phone with unlimited calls and data. Meal vouchers. Beer tokens. Literally, we give them *beer tokens*. Full flu screening and health care, of course, and vaccinations. Here. Have a look."

She was prepared to be polite about a photograph, but instead he handed her a VR headset. She was glad she knew what to do with it, thanks to the ones they used at space training, though this one was a lot lighter and slicker.

She clicked and was in a room. She looked around. The carpet under her feet was gray. The furniture was new, neutral colored. She was sitting on a sofa. Over to her left there was a kitchen alcove with a breakfast bar with stools. She could smell coffee, hear birdsong.

"Dad!" That was Harvey. "For God's sake."

She took the headset off and handed it back. "That's amazing technology," she said politely.

"You should do it properly. Walk round the whole place, go to the pub, everything," said BA. "It wins over the doubters, all right."

"Dad," said Louis, "Nina's in the middle of dinner."

"Yes," said Elena. "Not now, Ben. Please, my darling. So, Nina! I want to know about your family. Your brother was sick?"

"Yes," said Nina. "He recovered."

"That's wonderful," said Elena. "It's been a terrible thing. We've lost someone in the family. It's been just awful. I'm so glad your brother got better. How old is he?"

"Six."

"A full recovery? I'm so pleased."

A s soon as Nina was home, she video-called Shelly.

"You knew!" she said. "You knew who Louis is. I went over for dinner. That was a surprise. Oh, my God. Dinner with Ben Alford."

Shelly laughed. "Thank God for that. I thought he was never going to tell you."

"It was weird. What's the thing you were saying about his sister? We started talking about her. He said it was complicated, and then we never got a chance to finish the conversation."

"Oh, yes," she said. "The sister. Well, they won't talk about her around the dinner table, I imagine. She's the same age as Louis' brother. BA was married to her mum and having an affair with Elena, and got them both pregnant at the same time. Awkward. He left her for Elena, and then at some time after that, his first wife died. I don't know what happened. No idea where the sister lives now." She paused. "See if you can find out. There's something intriguing about the whole thing. Because she should live with her dad, but she seems to have disappeared."

TWENTY-THREE

Al left for work without a word. Rachel knew they needed to talk, but she didn't know what to say, so she watched him go, with Beth wriggling in her arms.

"Bye," she said, standing in the doorway. It was bitterly cold. The rain had turned to hail, and a gust of wind blew it into her face. Dots of icy shrapnel sprayed across her, and she turned so that her body was protecting Beth.

Al looked back, the hood of his flimsy coat pulled up round his face. He looked as if he were going to say something but decided not to. He gave a small wave, swung his leg over the bike, and cycled away.

It was bitterly cold indoors, too. The damp patch on the wall had grown. The wallpaper was peeling in lots of places. Some of those places were where she had taped the quarantine sheets, and she knew the landlord would say it was her fault. Others were just places where the wallpaper was falling off.

Today, she supposed, she would become a home educator. She saw the home educators out and about sometimes, when she was out with Beth. They were the people who refused to register their children for school for all sorts of reasons, ranging from concerns like calm rooms and uniforms to a refusal to give their children the compulsory vaccinations. Also, she now saw, they included the parents whose children just didn't fit.

Rachel had never imagined a day when she would join their ranks. She would have assumed she didn't have the energy or the skills to teach a child all the things they needed to know. However, today she had to have that energy, that skill, and so she would dredge it up from somewhere.

As soon as the hail stopped, she put her head down and walked to the park, both children insulated in all the layers of waterproofs and warm things they had. Billy wore his Wellies and stamped on the tiny balls of ice that were still here and there on the pavement. *Like a normal six-year-old,* Rachel thought, and she seized the moment and tried to hold it. At the park he pushed Beth on the baby swing, and for a while, everything felt normal.

Back at home they watched television, and Beth tried to crawl and cried when she still couldn't do it. Apart from the annoyance of having to say no to Billy about the computer every ten minutes, Rachel felt that things were going all right. They had baked beans on toast for lunch. She kept looking at the door, but no one arrived to take her children away.

Baked beans, she thought, would be all right if a social worker were to turn up right now to inspect their lives. They were protein. They were filling. Cheap but effective. She wasn't neglecting Billy or feeding him too much sugar.

Billy sidled out of the room, and fifteen minutes later, Rachel found him in Nina's room, tapping on the laptop.

Nina's room was an oasis of order. It was always clean, always tidy. Billy knew he wasn't allowed in there.

"You know tiny things," he said, in the most conversational of tones, as she came into the room, "as tiny as things can get? Well, the little, teeny bits can talk to each other. They do it by vibrations."

"Oh, Billy," said Rachel. "Give it here. You *know* you're not allowed on that."

"See." He ignored her. "Like this." He pointed to the screen, and she saw a Wikipedia page open for "quantum mechanics." "Delfy says this isn't completely right," he said. "But it's *a bit* right. It's maybe the rightest thing so far."

"Billy!" said Rachel. "I have no idea what you're saying. Stop talking like this. You said you were going to the loo, and you came here instead." She snapped the laptop shut and shooed him out of the room. She heard him stomping down the stairs.

"I came here *after*, not *instead*," he shouted. He was mutinous. She decided to hide the laptop, although there were no real hiding places in this house. For now she lifted Nina's mattress and decided to put it underneath.

Something was already there; it was a book with DIARY on the front. Rachel hesitated.

Of course she wanted to read her child's diary, to check she was OK, to find out more about Louis, particularly since Nina had been to his house last night. Of course she couldn't do that. She had really better not.

A diary, though.

Nina would never know. She, Rachel, might find things out. It would be high stakes because the only thing she wanted was reassurance; if there was anything terrible going on, she would have to tell Nina she'd read it or somehow get her to confide in her.

She touched the diary with the very tips of her fingers. It was a green hardback.

Nina was sensible. It was probably OK.

Rachel opened the cover.

On the first page Nina's neat writing said: *I am definitely going to keep a diary.* Rachel flicked through: every other page in the book was blank.

She put it back, mainly relieved, though now she knew that she was the sort of mother who would betray her teenage child by invading her personal space, so that was nice. While she was at it, she thought, she would look at the history on the laptop, because Billy certainly didn't get to have any privacy. She needed to check all of that because when social services came, they would probably take it away.

She thought of what he had said about quantum mechanics and wondered where her Billy had gone. There was something very wrong. She was watching her child spinning away from her, and it was . . . She wobbled, sat down quickly.

Focus. This was not the time to fall apart.

She replaced the mattress over the diary, sat on it, and opened the laptop. It took ages to come back to life, and Beth was shouting downstairs, and Rachel was about to take the computer down with her when the screen came back on, and she clicked on the history tab, just for a quick look.

She convulsed and almost dropped it. She realized that although she had been consumed by Billy and Delfy, she had been criminally neglectful.

She looked at the history.

She scrolled down it.

She stared.

She felt sick.

Her ears were ringing. Her vision was fading around the edges.

She tried to breathe. In and out and in and out. That was how it went. Breathe in and then breathe out.

She got to her feet. The router was on a little table on the landing; she unplugged the Wi-Fi as she passed. There was a hammer in the bottom drawer in the kitchen, and she got it out, ignoring both children, and took it upstairs, where she put the laptop on her and Al's bed and smashed it up. It took a while, but in the end, it was in pieces, and she was pretty sure the hard drive was destroyed. She put all the pieces into a plastic bag and tied the handles together.

She would get rid of it completely before the authorities came. Dropping it in the river would be best.

Rachel knew that she was the worst mother in the world. The laptop's history had been cleared a day ago, but even since then, without her realizing it, her six-year-old son had been looking at what had to be hard-core pornography on the Internet.

Rachel never looked at porn, but she knew enough about it second-hand. The horrific things that were normalized. The way it had bled into everyday life. The nastiness of it. The misogyny. The way it warped boundaries of what was first acceptable and then expected.

She had seen his search history. Her Billy had typed those words.

People sex

Animal sex

Animal people sex

Child sex

He had searched for the words "child sex." What had he seen?

She would throw the bag into the Thames, and Nina would not have a computer anymore. Rachel would make it up to her somehow.

Nina had a school iPad, although she never used it for anything other than occasional homework because she said it was too heavily filtered to be any use at all. She had a phone, and so did Rachel and Al, and there was the iPad that Henry had bought Billy, which Rachel would repurpose as the household one with every single parental control activated. They would manage. There was a computer at Henry's house that Nina could use, though Rachel needed to make sure that Billy couldn't. She would tell Henry that Billy was banned from all screens apart from the family television.

Rachel needed to take better care of Billy. This was her fault.

Hello there, darling," said Orla.

"Mum?" Rachel said, jiggling around from one foot to the other. "Can I come over with Billy and Beth?"

She just needed to get out of this house. Mum's was the obvious, cheapest place to go. Her resolution to keep Billy away from Orla because of the potential exorcism was overshadowed by the fact that she was cracking up and needed her mother.

"There's a church sale I was going to . . . ," Orla said, "but, oh, sure you can, my love. I'll go later. Shouldn't my Billy be at school?"

"No." She could hardly speak, and anyway someone might be listening on the line. "He's not well. He's back at home for a bit. I mean, he's not *ill* ill again or anything." Orla did not need to know about the referral, or about the Internet, or about the way Billy had charged into his school's staff room to ask the teachers about sex.

They shouldn't go. She saw that at once, as if the sun had come out from behind a cloud. It lit up the truth. *Don't go to Mum's.* Last time they went, something bad had happened. This time it would happen again. Bad things were happening wherever they went. It was a stupid idea.

"Actually," she said, "we don't need to come today. Don't worry. Go to the church sale."

"Well," said Orla, "you should really. You'll need to be back at work next week."

Rachel opened her mouth to contradict her, but she couldn't, because, she realized, it was true. "Oh," she said.

"So come over. If Billy's going to be off school a bit longer, he'll need to stay with me anyway, when you're working."

Rachel didn't know what to do, because her mother was right. She couldn't, though. She couldn't leave Billy with Orla and go to work. In the end, she got the children wrapped up again and took them straight over to Orla's on the Tube.

It was nice just to be someone's daughter. That was all she wanted: not to be the senior person responsible for everything. She wanted to drink tea and talk about other things. She would like Orla to tell her about Jesus. She didn't care what they talked about, so long as it wasn't Delfy.

Orla, wearing a short orange dress, made a pot of tea and poured it weak and milky as usual. Beth was happy for a while, playing with the

Lego Duplo that Orla had stashed away since Billy's babyhood. Billy was watching an episode of *Horrible Histories*, and Rachel was next to him so that she could be absolutely sure at all times that he was not doing anything other than watching an age-appropriate TV program.

"Chrissy said she was bringing her chocolate cakes, but last time they were dry," Orla was saying, and Rachel almost relaxed. That was the kind of thing she needed to hear. She needed minutiae to calm her paranoia.

It wasn't paranoia.

The worst thing she had done so far was to assume that everything was fine.

Rachel was out of her depth, and she had nowhere to turn, and she couldn't talk to her own mother about what was going on because the last thing they needed was church involvement. Graham Watson's offer of a hospital bed, which had seemed so jarring and unnecessary, suddenly felt like a lifeline. Watson had known that this would happen.

She started to imagine Billy growing up and Delfy never going away. He might end up in prison. She should call Watson back and see if his offer was still open.

"Go out again," said Orla. She stared into Rachel's eyes. "Clear your head. You're struggling. Leave them here with me. Look at him. You see? He's perfectly fine. We won't do anything to disturb anyone. And this little one—we'll get her crawling, shall we? That's what we'll do. Time to move, Bethie."

"But the last time he saw you . . . ," Rachel began.

"Not this time," said Orla. "We won't even talk about it."

"You promise? No exorcisms. Nothing?"

"Nothing, darling. Off you go. You'll be leaving them with me every day soon enough. Go and have an hour off."

Rachel felt uneasy as she waited for the lift. Billy was contained. No one loved him more than Orla did. Orla had promised not to try to exorcise him, not to talk about Delfy. She was just giving Rachel a break.

Billy, for his part, had agreed that Delfy wasn't going to attack Grandma and had frowned for a while, then announced that Delfy agreed to it, too. Rachel was only going out for an hour. All the same, the panic wriggled inside her like a creature trying to escape. It was like a thousand spiders. She hated being away from the children. But Mum was right: she was going to have to get used to it.

She went to Canary Wharf again, putting her head down and passing a group of men who demanded spare change, walking into the shopping mall, trying to imagine herself back at work next week. On Monday. The date had been fixed before she left to have Beth, and she knew it was non-negotiable. She had been extremely lucky to have a generous maternity allowance, even though most of it was unpaid, and she knew that the bank that had employed her could not have expected that she would actually use it. No one had thought she would leave to have a baby at the age of forty-two, when she already had two children.

Although she couldn't afford to buy a coffee, she ended up in a branch of Cafe Rosso, in the basement of the building. It was a windowless space whose walls were covered with photographs of people at cafés in what seemed to be Italy in the middle of the twentieth century, but its ambience was relentlessly corporate: the few other customers were in work clothes and carried bundles of papers. A couple of men were having a low-level confidential conversation away from their office, and a man and a woman were meeting for an illicit coffee, rubbing their legs together and holding hands under the table, both wearing wedding rings.

Rachel took a paper cup, filled it with water from one of the jugs that were on a counter, and sat down. She was almost certain no one would notice that she hadn't bought a drink, and she leaned back and exhaled. No one was following her; she had been checking all the time.

It was difficult to clear her mind. The pressure of the unexpected time alone was too much, and her head was full of Billy searching for animal porn and talking about sex at school. Searching the words "child sex." That made her retch. He would have seen whatever the results of that search were, and she couldn't search the phrase herself to see exactly what they were.

After a while, she clicked on social media for distraction and stared at a load of updates from people she vaguely knew. She read about politics and viruses and space colonies, and scrolled past photos of pets and children. She didn't care about any of it. The only thing that mattered was Billy, but the normality of all this was soothing.

She clicked a link to the secret group she belonged to, the school one. It was full of the most boring secrets there could be, and she looked at it only when it occasionally showed up on her timeline to remind her about a nonuniform day or to check arrangements for a school trip, but she opened it now out of paranoia, and then discovered that, again, she hadn't been paranoid at all.

Anyone know what happened at school today? began one of the mothers in a message written the previous afternoon. She was a woman Rachel barely knew. **Apparently it's all kicked off,** she continued. **I mean, we all know who we're talking about, right? #lipssealed #getawayfrommykid #emergencyreferralplease #probablythestepdad.**

A load of others had piled in, in the same vein. Nobody mentioned Billy, Al, or Rachel by name, and she actually wished they had because the coyness of "my lips are sealed" made it worse and impossible to refute. They swapped stories:

> **The school has actually has called social services.**
> **Enough's enough—I'm not sending my child to school to learn about p*rn and s*x from a 6 year old!!**
> **It's sick.**
> **he asked Miss Jones if she shaved her bits! shudn't laugh, but can u imagine???**
> **Yeah, but it's not really funny. I mean it would be if it was someone else's school, u no?**
> **Are they going to expel him?**

I saw his mum in the playground.

U can only blame the parents

the parents

the parents

the parents

Poor boy. He must of been abused.

The stepdad

There it was: everything (badly) written down, giggled about, and archly hashtagged. The sheer delight everyone was taking in the gossip was the second-worst part. The very worst thing was that it was real and about her own family.

This meant Billy had left the school forever. She was not putting him anywhere these parents might see him and whisper about him. And yet Rachel had to go back to work. She couldn't take Billy to the office with her. Henry couldn't look after him, and neither could Al, or Nina. As Orla had said, she would have to look after him and Beth together. That, right now, felt like the only plan Rachel could possibly come up with.

Her finger hovered over the screen. Every part of her longed to write a string of expletives, but she knew she mustn't because they would love it so very much if she did. She tapped LEAVE THIS GROUP instead and exhaled in relief when all the words went away.

Perhaps Henry would pay for a private school.

She remembered Graham Watson. He was the only person who might understand.

She got through first to a switchboard that said her call was important, and then to Lauren.

"It's Rachel Jackman," she said, standing up and walking out of the café.

"Oh," said Lauren. "Hello there! How are you, Ms. Jackman?"

Rachel found a tiny space in her brain to be impressed that Lauren knew, at once, who she was and got her title right.

"Fine," she said. "Well, actually, no. Not fine. No. Professor Watson said we should call if things got worse, and they have. They have. They really, really have." She stopped and wrestled herself under control. She was still filled with spiders. They were trying to climb up her throat and out of her mouth. "So I wondered if I could speak to him? I mean, I spoke to him yesterday, but I was a bit . . ."

"Oh, I'm so sorry to hear that," said Lauren. "Yes. Of course. He's in a consultation right now, but I'm sure he'll want to speak to you as soon as he has a moment. Is this the best number for him to call you on?"

Rachel looked at the phone in her hand and nodded. Yes. This was the only way he could call her back.

"Yes," she said. "Thank you."

"Brilliant. He won't be long. Thanks, Ms. Jackman. I know he'll be keen to chat."

Rachel felt marginally better as she waited at the bus stop. Her phone had plenty of battery, and she turned the volume right up.

TWENTY-FOUR

In spite of everything, it didn't occur to her that there was anything wrong when no one answered the buzzer. She pressed it again, imagining the Beatles playing, picturing the three of them dancing up on the fifteenth floor, too happy to hear her ringing. On the fourth ring, she was starting to wonder, but then Billy answered.

"Mumma?" he said in a burst of static.

"Let me in, darling!"

The buzzer sounded, and she pushed the door. She fidgeted in the lift, looking forward to seeing her babies. It jolted to a halt on floor nine and refused to budge from there, so she walked up the final six flights of stairs, huffing and eager for a cup of tea.

The front door was ajar. Beth was screaming inside the flat, and Rachel ran to pick her up, following the cries straight into Orla's bedroom, where she found the baby strapped into her pushchair, yelling. She was writhing around and struggling to get out.

"Oh, poor Bethie," she said, unstrapping her and picking her up, holding her close until she stopped crying. "What was Grandma think-ing? Where is she?"

"Mumma." Billy was standing behind her. He wasn't exactly crying, but his face made Rachel freeze. There was something in his eyes.

"Where's Grandma? What's she doing?"

Beth was pulling Rachel's hair. She was hiccuping, taking shuddering breaths, gradually calming down.

"She's here. Mum, you need to see. Mum. We're sorry. I didn't want to." He gasped and let out a wail.

Rachel's hands were busy with the baby, but while she was trying to get an arm free for him, Billy squirmed away and pulled her along by the edge of her coat. He took her into the living room, where Orla was asleep on the sofa with a cushion over her face, and stood back.

Rachel could see at a glance that Orla wasn't asleep, but she pretended otherwise because she didn't know what else to do.

"Mum," said Rachel. "Hey, Mum. Wake up!"

She stepped closer.

She looked at her mother. She held the baby close. She took the cush-ion away, looked at her mother's face, and put it back.

A paramedic arrived forty minutes after she called, and he rang the police and got out a body bag. Even then, Rachel wasn't able to face the truth. She busied herself instead with looking after the children.

If something had happened to Mum, she thought, it must have been a heart attack. She fixated on that while she fed Beth, played with her, changed her nappy. When Billy tried to tell her what had happened, she didn't want to hear the words he said, so she stopped him from speaking. He was calm and pale. She knew the man was zipping Orla into the bag, but if she stayed in the bedroom, she could pretend he wasn't. Beth was restless, trying to crawl across the carpet. And Billy was saying the same things over and over again.

"I'm sorry," he said. "We are sorry."

"You didn't do anything," said Rachel. "Shh. It's OK."

It wasn't OK.

"She did try to do an exercise thing for Delfy."

"An exorcism," Rachel said. "And the strain of it must have . . ."

"Delfy didn't like it."

"So Grandma's body must have given up," Rachel said. She said it to Billy over and over again. She didn't want anyone to entertain any other possibility. He had to say that Orla had just died. That was the only thing that could have happened. After a while, Billy lay on his back and stared at the ceiling.

But then the police turned up, and she had to speak to them. The man looked about Nina's age and the woman was in her forties with a kind smile that sent a sword of ice through Rachel's stomach. She was being kind because Rachel made a pathetic spectacle, sitting on the bed with her two babies, pretending that her mother's body wasn't in the other room.

"I'm DCI Meadows," the woman said. "I'm terribly sorry about your mother. We do have to attend a scene when there's an unexpected death. It's a formality. So, your mother just . . . ?" She was too delicate to complete the sentence.

"Yes," said Rachel. This was her chance to be firm about it. "She just died. I wasn't here. Mum was looking after Billy and Beth, you see. While I went down to Canary Wharf. I work there, or I did, and I'm going back after maternity leave next week. Mum's going to be looking after Beth for me. She was going to. I mean, I suppose she won't . . ." She kept trailing off. It was impossible to make sense of this.

"Right," said DCI Meadows. "So she was alone in charge of the children when this happened?"

"Yes. Yes, she was. I came back, and Billy pressed the buzzer to let me in."

DCI Meadows turned to him. "Clever boy."

Billy shook his head. "No, police lady," he said. "No, I'm afraid I'm not a clever boy, because, you see, it was me that killed her."

Rachel felt herself splitting in two. The real Rachel floated off to the ceiling and watched the shell that was left behind shouting at them that Billy hadn't killed Orla, that there had not been a cushion on her face. She kept saying, "Heart attack."

Someone handed her a cup of sweet tea, because that was what people did, and she sipped it without noticing.

"What do you mean?" said the policewoman to Billy.

"I putted a cushion over her face, and that did stop her talking and breathing."

"I see. Why did you do that, Billy?"

Rachel tried very hard to focus on the answer, but she couldn't do it. There was no part of her that could bear to listen to this. She stayed on the ceiling as far away as she could.

She heard it all through a ringing sound that fenced her off from everything outside her head. She tried not to hear the baffled police officers trying to make sense of Billy's explanation of Delfy. They seized on the exorcism, and Rachel thought she saw some sort of understanding cross the woman's face as she found a narrative that made sense.

"She was very religious, was she?"

"Yes," said Billy. "She did want Jesus to come. She thought that Delfy was the devil."

"Right." The woman wrote that down. "She was attacking you?"

"Not me," said Billy. "Delfy. She putted her hands on my head and said there was a lamb and a snake."

"Right."

Rachel tuned out again.

Billy Stevens," said the young policeman at some point a bit later, "I'm arresting you for the murder of Orla Jackman. You don't have to say anything—"

"No!" Rachel screamed, and flew at them, putting herself between Billy and the police. "You can't do this. It wasn't Billy! He's six! You can't arrest him!"

The policewoman put a hand on Rachel's arm. It was a firm grip, disguised as comfort.

"Don't worry, Rachel," she said. "We just have to follow procedure. As you've heard, Billy has repeatedly confessed to this and clearly explained what happened."

"You can't take Billy away! You can't! I won't let you!"

Beth was crying. Billy was looking at her with wide, darting eyes. For once, she wanted to see the dilated pupils and the stiff posture that meant Delfy was in charge, but it didn't happen.

"Mumma," he said quietly. "Mum. We're sorry."

The legal change had happened only last year: after a group of homeless children had killed a policeman, the age of criminal responsibility had been lowered to five. Billy, at six, was old enough to be tried as an adult. To be sentenced to decades of imprisonment for murder. To grow up in a youth prison and be transferred to an adult one as soon as he was eighteen.

Rachel screamed and shook the other woman's hand off her arm, ran. Picked up Billy and clung to him.

"No!" she said. "You can't take him. You can't!"

B ut they could.

T hey held Rachel back (they were strong, the police), and they took Billy away. She wasn't allowed to go with him: she was left, instead, with a woman called Felicia, who was a family liaison officer. Rachel could see, through the fog, that her own position was ambiguous. She was, at the same time, the daughter of the victim, so in need of help and comfort, and the mother of the perpetrator, which made her evil. *I blame the mother.*

That was what people said reflexively when anything like this happened. She imagined the Facebook group and shuddered.

She walked around her mother's house, screaming for her son at the top of her voice. Beth sat silent in the middle of the floor, her face crumpling.

"I'm sorry," said Felicia, who was young and beautiful. "This is distressing, I know. For what it's worth, I think Billy will have mitigating circumstances. It might not be the worst outcome for him."

"But that would be"—Rachel forced herself to say the words, as surreal as they were—"at a . . . trial. Will you keep him until then?"

"Yes," said Felicia. "I'm afraid we have to."

Rachel's phone rang. The screen said *Graham Watson*. She had called him earlier! Oh, thank God. Oh, God, she had turned down a residential treatment. This wouldn't have happened. Oh, God.

"I have to get this," she said, and Felicia nodded.

"Of course."

"Sorry it's taken me so long to get back to you," said the doctor's deep voice. "Lauren says things have become difficult with Billy."

Rachel cried and told him everything. The words fell out on top of one another, but he understood.

"OK," he said. "Leave this with me. Which police station is he at?"

Felicia said she would drive Rachel and Beth home. There had been four of them, and now there were two. Orla was dead, and Billy had been taken. It had unraveled.

Rachel needed to tell people. She had to tell Henry, and he could go to wherever Billy was because she knew she wouldn't be able to get her head straight enough to do everything that was needed for him. She had to tell Al. To tell Nina that her grandmother was dead and her brother had been arrested for murder. The news would travel out and out and out, and she was the one who needed to start that process, and the only person she had told was Graham Watson, and she couldn't do any more than that. She could not begin the process.

But she had to.

*M*um? she said internally. You never knew. Perhaps Orla would take up residence in her daughter's head as Delfy had with Billy. Right now she would take her mother's voice in her head for all eternity, because that way she would still be hearing her mother's voice.

*S*he called Al at work before they left the apartment. He didn't answer, so she tried to leave a voice mail, but no words came out, so she hung up. She called Nina's phone, but Nina didn't answer either, and a moment later, a message arrived saying: Mum! my phone went off in geography!! I'll call back after.

Rachel managed: please do. xxx

She stood on the landing and waited for the lift. It was raining outside again, and the whole of the city was smudged below her, with wisps of clouds floating over it. Felicia was holding Beth, and someone else from the police had the pushchair, and Billy wouldn't be walking beside her as she pushed it because he was with the police. He was under arrest.

And Rachel was an orphan. Perhaps she could go and live in an orphanage now. Nothing would be expected of her. She would sit at a long table and eat gruel and sew clothes or something; that much she could probably manage.

I can be around to help out for a few days, if you'd like that," said the woman. Felicity. Felicia.

Rachel had no idea what she said, but her phone rang as they were at the base of the building, and it was Al, and by that point, she was holding the baby, so she couldn't answer it, and so the woman whose name she had forgotten tried to take Beth from her, but Beth shouted and clung to Rachel's hair, and the phone stopped before she could answer it.

They walked quickly away from the base of the tower block. It was cold, and her mother was dead.

TWENTY-FIVE

Graham took a taxi to the police station, which was a boxy building in East London. He struggled to believe that a society that considered itself civilized would lock up tiny children. He knew it happened, but it hadn't happened to one of Graham's patients in years. His current young inmates were responsible for a whole collection of horrific things, but none of them had insisted on confessing to the police, and largely their families had had enough money to ease it all away.

Graham needed to make this go away for Billy. His knees hurt, and he was tired, but he was on a mission. If it seemed that Billy really had done this thing (his mother had been so distraught, it was hard to tell what had actually happened), Graham had a plan B, and he thought it would work. He had put on his tweed jacket for extra authority.

This was his fault. He had tried to offer Billy a place in the ward, but had retreated in the face of Billy's mother's instinctive refusal, rather than pressing his case and scaring her with possible scenarios. He had known Billy was going to do something like this, but he had stepped back and let it play out.

He walked into the reception area. It was populated with sad-looking people waiting on chairs, and there was no one behind the desk. There was, however, an old-fashioned bell, the sort you hit with your hand.

He loved these. He gave it three sharp taps and, when no one came, three more.

"All right!" said a voice. "Hold your horses." A middle-aged man appeared. "Can I help you?" he said, looking pissed off.

Graham nodded. "You certainly can. I'm here to see a patient of mine who has been illegally taken into custody." He showed his card. "I'm here for Billy Stevens. He was brought here a short time ago."

"Illegally" was an out-and-out lie, but he knew it sounded good.

The man nodded. "A very short time ago indeed," he said. "He only just arrived. Hang on. Can I take your card?" He looked at it. "You're a professor or a doctor?"

"Both. But for these purposes, I'm Billy's doctor."

The man disappeared, and Graham sat down, nodding hello to a woman sitting on the next chair. She smelled strongly of spirits, and she just rocked back and forth and muttered under her breath.

A n hour later Graham was in a tiny room, when Billy was led in between two police officers, a man and a woman. He looked lost. He stared at Graham and then looked down, and Graham realized he must have been hoping for his parents.

Graham stood up. "Hello there, Billy," he said. "How are you doing?"

Billy's eyes were staring at something Graham couldn't see. "Not very good, I don't think," he said after a long pause.

Graham wanted to pick him up and carry him out of there. He wanted to take him home to his mother. "Nice of you not to handcuff him, at least," he said instead. He was aiming for an acid tone, but it was lost on the officers.

"Our handcuffs are too big," the male one said. "No point."

"For God's sake," he said. "He's six years old!"

There was a commotion outside, and then the door opened, and someone ran into the room and tried to pick Billy up before being pushed back by the officers.

"Billy!" said Henry Stevens. "Oh, Billy! What the hell is going on?"

"I didn't mean to do it!" Billy shouted. "I didn't want to hurt her. It was Delfy. Delfy did it."

G raham found that he and Henry made a better team than he would have expected. Henry was a lawyer, and although this was far from being his area of specialty, he, like Graham, was able to say the right things.

"Utterly unacceptable," Henry said. "This is my son. He's been very troubled. The NHS has declined to help. His school has washed their hands, effectively expelling him for being ill. Thus, the state has turned its back on him until now, and so we've done what we can. He's seeing this very eminent doctor in Harley Street. He is a sick child. Whatever he has done, he is emphatically not going to prison. It would be catastrophic."

Graham nodded and took over. "I have a proposal," he said, "as an interim measure. I run a psycho-pediatric ward at the Harley Hospital." He felt Henry turning toward him, surprised. "There are currently six residents with round-the-clock care and security. I can offer Billy a secure private room and medication that will ensure he's unable to harm anyone. A secure, private children's hospital is a much more appropriate place for him. I realize it will only be until the trial, but that's likely to be months away, isn't it?"

The woman nodded. "Next year, most likely."

"I cannot have my patient held in custody for that time."

It sounded straightforward when he said it, but of course it wasn't, because someone who had been accused of murder couldn't be moved to a secure hospital without all kinds of paperwork being done and ultimately the approval of a magistrate. He had done all this before, of course, with Kitty, but that had been thirteen years ago, and the law was different now. Nonetheless, it was the fact that he already had a long-term patient in residence with him, another child who had murdered someone, that made them agree to it.

All the same, sorting it out took hours. Hours and hours and hours. Billy couldn't be on the ward. He would have to be, like Kitty, in a separate room with at least two locking doors between him and the other children. (*If only they knew,* Graham thought, *about the other children.*) The negotiations continued as Billy was taken away. Apparently he was fed and went to sleep in a little cell on his own, and Graham, Henry, and the police carried on working it out.

Just after Billy was taken away, Graham flagged. He needed to sleep: he was too old for this. But there was a small child in a prison cell, a boy who, however newly, was his patient. He tried to find the energy to keep at it. He couldn't. The energy wasn't there. He closed his eyes for a second, but he knew he mustn't tune out. He tried to focus, but he didn't have the capacity to focus.

He needed strength. He needed something more than coffee (though coffee would have been a start). He needed . . .

Imogen? He made sure not to say it out loud. Henry and someone high up from the police were arguing a point. Graham closed his eyes again and focused inward. He needed, somehow, to summon his dead wife and to ask for her help, like she had said.

He waited.

Someone tapped him on the shoulder. He jolted back into the room and looked around, guilty. And there was Imogen beside him.

She was looking impeccable, as always.

I like your hair, he said, with his mind.

Thanks. She touched the edge of her sharp bob and smiled. *Come on, Graham. Don't be a twat. You can do this. Fight for him! Fight for him like we fought for Kitty.*

She reached over and took his hand, and he felt himself fill with the most extraordinary power. It surged through him like electricity. She kept hold of him while he tapped the table and said: "Gentlemen! Why don't we just cut through the crap and get this done right now?"

A solicitor turned up to draft some paperwork. Graham had to swear an affidavit saying that Billy was mentally unfit to be kept in the cells (*BECAUSE HE IS 6,* he wanted to scrawl underneath those words), and Henry gave parental consent to everything Graham proposed. They were on fire.

"We'll have to keep Billy overnight," said the policewoman, the one who had arrested Billy in the first place. "This needs to be actioned by a magistrate. We can't do that this evening."

"Can't we?" Graham looked at Imogen, who nodded her encouragement, and then at Henry, who took out his phone.

"I reckon we can," said Henry.

A t midnight, a sleepy Billy was between Henry and Graham in the back of a police car. Henry was on the phone to Billy's mum. Imogen was riding in the front seat, trying to switch on the siren.

"We did it," Henry said. "He's out of the cells. I told you we'd do it tonight. Graham and I made it happen."

Graham could hear Rachel, even from here, crying down the phone. What she didn't know was that they had had to agree to an enormous dose of antipsychotic medication to incapacitate Billy. This wasn't the moment.

Henry passed him the phone and said, "Billy's mum wants a word," and when Graham took it, Rachel Jackman thanked him a million times through her tears and said she would be over to visit Billy first thing in the morning.

He wanted to say that visits from family were strictly limited but decided that it wasn't the moment for that either. Of course she could come tomorrow.

By two in the morning, Billy was in a different sort of cell, fast asleep. He had barely said a word. Graham looked at him in the bed and wondered what the hell his life was going to be like. They had broken him out of prison for now, but he had a feeling it was going to be a very, very long time before Billy saw daylight.

He had killed someone and admitted to it. Children were being tried as adults. Unless someone could prove beyond reasonable doubt that this was Delfy's doing and that Billy had been controlled by an independent force, Billy would spend decades behind bars. And if they could prove that, he would still spend his life in a hospital. What was needed, Graham thought, was proof that Billy had acted on the instructions of the voice in his head, coupled with proof that the voice had now stopped talking to him.

And that seemed unlikely, as it hadn't.

TWENTY-SIX

Rachel left Beth with Nina, who said she wouldn't have gone to school anyway, and set off to visit Billy. She caught the bus with a canvas bag that contained his rabbit, his pajamas and toothbrush, some books, and a selection of other things from home.

She thought private hospitals had family rooms. That sounded like a luxurious thing, so it probably existed. Maybe Graham Watson would let her sleep there twice a week. Something like that, at a time when Al could be home with Beth. She would ask.

She caught a bus even though the Tube was quicker, because she didn't want to go underground: she'd had a dream about creatures running out of the tunnels and couldn't shake it off. The bus flew through the bus lanes and sprayed pedestrians with puddle water, and she gazed out the window and knew that she was nowhere near assimilating what had happened, and she would probably never be able to do it. Not properly.

She saw her own face reflected in the window and closed her eyes to make it go away. Suddenly she looked like her own mother. She was an old lady with a jowly face, her hair gray and bird's nesty, her cheeks hollow, her eyes wild. No one was sitting next to her even though a few people were standing up. She must have appeared mad.

She looked like Orla, because now she was Orla. She was the matriarch, the oldest woman in the family.

Mum is dead. That was the secondary fact to all of this, but it had pulled away a building block of her world, and everything had fallen down. She had to be strong for Billy, who was at the center of the biggest crisis there could possibly be, but she didn't know how to do it. She had taken Orla for granted, had complained about going to her house for lunches while cheerfully using her for free childcare. And now there was no more Orla. Rachel was going to have to organize a funeral, at the same time as being the mother of the killer.

She vaguely knew that she was making a high-pitched keening noise and supposed that this was why no one wanted to sit beside her. It didn't matter.

It was impossible to get into the hospital, so much so that she almost gave up. She kept pressing the wrong buzzers and annoying people who worked in other parts of the building. She had thought Graham Watson had said the hospital was downstairs, but the BASEMENT button got her the offices of a facial plastic surgeon, however many times she pressed it. In the end, she got out her phone to call Lauren and found that she'd written a note to herself with the instructions. She followed them and found herself in a tiny lift that seemed to go to the center of the Earth.

When she got out of it, she discovered that it had been a portal into a different universe. The air was warm and fresh, and it appeared to be daylight even though she knew it couldn't possibly be. The carpet was thick under her feet. The walls were white but not quite. It was like being on a spaceship from an old film.

"Hello, Ms. Jackman," said the woman on reception. "We just need to go through some security procedures, and then you can visit your child."

They photographed her eye, took her fingerprints, scanned her face.

She signed things and promised things and let them X-ray her bag, and wondered what the hell had happened, why she had to do this to get to her Billy. Then she remembered.

She zoned out of it all and forgot to answer a few things, but in the end, she was through, following a woman in a nurse's uniform down a corridor. The doors swooshed open, spaceship style, as they approached them.

There were doors all the way down this corridor. One said GYM on it. Several read NO ENTRY TO UNAUTHORIZED PERSONS. Then, incongruously, she came to a door with a picture of a giraffe on it. Only one door, however, had a policeman sitting outside it, reading a book. He stood up as she approached and took a step sideways to bar the door itself.

"I'm Billy's mother," she said.

"I need to see your pass," said the man, and she showed it to him. "Yes, you can visit, but I think he's sleeping."

"That's OK," said Rachel. "I'll just look at him."

She went in. The room was bigger than she'd expected and white like the inside of her imaginary spaceship. Billy was tiny in his bed. He had purple bags under his eyes, and his hair was knotted, but his breathing was even, and at least he was safe.

Henry had said Billy was going to have to stand up in court, accused of murder. He had said it would happen next year. Rachel couldn't think about it. When she tried to imagine it, it was like looking into the sun. She couldn't do it.

For now, she was here, at Billy's side, and so life was not so different from the way it had been when he was ill. He lay there, and she sat beside his bed and stared at him and tried very hard not to think ahead.

TWENTY-SEVEN

Nina desperately wanted to write all this down. She needed to pour it out onto her blog, but when she looked for the laptop, it was gone.

She looked everywhere. It had completely vanished. There was no computer in the house, and she couldn't use her school iPad, because it was so heavily filtered and monitored that it was more useful as a tea tray than anything else.

She couldn't focus. She had created the perfect place to pour all of this out, and her access to it was gone. She couldn't ask Mum, because Mum was visiting Billy in the hospital that Dad had somehow fixed up for him as an alternative to prison (much respect to Dad for that). She couldn't ask Al because he was at work and couldn't be contacted there unless it was an emergency, and anyway she didn't quite want to demand her computer when Billy had murdered Gran.

She took Beth around the house, looking everywhere. It was like acting out one of those picture books Beth had: "Is it under the bed?" Pause while she looked under the bed. "No!" Beth giggled every time and tried to help out by pointing at things, but they were never the right thing.

The clues turned out to be in Mum and Al's room. It felt weird going in there when they were both out, a bit of an invasion of privacy. The duvet was piled on the bed, bunched up so tight that Nina had to shake it out to make sure no one was hiding under it. She sat Beth on the bed and looked everywhere else. There was a stash of nappies on the floor, a heap of sci-fi books beside Al's side of the bed, a pile of clean washing on the cot. And right there, a hammer. It was on the floor, half under the bed; there was no reason for there to be a hammer in this room.

Nina got down on her hands and knees and checked the floor; there were a shard of hard plastic and a piece of metal.

"Oh, look, Bethie," she said, holding them up. "Oh, Beth. I have a feeling that this is all that's left of my computer."

Beth pointed at it and shouted.

Nina messaged Louis, who was at school but managed to reply anyway.

I've lost my laptop, she said. Social services were going to come and visit Billy so I reckon my mum panicked and destroyed it. No idea how I'm meant to do my homework. I can't exactly kick off about this right now, can I?

Shit, wrote Louis. I can get you a spare one from home?

You sure? She remembered his home and smiled to herself. Of course he could. It would feel weird taking a thing like that from the Alfords. Ideally she wouldn't do it.

100 sure.

But nothing about right now was ideal, and she desperately wanted a computer—not just for her blog, but as a link to the world, a thing to look at to stop her thinking about everything else. Billy was in a secure hospital, Gran was dead, Mum was unraveling, Al was stressed, and Dad had unexpectedly stepped up.

Just as a loan? she wrote.

If you like. Meet you later with it?

Nina sighed.

Thank you, she wrote. You are amazing.

There was a long pause before he next replied. By that point she and Beth were downstairs playing with Beth's favorite toys, the pots and pans.

Just pleased I can do something, he wrote, two hours later. Sorry. Teacher caught me and took my phone away.

M um stayed out at the hospital all day. By the time she came home at seven, wild-eyed and jittery, Al was bathing Beth, and Nina was sitting at her desk in front of her new, very up-to-date computer, logged in to her site and starting to write.

A terrible thing happened to Josh this week, she wrote. She paused. No one was going to read this. She would move the text out before she even submitted the site itself. It was just going to feel incredible to write it down, to tell it to the ether.

He killed our grandmother.

The relief at writing those words was so immense that she burst into tears.

TWENTY-EIGHT

Rachel was at the park with Beth. She was sitting on a bench, and the baby was on the ground at her feet, at her own insistence. Rachel's office had offered her an extra month of unpaid leave, but she had thanked them and told them to hire someone else, because there was no way in the world that she would be able to go back to work and answer phones and file pieces of paper and act as if the world had some order to it when it didn't. They would only have had to fire her. She would inherit Orla's flat at some point, and then they could move into it; she just couldn't bring herself to care about money.

She went to the underground spaceship to visit Billy three times a week, because that was what she was allowed to do, and even that was a concession because the actual rules said twice. The rest of the time, she tried her best to get through the days. She knew that if Graham and Henry hadn't stepped in, Billy would have been in one of those god-awful places where kids starved themselves to death as the only way out, the ones you saw in TV exposés. She was so grateful to Graham that when she saw him, she couldn't look him in the eye. It was too much. And Henry, too. Henry had got a magistrate out of bed and assembled an emergency hearing just so Billy didn't have to spend one single night in the cells, and she was so grateful that she didn't know what to do with herself.

The autopsy results would be back the next day, but she didn't need to wait for them, because she knew—everyone knew—that Billy had killed Orla. Her son had killed her mum. It went around and around in her head all day and all night. She couldn't be the killer's mother properly while she was also the victim's daughter, and vice versa.

She stood in the park with Beth in the rain and tried to remember what she was doing here. Her phone rang. She didn't answer it because it wasn't Al, Nina, or anyone calling from the hospital. Her phone had rung a couple of times with this same number, and she always ignored it.

She found herself imagining and reimagining Orla's death day and night. Her son had murdered her mother because she was trying to get the voice out of his head. It was nightmarish. There was no bright side to look on, no chink of light. She woke in the middle of the night, rigid with horror. During the day she tried to act the way she thought previous-Rachel would have acted, and she didn't think that even Al could see how much she was faking it. She made an effort to say and do the right things while the small Rachel inside her, the kernel of her, was ceaselessly obsessed with her mother's death and the voice in her son's head that had made him do it.

She had never believed in Delfy as a thing separate from Billy; sometimes it had felt that way, but she had always known, really, that Delfy was a thing that had sprung from Billy's own brain. Now, though, everything had changed. She needed to believe that Delfy was a spirit, a demon, a ghost. Mum had been right: Delfy was something from the outside. She was not part of Billy. She was not.

She sighed. It was time to pull herself together. She reached down to pick up Beth, but the baby wasn't there.

She had been on the ground at Rachel's feet, and now she was gone.

Rachel had been staring into space, distracted, catatonic, and someone had stolen her baby. They had taken Beth.

She had lost Orla.

Lost Billy.

And now she had lost Beth.

"Where's my baby?" she yelled. She screamed it with all her might.

A man was walking a dog nearby. He turned and smiled.

"Over there, love," he said, and she looked at where he was pointing and realized that he was right. Beth had chosen that moment to work out how to crawl. She was halfway across the muddy grass. When she saw Rachel looking at her, she stopped, sat back on her bottom, and applauded herself heartily.

A day later, the autopsy showed that Orla had died from asphyxiation. It had not been a heart attack or a brain hemorrhage or any of the other things that made people suddenly die, and so the last spark of hope was extinguished. She had been killed, and as the building's CCTV showed that no one else had come in, she had been killed by Billy.

Billy would be tried next year, and he was staying in the hospital until then, and Rachel was more grateful to Graham than she could possibly have said. Billy had asked Graham to ask her to bring Beth to visit him, and she was delighted to be able to do that. It would be good for the two of them to see each other. Nice and normal.

She was at home, standing at the window, looking at the brand-new cobwebs that had appeared, when she heard Al come into the room.

"Hey!" he said. "How did you get all the way up there?"

"I'm not up . . . ," she started to say, but when she turned, she saw that he was talking to Beth, that Beth had managed to climb onto the bed and was bouncing on it on all fours. Rachel hadn't noticed.

He closed the door and sat on the bed. "Rachel?" he said. "Look. I'm really sorry. This is terrible timing. But. We . . ."

She came to sit next to him. He paused for a long time. She waited. She could see that he was finding this difficult, and that made her dread what was coming.

"Mmm?" she said when she couldn't bear it anymore.

"Just. God. Your mother. And Billy being in hospital. And you resigning from your job. All of that. I didn't want to say this until things had settled down a bit, but I'm not sure when that will be," he said, and their eyes met. She knew. This was about money, and he was right. He was always right. "Me taking half a day off for the funeral affects our budget for the month. That's the kind of margins we're operating under. Darling, I'm afraid we just don't have enough money."

"Childcare," she said because she knew exactly what he meant. "I'm already supposed to be back at work. We can't afford for me to stay at home, and if I do go back, then without Mum's help, we have to pay for childcare, and we can't do it."

He looked agonized. She shifted along so she was closer to him, so their bodies were touching.

"I know this is the shittiest time for this kind of discussion," Al said. Beth was pulling his ear. "And Billy's in the best place for him at the moment, if he has to be away from home. However barbaric that is. Nina's self-sufficient. But Betty won't go to school for, what, four years? I don't know what we can do. I mean, you said you'll inherit the flat. Is that for definite?"

His question hung in the air. Al would not have said the words *I don't know what we can do* unless he had tried very hard indeed to find a solution. Nobody solved things better than Al.

"Yes," she said, "but I don't know when. I've been thinking about it, too. It's not been at the top of my list of worries." She forced a smile. "Not even in the top five, really. Ten. But you're right." She thought she should spell it out to make sure they were talking about the same thing. "Even if I did still have my receptionist job, it pays the minimum wage, and that's not enough to cover a nursery or a childminder. Right?" He nodded. "Billy's going to need a lot of care, a lot of visits and input and energy, and I'm not really in a position to work nights or anything."

He sighed. She put her head on his chest and listened to his heart beating. They were responsible for three smaller humans, and the only safety net (Henry's money) didn't apply to Beth. Beth was expensive because of nappies: they used cloth ones, but the water and electricity and washing powder added up. Nina was expensive because she was sixteen. Billy was something different altogether.

"I've asked the solicitors to let us know about the flat," she said. "We could move in. Two bedrooms. We'd manage. Or we could sell it."

"Did she pay off the mortgage?"

"She did. So this is temporary."

There was a long pause before he spoke. "Well, I do have a plan," he said, "to get us through until that point, because those things take a lot of time. It's going to be just about OK if it's temporary. I can get a new job that would include accommodation. Three bedrooms, like we have here. No bills. No rent. Lots of things thrown in, including childcare for Beth. I'm pretty sure I'd get the job. A change of direction and pretty menial, but I could do it. You wouldn't have to go back to work."

She felt sick. She knew what this was.

"Worklifeplus," she whispered. He nodded. "But you hate that."

"I don't have that luxury anymore."

"I could go back to my old job," she said. "My career." But even as the words came out, she knew they were hollow. She was in no position to go back to work, and least of all to update her legal qualifications and head back to work as a contract lawyer. It had been terrible for her the first time around, and now it would be infinitely worse. Still, she kept talking. "I trained as a lawyer, didn't I? I'm sure I could go on a course to get back up to speed, and however difficult it was, it would be better than selling out to Ben fucking Alford."

Al touched her arm, stopping her. "Hey," he said. "It's OK. Stop it, my love. Stop talking. You're not doing that. Honestly, it'll be OK. I promise.

We'll let Ben fucking Alford bail us out. It's the least he can do. You left the law because you had a breakdown. Things are hard enough already without you plunging back into that."

She took a deep breath. "But maybe I need to. Something to focus on. The breakdown was about other things really. And it would be better than the other options."

"No," he said. "It wouldn't. Look. I've got details of the flats they offer."

It looked tiny on the screen of his phone. Just a collection of rooms with gray carpet and white walls. Nice clean rooms that would probably be warm, and no rent and no bills.

Al had, it turned out, already filled in an application form. He hadn't sent it because he had been waiting for Rachel's approval, but as soon as she gave the smallest nod, he pressed the SEND button. It would have been easier, of course, to do this on a computer, but they didn't have one anymore (though Nina seemed to be using a shiny one that she must have got from Henry).

While Felicia and a young male police officer were working shifts to ensure one of them was with Billy at all times, other, less gentle officers had been to the house to look at everything. Rachel was more pleased than she could possibly have said that she had destroyed that laptop. Nina's new one escaped, as she'd had it at school with her. They took away Billy's iPad, and although it never came back, nothing was ever said about it. The filters must have done their work.

"When will you find out about the job?" she said. She didn't know exactly what the job was. It didn't matter. It would be something Al could easily do.

The homeless community would miss him.

"Couple of days," he said.

"I'll have a look through my stuff," she said. "There must be things we can sell online or something. To give us a bit of a break so you can take time off for the funeral."

She was thinking of her old wedding and engagement rings. She thought Al was thinking of them, too, because he said what she was thinking: "I wish we could afford to get married."

"Me, too."

"If you do sell something . . . Well, you should see your friends, you know? Arrange an evening out. Do something for yourself, because you never do. Take yourself out of it all for an hour or two. I'm worried about you."

She hugged him. "That might be nice, actually," she said. "Let me see what I can dig up."

"It'll be OK, you know," he said. "We'll be all right. This won't be so bad." He kissed her, and Beth giggled and slobbered all over her other cheek, and for a moment, she let herself believe him.

TWENTY-NINE

Nina let the music wash over her. It was electronic and sounded a bit spooky, and it came from a man standing in front of an old-fashioned keyboard, pressing buttons. The music, she supposed, was probably evangelical tunes that she didn't know. Her heart was pounding, and she hoped her hand in Louis' wasn't too sweaty.

The church was packed, but she kept hold of Louis and didn't look round. It was wrong to think it, but he looked gorgeous in his suit. He looked like someone in a Mafia film, but in a good way. He had had his hair cut, and it was still long enough at the front to tuck behind his ears, but it was short at the back, and she loved looking at his neck.

Nina was getting used to the idea that Louis was Ben Alford's son. She hadn't told anyone: not her friends at school, not Mum, not Dad, not Al. She had discussed it only with Shelly, and that was because Shelly already knew. Shelly, it transpired, had done what she called "deep research" into everyone on the space program; she was a computer geek, and this was what she did. "It took me about seven minutes to discover who Louis Ricci really was," she'd said. "I mean, it's not rocket science."

Nina realized that the music wasn't evangelical hymns, but a plinky sort of arrangement of the Beatles song "I'll Follow the Sun." That had been Gran's favorite.

Nina knew that even though the funeral was supposed to be only for family and friends, the place was packed with journalists and bloggers. They could easily pretend to know Grandma from church or from the neighborhood, and it was impossible for the family to know who was genuine and who was lying. That was the way these things worked.

She looked at Louis and tried to shut out the rest of it. Mum, on her other side, was still and silent. Mum was in her own world these days.

They were going to move into worklifeplus. Nina hadn't told Louis yet, and she could hardly bear to imagine how the conversation might go. It was the most humiliating thing. She, Louis Alford's girlfriend, was going to be living in one of his dad's workhouses. She knew you weren't supposed to call it that, but that was what it felt like. Starcom took advantage of spiraling living costs, and accommodated their workers in a way that felt almost socialist, except that rather than working for the collective good, they were working for the Man. And the Man was Ben Alford, her boyfriend's dad. She knew what to expect from the flat because he had shown it to her on a VR headset.

She was not proud of this, but her initial reaction had been to decide to spend a lot more time with Dad. Soon after that, though, she'd imagined leaving Beth and Mum and Al in their workers' accommodations, as well as Billy, if one day he was allowed to come home, and she'd known she couldn't do it. She would divide her time as she'd always done.

Nina sat in the church and tried to decipher why she found the whole concept so offensive. It was, she thought, the fact that, rather than using his power to work for a fairer society, with rent control or whatever, BA was buying up all the houses, making the crisis worse, and then dispensing them as he saw fit. He was making himself into a dictator, an overlord, and keeping all the money. She hated him.

And she loved his son. She squeezed Louis' hand. At least Louis had met Mum now.

Billy wasn't at the church. He should have been here (as Orla's grandson) but he wasn't allowed (as her killer). His absence was a gaping hole. She saw that Mum kept reaching out to touch him.

Nina was still writing everything on her private website, and now she was wondering whether to make it public. Graham Watson had told her to before this even happened. He had known something like this was on the way. She decided to try to speak to him again.

If she made her story public, maybe she could counter the narrative that was currently everywhere. She had tried not to look at the coverage, but it was impossible to avoid it. The newspapers had it on the front pages. *Tragic Gran killed by kid. "Voices in his head told him to do it," say sources.* That kind of thing was leaked, presumably, by the police. She had asked Louis to check what people were saying online. Louis had reported back that she should definitely never read any of it, and had offered to set up parental controls on her new laptop to stop her.

The fact that Billy was held as responsible for his actions as an adult was a grotesque injustice. It made Nina rage. Apart from the viciousness of the policy, she felt that if anyone understood what it had been like for Billy, from the moment that Delfy had come along, they wouldn't be caricaturing him as the "killer kid." It wasn't Billy. It was the voice in his head.

But the voice in his head was Billy. It was a part of him. This was horribly complicated.

She kind of preferred Grandma's church to the normal kind. This one didn't look like a church: it was an ordinary building on the outside, and inside the aisle was lined with scratchy blue carpet. The pews were pale wood; before they were there, there had just been rows of plastic chairs, and Grandma had fund-raised ferociously for the new seating. Even Nina and Billy had ended up handing over scraps of pocket money to her "pew fund." It had driven Mum mad. Nina was glad the pews were there today. Maybe that was the thing that had made Grandma fund-raise so relentlessly. Perhaps, Nina thought, she had subconsciously wanted the church to be looking like its best self for her own funeral.

She squeezed Louis' hot hand. His first meeting with Mum and Al had gone well, in that he had said how sorry he was about what had happened, and they had said thank you.

It all felt so surreal. Nina was sitting on this pew, wearing a black dress she'd got Dad to buy, listening to the music, and underneath all her worries was the stark reality: Grandma was dead. She had seen Grandma approximately once a week for sixteen years, and now she was never going to see her again. Her problematic, adoring grandmother was in a box, and she was going to be burned into ashes, which were going to be scattered in a place as yet undecided. Actual Grandma. That was not something Nina could get to grips with. She couldn't make it work in her head, and that was without even trying to assimilate the Billy–Delfy side of things.

No one she had been close to had ever died, though plenty of people she didn't know well had gone lately. Eleven students from her school had died of flu this year, as well as two teachers, and that had been horrific. Nina had watched the livestreams of the funerals and sobbed with her friends. Grandma, on the other hand, had lived into her seventies. Grandparents dying was the natural order of things, even though the manner of her death very much wasn't.

The organist segued into the national anthem. Every day at school began with this, and every gathering had to play it. Nina hated that.

The vicar, who introduced himself as Father Mike, stepped up to the pulpit, adjusted his microphone, and said: "Hello and welcome on this sad, sad day. We are here to celebrate the life and lament the death of our dear friend Orla Jackman. Orla was a true friend of Christ. . . ."

Nina tuned out. She couldn't help it. Father Mike talked about Orla as a "beloved worshipper, mother, grandmother, and friend" and then went on and on about everything she had done for the church and emphasized that she was now living in eternal bliss. He did not mention Billy, except, glancingly, when he said "three adored grandchildren." No one said that her grandson had suffocated her with a cushion over her face. It would have been a hard thing to work in.

The pub was a normal one, not too posh and not too scary, and the wake was in a room upstairs that had tables and chairs around the edges and an empty floor and bowls of crisps and little sandwiches and slices of quiche. Mum said Gran had ordered all the food herself years ago, had had it sitting in a shopping basket on a supermarket's website, ready to go at the click of a mouse.

There were lots of people here, looking like extras from a casting agency, and a few of the family from Ireland but not many, because most people were still too nervous to travel. Nina didn't have the strength to talk very much to any of them, particularly when she didn't know who people were and didn't trust them.

She sat in a corner with Louis.

"I'm so glad you're here," she said. "We don't have to stay long. I don't know many of Gran's church friends, and I don't know the Irish side of the family. I keep expecting her to walk in and introduce everyone to one another."

Louis looked at the door. "Now you've said that," he said, "I do, too. And I never met her. I feel I know her, though."

"Do you think," she said, "that I should put my diaries about Delfy online?"

He frowned. "What?"

"You know I've been writing it all down. I want the people who are screaming for Billy to be locked up for the rest of his life to understand. What do you think?"

"Well," he said carefully, "I'm not sure. Let's give it some thought. I'm not sure you want to invite that kind of attention." He stroked her hair and tucked it behind her ears. She loved that.

"We can leave in a minute," she said. "Let's just go and see Mum."

They made their way, among church people and Grandma's neighbors and random people Nina didn't know, to Rachel and Al, who were standing in a corner, looking miserable. Al was holding Beth, and Mum's hand kept jerking, still trying to reach for Billy. They had asked if he could come to the funeral, but the answer had been unambiguous. Nina looked at Mum, who was tired and defeated. Her face was craggy, and it had new lines on it. She hadn't brushed her hair or put on any makeup, and her black clothes were old work ones that didn't really fit her anymore. She had a glass of wine next to her on the table. Mum never drank.

"He's a lovely boy," said Mum, making a visible effort and nodding at Louis, who was talking to Al and Beth. "It's good of him to come along today. That means a lot."

"He *is* a lovely boy," said Nina. "Yes."

"Bring him to the house? Sorry, darling. I always say that, don't I? I mean, bring him soon while we still have a house."

"I know. Yes."

"Nina," said Al, "you OK?"

She smiled at him. She liked Al more and more. He was, she had decided, an awesome stepdad, and he was much more straightforward than her actual dad, who, after talking about it for ages, had finally decided not to come along today. Thank God.

"Yes, thanks," she said. "And, like, thanks for looking after Mum. She needs you, and I'm really glad she's got you. And I know you're doing a really difficult thing." She looked at Louis, who was now talking to Mum, and then quickly said, "With the move."

Al nodded. "It's temporary," he said. "And it's for all of us. It's actually a godsend as a fallback position. One day at a time." He lowered his voice. "Your mum's struggling. It's an impossible situation."

"Yeah." Nina reached out her arms, and Al hefted Beth into them.

"Thanks," he said. "My God, she's heavy." He stretched his arm out. "That's better."

Beth grabbed Nina's nose because she loved noses. Nina pulled her hand away and went to sit on one of the chairs with the baby on her lap. Within seconds Louis was next to her.

"Gaaaahhhh!" yelled Beth, delighted to see him. She was wearing a pair of navy blue dungarees, which were the closest thing she had in her wardrobe to black, and a lighter blue cardigan that Grandma had knitted for Billy years ago.

"Gaaaahhhhh!" said Louis.

Nina thought she had better say it, too, or she would be left out. "Gaaaaaahhhhhh!" she said.

All three of them were pleased, even though a man nearby, who could have been church, neighbor, or nosy stranger, turned and frowned.

"Disrespectful," he said.

"Fuck off," said Nina.

THIRTY

Graham walked down the corridor toward Billy's room, with Kitty skipping at his side. Kitty broke Graham's heart: she had grown into the kind of eccentric, unselfconscious young woman who would have made her mother proud. She was tall and heavyset, with long blondish hair and a love of doughnuts, television, and punk music. Even though she was too old for that kind of thing, she had a pet rock that she carried around with her. It was the only thing she had brought with her from her old life; he saw the bulge it made in the pocket of her hoodie.

The iceberg hospital was, objectively, weird, though it was normal to both Graham and Kitty. It currently felt like spring, and the sun always set at seven o'clock. There was a breeze that smelled of jasmine. (Alternatively it could be woodsmoke, cut grass, or laundry.) The daylight effect was astonishingly convincing. It was like walking through a dream, though in this dream you were likely to meet psychotic children.

At the threshold of Billy's room, Graham put out a hand to keep Kitty back for a moment. Billy's room was stocked with carefully vetted games, toys, and books, but however much he filled it with things that should have been luxurious, Graham couldn't shake the feeling that he had pumped in sadness instead of jasmine. Misery and sickness hung everywhere. Of course it did: he and Henry had worked hard to get Billy in here, and the victory had come with conditions.

This was better than the alternative; however, it was worse than almost everything else. Billy was isolated and guarded, and he had to be specifically kept away from Lulu, even though she was essentially the same as he was. He could play with the other children only under close supervision even though he was no danger to anyone. Any one of them, Graham thought, could have done what Billy did. All of them were medicated, and they were supervised at all times by multiple nurses, guards, and surveillance cameras.

Only Kitty had the leeway to pop in and visit whenever she wanted, partly because she was an adult, but also because no one really remembered that she was here. Graham looked out for her; Kitty missed Imogen almost as much as he did. Imogen had visited her almost every day until she got ill, and Kitty was distraught to have lost her. She and Graham had cried together; it was the only time he had allowed himself to do it.

Billy was kneeling on his bed, looking almost as if he were praying. His head was bowed, and Graham couldn't see his face. Billy wasn't holding anything, wasn't looking at anything. That was because he was under such heavy sedation that his body would be heavy, his mind drugged into nothingness.

Graham forced a smile. Kitty was breathing heavily in excitement next to him.

"Hey there, Billy!" he said in the fakest of all the fake cheerful voices. "How are you doing, young man? Everything OK?" He went to sit in the chair next to Billy's bed. Kitty followed him, then took a step back, suddenly shy. "Billy," Graham said, "I want you to meet Kitty. Kitty is your friend. She lives here, too. She has a voice in her head, though it's very quiet now."

"It went away ages ago," Kitty said, speaking just to Billy. "But no one believes me."

Billy turned his face to her. "It went away?" he whispered.

"It really did, mate," she said, sitting down. "It just faded away, and then it was gone. It got sick, in my head, and it died."

"You should be at home with your mummy."

"I don't have a mummy, and the rest of my family are cunts. I live here, like the big man said. I can hang out with you anytime you like." Billy stared at her. He put his hand out, and she took it. "Don't worry," she said, suddenly serious. "It's cool here. They bring me doughnuts. I go out every day. There's a gym for when you feel like getting up and about."

There was a tiny smile on Billy's lips.

"Doughnuts?" he said.

"Chocolate ones," said Kitty. Graham nodded at her, and she left the room.

How are you feeling?" he said. Billy shook his head. Graham knew that if he adjusted the dose, it would get better. All the same, he felt the malignant presence, the psychotic part of Billy's brain, more strongly than he had felt it before, and it scared him.

"I'll change your pills a bit," he said. "That will feel better."

It sounded terribly lame. He looked at the door. It was still a bit open, and Kitty was out there, chatting to the policeman. They were both distracted. He looked up at the corner of the room and saw the camera blinking.

Billy said something, but it was just a whisper. Graham went closer, trying to hear. Billy's little hand grabbed Graham by the collar of his shirt and yanked him closer still. Graham found himself pulled forward, taken by surprise, and then Billy's mouth was right next to his ear.

And then he could hear what Billy was saying.

"I want to talk to you, Graham Watson," Billy whispered. Then he let go, and Graham pulled back, more spooked than he should have been.

"Is that *you* speaking, Billy?" he said, holding eye contact. Billy's eyes were a very unusual green, he noted.

Billy shook his head. "Delfy," he whispered. His eyes were huge and scared. "It's Delfy."

Everything in Graham tingled. The psychosis was speaking—the monster that Billy's brain had conjured, somehow, from the virus. And it wanted to talk directly to him.

"Right," he said. This shouldn't happen. He knew that: antipsychotic medications (not really suitable for children, but desperate times and so on) should have suppressed the voices, not amplified them. He seemed to have suppressed Billy and set Delfy free.

"Do you want to talk to me now, Delfy?" Graham said. He looked at the door, knowing that the police officer was outside. "I'll need to go and fetch my notes and my notebook, and if you don't mind, I'd like to record it, too. I'll need to cancel my next—"

"Now," said Billy. "Sit down."

Graham sat. His phone was in his pocket, so he set it to record and put it on the bedside table.

"What would you like to say?" he said.

The Delfy voice came only in a whisper, and it didn't sound like Billy, even though it was. "You need to help us," it said.

"I hope so," said Graham. "How?"

"This place is good. We need the other children. Bring all the children here. All of them."

By the time Graham managed to reply, Billy was asleep.

t felt odd, going up in the lift and emerging into the real world, with its smells of pollution and shit, its murky, cloudy daylight. Graham loved its imperfections. Admittedly, floor two wasn't exactly the slums, but it was recognizably part of the real world, not the dreamlike underworld.

Bring all the children here. He shuddered. He wondered how one would go about such a thing and exactly which children Delfy wanted. She couldn't really want *all* the other children.

Lauren was on the phone, but when she saw him, she covered the receiver and said, "Prof, there's a message on your desk. I think you'll want to see it." She turned back to her conversation. "Sorry. I'm afraid you'll be looking at a wait of around four weeks."

He nodded. He and Lauren were turning potential patients away faster than he had ever done before. Delfy would be displeased with that.

Bring all the children here.

It was good, he thought, that Lauren had told him about the message, because even though she'd left it on his keyboard, he would just have tossed it aside with the other pieces of paper. It was a page from a notebook, folded in half.

Graham, it read, in Lauren's beautiful hand. *We need to talk. BA.* He sighed. Underneath those words, Lauren had written: *He told me to write exactly that. Call him ASAP on his personal number.*

He picked up his phone and made the call.

"Graham!"

"Hello, Ben." He refused to address him as "BA." It was stupid. There was a moment when he thought Alford was going to correct him, but it passed.

"How are things in Harley Street?"

"Fine."

"I need to see you."

"Busy," said Graham. "Sorry, but I can't drop everything right now."

"This evening?"

Graham thought about Alford, about their long association, the webs of obligation that ran between the two of them. He knew what this was about and had been mildly dreading it for a while. He had to face it.

"I suppose I could manage an hour at seven," he said.

"I'll send a car," said Alford. "Outside your office at half six."

Graham sighed. He knew what that meant. It would be bloody Harvey driving him across London again. Imogen used to refuse to get into his car. Maybe he should channel her and do the same.

. . .

Graham was keeping the last bed in the main ward free because he knew he would get the security loosened enough to move Billy in with the others. Their various health insurances, or in a couple of cases the parents, were paying huge amounts of money for their care, and he was seriously considering opening up another ward. They'd call it zebra or penguin or something. It would fill up and so would another. That was what the voices wanted him to do. He could dedicate this whole level to these kids.

"Would you like it if there were more children like you here?" he said to the children around him. He was sitting on a beanbag, his knees up around his ears. They loved sitting on the beanbags.

"Yes!" they all agreed. They were enthusiastic, part childish and excited, part serious. He watched them closely. They looked at one another, communicated without speaking. Anita was wordlessly appointed spokesperson.

"We think that would be a very good idea," she said in the formal voice she used sometimes. "We would like you to find all of the others. Bring all the children here."

"Also," said Louisa, "we'd like to do some knitting."

He had no desire to be the keeper of psychotic children. He wanted to work out what was going on and how to make it better, rather than hoard kids in an underground bunker so they couldn't kill anyone.

"Knitting?" he said. They all nodded. "I don't think I can let you have knitting needles under the circumstances. Sorry."

"Something else, then."

They wanted to be hoarded. They wanted to mass together and gather strength so that they could . . . Well, he didn't know what they thought they could do.

"You could do some . . . crochet, maybe?" he said. Imogen had crocheted, and her crochet hooks had been tame things with no spikes or anything. They all nodded.

He forced a smile.

"OK," he said. "I'll work on it. Meanwhile, I'd really like to get some more ideas about what triggered this for you." This was what they talked about several times a week. He was certain it was the J5X flu *plus something* that led to voices, but so far, even with this tiny sample, he hadn't found a link. And that was without taking Kitty, the outlier, into consideration. "We all know that this comes after the flu, but there's something else. I know we've spoken before about medication and food, but today I'm thinking about environments. Places. Can you write down absolutely everywhere that you went to in the last year before you came here? As much as you can."

He handed around pieces of paper. He had, of course, looked at this before and found no common ground. But there *had* to be a link, and so he had to keep asking.

"I've done what I can," Louisa said after a while. "But I forget what places are sometimes. There were always these people. Security. You know—these guys." She waved a hand at her bodyguards without looking at them. "That's why I didn't know about the food, too. It's always cooked for us. Do you guys have cooks?"

Most of them did, and they started hypothesizing about a union of domestic staff conspiring to drug them because they were jealous of the children.

"It's not that," Graham said. This wasn't the kind of talk he wanted to hear. "Let's not go in this direction. Thanks. I'm not thinking that anyone's done it on purpose." He was pretty sure of this: the psychosis didn't benefit anyone. If a pharmaceutical company were to turn up with a miraculous cure, then that would need scrutiny, but for now he couldn't think why it would be desirable for anybody to have things like this happening. If anyone was doing well out of it, it was Graham himself, and he pulled away from a line of reasoning that would make him the prime suspect.

"Could it be from the air, Graham?" said Majid. "I mean, maybe if we breathed it at the same time we breathed in the flu?"

"Exactly," Graham said. "Let's see. Could you all have been outside at the same time before the flu? There haven't been any huge environmental catastrophes that we know of, but there's bound to be a lot we don't know."

They started talking. Because these were children from unimaginably wealthy families, their diaries were startling, but gradually they homed in on something.

"Remember that plane crash?" said Louisa. "I was outside then. We had just finished school, and I was doing netball because I'm in the squad and we had a match. So I was outside, and there was this huge flash in the sky. BOOM! It wasn't really a plane. No one knows what it was. Not even the secret service." Again, the wave of the hand.

"Yeah," said Majid, "I think it was a bomb. Maybe one that went wrong. Maybe it got intercepted. I was out marching in army cadets."

Graham looked at Anita.

"I was on a school trip," she said in her clear voice. "We were at the Tower of London."

Graham leaned forward. "Were you outdoors when the thing happened?" He had always assumed that the explosion had been a plane crash, but it clearly hadn't been a legitimate plane. Beyond that, he hadn't really wanted to know. He could have asked Ben, but he had chosen not to.

He remembered sitting in a café with Imogen when the sky lit up. Grabbing her hand, thinking of nuclear war. He imagined that now; being able to take Imogen's hand for comfort had been the most impossible luxury, and he'd had no idea.

"Yes," said Anita. "You know I go to boarding school in Devon. But we were on a three-day visit to London, and at that point we were having an ice cream outside the Tower. It was a nice ice cream even though it was a cold day, but then everyone panicked, and lots of people dropped them. I didn't."

"OK." Graham turned to Peter. Little Peter, just a bit older than Billy but far younger in lots of ways. Peter, who Graham knew was faking the voice in his head because he had been sent across the world to boarding school when he was barely more than a toddler, and he was so unhappy that it had seemed to him like an escape route. Peter was always watchful, always holding back until the others had spoken, and in his one-to-one sessions, he was different from the others. Graham was sure that Peter had seen someone else leaving school because of a voice and copied it. It was heartbreaking.

However, Graham was happy to take the money. Peter's parents paid their bills on time (actually paying with real money, rather than health insurance), so Graham wasn't going to rock the boat and have him sent back to the school he had hated. He seemed happy enough here.

It turned out Peter was the only one who hadn't been in London at the time of the plane crash: he had been at home in Malaysia, busy being a six-year-old kid getting prepped to go to British boarding school. It seemed OK to discount his data, under the circumstances. So, Lulu had been playing netball. Anita had been standing outside the Tower of London. Majid had been marching up and down a parade ground. Suki had been walking to her violin lesson, a few streets from her Hampstead home, with her nanny.

All of them had been within five miles of one another, and all of them out of doors. He didn't know whether there was anything in it, but it was the best lead he'd found so far.

The only thing everyone agreed on was that there had been a cover-up. There could have been anything on that plane.

G raham sat on Billy's bed and pulled one of the buds out of his ear.
"Sorry," he said. Billy turned his blank gaze on him. "But you remember the plane crash? The one no one thinks was actually a crash?"

He hoped he was getting Billy, not Delfy.

"I think I went to Lola's house," he said. Billy, in his normal voice.

"Sure. Where were you when it happened? Were you outside?"

Billy's forehead furrowed, and Graham resolved to change his dose radically. The magistrate had approved the original dose, but Graham felt that he could adjust it without having to get Henry Stevens to get his friend out of bed again.

Billy's mind was working slowly, but it was working.

"Yes. Outside," he said. "I was supposed to have gone to after-school club. But I did run outside instead to play on the field. I was with my friends. Then the sky was light and dark. I ran to the middle of the field, and I put up my arms." He raised his arms above his shoulders. "And I shouted at it."

"Thank you, Billy," said Graham. "That is incredibly helpful." He rubbed Billy's shoulder and handed him back his earphone.

"Bring the other children, Graham Watson. Or else you will be sorry," Billy said as Graham left the room.

The other children. Graham imagined level minus seven, populated by twenty, fifty, a hundred psychotic children. He shuddered. These children, even medicated, were alarming. Having seven of them here was worrying enough.

Billy had killed his grandmother, but he wasn't the only one. Kitty had killed her own mother and then half-strangled her baby brother when she was six.

Two of the others had killed animals. Two more had attempted to kill other humans, and Suki, like Billy and Kitty, had succeeded.

That poor nanny.

THIRTY-ONE

Rachel put her key into the lock, half-expecting that it wouldn't work. It turned, but it didn't seem to clunk open. She turned it back and tried the other key, but although it worked, the door was still double-locked.

"Nearly in," she said to Beth. The door hadn't been double-locked in the first place, although it should have been. She sorted it out and pushed it open, and then they were there. Rachel guided the pushchair over the threshold into her mother's flat.

She was trying to face the future. Realistically, she thought, Billy wouldn't be home for a few months at least. When he did come home, it would be either to this flat or to somewhere he didn't know. Al had got the job at Starcom, and they were moving as soon as possible, because it turned out that Starcom liked things to happen immediately. They were packing up and planning to move next week. When Billy came back (soon), he would have to go to a different school, which was one of the things that felt like a blessing.

She had a horrible feeling that once you moved into worklifeplus accommodation, it would be next to impossible to get out of it. She was supposed to be packing things up right now and arranging for charities to come and collect their old furniture, because everything they would need was already there. The flat they had been allocated, on the third floor of a purpose-built block, was furnished. Its kitchen was equipped. It was all ready for them.

When they moved over here, they would use Orla's furniture, which was much better quality anyway. That was partly why she had come here today.

"Here you go, baby," she said, and she put Beth on the floor. The baby crawled away fast, not apparently affected by the terrible thing that had happened the last time she had been here. Rachel watched her vanish through the door toward the bedrooms.

The flat smelled weird, but even though it had been unoccupied for almost a month, and despite the fact that it had been a crime scene, it was still completely Orla's flat. All her stuff was here. There was even a trace of her incense in the air.

Memories were trying to assault Rachel, but she pushed them aside. She was here to sort through Mum's things, to find keepsakes for the children, and (she had not spoken this last bit out loud) to see if she could find jewelry to sell so they could buy food.

Also, she wanted to look at the flat through different eyes and try to work out how they would all fit in. She, Al, Nina, and Beth could live just fine in two bedrooms, but she would never, never live in a place that didn't have a bed that was made up and ready for Billy.

Anything that might help her family was fair game now, she thought. Mum would have wanted that. This apartment was filled with things, and Orla would have given every one of them to her grandchildren in a heartbeat.

Mum's decorations were still all over the walls. No one would have come to take them down because now that the police had finished in here, nobody was interested.

"Hi there," she called to Jesus, who was still there, in His place on the wall.

"Hello, love," He replied.

She screamed and followed the voice into the bedroom, where she discovered the man who had taken her mother's funeral, Father Mike, holding Beth and smiling. Beth was giggling. Rachel snatched her from his arms.

"You're from the church," she said. She didn't want to say his name.

"Hello, Rachel," he said. "And the lovely Beth. I'm sorry to startle you."

"What are you doing here?" She stepped backward. She wanted to get away. She didn't trust him.

He put his hands up and took a couple of steps toward her. Father Mike was an older black man, and he smelled lovely: he was clearly wearing an expensive cologne. *Focus,* she told herself. *It doesn't matter what he smells like.*

"Shall I make tea?" he said.

"No. I'd like you to leave my mother's flat, and I'll need your key back," she said.

"Oh," said Mike. "I'm really terribly sorry. Look, let me make you some tea. We need to have a chat."

"We don't." She followed him back to the kitchen anyway, carrying the squirming baby. Mike put the kettle on, and Rachel looked around. Now she looked properly, she could see that he was sorting out Mum's stuff. He was piling things, bagging them. He was interfering. Maybe, she thought, he was looking for everything he could sell.

"How's your little boy?" said Father Mike.

"Terrible," said Rachel. "Obviously."

"I'm sorry. It's a dreadful tragedy."

She sat down and tried to breathe deeply. He handed her a cup of tea. Last time she had sat on this sofa, a policewoman had handed her the tea.

She looked across at the other sofa, where her mother had been, with the cushion on her face, and shivered.

Beth wrenched herself free and set off, crawling around the room at top speed.

"Why are you here, though?" Rachel asked.

"I'm sorry," said Father Mike again. "I'm so sorry to have startled and upset you. Oh, I do apologize, but I need to get straight to the point. Rachel—have you seen your mother's will?"

She froze. "Not yet," she said. "It won't be complicated. I'm an only child, so there's no one else." She looked into his sympathetic eyes. "No one else for her to leave it to," she said with less certainty.

"I'm sorry to say," he said, "that I've been contacted by your mother's solicitor, who said that she willed this flat to . . . well, to the church. But you must take everything you want from it! I was starting to sort the contents before we put it on the market, but of course, you have first refusal on everything." He looked at her face and backed off. "Why don't I make myself scarce? I'll leave you to have a look at everything. I'm sorry."

She looked at him, standing under the outstretched arms of Jesus, and everything boiled over.

"You fucking bastard!" she said. "You made her do it. You don't need it. We need it."

He was unperturbed. "She chose to do this," he said. "It was God's will."

This was it, then. There was no safety net. Rachel's fury with her mother was white-hot and burning.

"How could you, Mum?" she muttered as she piled up her mother's clothes. "How fucking could you? How could you choose the church over your grandchildren? We're living in poverty! We're moving into the workhouse! You've done that to Beth!" She was determined to take every single thing from this apartment because otherwise Father Mike would sell it to fund new prayer books or whatever.

She sat Beth in front of the TV, which seemed to be signed on to a Christian streaming service, but she found a pious children's channel that would do. They had long since stopped paying for all their TV accounts at home, so they watched nothing but the scant offerings of Freeview. There would be plenty of TV at their new home, she supposed. It was one of the things they always said about it. A selling point. Lots of telly, though the downside was in the small print: it was in a communal TV room, and she didn't think she'd have the confidence to go in there. If she did go in, she wouldn't relax.

The jewelry was more cheerful than priceless, but she took all of it anyway, hesitating over the horrible spider brooch before tucking it into the bag. Billy liked spiders, and the brooch made her feel close to him. She would take Billy giving her a box of spiders in a heartbeat.

She packed up every single thing from the kitchen. She would take that now, and she would bag up everything else and come back for it another day with Al and Nina to help her carry it.

For two hours she went through every piece of paperwork she could find, but she didn't call the utilities people to cut things off as she had planned because that was none of her business now. She found a stash of old drawings and paintings by Nina and Billy that made her cry. She looked through photo albums and packed them into one of her bags, even the one that was filled with photographs of herself as a child wearing dated clothes and looking terrified. She felt anxious just looking at them, but she couldn't bear to throw them away, and she wondered why no one had ever told her to smile for the camera. She looked at her parents' wedding photo and tucked it into a bag, too. It was the past. It was where she had come from.

In the drawer by the telephone, she found a credit card. It had a piece of paper wrapped around it with an elastic band, and the number 4938 was written on it; although this was old technology, most places still accepted chip and pin.

ATMs certainly still liked them.

She stood and stared at it. Would this be theft?

Beth was starting to whine. They had been here for a long time. Rachel put the card into her pocket. If Orla had left her flat to the fucking church, then this credit card was the least she could do.

Rachel went back into the kitchen and found Mum's bottle of brandy, then shoved it right down inside one of her bags, and they left before Father Mike could come back.

THIRTY-TWO

Graham waited outside his office. No one had had a car in London for a million years; Graham traveled by bus, foot, or taxi. (He'd given up the Tube years ago because, ironically under the circumstances, he didn't like feeling he was trapped underground.)

Ben Alford, however, had cars and drivers and liked to throw his weight around by sending them to pick people up and bring them to him. Graham loved it when he got a sleek car and a uniformed driver, because that was fun. When a battered blue Fiat pulled up next to him he sighed. He should have taken a taxi.

Graham opened the passenger door and lowered himself in. There were three drink cans and a collection of chocolate wrappers by his feet. He kicked them out of the way.

"All right, Graham?"

"Hello, Harvey," he said. "Dad still making you do his driving?"

Harvey had grown up to look exactly like his father. Poor boy. "Only for 'the inner circle,'" said Harvey. "He never lets me drive anyone he needs to impress."

"Good to know where one stands."

Harvey was still a truly terrible driver. Graham tried not to show it, but he clutched the inside of the passenger door ready to make a quick exit if one were needed, and his foot kept pumping down on an imaginary brake. They wove in and out of bus lanes and ignored pedestrian crossings, and Harvey swore often.

"You've passed your test," Graham said in the mildest tone he could manage. He imagined Imogen shouting, *For Christ's sake, Harvey! Stop the car right now. I'll drive.* He looked at the backseat in case she was there, but she wasn't.

"First time," said Harvey. "Oh, shit. Sorry!" he yelled out of the window. He turned back to Graham. "I know I'm crap. I shouldn't have passed. I reckon Dad pulled some strings, or maybe the examiner saw my name and was scared."

They swerved across Vauxhall Bridge, drove through some red lights, and pulled onto Trillionaires' Row. Ten minutes after that, Graham was in a sitting room overlooking the river, a much-needed glass of wine in his hand, still trying to catch his breath. Ben was red-faced and laughing.

"Harvey's a shit driver. Right?" he said. "I want him to feel useful. He only drives for the inner circle. Anyway, you're here in one piece, so no harm done."

"I wish you'd stop doing that," said Graham, feeling wobbly, "sending Harvey for people. It's unnecessary, and that boy really shouldn't be behind the wheel."

"That's what Imogen used to say."

"She was right."

"How are you bearing up?"

"Oh," said Graham, "you know." He gulped back half his glass of wine in one go. "Have you still got your houseguest?" he said, wanting to talk about something easier.

"Of course."

This was the first time Graham had been here since Imogen died, and he was extra jumpy because this was exactly the kind of place she would haunt. He kept looking around, trying to spot her. He thought he caught a glimpse of her scoffing at the bookcase, but it probably wasn't actually her. He just knew those books in the bookcases were fake, and he knew how ridiculous and classless Imogen had found that fact. He remembered the note she had left him, the one he had found in the flat.

"Yes," said Ben. "OK. To business. What the living fuck is that murdering kid doing locked away with my daughter?"

Graham sat back. "I thought it might be that," he said.

"So? We pay you handsomely for Katherine's care. I was under the impression that at least part of your obligation was to keep her safe. Not to put some little psycho kid in the next room."

"Billy's not in the next room," said Graham. Imogen had been right: he did tend to find himself in thrall to this man. It was very complex. He decided to channel her and try to do what she would have done. He felt her energy even though he couldn't see her. He thought of Kitty, thought of her father's coldhearted abandonment, and remembered Imogen's outrage. He leaned forward and topped up his own glass. "Not that you'd know," he said. "I checked the records before I came out, and you haven't visited in over three years."

Alford bristled. His face reddened. "I stopped visiting my daughter," he said, "when she called me obscene names to my face, knocked me over with some kind of karate kick that she'd learned from the Internet, and had to be restrained by your staff."

Everyone remembered that. It had caused great amusement in the building and then passed into legend.

"But you're her father," Graham said mildly. "You know she's troubled. You don't get to sulk."

"I'm not sulking! You know how difficult this has been for me. I'm her only living parent. Elena refuses to have her in the house. Katherine is a psycho. What am I meant to do?"

"There!" said Graham. "You said it yourself. You can't call your own child a psycho, commit her indefinitely to a psychiatric hospital, and then complain when other troubled children are treated in the same establishment for the same condition." He hesitated, wondering whether to carry on. Imogen appeared, perched on the arm of his chair, and he wondered why Ben couldn't see her. *Go on,* she said. *Go on. Say it. Hit him where it hurts. He will hate this!* So he carried on. "And to be frank, you don't pay enough to buy out the entire hospital, so you don't get to exclude children you don't know from a place you never visit."

Imogen stroked his cheek with electric fingers and vanished.

Ben half-stood up. "Graham! How dare you . . . ?" He paused, reaching for words. Then he deflated and sat back down. "Oh, Christ knows," he said. "I know I've fucked up with Katherine, but I have no idea what I'm meant to do. It's the only area of life in which I feel I'm staggering around in the dark. Yes, of course, what she did is the same as the thing that boy did. I suppose I'm just so used to demanding the best for my children. With the boys, it's easy."

"Imogen wanted Kitty to come and live with us," Graham reminded him. "I would have been happy with that. She needs to learn about the real world. Imogen would have looked after her. But you vetoed that. I'd take her now happily."

"Elena is convinced Katherine would go to the press and dredge everything up again. The boys barely know she exists. It's complicated. I think . . ." He sighed and looked out of the window. "I think it's better this way."

"Really? You'd leave her in an underground hospital, when there's nothing wrong with her, because your wife tells you to?"

"Under the circumstances, I think it's best."

They stared at each other a bit longer. Graham used all of Imogen's strength and didn't say anything conciliatory, as he would normally have done. He made Ben sit in uncomfortable silence. Two clocks ticked, slightly out of sync with each other. Finally, the other man couldn't bear it any longer.

"So," said Ben, "anything else going on?"

Graham exhaled. "There is one other thing." Ben was exactly the person for this. "What was that plane crash really about? I think it might have some bearing on what's going on now."

Ben stared at him. "The crash? Seriously?"

Ben talked with more animation than he would normally have done, seizing on the change of subject, but he effectively told Graham nothing, in a very long-winded way. Graham hadn't really expected him to help. When he left, he felt Imogen's approval all around him. Finally, he had stood up to her brother.

THIRTY-THREE

Nina and Louis were sitting on either side of Billy, who was a lot more wide-awake than he had been the last time she had seen him. Dad said that Professor Watson had halved his dose of tranquilizers, and Billy certainly had more strength, though he was miserable.

The room was shocking. Walls that had once been white and calm were now covered with words, some legible and some not. None of it made much sense to Nina. There were pictures of spiders. There were passages that must have been copied from somewhere:

When multiple spiders work together to subdue prey, they can catch and eat larger organisms such as birds.

He had a box of wool and silk and a crochet hook beside the bed, and he had tangled the wool up into nests of knots.

A young woman was standing in the doorway, watching them. She was wearing a football kit and was singing along loudly to the music in her headphones. Louis got up to close the door, and the two of them stared at each other for a long time.

"Sorry," he said. "But this is private."

"You're mean," she said. They seemed transfixed by each other.

"Nina. Take me home, please, Nina," said Billy. "I want to go with you."

"Oh, darling," she said, "I want to take you. I want to get you out of here. We'll do it. I promise you, we will." She paused. "You know, when we do get you home, it will be to a different house? A flat? But it'll still be home, because we'll all be there. And Dad's house is still the same."

Billy nodded slightly. " 'Kay."

"What's Delfy been up to?" said Louis after muttering something to the girl outside and closing the door. He gestured at the walls. "She seems busy. Still spiders?"

Billy looked at him. "Yes, she is busy," he said. "Yes, it is still spiders. She makes me write things and try to make things. She can talk to spiders. I don't like it. She is much more strong, but my body isn't strong, and we are in prison here, so she can't do things, and that makes her angry. We need Graham to bring the other children."

"Do you get to play with the other children?"

"Sometimes," said Billy. "Kitty comes in. That was Kitty there. She is my friend. I see the other children with lots of guard people so I can't hurt anyone." His eyes filled with tears. "They don't understand! We wouldn't hurt them. And it's not just me that has done something bad. And I didn't want to." He stopped and burst into tears.

"Sorry," said Nina, stroking his hair. "Oh, Billy, this is so screwed up."

"If I have to stay here, I would like to live in the ward," Billy said through his tears. "It's not fair. They have a room together like in Hogwarts, but I'm not allowed. It's Delfy's fault. I want to see Grandma again, and I can't because of Delfy. I miss Grandma so much. I hate Delfy! She has spoiled everything."

He went rigid, and his eyes changed. Nina thought that Delfy hadn't liked him saying that.

"Oh, darling," said Nina, "I know she has. Oh, Billy, I hate Delfy, too. One day she'll go."

"No, she won't," said Billy in an expressionless voice. "She lives here now. She lives here always."

"We want to work out where the voices came from," said Louis.

Nina realized she had never quite asked this before. "Does *Delfy* know where she came from?"

Billy frowned for a moment, then said, still in his odd little voice, "She camed from the flu. Not exactly. It's complicated. She is saying lots of things, but I can't work them out into our words. She is using me as her home. It's like I'm her robot."

"Shit," said Louis. "Like, she's your Harmony?"

"What?"

"Your AI?"

Billy shrugged. Nina leaned forward. "The medication isn't helping, is it? It doesn't make her quiet."

Billy shook his head, and a tear ran down his cheek. "No, Nina. The medicine does calm *me*, not Delfy. In my head, it is almost all Delfy. She can't do anything because I'm not strong anymore. She's very cross. I can't even understand her."

"Oh, Billy." Nina reached out and took his hand. "Look, Bill. A while ago I started writing about you and Delfy. I wrote down everything I felt about it all. It was just for me. Is it OK if we let other people read it? That way we can find the other children like you, like you said. The ones whose parents can't afford this treatment. The kids here must be really rich, right?"

He nodded and whispered something about Lulu.

"I think," Louis said, "that if we can prove that this happened to lots of kids all over the world—or work out where in the world they are—then we can make people see that what happened with your grandma wasn't your fault because you're part of an epidemic. You're a victim, too. It's a huge mental health crisis."

"Yes," whispered Billy.

"Are you OK with us doing that?" said Nina.

"Yes, I am," said Billy, visibly happier. "And so is Delfy. Find all the other children, and tell them to come here. Tell them to come to London, Nina."

"We'll make sure it doesn't have your name in it."

"I don't care if it has my name," said Billy. "I don't care about that one tiny little bit. Tell them to come to London."

They were ushered out through all the security in reverse and into the little lift, which was shiny and metallic, like an elevator from the future. Nina looked at the buttons and pressed the 2 for Graham Watson's office. Nothing happened. She pressed the G for the ground floor, and the lift started to move.

You would never have known from the building's entrance hall that there was a state-of-the-art hospital beneath your feet. Those iceberg basements had been banned years ago, and Nina thought this hospital was incredibly lucky to exist, as well as completely weird. She was glad there were only a few places like this in the city. There were houses in places like Louis' road (but not there because it was too recent) that were immensely bigger underground than they were above it. Some had cinemas and tennis courts underground, and this one had a hospital.

Up here, though, it felt exactly like a smart town house, with a slightly worn old carpet, polished wooden paneling, and old-fashioned windows. There were landscape paintings on the wall. Everything was set up to look staid and reliable—to hide, she thought, what was underneath.

Nina took Louis' hand and led him straight into the lift next door. It was a much bigger one, with a mirror and a little seat in it. This one was for the public, and when she pressed button 2 in here, they went straight up.

"I'd like to speak to Graham Watson," she said to the receptionist, who looked startled.

"I'm afraid he's out of the office," she said. "What was it regarding? Oh, hello, Louis!"

Louis had known Watson all his life. Nina was banking on that connection to help her.

"I'm Billy's sister," she said, and she was filled with fire. "I'm Billy's sister, Nina Stevens, and we really need his help. I don't mind waiting here until he's free. We'll just sit and wait."

"Oh," said the assistant. "And, Louis, you're here with Nina?"

"I'm her boyfriend," said Louis, and Nina loved how proud he sounded.

"Lovely! I'm sure he'd be more than happy to see you, but he really isn't here. Let me speak to him and see what we can do."

Graham Watson told Lauren he would call them and took Nina's number again and so they went home to Mum and Al's. This was a thing Nina had been dreading, had managed to put off until their very last night in the house. She still hadn't told Louis where they were moving tomorrow. It was easy enough to divert the conversation when he asked by saying things like "West London," but now, she knew, it was going to have to come out.

She didn't know what it would be like there. She'd seen glossy photos of hotel-style bedrooms and people laughing, but discounted them. She had seen that VR and known that it was just an advert. She and Al had railed against worklifeplus ever since it had become a thing, had been furious at the court case months ago, and now they were moving in, and not only that, but it was an absolute lifeline, so she couldn't even hate it anymore. She was, by necessity, grateful.

Mum had said it was going to be nice. Louis' dad, who she supposed was now their boss, loved to talk about how great it was, though he was seeing it as a landlord rather than as a tenant.

They were nearly home. Nina was talking fast about the blog, determined not to be nervous about her boyfriend, who lived in an actual palace, visiting the falling-apart rented home they were just about to leave because they couldn't afford it anymore. She told herself it didn't matter. It didn't matter because no part of her believed he was morally better for having been born into riches. Mum and Al worked hard, and their home was filled with love as well as weirdness. She knew that extreme wealth was the thing that carried moral bankruptcy, not poverty.

She knew all that in theory, and yet she was mortified. Louis could never have been to a house like this before. What would it look like to him? And that was before he even knew what was coming next.

"So you can get the Twitter account up and running," she said to put off the moment when she would have to tell him. "And we'll arrange to talk it through with Graham and see if he'll help. I need to change the name. It was called 'Delfy.' It needs a name that's a lot more grabbing than that. Something that gets across the sense that it's about voices in kids' heads that don't feel like a part of them at all. Something to show that there are lots of them it's happening to."

"OK," said Louis. "We'll think of something. And we need to go over everything and change the details. I know Billy said he didn't care, but . . ."

"Yes, obviously we need to," said Nina. "And it's difficult, because all the stuff with Gran got quite a bit of publicity, and there's his trial coming up. I think I'll change it so that he killed a pet or something. I don't know. Does that work? He did kill a few spiders when he made that present for Mum. Most of them were alive, though." She shuddered. Nina admired spiders, but even she didn't fancy a box of them.

"Yeah," said Louis. "It doesn't matter what the incident is. Those other kids have done things, too. All of them, I'm sure. So all we need to get across about Billy is that he did something out of character and violent, and is now in an underground bunker, drugged up at the behest of the state."

"Shit," said Nina. "He is." She stopped, and Louis stopped next to her. She looked up into his face. "I don't know if this is a good idea," she said. "His story is identifiable. You saw what it was like at the funeral. All the people crowding around, filming. Good for their social media. They love scary children. All that shit. I don't want to give them more to gossip about."

"You're doing it to find other kids. To show that Billy's not a lone killer but a victim of the virus. And . . . well, I'm doing it for the same reason. Something like that happened to my sister. My half sister. It all happened when I was a tiny baby. She did something violent and then just disappeared."

"Hang on," said Nina. "You mean . . . Are you thinking about that girl we saw today?"

"I don't know," said Louis. "I mean, possibly. I know she's still alive because Auntie Imogen used to talk about her all the time."

They carried on walking. Nina tried to make sense of it all. Could that girl have been Louis' mysterious sister? She was older than Nina. Could she really have grown up underground? Surely Graham and his wife, Louis' beloved auntie Imogen, wouldn't have allowed that?

They were nearly at the house when Louis took a deep breath and changed the subject. "I spoke to Shelly. I know you've got security, but we can quadruple it. We can put it through a proxy server and all that. Change the details so much that it doesn't sound like the same kid, because there are so many kids out there, no one will know. We can say we're in—I don't know—Toronto. Or something."

"OK." Nina felt around inside her pocket for her key. "We'll change the location and focus just on the voice."

She looked at the outside of the house. It opened straight onto the pavement, and the paint was peeling. An electric cable had fallen down from the front of the house next door and was blowing in the wind. There was a TO LET sign outside, and someone had already written the letter "i" into the middle of it. The flats loomed behind the row of houses.

Louis didn't seem to notice any of it.

"Exactly," he said. "No one else has made a space to talk about how a virus can do this to people, and to pool experiences. Connect with other people who are going through this. Work out how long it's been going on for. The detail doesn't actually matter."

She opened the door. The voices were absent from the official J5X narrative, and she loved the idea of taking a hand in crafting the alternative, the real story.

There were certainly other people out there, and the Internet was probably the place to pool experiences, but she didn't know how to stop it tipping over into real life. She didn't trust people, and she certainly didn't trust online anonymity. A dedicated hacker could find anyone once they started writing about it. She thought of Shelly. Shelly was a brilliant hacker. If she was in on this with them, that would be something.

"Hello!" she called into the house.

Mum answered, "Hey!" from the kitchen, and her voice was so enthusiastic and polite that Nina knew she was making an enormous effort, and she wanted to cry. Nothing Mum said or did would make things any better or worse with regard to Louis' perception of their home, let alone what came after it, and she hated that she and Mum both felt they had to try.

Mum came out of the kitchen, past the bottom of the stairs, and met them in the hallway. She was wearing a dress and lipstick, which never happened. The hellos and hugs were a bit awkward but everyone said the right things. Nina looked at Mum through Louis' eyes and saw that she was wrecked. Of course she was: one of her children was drugged in a mental hospital, and she couldn't afford to live independently anymore.

There were towers of bags and boxes in the hallway; everyone had to squeeze past it all.

"Come through," said Mum. "Beth and I made a cake. We had to use up the bits of food. So how about that?"

"You made a *cake*?" said Nina.

No one did any baking at their house, because although homemade cakes were cheaper than shop-bought ones, packets of budget biscuits were cheaper still, and no snacks at all were even better than that.

Mum laughed a bit. "I know. Honestly, I just wanted the distraction.

Beth was happy. Don't worry: I washed her hands first. Beth is into everything since she learned to crawl." She said that last bit to Louis, who nodded. "And also we took all the kitchen stuff from Mum's flat, and I don't know how long it's been around. It was all going to go off, if flour does go off. I don't know."

"I think it can get mites in it," Louis said. "Little weevily things."

"Yes. Exactly. Those things. Luckily Gran had loads of sugar and cocoa powder, too, but of course I had to throw out the rancid butter, so that was all I had to buy for this. Well, not butter. Cheaper stuff. We did it without eggs because have you seen the price of them? I could never bring myself to buy the caged ones. Mum had a jar of applesauce that was still in date, so we used that instead. So I hope you appreciate Beth's first ever chocolate cake. Chocolate and apple."

Mum was flapping, working herself up as she talked too fast, but there was, indeed, a cake on the table. It was as flat as you'd expect an eggless cake to be, but it was definitely made of cake. Beth was in her high chair staring at it, and she shouted with joy at the sight of them. All Nina could think, as she leaned down to kiss her sister's chubby little cheek, was that Billy should be here. Billy would have loved to bake a cake. There was a gaping hole in the family.

Nina made some tea, poured Beth a cup of water, and got out plates for the cake. She saw Louis, from the corner of her eye, sizing up the house, and she worked hard on herself. She was not going to cringe. All the pictures were down from the walls now, and she could see just how much they had been hiding. There were patches of actual green mold and black marks and cracks. The paint had peeled away. There were spiderwebs running right across the ceiling, probably made by all the spiders Billy had brought home. It looked, she could see, absolutely shit. It had somehow become a hovel, right around their ears.

They lived in crowded, substandard rented accommodations because of people like Louis' dad. *He* should have been mortified, not her. It was difficult to hold on to that right now.

She could not allow Mum to find out who Louis actually was. It made Nina paranoid; God only knew what it would do to Mum.

Nina knew Mum would be upset about Grandma for a long time, but it was Billy and Delfy who had broken her. Nina was upset about Grandma, too, but she knew that it was the order of things. The elder generation died, and new people were born. That was how life worked. It was the Billy situation that had let loose all the demons at once and that had made Nina determined to do everything she could to help. Mum was pretending like mad, but Nina could see below the surface.

"Sit down, Louis," said Mum. "It's lovely to have you here. I know our house is a bit . . ." Her voice tailed off.

"Don't be silly," said Louis. He was good with people, and Nina loved him for making this a bit easier. "Your house is a real home. And it smells amazing."

Mum relaxed a bit. "You wouldn't have said that earlier," she said. "Beth's nappy. Well, enough said."

Nina laughed and Louis did, too, even though it wasn't really funny. Mum picked up a blunt knife to cut the cake.

"The knife isn't sharp," she said, looking at it, running her finger along it. Something about the way she was doing it was alarming, and Nina got up to find a sharper one, but didn't hand it over.

"It's OK, Mum," she said. "Sit down. I'll do it."

The cake was the best thing she had ever tasted. It was nice, even by the standards of real cakes. Mum and Beth had done some magic somehow.

"Thanks," said Louis, sipping his tea. "And thanks, Beth. This is literally amazing."

"Maybe Beth can be a baker when she grows up," said Nina, looking at the baby's happy face. "She could have a cake shop. Make cakes all day long. You could help her, Mum."

"Yes," said Mum. "Let's make cakes all day long, Bethie. I'll work for you. You can pay me in cake."

They carried on talking, and Nina tuned out a bit and sipped her tea. She was thinking about the reality of getting their website out there and particularly about the fact that Louis must have access to all sorts of security.

She had checked, and there was very little about Louis and Harvey on the Internet, and no photos of their childhoods at all. There were, however, a few staged photos of Ben Alford, his first wife, Anna, and a puddingy baby called Katherine Maria Alford.

M um," Nina said in a soft voice when they had finished the tea and most of the cake was gone. "Mum?" Mum looked at her. "Go to bed," said Nina. "Seriously. You look knackered. We'll look after Beth. Seize your moment. We've got this. You're moving house tomorrow!"

Louis looked up. "Yeah," he said. "Moving is a massive thing! And you've done all this packing and made a cake. You should get some rest, Mrs. Jackman."

Nina and Mum both laughed.

"*Rachel,*" said Mum. "None of this 'Mrs. Jackman' for me. Thanks. That was . . ." She stopped suddenly.

Nina finished the sentence in her head. *That was my mother's name.* She saw Mum's eyes fill with tears.

A s soon as Mum had gone upstairs, Nina took Louis and Beth into the sitting room, which was below Nina's and Billy's rooms, so Mum wouldn't hear them talking. She put on the telly for extra sound camouflage and bounced Beth on her lap.

" 'We Hear Voices,' " she said to Louis. "That's what I think we should call it. Let the children speak. That's what they want to tell us, isn't it? They hear voices."

"Sure," he said.

"I'm going to say he threw a cat out of an upstairs window. In Toronto. And then we can appeal for other people to get in touch with us and start to put information together. Make a database. I can't use my normal phone for this. Louis, can you get us burners? No one can know apart from us. And Shelly. And Graham."

"You want to bring Shelly in?"

"Yeah. She's good at this stuff, too."

"I agree. I don't think she likes me much, but she's really good at this."

"She knows who you are. She researched you."

Louis opened his mouth to say something and then closed it again. He shrugged a bit and changed the subject. He changed it to the thing Nina had been dreading the most.

"So," he said, "where are you moving to anyway?"

THIRTY-FOUR

Rachel sat up in bed, looking at the door, the duvet over her legs. She hoped she had done all right with Nina's boyfriend. She had tried, but it might not have been enough. He was nice.

She had hated this house for years, and now that they had to leave, she was realizing that it was a haven. She had brought Beth home from hospital to this house. It was the first home she and Al had lived in together. Billy had been ill here, and then well again, and then ill. It was full of mold and peeling paper and appliances that didn't work, but it had been theirs. It had been their landlord's house but their home.

And now it wasn't theirs anymore. Most things were packed into boxes, ready to go tomorrow. Worklifeplus was sending a van tomorrow afternoon to pick up everything they were taking with them, which wouldn't be much. Al's charity was picking up all the furniture, and she would probably just pile everything else up on the street with a note telling people to help themselves.

Nina and Louis were looking after Beth, and right now everyone was fine. Billy was safe and cared for, and he was OK, considering. Rachel had a lot of things to do, but whenever she stopped, two things swamped her.

Her mother. Billy. Her mother. Billy. One, and then the other, or some-times both at once. Motherbilly. Billymother.

Mum had left her flat to the church. Rachel hadn't been told that fact by a lawyer yet, but she knew it was true because she was sure Father Mike wouldn't have been in there otherwise. When they moved into their corporate accommodation, it was going to be difficult to move out. The only person who could get them out was Rachel herself. She would make it her mission.

She had thrown away the bottle of brandy she'd taken from Orla's flat. She had been tempted, but there was no time to indulge herself now. She needed to get back to work. She had brought a cup of tea upstairs instead.

It was going to be an odd setup in worklifeplus. Al's job was doing something with data for the telecoms division, and he would of course do it brilliantly, but it would take all his time, and his wages came in the form of the apartment and a phone and food and tokens for beer and clothes. He was not going to be able to save anything to get them out of there, because it was a job that paid literally no money at all.

However, Rachel had read the rules again and again and again, and she was pretty sure she had found a loophole. As a resident, she was obliged to work for the company. She had already signed her rights away on that front: she could work outside Starcom only if they didn't have a job available for her.

As the mother of a baby, though, she didn't have to work until Beth was three.

And they made a huge point of saying the day care was available to every child from the age of nine months up.

Therefore, technically she was allowed to put Beth (ten months old) into free childcare and go out to work. She would do that, and she would go back to work as a lawyer and save every penny she earned. She was trying desperately to control her anxiety at the idea. It was her way of getting the family their life back. With Billy locked away in hospi-tal, and with his visits severely limited, she needed something else to focus on. Otherwise she would spend her time being furious with her mother for making such an awful will, and feeling like the worst person in the world for the way she had failed both Orla and Billy. She had walked away from the tower block and left them together. It had been her fault. She had effectively killed her mother and made her child a murderer.

She cradled her teacup between her hands and wished she'd kept the brandy.

Last time she had worked as a lawyer, she had had a breakdown. That was a fact. She shook her head and refused to allow herself to revisit it, but she knew that it hadn't been *the law* that had done it. It had been Henry, and above all, it had been her younger self. Everything had spiraled out of control until she couldn't do any of it for a moment longer. She could pull the work part out of that. That strand would be all right on its own.

She sat up in bed and tried again to get her head around the idea. She had a professional skill, although it needed updating. She would get it up to speed and then use it until Beth was three. She needed to stockpile the most money possible to get them a new life, and a professional job, rather than a minimum-wage one, was the way to do it. She wanted to do it. She was going to do it. She had to do it.

She had made an appointment at a specialized jobs agency on Monday morning. This was her last weekday as a former lawyer, as well as her last afternoon of living in this house. She had to pull herself together. She was on a mission now.

The pub had been totally revamped since Rachel last saw it. She noted that Nina was right: it was now called the Elizabeth II. The old carpet had gone. The floor was pale wooden floorboards. The dark varnished tables with their scratches and stains had been replaced with pale wooden ones, and the windows seemed cleaner and clearer.

Sami and Emma weren't here yet, and Rachel found a tiny table in a corner. The sound track was strange, plinky jazz, like elevator music, and she felt disconnected, as if she were in a waiting room to the afterlife. She looked at all the people and thought that they must be dead people. Look at them. Sitting there, drinking, laughing. Their eyes were weird, she thought. They were different. All falling apart, all dead. She must be dead, then, too. It felt possible.

She went to the bar for a soda water, but somehow came away with a bottle of wine, paid for by credit card.

Rachel's dad's binges had made her hate alcohol before she knew what it was, and so she had never been interested in drinking. It had been a logical and uncomplicated position, through her divorce, through Billy's illness, through everything. Yet she had had some wine after Mum's funeral and that had been fine. Now here she was, on her last night of her old life, doing it again.

Rachel!" said Sami, and she kissed her cheek. "So sorry. Babysitter. Anyway I'm here now. Oh! You're drinking?"

"Yes," said Rachel. "Don't worry. Just a couple of glasses. It can't exactly make things any worse."

"Fair enough." Sami sat down and poured herself a glass. "Well, cheers, if that's appropriate. I'm gutted you're moving."

Emma joined them, and Rachel realized that she liked her friends very much and that she ought to see them more. That was an impractical decision to make when she was about to move across London to an area in which she knew no one.

"How's Billy?" said Emma as soon as she sat down.

"Terrible," said Rachel. "I can't bear to talk about it."

They talked, instead, about other things, and the evening flew by. They finished the bottle, and Emma bought the next one, but Rachel moved on to soda water. It felt like the most liberating thing to drink some wine and then stop. She wasn't an alcoholic. She wasn't her father. She had a wonderful evening with her friends, a little glimpse into a different world, and when she got home at half past eleven, she felt she was ready to tackle everything.

THIRTY-FIVE

On Sunday, they spent the afternoon having a seminar about radiation in space. It was alarming.

Nina was struggling with her future plans, and she had never felt as detached from the space program as she did today. She had longed with all her heart to live out most of her life in a space colony, to leap across the universe with whatever the technology was going to turn out to be and set up life on a new planet. But now she felt that Mum would always need to lean on her. And she wasn't going anywhere until Billy was free.

You could go to live on the Rock and pop back to visit your family regularly, because it was between here and the moon. It was no distance away at all. But the people who went to the next planet would be making a one-way journey. There was a lot to think about.

She had never felt this grown-up before. It was fucking depressing.

The moment the session finished, at six o'clock, she, Louis, and Shelly gathered their stuff together and set off to sort out the blog. They were doing it at Dad's house. He had a hyperfast Internet connection, and crucially, he was always at cycling club at this time on a Sunday. His was the only house that was guaranteed to be empty.

The three of them traveled by Tube in silence and walked down the road in almost silence, and Nina held her breath as she opened Dad's front door, praying that he wouldn't be there. The long tone of the alarm told her she was safe, and she nipped inside and put in the code.

"Come in," she said, and she breathed in the cleaning-fluid smell and thought guiltily how straightforward a space Dad's house was when he wasn't in it.

When they had everything set up, Nina thought she should set out the basics.

"So," she said, "this is to help Billy, because we suspect the voices are a part of the epidemic that's been suppressed, and we need to gather evidence to show that it's not him being evil. It's to help Graham because he needs more data for his research. It's for Louis to work out if there could be any connection with what happened to his sister. And it's so we can feel we're doing something. 'We Hear Voices' is written and edited, and as soon as you guys say it's OK to go, we'll start to try to get it to as many people as we possibly can. If we do hear from anyone else, I'll deal with the messages and contact people on my new phone, unless there are too many, in which case I'll get you to help."

"Absolutely," said Louis.

"What has this to do with your sister?" said Shelly.

Louis tensed up. "I don't know," he said. "But everything I've seen about Billy feels like an echo of what happened to her. My parents will never talk about her. Mum refuses to have her name said aloud. Auntie Imogen used to talk about her all the time, though, so from what I've pieced together, my dad was married to her mum, but he got my mum pregnant with Harvey, and he ended up leaving his first wife and daughter. Then Katherine got ill, and she did something bad."

"She probably killed her mum," said Shelly. "I mean, Anna Alford died around then, didn't she?"

"Fuck," said Louis. "I mean, yes. She probably did kill her mum, and I've been thinking that for a while, but I've never said it out loud before. Yes, given what's happening now, I'd say she probably did."

"So that could well have been her we saw the other day," said Nina. "Kitty. Katherine."

"Incredibly likely," said Louis. "Mum hates her, and Dad would totally just have got Graham to shut her away out of sight and out of mind. And I actually met her, and I told her to go away and I shut the door in her face."

Nina raided the fridge, coming back with a plate of cheese and tomatoes and a baguette that she had found in the kitchen and that Dad had almost certainly been saving for later. If he knew he was feeding BA's son, she thought, he would be absolutely fine with it. He would run out and buy all the rest of the baguettes in the shop for Louis Alford.

She hadn't actually been to the new flat yet. She felt a bit shabby about that, but she'd go there tonight. She would do all she could to make it OK. When she had finally told Louis where they were moving, there had been the most awkward moment they had ever had (or at least, it was up there with the time he'd told her who his dad was), and then they'd agreed not to talk about it. That was OK for now, but it obviously wouldn't really be all right when she was living there. She didn't want to be in a relationship in which she couldn't talk about her home.

They ate and worked and talked and worked and ate, getting through all the food without even really noticing, and after a couple of hours, Shelly ran through a checklist.

"Nina," she said, "are you happy with the content? The 'We Hear Voices' logo, the appeal to contact us, the story of Josh? And your list of questions for anyone who gets in touch?"

Nina cast her eye over the screen in front of her. "Yes," she said.

"Louis," said Shelly, "you're happy with the site security, and you've got all the social media accounts and press releases ready to go?"

"Yes," said Louis.

"And how about you, Shelly?" Shelly said to herself. "Are you happy with the absolutely awesome job you've done of setting this up to run through private servers so it pings all around the world and no one will ever be able to trace it back to us? Why, yes, Shelly. Yes, indeed, I am."

Nina stood behind Shelly and leaned over to hug her. "You're amazing," she said. "Thank you so much for this."

Shelly turned around and grinned at her. "I love a project, Nina. I do love a project."

They were thinking about opening some of Dad's wine when Nina heard his key in the lock. She had forgotten that he would, of course, be coming home, that he didn't stay out cycling around South London for the entire night.

"Ah!" he said, standing in the dining room doorway and rubbing his hands together. He looked ridiculous in a padded Lycra suit, with red face and sweaty hair. "Welcome! Make yourselves at home."

"Hi, Dad," said Nina, hoping for the best. "This is my dad. Dad, this is my friend Shelly, and this is Louis."

"The famous Louis!" he said, striding over. "At last! It's a delight to meet you." Dad laughed and held out his hand. Louis shook it, mirroring Dad's smile, and Dad turned to Shelly. "And you, too, Shelly. You're Nina's friend from space cadets—am I right?"

"You certainly are," Shelly said. "Thanks for letting us use your house, Mr. Stevens. It's a lovely house. I mean, I know you didn't know we were here, but we're grateful all the same. We ate quite a lot of your food."

"And you are welcome to it," said Dad. "Are you doing space work? Launching rockets remotely?"

"Something like that," said Nina. "Anyway, we've just finished."

Shelly snapped the lid of her laptop shut.

"Then," said Dad, "I just have one question for you. Red or white?"

They migrated to the kitchen and had a glass of wine, and Nina decided that she liked Dad a lot more lately than she ever used to. He was barely embarrassing at all.

And the website was out there in the world.

And now, even though she wanted to stay here drinking wine with Dad and her friends, she had to cross London and go to the worklifeplus apartment, because she had absolutely promised Mum and Al that she would, and she couldn't hide away from their new life for a moment longer.

THIRTY-SIX

On Monday morning, it took Nina ages to remember where she was. She switched off the alarm and lay still, heart pounding. This was a different room, and it had a weird smell. She was lying in a single bed under a thin duvet, and the air was uncomfortably muggy.

She wasn't at home.

She *was* at home.

She sighed and got out of bed. It was "home." She had lived here only for a few hours, but so far it was freaky and she hated it. She needed to put up all her pictures on the wall; they were in a box on her desk. It would feel better when her stuff was up. When she had looked at a place like this before, through that VR headset, it had been entirely different.

Then she remembered the website. It was too soon for anything to have happened, but she took out the new burner phone Louis had got her and checked it.

There had been five e-mails overnight, all of them from readers. She smiled and skimmed the messages. All of them were saying: "This happened to my child, too." It was phenomenal.

She pulled on her dressing gown, smoothed her wild hair, and walked as quietly as she could to the bathroom for a shower. Today she had a lot of things to do, and even though it was Monday, going to school most certainly wasn't one of them.

Their new home was on the western outskirts of London. It was just another neighborhood, not particularly better or worse than their last one, but a lot farther away from school, as well as from everything else apart from Heathrow Airport, and it meant she needed to leave at seven to get to school by half past eight. Or she would need to do that when she did go to school.

At seven fifteen she was making a cup of coffee in the . . . not a kitchen, but a corner of the living room that had a kettle, microwave oven, and sink. She could hear the people upstairs walking around, and the people downstairs were playing music. The real kitchen was a shared one on the ground floor. There was a television room there, too, but Nina knew she would never sit there with the neighbors arguing over what channel they should all watch.

Al came into the room and stopped in the doorway.

"Hey," he said in a voice that was almost a whisper, "Nina. You OK?"

She nodded. "Would you like a coffee?"

"That would be great. Thanks. Jesus, I'm nervous!"

She went over and gave him a hug. "I'm sure it'll be fine," she said carefully. "I hope it's not too boring."

He laughed and came over to get out another coffee mug. These were dull ones, all the same corporate green color. Mum had brought three with them from the old house, all of them with some version of WORLD'S BEST MUM on them. Other than that, neither Nina nor Al had felt they were attached to the chipped old mugs they'd had forever, though now Nina thought that perhaps, in fact, she had been.

"I can handle boring," said Al. "I just . . . I guess I've spent all my life resisting this. And now here I am. I thought I was different, thought I had a vocation, that I would never succumb to working for the Man. I would spend my life fighting injustice. Maybe I had a bit of a superhero complex. Perhaps I needed bringing down a peg or two. You know, time to be reminded that actually, mate, it's better for everyone if you just do . . . some data thing that I still don't completely understand. Hopefully I will at some point."

"Stop it!" Nina was outraged. "You absolutely didn't have that complex, Al. You were great at your job and society was lucky to have you doing it. This is just bullshit, isn't it? All of it. But at least there was a safety net." Her voice had risen, and someone upstairs banged on the floor. Great.

"Yeah," said Al. "At least that, I guess."

She plunged down the cafetière (they had brought that with them, too) and poured two cups of coffee.

"Shall I make one for Mum?" she said.

"Yeah. Please. Big day for her, too."

"Job interview?"

"Interview with an agency about going back to legal work. I don't want to put pressure on her, but she was so gutted about your gran's flat. This was supposed to be a stopgap until she inherited it, and now she thinks she has to do something to stop us from being here forever. I'm not convinced about the loophole she's found, but she's the lawyer. When she goes back to work after Beth is three, she's supposed to work here, but there's nothing about anything before that. She can do it for a bit, I'm sure."

"And Beth is going to Starcom day care?"

"Beth will show them how to run their silly day care. You OK getting to school from here?"

"Yeah," said Nina, "I am today. I have a free period first thing, and even though we're meant to go into school for them, no one will notice if I don't. Just this once. Or rather just this every Monday. I might stay at Dad's tonight, though."

"Sure," said Al. "Twenty minutes to school from there, right?"

They smiled sadly at each other.

Nina let herself into Dad's house, switched off the burglar alarm, and changed out of her school uniform and into jeans. She'd had seven e-mails now, and that was far more than she'd expected to happen this early. There were more important things than school today, even though exams were coming up, and even though they were important ones that she had to pass well for her future plans to work out.

This felt more important than that, which was something Nina would never have expected to find herself thinking. When she was dressed as an ordinary person, she went back to the Tube and headed into the center of the city.

This time she went straight up in the normal lift to floor two. It was odd to think that Billy was far down beneath her feet, and she found that she liked the idea that Katherine Alford was potentially there with him. Lauren gave her more coffee and a biscuit, which was nice because Nina had been so preoccupied that she'd forgotten about breakfast. The biscuit was a tiny little thing, though, and melted in her mouth before she could enjoy it, so she went and stood in the doorway of Lauren's office and cleared her throat.

"Oh, hi," said Lauren, looking up from her screen. "You OK?"

"Yep," said Nina. "Sorry. This probably is against all the etiquette, but could I have another one of those biscuits? I'm really hungry, and I didn't have any breakfast."

Lauren laughed and opened a drawer. "Of course you can," she said. "Makes a change from people who refuse anything with carbs or sugar. Have as many as you like. Do you fancy some chocolate, too?"

"Always," said Nina, and Lauren gave her the rest of the pack of biscuits and a box of Rockolate Planets. Nina didn't get a chance to try one before Graham popped his head out of the door and said: "Ah, Nina. Come on in."

"Right," said Nina. "Lots of things." She was nervous, but was trying not to be, so she was probably overcompensating by being brisk. "I know your time is valuable and all that, so thanks for seeing me."

"My pleasure. Go ahead."

"Do you remember when I spoke to you ages ago on the phone?"

Graham inclined his head. "Of course."

"Well, I've done it. I've started a website with Louis and our friend Shelly to gather people's experiences of the voices," she said. "We launched it properly last night, and we've already got forty-three comments, and I've had e-mails from eleven people wanting to talk. So I guess I need to see you because you wanted this data. I have a feeling we're going to end up with lots of it."

Graham leaned back in his chair and nodded. "Does Louis' father know about this?" he said.

"Oh, God, no."

"Good," he said. "Well, this is fascinating, Nina. May I have a look?"

She got out her laptop to show him the site, then forwarded him all the messages she'd had so far. They were from the US, Japan, and a handful of European countries. They talked it through.

"In confidence," said Graham, "here is the thing. Yes, we can show that this is far more widespread than you'd think, and we can link up a thousand local stories of children behaving badly into something much more . . . interesting. But then what? With someone in Billy's situation, yes, we can make sure he's not held criminally responsible for what he did, because it's part of an illness, and let's put all our energies into doing that. But he can't go home because he's likely to do something else. What the hell do we do about it, short of medicating them so they become zombies? You've seen Billy. Whatever medication I give him seems to subdue *him* but not the bloody voice. The rest of them down there are better because when they socialize, they get to control it a bit more, but when it comes down to it, I have no idea how to get these voices to go away."

Nina decided to try something. "Does Katherine still have a voice?" she said, looking at her fingernails, which really needed some attention.

"I'm sorry?"

"Katherine Alford. Kitty."

"Why would you think that?"

"Louis knows she's here," she said. "I think because of what your wife used to say. That's her, isn't it, down there in the football shirt?"

"Well," said Graham, "I can't speak about my patients." He hesitated, about to say something, but stopped himself. Then he took a deep breath and said, "Hypothetically, if I'd seen an early case of this some years ago, I think I would probably have observed patient recovery in adolescence."

"Adolescence," she said. That was something, but Billy was only six. "Well," she said, "maybe we can stop Billy from having to go on trial, like you said."

"That would be a magnificent achievement," said the old man. "He's not even seven years old yet, and he's been taken away from his family after a series of traumas. He belongs with his mother in particular, and until he has some degree of security, he won't start to heal. I'm very troubled, Nina. Very. I'm glad you're trying to gather the stories together. Do tell Louis to come and chat with me."

He looked as if there was more he wanted to say, and Nina knew that she had no idea of the things that went on in places like this. She watched as Graham rummaged around in his drawers until he found a bright red bag of Maltesers, opened it, and put it on the table between them.

"Have a sweet," he said. "My late wife loved these, and she was a wise woman."

Nina shrugged. "Sure," she said. "Thanks. She sounds brilliant. Louis loved her. Was she his dad's sister?"

"And his harshest critic."

"Sorry that she died. Do you have children?"

He looked surprised. "Yes. Three sons. A handful of grandchildren, too."

"Are they all healthy?"

"I believe so."

"You're incredibly lucky," she told him. "I hope you realize that. I mean, it's awful that your wife died, but you have a family. So, I need to talk a few things through with you if that's OK."

"Right," said Graham. He took a Malteser and looked at her, waiting for her to continue.

"I need to call these people back. Can you check my list of questions?" She pushed it across the table. He looked at it and made notes on it while Nina ate all the rest of the Maltesers.

"Shouldn't you be in school?" he said.

"I should. So." She looked at what he had written. It looked logical apart from one thing. "Ask about the plane explosion? Seriously? What about the ones who don't live in London?"

"I know, I know," said Graham. "It was an observation I made with the kids down there. I make what connections I can. It's imperfect."

Nina tried to imagine something in the crashing plane that was in the air, breathed in by people, so some substance was in their bodies when they later got the flu.

"OK," she said. "Any London ones, I'll ask them."

Graham Watson sighed. "I'd love to see your data, no matter what you come up with. Obviously a map would be helpful. I guess you'll be recording your calls?" She nodded. "I'd like to look at it with you. If that would be OK? I want to get to the bottom of this as much as you do."

"Can I go down and see Billy?" she said.

"Technically no," said Graham. "Visits are strictly limited. I wish they weren't, but there we go. However, he'd love to see you, and I'll escort you down right now. We can sidestep the rules this once."

. . .

Billy was sitting on his bed, twiddling with his crochet hook and a ball of wool, along with two girls. One was small with tangled hair and was wearing an excellent silver tracksuit. The other was Louis' sister, and Nina saw Graham stiffen at her presence. There were more security people in the room than there were children.

"Hey, Nina," Billy said as the policewoman nodded her in.

The little girl looked round, and Nina thought she looked familiar. It was Katherine Alford, though, who was the interesting one.

"This is my friends Lulu and Kitty," said Billy, and he looked more relaxed than he had for a long time. "Lulu and Kitty, this is my sister Nina."

"Hello, Nina," said Lulu, and Nina began to think she knew who she was. Surely not, though. That wouldn't make any kind of sense. Princess Louisa had died before Christmas. This girl just looked like her.

"Hi, Nina!" Kitty was looking at her intensely, almost hungrily. She put down her ball of wool and just gazed at her.

"Hello, Kitty," Nina said, and she smiled at the security people, one of whom smiled back.

"Kitty has been here for a long time," said Billy. "And Lulu has been here a bit more than me."

Nina looked at Billy and Lulu playing together and laughing, and although she had a million questions for both of them, she didn't want to interrupt. She was pleased Billy looked happier, but there was something about these children, the way they looked at one another, the unknowability of them, that chilled her.

"They're freaking awesome kids," said Kitty, seeing her looking. "Do you want to be my friend?"

"Sure," said Nina.

Kitty moved closer. Graham caught Nina's eye and signaled to her silently not to ask about Kitty's family. As if she would have right now.

"You can join in if you want, Nina," said Billy. "It's fun. We're making spiderwebs."

"Are you all into spiders?" That was a silly question, given the spider facts that were written on the walls all over Billy's room. All three of them nodded. "Well, you'll have to teach me."

"You just take this hook," said Lulu, passing one to her. "And look. You do this."

Nina couldn't get the hang of it at all. The others were brilliant at it.

THIRTY-SEVEN

When Rachel woke, Nina had already left. Al said she had gone to school late, but it still felt early to Rachel. Everything was weird here. She didn't understand it. There was scratchy gray carpet throughout the house (even in the bathroom), and they were supposed to cook and watch television and do everything else that people did in their downtime communally with the other workers. The kitchen and the TV room were downstairs, and there were a shop and a bar that took tokens at the end of the street. They couldn't shop anywhere else because they had no money. They were totally under the control of the corporation, entirely tied into it.

The thing about this apartment was that it was tiny. Knowing that they didn't have the luxury of looking around and changing their minds, she had seen it only in the brochure before they moved in. In reality, there was no space for anything. The bedrooms were cramped and gray, the living room tiny with a demi-kitchen crammed into one side of it. The bathroom was the size of the loo on a train, but with a shower cubicle stuck on the side.

She felt like a bee or an ant. It was suffocating. This could never be her home, and she had just over two years to amass enough money for them to get out of here.

She opened the blinds. They were on the third floor, and the bedroom window looked out over a busy road. For a few seconds, she just stood and watched the traffic, remembering a different window and a spiderweb, and then convulsing with horror as every molecule in her body longed, longed, longed for Billy.

"Where's Beth?" she said, walking into the living room. She stopped and did a double take at Al. He was wearing a bright white shirt that still had the creases from the packet and a thin purple tie with synthetic black trousers.

"Wow," she said. "Have you seen my boyfriend?"

Al looked down at himself and made a face. "He's in here somewhere," he said. "I hope. Jeez—state of me."

"You still look gorgeous, though," she said, and she walked over to kiss him. "Good luck."

"I'll need it."

They stood together and surveyed their new quarters, and Rachel thought that if she didn't have Al, she would have absolutely nothing, and she would definitely not be able to cope. Beth crawled over to them and pulled herself up on Rachel's legs.

"Good luck to you, too, Bethie," said Rachel, picking her up. Beth was going to the day care today, and Rachel really, really hoped she wasn't going to hate it.

Al put on his purple jacket and set off to catch the minibus to work, and Rachel dressed Beth as tidily as she could and took her down the road to the corporate nursery. Beth wriggled and wanted to get there under her own steam (or get somewhere else, more likely), but Rachel kept hold of her and carried her down the road to day care.

Corporate responsibility was a good thing. That was what Rachel told herself. This was an enormous safety net, and they were lucky. It was an adjustment. That was all.

Her phone rang, and she shuffled around to find it, but it was a number that she didn't recognize, and she had a bad feeling about it, so she ignored it. She'd deal with that later.

It took a couple of minutes to walk to the nursery. She put Beth down while she filled in the forms, and when she looked up, her baby daughter was on the other side of the room, standing up, leaning on a little table and driving a toy car up and down.

"Look at her!" said the woman. "Oh, I love it when this happens. We'll see you in three hours."

"Yes," said Rachel. "Thanks." She waited for Beth to look round so she could at least wave good-bye, but she didn't, so Rachel just left. She had never left Beth in a place like this before, and Beth didn't care at all.

The phone rang again as soon as she was off the Tube, and it was the same number. The number gave her a bad feeling. She couldn't even articulate the thought properly because it sounded so mad, but she thought it was Delfy calling from hospital. Delfy had killed her mother; why wouldn't she torment her by phoning her?

If Delfy had murdered Orla (which she had), then she would be able to make a phone ring. Rachel looked at the number. If you read it upside down, and converted sevens into "L"s, and a four into a "D," you could make it spell out ITS DELFII.

Her head was pounding, though she wasn't ill. With Beth at day care, there was nothing to ground her. She floated along, disconnected. Nina was at school. Al was finding out what data processing actually meant. Rachel was surplus to requirements.

Next time she thought she might answer the call without saying anything. A tiny part of her thrilled at the idea that she might hear Delfy's voice if she did. It would be a voice that wasn't a voice. A nonhuman voice. She imagined it coming down the phone.

At that moment, it rang again. Her hand trembled as she answered it. She didn't say anything. There was silence on the other end, too.

"Delfy?" she whispered. Nothing happened. It *was* Delfy.

Or maybe it could be . . .

"Mum?"

More silence. Rachel trembled all over. She started to whisper all her secrets.

Then a voice came onto the line. "Rachel Jackman?" it said. "I'm calling from the East London Legal Center. It's a courtesy call about your late mother's will. As I think you're aware, she left her flat to the Ch—"

Rachel didn't hear the rest. She shouted all the obscenities she knew into the phone, threw it on the ground, and stamped on it. A minute later she went back and picked it up and brushed it off. Luckily it still worked.

"Thanks, Mum," she muttered. In a way, it had been her mother on the phone, calling to say *Fuck you*.

Rachel was in a small waiting room with green carpet in squares, and she sat on a wobbly chair, feeling more determined than ever. She had no choice but to make this work. A woman in a gray suit came and looked into the space above her head, then around the room, and said, "Rachel Jackman?" in a loud voice, into the room at large, even though Rachel was the only person in it.

"Hi," she said. "That's me," she added, immediately feeling silly.

Rachel's tight skirt and cheap work jacket were uncomfortable. Her shoes rubbed the backs of her ankles, and her waistband was squeezing her flesh. Still, she was dressed in approximately the same manner as the woman interviewing her, which was good. They were about the same age, too, but when Rachel smiled, all she got back was frost.

"Nadia McGovern," the woman said, and when she turned, Rachel followed her into an interview room that was much smaller than the waiting room. There was a poster of a fjord on the wall with the words STRIVE

FOR EXCELLENCE written across it, and a picture of a kitten and a ball of wool that said: ONLY BY CHASING RAINBOWS DO WE ACHIEVE OUR DREAMS. On another wall were a few of the old flu information posters. It didn't look much like a lawyer's office. Rachel had imagined shiny efficiency, and this was not it.

"Nice to meet you," said Rachel.

"So, you're hoping to get some legal work? Well, you've come to the right place, I suppose." Nadia tapped a pen on the desk, again and again and again, until the sound of it was all Rachel could hear. It felt like someone knocking on her skull.

"I'm sure I could get back up to speed." She spoke loudly to hear her own voice over the sound of the pen, which was so loud now that she looked round in case there was a drummer in a corner of the room. "I've been out of the game for a while."

"Raising a family?"

"Yes. Well, my youngest is still very small. She's just started at nursery."

The interview got better (though Rachel felt bad for talking about her two daughters and not mentioning Billy, but she couldn't—she just couldn't), and in the end, Nadia said: "The thing with parents is, they know how to get things done. I should know: my twins are twelve. I'm not supposed to say this kind of thing, but from what you've said, you have reliable childcare with that nursery and backup from your elder child. Those living spaces are weird, but they can be a godsend, and I'm glad, and a bit surprised, that they let you go out to work elsewhere. As long as you can be committed, we'll take you on. I can only offer admin work to start with. If you want to go back into contract law, you'll need to take a course, and that will cost five hundred pounds. With that under your belt, you could pick up work year-round covering for holidays and illness."

The pen was still drumming. The sound carried on even though Nadia's hand and the pen had stopped moving.

Five hundred pounds.

Rachel did not have five hundred pounds.

She had taken the credit card to help her support the family, and now she would use it to do exactly that.

Is that OK, Mum? she said, on the inside, though she knew it was. Her mother's ghost owed her. She owed her big-time.

She made Orla's voice reply in her head. *Yes, love,* it said. *Of course. It's the very least I can do for you.*

Too right, she told it.

"I'll do it," she said. "The course, I mean. I'd love to. And before that, I'd like to do some admin temping, like you said."

"Great. Well, I've got two sets of forms for you to fill in, in that case. Coffee?"

Rachel drank a cup of filter coffee that was somehow stale even though it was still dripping through the machine, and she put herself onto the books of the LegalEagles agency. The admin work she was signing up for was paid at the exact same rate as her old receptionist job, but at least this would demonstrate (to herself, to Al, to Nina) that she meant business. At least she would be able to hoard every single penny of it.

Nadia booked her onto a refresher course for contract law, which involved turning up at a classroom once a week and doing lots of work at home in between, and she paid five hundred pounds on her mother's credit card, praying it would go through.

The word **AUTHORIZED** appeared on the screen. It was done.

As she walked to the Tube, she examined her feelings about the credit card. She supposed she was stealing from the financial people by using a stolen card, but they were a massive corporation, and she was going to pay it back. If she got in trouble, she would say Mum had given her the card years ago, and no one would be able to prove otherwise. She wouldn't mention it to Al at all because he had enough going on as it was.

She stopped to stare at some pink blossoms on a tree.

Mum? she said, in her head. *Look at me, Mum. Going back to the law. Thanks to your stupid will. If this goes wrong, it'll be your fault.*

She made her mother's voice in her head say: *You're right. Take all the money you need.*

She kept walking. She was feeling odd. Everything was where it shouldn't be. A postbox sprang up in front of her where she was sure there hadn't been one before. She kept walking toward the Tube, but she felt as if she were watching herself stumbling down a street. She wasn't even visible. Maybe she had died, too, and hadn't noticed she'd become a ghost, like in that movie. She was insubstantial, and none of this mattered. A pigeon landed in front of her and pecked at some dried-up vomit on the pavement. She walked past it, and it didn't even flinch. That was how flimsy a presence she was.

This was how it had started before. When she had had her breakdown.

S he had booked a visit to Billy for this afternoon, and when she sat by his bed and looked into his eyes, something inside her flickered back to reality. Billy was there. She could see him.

"Hello, Mummy," he said.

"Oh, Billy." She blinked, looked at him. Pulled herself together. She tried to make her mind fit into her body. She had to be strong for him.

"Can I come home?" he whispered. "I know it's a different home. But can I come to it?"

"Yes," she whispered. "I hope so. Soon."

"Nina says she will sort it out. She is finding other people's stories, and her and Graham will tell everyone it's not fair. Nina was here just now, Mummy. She only just left. We did crocheting with Lulu and Kitty. It was so funny, Mummy. Nina was so bad at it! Lulu and me are good because we do it lots. So does Majid, and Suki, and Anita. And Kitty, too. Lulu is the best, but that's OK because she's going to be the queen."

Rachel frowned and tried to untangle what he was talking about. Billy had hallucinated a visit from his sister, who was at school, because one thing that was certain was that Nina went to school on Mondays.

Rachel looked around. "Can I have a go, too?" she said. She saw that, in one corner of the room, there was a pile of silver crocheted rope.

As she was leaving, Lauren intercepted her and told her that Graham had applied to court with evidence that Billy was sedated enough to be moved onto the main ward, and that he would be moving as soon as the legal paperwork came through.

"It's highly unlikely there'll be any problems with it," she said. "And Graham thinks it'll do Billy a world of good to be with the other children. They've already become firm friends. It'll be a very positive thing indeed."

THIRTY-EIGHT

Nina was sitting on a sofa at the very back of an anonymous café in Soho. She was trying to breathe properly because she was a bit scared by what she had started. There was a pot of tea in front of her; she had definitely had too much coffee.

She checked her phone and tapped her foot. Shelly wasn't even late, but Nina felt like she was, because it was strangely hard to fill a day when everyone else was at school.

She wanted to break down and cry. This was too much; it was only Shelly's imminent arrival that kept her hanging on. She was swamped by voices, and these same voices had murdered her grandmother. She didn't know why she had thought she could do this.

She should have gone for a run this afternoon, but then she'd have had to go back to Dad's to get showered and changed. Instead she'd just walked around the city for hours, thinking and talking on her new phone. She'd spoken to two parents of children with voices, but she needed to find someone to translate from Japanese.

Her blog phone was on silent, but when she looked at it, it had had a further ten e-mails from people who wanted to share their stories. She was seriously going to need to take another day off from school, to stop going to school altogether, if she was going to stay on top of this. The calls she'd made had been difficult: she had asked all the right questions, but it had been much harder than she'd imagined, and emotionally it was almost impossible. There was story after story like Billy's, and Nina didn't know how to deal with the way they made her feel.

She took a sip of tea, and then Shelly was there, beaming and saying, "What's up, girl?" and Nina had never been so pleased to see anyone in her life.

"Hey," she said. "Want some tea?"

Shelly had come straight from school and was wearing tight black trousers and a white shirt that was unbuttoned a bit further than her school had probably intended. She was the only person Nina knew who could make a uniform look intensely cool.

"Tea?" Shelly said, and made a face. "No."

She was back a couple of minutes later with a bright green drink with bubbles in it.

"So," said Nina.

"So?" said Shelly. "What's happened? Is Louis coming?"

"No," said Nina. "I actually wanted to see you without him."

Shelly gave her a look. "Oh?"

"Yes. I've had thirty-seven e-mails, and I've spoken to some of the people and written down their stories, but I'm going to have to find a new way of doing it. I can't talk to all of them, and even if we took a third each, I still don't think we could do it. And it's difficult, Shelly. It's too hard, hearing those stories again and again and again." She paused and managed to say: "They killed my gran." She felt emotion bearing down on her and struggled not to succumb to it. She gasped, and Shelly took her hand and squeezed it hard. "Also we need someone who speaks Japanese."

"OK," said Shelly. "I can sort that bit. And of course it's impossible for you to do it alone. We didn't really think this side through, did we? Let's put together a questionnaire and let them fill it in and send it back to us. Numbers-wise it's doing well. They're climbing faster than I thought they would. I saw Louis has been running the social media from school today, so that's good. So, what else? Why do I get to see you without your boyfriend?"

Nina threw herself back in her seat. "Oh, Shelly," she said. "Right. I went to see Graham Watson. I met Louis' sister, Kitty. Billy adores her, and it seems like she's really good to him. She's a strange girl, but I liked her because she was brilliant with Billy. Graham said—or kind of implied—that she'd had a voice, but that it went away as she grew up. I mean, she's older than us, and she's lived in that hospital since she was a tiny kid. Her family won't have her home."

Shelly frowned. "Jesus," she said. "She just vanished from view. Her mother died." She paused. "Kitty did kill her, didn't she?"

Nina sighed. "That's the only thing that makes sense, considering where she is and what she's been through. So I just wanted to talk it through with you before I see Louis. Because it's really complicated. It took me a while to realize that Louis' auntie Imogen, who died, was Graham's wife. I thought Graham was just an old family friend."

"Oh, seriously?" said Shelly. "Sorry. I could have told you that. It just never came up."

"So, Imogen was Ben Alford's sister and that's why she cared so much about Kitty, and why Kitty's grown up in Graham's hospital."

"Imogen Alford-Watson was a magnificent woman," said Shelly unexpectedly. "Totally unfair for her to be defined by her brother or husband. She was a fantastic physicist, and then she gave it up to have kids. She never quite went back to that, though she did work on the current Harmony prototype. Then she spent the last twenty years doing incredible community things. She set up a foundation that gives disadvantaged London girls a leg up. I used to go to their community center after school, and that's where I started to learn coding. She is incredible. Was."

Nina stared at her. "Really?"

"Yep. Shame for her that the world only sees her wanky brother and her uptight husband. Because she was the shining star among them all, and it's so, so unfair that she's the one that died."

"Oh, my God. I had no idea."

"Yeah. No one does, because what's a network of safe community centers for girls when you could be buying up all the homes or running a weird hospital?"

"Right. So, she was Louis' aunt, and from what he said, she was the only one who worried about his sister. So we probably need to talk to Graham again. He won't speak to us in any detail, of course, because of patient confidentiality. But he might speak to Louis, as he's family."

"Good point."

"So we'll need to talk this through with Louis. It's probably a sensitive topic in their house. We'll need to tread carefully."

"We will."

"Oh." Nina remembered something else. "Graham said to ask anyone in London if they were outside during the plane crash. A couple of them were in London, and actually two of the others, in England and Scotland, happened to have been in London at the time, too. It sounded like a bit of a weird question, but then I guess they can tell we're not in Toronto when they hear my voice anyway."

"OK. Potentially interesting. Was Billy outside?"

"Yes. He was at school. I remember him saying that he ran out onto the playground and shouted at the sky."

They stared at each other.

"That wouldn't make any sense," said Shelly.

"No," said Nina. "Would it?"

"I have no idea," said Shelly. "And that, my dear, is why it's fun."

THIRTY-NINE

When Louis called, Nina felt guilty for talking about his family behind his back.

"Hi!" she said, too brightly. She was walking to the bus stop in some unseasonal sunshine. "How are you?"

"I'm great," said Louis. "So, do you know how many people have read it?"

"Lots?" she said.

"Yeah. Lots." He went through the numbers, and she tried to get her head around the fact that hundreds of thousands of people around the world had looked at the thing that had started as her computer science homework. She told him about the people she'd spoken to, about how difficult it had been.

"Well done," he said. "You're brilliant. We can help. So, what happened with Graham?"

"Oh," she said, "it's complicated. I mean, nothing very much, but he was really helpful and pleased we're doing it. He's on board. But he doesn't know how to get rid of the voices. He said the tranquilizers just calm the children and give the voices free rein. So it can look like everything's calmed down, but actually the child is being tortured on the inside."

"Jesus. Does he have any ideas about what it actually is?"

She hesitated and decided not to talk about Kitty on the phone. "Weirdly," she said instead, "he says all the kids he's treated in London were outside during that plane crash. I mean, it doesn't make sense, but that's something." She took a deep breath.

"Oh," said Louis, "right. Lots to think about. Did you see Billy?"

"I did." Nina saw her bus coming and decided not to run for it. "He was crocheting loads of strands of stuff with . . . a couple of the other kids."

"Oh, that's good. And how's home?"

She sighed and stepped out of the way of someone coming down the pavement on a mobility scooter. "Bizarre," she said. Her entire conversation with Louis was, somehow, full of land mines. She wanted to find her way back to the way they used to be. "I mean, it's a lifeline. But weird."

"I'm sure." There was a bit of a silence. They never usually had silences. Then Louis spoke quickly.

"Nina, do you want to come and stay at mine? Maybe on Saturday? We can get all our first week's data collected and have a bit of breathing space together. Mum told me to invite you when I said things were difficult at home for you. It'll be separate bedrooms and stuff, obviously. They're really strict on that."

Nina thought about it. She thought about her conversation with Shelly. She thought about Ben Alford's first wife, about Kitty, shut away seven floors underground for fifteen years or so. She thought about Alford's brilliant sister, Imogen.

She wouldn't even need to tell either of her parents what she was doing. They never spoke to each other; she could just tell each of them she was with the other.

"Yes, please," she said. "That would be lovely."

FORTY

Rachel stood in front of a glass building by the Thames, her breath puffing in a cloud in front of her. She could do this. It was an admin job, no different really from her old receptionist work. It was in a law firm, but she wouldn't be the lawyer. It would be fine.

Thanks to the credit card, she had bought a set of bigger work clothes. She could do up the waist of this skirt without leaving red marks on her skin. She had got Nina to help with her hair, and so she was wearing it in a bun, and she felt efficient, like a parody of a secretary.

She walked in, pretending to be confident. The floor was made entirely of shiny marble, the walls of glass. Her heels clacked as she went, and she liked the businesslike sound. It proved that she was really here.

The woman at reception looked up.

"Hi," said Rachel with an ingratiating smile. "I'm from the Legal-Eagles agency. I'm here to work at Dowling's for two days."

"Sixth floor." The woman turned back to her computer.

The lift was glass, and Rachel enjoyed watching its mechanism working as she went up.

"Hi," she said again at Dowling's reception. "I'm Rachel Jackman from LegalEagles."

This woman was more interested. "You're the temp?"

"Yes."

"OK." The woman looked a bit surprised.

"I used to be a lawyer," she said. "Stopped to have kids."

"Oh, right," said the woman. "Same here."

They smiled at each other, and the woman gave Rachel a lanyard and directed her to an office down some corridors. Someone else gave her a place to sit and put her to work, and she tried hard to concentrate on things because her brain kept skipping away from them.

It was Wednesday. Al had spent his first two days at work working with AI. He was training it, teaching it how to have an in-depth conversation by talking about things in the news and the royal family. The idea was that it would be impossible to distinguish it from a human in every single interaction.

"In its way," he'd said, "it's almost fun. Sinister, yes, but I'll be OK."

Beth was almost annoyingly happy in day care, and Rachel was pleased even though it was a wrench. She wasn't allowed to visit Billy until tomorrow, and when she went, after work, she wanted to be able to tell him about her new job, which would already be over by then.

She did some filing and organized a "fee earner's diary," which meant writing someone's appointments on an online calendar, which was not at all difficult even when your mind was elsewhere. Even the most straightforward of tasks gave her a sense of achievement.

The other people mainly ignored her. Her desk was near a window, but she could see only the fire escape at the back of the building. She felt more like an alien observing human life than like an actual part of it.

At lunchtime most people got food from their bags and carried on working while eating, but Rachel knew she wasn't being paid for an hour in the middle of the day, and Nadia had said, "Make sure you get out at lunchtime. They'd love you to work straight through, but if they want that, they should pay for it."

She sat on a bench and looked at the river. There were hundreds of people living out here. Their homes were terrifying-looking salvaged or homemade boats, and whenever the police came close, they would motor or row away, their engines, if they had them, belching smoke. Today there was a row of people fishing. The tide was high; the river must have been deep, even at the edges.

At least, she thought, *we don't live on a leaky boat.*

She stared across to the South Bank. Half of it was pristine, and the other half was fenced off and filled with cranes.

Nina went there every week, of course, and she did it so quietly that Rachel always forgot about it, but in fact Nina was doing something extraordinary. She had seen the world and decided to get ready to bail on it and that, too, broke Rachel's heart.

Rachel ate her sandwich while watching a man on the other side of the river trying to climb up the side of a crane.

Kids on a school trip walked past her bench; the children were not much bigger than Billy. They were wearing high-vis jackets that were too big and were walking in pairs. A frowning female teacher was leading them along, with a bearded male one at the back, and they both looked stressed. *Teaching,* Rachel thought, *might be a worse job than contract law.*

As she watched, one of the children pulled away from the boy she was walking with and ran over to the river. She climbed quickly onto the wall, and then she jumped down, straight down, shouting something. It all happened so fast that it didn't seem real. Rachel seemed able only to stare. The male teacher ran to the wall and looked over it. Rachel imagined it was Billy, and that made her get up and run to the wall, too. The girl was in the water with just her head poking out, a determined look on her face. The people on the nearest barge were pointing and laughing. Filming.

Don't just stand there, said Orla's voice. *Rescue the poor girl!*

Rachel thought that the look on the girl's face was the expression of someone who was being instructed by a voice in her head. She knew that the voices told children to do things they didn't want to do. She imagined the little girl telling the voice she didn't want to jump into the river, but being compelled to do it anyway. She had the same expression Billy had when things were bad.

Rachel hadn't been able to save Billy when the voice had taken control of him. She could, however, save this girl.

Rachel didn't realize she was going to do it until she was flying through the air and then landing in the water. In fact it wasn't deep, and it hurt her legs when she landed, but then she was able to wade in (it was very smelly, she noticed, with lumps floating around) and she reached the girl easily.

"Hello," she said.

"Who the fuck are you?" The girl was already striding back toward the shore. She was older than Rachel had thought, closer to Nina's age. "You owe me chocolate!" the girl shouted at someone.

"My name's Rachel. Are you OK?"

"Yeah."

"Why did you jump in?"

The girl shrugged. "A bet. I wanted his chocolate. Why did you?"

"To rescue you."

The girl laughed. "You're a crazy lady."

"Did you have a voice telling you to jump?"

"Yeah. Ahmed's voice." She pointed.

It was there in her eyes, though. Rachel could see it. She thought she could see it.

"I understand about the voices," she said. "My son hears one." But then the teacher was there, standing on the wall from which they had both jumped.

"Jamelia," he shouted, "what the hell did you do that for?" He glanced at Rachel and looked away. "Also, don't speak to strangers."

"*Excuse me.* I was trying to rescue her."

He laughed, and Rachel realized how stupid she looked, knee-deep in filthy water, intent on saving a child who had never wanted or needed to be rescued. A child who had jumped into the water to win a bet and get someone's chocolate, because that was the kind of stupid thing people did.

Rachel stood on the pavement, her bottom half drenched with filthy water, and she was so shaken and felt so stupid that she didn't think she could possibly go back to work.

But she remembered the scratchy carpet, the tiny rooms, the oppression of knowing that she was the property of a corporation and so was her baby, and she knew she had to. She looked down at her skirt: even if she could manage to stay behind a desk all afternoon, she wouldn't be able to pretend nothing had happened, because her clothes below the waist had an overpowering stench to them, quite apart from the fact that they were soaking wet and uncomfortable.

She was supposed to be back at work in twenty minutes. This was it. She could either give up or she could find somewhere to buy a skirt and new tights and shoes. And she could go back to work and get on with it.

Billy was in hospital and heading for prison, and Mum was dead. They lived in worklifeplus: the humiliation of that, particularly for Al, made her want to throw herself into the river all over again.

She looked through her bag, checking for her purse, making sure she had the credit card (even though she knew she definitely did), and then she found something else. There, at the bottom of her bag, was a piece of green paper.

It was a medical prescription. She stared at it. It had her name on it, and their old address. It was signed by Dr. Singh.

And then she remembered. Right at the start, when the worst thing Billy had done was flying at Mum because of chocolate, Dr. Singh had suspected the whole thing was a problem with Rachel's anxiety.

Anxiety medication might be just the thing.

. . .

She used the credit card to buy a skirt, a pair of tights, and some horrible shoes made of plastic that dug into her feet and made them feel as if they were bleeding straightaway. She asked if she could change into it all as soon as she'd bought it. Then she wrapped her old clothes and shoes in the paper bag her new stuff had come in and stashed them in her handbag, because she certainly couldn't afford to throw them away. There was a laundry somewhere at their new home.

She found a pharmacy a couple of doors down and paid for her new tablets. The pharmacist told her to take one a day, at the start of the day, and to go back to her GP after three weeks to get the next prescription. She nodded. She would do it.

Rachel got back to her desk fifteen minutes late, hoping that she didn't smell of river water, and spent the afternoon pushing pieces of paper around while the sun shone hotly into the office. She got everything done, and it was very boring, but she got away with it. She stayed an extra fifteen minutes at the end of the day, to be scrupulously fair.

"See you tomorrow," said the nice woman on reception as Rachel left on the dot of five forty-five.

FORTY-ONE

Beth had again had a wonderful time at nursery, and she grinned and speed-crawled over when she saw her mother arrive, then sat on the floor in front of her and lifted her arms, shouting, "Mama!" That made Rachel feel better, and she held both of Beth's hands and walked behind her, letting her stagger back up the road to the flat. They made slow progress, but it wasn't far. The sun had gone in, and it was improbably cold now, but Beth didn't care and neither did Rachel, really.

Every building on this street was part of Starcom. Every person here worked for them, and all the children went to their nurseries and then, Rachel had recently discovered, their primary school. She had broken the rules, in spirit if not by the letter, by doing a day's work out in the real world, and she found she wanted to break more and more and more of them. She wasn't going to be a drone. Today's job was scheduled to last two days, and after that there would be other offices to visit, more places to go. Her first law lesson was on Monday. She felt, all of a sudden, that she might be able to do this. The medication was in her bag; she would take her first pill tomorrow. It might work.

The flat hadn't got any bigger since this morning, and she couldn't bear to go downstairs to the bigger kitchen, where names were taped to cupboards and where people were (she was sure) fiercely proprietorial about their packets of noodles and their milk in the fridge. Instead she made herself a cup of tea and sat down to breastfeed Beth.

Nina had been at Henry's all week, and she wasn't coming home until Sunday. It was very quiet. She missed her with all of her heart, and she missed Billy more than that. She was a bit hazy about how her potentially earning money would pull him out of hospital (she knew she was missing the part where Delfy disappeared), but she knew she had to try. You could do more things when you had money in the bank than you could without it.

Beth finished quickly and pulled away, twisting around, asking to be put on the floor. Beth, Rachel thought, didn't mind being here at all.

Rachel was wondering what to make for dinner without going down to the kitchen when Al arrived home, still looking as corporate and unlike himself as he had in the morning. He kissed them both. Rachel noted that he looked as stressed as she felt.

"You smell nice," he said. "How was work?"

"It was OK." She couldn't tell him about her lunchtime adventure, though she would tell him about the medication later. "How about yours?"

He shrugged and made a clear effort to make himself look happier. "Fine! Chat bots are scintillating company. But it was all right. The time passed. Basically I'm a human doing a job that will ensure future humans don't get to have jobs."

"Drink? Tea or something else?"

He looked at her, then said: "That sounds nice. And I *do* have three tokens for drinks at the bar."

"Free?"

"Yep. Well—earned."

"Nearby?"

"Two streets away, I think."

. . .

The pub was called the Thirsty Centipede, and it wasn't a real pub at all. It was an old terraced house that had been repurposed, its ground floor stripped out and made into a bar area filled with Formica-topped tables. Rachel saw that Starcom had bought out many streets around here, and she wondered whether, if she could fast-forward twenty years, it would turn out that they owned the whole of London and everybody in it, and there wouldn't need to be elections anymore because Ben Alford would be their supreme ruler for life.

Beth was happy, gazing around at everyone. Rachel found her a high chair and sat her in it, handing her a cup of water, while Al went up to the bar.

She watched him, feeling the most intense romantic love she had felt in her life. He had done all this for her, for the family, and now she was doing what she could for him. He said hello to another man at the bar, exchanged a few words, laughed. He ordered three drinks and handed over three tokens, which were plastic, like gambling chips. It was the most infantilizing thing in the world.

She looked around at the other people; she had expected them to be blank-faced cult people, but they were just normal. Some were laughing. Some were arguing. A lot of them seemed as if they had been through hard times. They were all ages, a cross section of the poorer people in London.

And then Al was back, and it was just the three of them, the family within the family, and she and he were both drinking wine, while Al added a bit of juice into Beth's cup of water, an outcome of which she thoroughly approved. They said, "Cheers," and clinked their cups together, Beth smashing her plastic cup against theirs and giggling.

"So it was OK?" He read her face. "You are allowed to drink, you know, if you want to. It's only *you* who decided you had to be teetotal. Why do you smell different, by the way?"

"I brought some of Mum's soap from her flat. I'm using it instead of the stuff that's here. So, is this job going to be OK?"

"I guess." He put his head down on his arms and said, his voice muffled, "You know. It's still standard *first week at work* stuff. 'Where's the loo?' 'What are you talking about?' 'What do we do now?' 'Why are you doing this?' 'I don't understand this.' 'I don't know where this is.'" He raised his head and grinned at her. "I guess that's what your temp work is, isn't it? One long round of being new."

"I am a professional new girl," she said. "Yes. Fun!"

"This one, though," he said. "It's OK? And you'll start the retraining thing next week?"

"It's fine." She lowered her voice, knowing they were in a gray area here. "I reckon by the time Beth's three, I'll easily be able to rent us a place."

Al nodded. They stared into each other's eyes for as long as Rachel could manage before she remembered that she had to tell him something else. "And I've picked up some antidepressants," she said. "I had a prescription from ages ago. I just felt I needed them to be able to get through the days."

He took her hand. "Good idea," he said. "I wish I had some of them myself."

FORTY-TWO

There were three children loitering on Harley Street. The weather was warmer than it had been lately, and the small trees that had survived the winter were blossoming. Graham was vaguely pleased to see people outside, until he drew close to them. He stepped to the edge of the pavement, impatient to get past, but stopped when someone pulled his sleeve.

"You're Graham Watson," she said. He stopped and looked down. It was a little girl, perhaps ten or eleven years old. Close up, she looked tired and dirty.

He looked at the other two. They were boys of about the same age.

"Who are you?" he said. He hoped he was wrong.

"The other children," they said, speaking almost in unison. "We are the other children."

"Where are your parents?"

"We want to see your children. We need to go to them. Downstairs."

"Where do you live?"

"We need to see your children. We need to go to them. Downstairs."

"Look," he said. "You hear voices in your heads. Is that right?"

"We hear voices," said one of the boys.

"I can't take you in." He looked up and down the street, as if help might be there somewhere. Of course, it wasn't. "You really need to go home. Where are your parents? If you get your parents to speak to me, I'll do what I can to help. I'm interested in this, but this isn't the way to do it. Tell them to ring me." He fumbled in his pocket and found his card, which he handed to the girl. "I can't just take you in. For all kinds of reasons. It doesn't work like that."

They all frowned at him for a few seconds. Then they sat down on the steps to his building.

As soon as he got in, Graham called the police, who laughed and declined to come out to talk to some children who were sitting on steps in a public place, breaking no laws. He was unnerved, even more so when he went down to the ward and all the children rushed at him to complain.

"You have to let in the other children," said Anita.

"How did you . . . ?" He shook his head. They were not telepathic; he knew that logically. It felt like it sometimes. "Yes, there were some children outside who wanted to come and visit you. I have no idea who they are, but I can't let them in."

Suki looked up from her crochet. "Graham!" She was disappointed in him.

"We'd *love* it if they could come and visit," said Majid. "You wouldn't need to let them stay. Not straightaway."

"Yes," said Peter, who was attempting to join in the crochet fad, but who was terrible at it. He frowned and pulled his thread out of the hook.

"Look what I made," said Billy, who was hooking away and had made a coil of gray twine. "Like a spider."

"Like a spider!" said Louisa, and they all laughed and looked up at the ceiling. Graham looked, too, expecting a web, but there was nothing.

"Nice work, Billy, my man," said Kitty, coming into the ward behind Graham. "Spider boy!" She threw herself down on the beanbag next to him and handed over a whole load of crochet that she had made, too. Hers was black.

"Whoa, Kitty," said Louisa, wide-eyed. "You could stitch that together into the best spider ever."

When Graham left the office much later, the three children were still on the steps, but they had been joined by . . . He counted. Six more. There were nine children sitting there, and it was nearly dark.

"Graham Watson," they chanted as he passed them, but this time he didn't stop. He put his head down and walked as fast as he could.

FORTY-THREE

The job by the river ended, and Nadia McGovern called with another position on Friday morning. Rachel had been secretly hoping for a day off, particularly after her visit to Billy yesterday evening. That had been unnerving and she wanted to think about it. Yet at eight her phone rang.

"It's a tricky one," Nadia said. "I mean, they're absolutely desperate. They lost three people to the flu last year. Not lost *them*—I don't think—but people leaving to look after family members and not coming back. What I'm trying to say is . . ." She paused, took a deep breath, and said: "Could you work in a job that goes beyond secretarial work? They are absolutely desperate for someone to sort out a load of contracts, and it's going to last at least a couple of months. I mean, I'm not sure what because it's not my expertise, but you get the idea. I know you haven't even started your legal course yet, but you can wing it, right?"

"Yes," said Rachel. "I'll give it my best shot."

She knew Al was just about to leave, and she got up and shouted, "Al!"

Beth shouted her version of his name, and the two of them looked at each other and laughed.

Al came out of the bedroom, ready for work.

"I've got another job," she said, the words tumbling out over one another. "It's a good one. Admin but also contracts, even though I'm rusty. It's going to last a couple of months. Maybe more. I have to be there as soon as possible, in town, so I'll get ready right now and drop Beth off."

Al was grinning. "See?" he said. "You've got this. You're totally going to show them. Nail it. Good luck." He paused and then said: "Do it for Billy."

"Yes," she said. "When he's better, we'll have a home for him. Maybe outside London. Somewhere new. Somewhere quiet. Where you don't have to wear a purple blazer."

"Exactly," said Al. "Shall I drop Beth off?"

"She's not ready. Don't worry. I will."

He left, and soon afterward she did, too. She had dressed in her corporate clothes, but added her mother's spider brooch. Somehow it didn't freak her out anymore, and when she was wearing it, she felt she could do anything.

B eth scampered off as usual, the moment they reached the day care, crawling over to the book corner, grabbing a book and sitting down and opening it. When another child tried to take it out of her hands, she pushed the toddler away without even looking up, and he sat down suddenly, looking confused.

"You look smart," said one of the nursery workers, smiling at her. "Love the spider." Her badge said that she was called Natalie.

"Thank you," said Rachel. "First day at a new job!"

"Ooh," Natalie said. "Good luck. No uniform? Which division?"

She realized her mistake. "I'm not quite sure yet," she said. "It's more of a chat."

"Oh, right." Natalie raised her eyebrows and another young woman, walking past with a baby on each hip, paused, too, but didn't look round. "Well, good luck."

Rachel cursed herself. Why hadn't she just thanked Natalie for saying she looked smart and left it at that? Now she would have to worry that they had seen through her.

They couldn't have done, though; she hadn't really said anything.

Had she?

She left, feeling uneasy.

The job was in a part of North London that she had never visited before, just off a main road and next to a theater. The buildings were old warehouses, and the legal office was located between a radio station and a graphic design company. The windows were huge, the pot plants polished. It didn't feel like a legal office at all, and though she was so nervous she could barely speak, Rachel liked it and really, really hoped she would be good enough.

The five members of staff were so grateful to her for being there that she found herself reassuring them.

"Honestly," she said, "I'm grateful to *you* for having me. I've been wanting to get back into this. I need regular work, and I promise I'll work hard."

She was powered by coffee and desperation. They were powered by the terror of knowing that they had taken on more work than they could actually do. She was going to work as hard as she could until half past five. This time she didn't take a lunch break.

FORTY-FOUR

G raham had been on the phone to his son Nick for longer than he'd realized. He'd been so excited by the sincerity of the invitation to visit them in Australia that he'd asked question after question about their lives, and discovered all kinds of things he'd never imagined about his grandchildren, who had suddenly become three-dimensional people to him. None of them heard voices. He had been careful to establish that.

There were still children outside the building. He and Lauren pointed the police to them whenever they could, because whoever these kids were, and wherever they were coming from, they needed to go home. But when they saw the police approaching, they would scatter, and then soon they reappeared.

He was fifteen minutes late to the ward, and he always tried not to keep the kids waiting. He tapped out a rhythm on the lift's wall as he waited for the doors to open on level minus seven. He pictured himself just taking a holiday like a normal person and going off to visit his family.

Imogen had died, and he hardly even saw her ghost now. He wanted her to sit outside with the unnerving children and help him understand what was going on and what he should do, but she never did. She flitted around corners, smiling and vanishing at his approach. However, he had never appreciated that she lived on in their three sons and their seven grandchildren. It almost felt like magic: his children were half-made of Imogen! He had seen them being born from her body. They were his link to her. He heard her in things they said, in the way they laughed at him. And all those girls out there, the ones she had helped. She lived on in them, too. She had left an imprint on the whole wide world.

He was smiling as he went through security. He heard Kitty singing in the gym as he passed the door, and decided to pop in for a chat once he'd checked in with the giraffes. They really needed to work out a plan for her future.

The sign on the door had changed. That was the first thing he noticed. They had stuck a hand-drawn sign over the old giraffe one: now they were calling themselves "spiderlings," complete with decorative webs. He smiled. That, he supposed, was fine. It was nice to see them working together on something wholesome, even if they did all seem to be a bit obsessed with crochet and spiders right now.

He pushed open the door. He wasn't expecting anything unusual.

A t first it looked as if they had just decorated the room, perhaps for an unseasonal Halloween. They had used all the crocheting they'd been doing and twisted it together and stuck it all over the wall. They'd moved the TV off the wall to make space. All he saw, at first glance, was a tangle of silvery wool.

Actually, it was arranged into a tangled-web shape. And some of it looked like actual spiderweb. There were tiny creatures scuttling away, all heading for the games cupboard. Most of this web, though, was made from wool, with real cobwebs over the top.

And then he saw what they had caught in the web. Graham waited for something to happen, looked around for the other adults, wondered why no one had raised the alarm, but no one was there. There were six children in the ward. Five of them were sitting in a row, on beanbags, looking at him. He looked at each of their faces. There were Majid, Billy, Lulu, Suki, and Anita. Each of them was gazing at him with the same blank expression. Each of them was sitting at attention, straight-backed.

He took a small step away from them.

He looked at the web on the wall and tried harder to process what he was seeing. He knew, really. He just couldn't bear to acknowledge it. Instead, he looked around. This ward was heavily staffed. There should have been medical staff, hospital guards, and Louisa's bodyguards. They were always here: at least four people were on duty in this ward all the time.

How had they got rid of the adults? That was an easier question to tackle first. He looked around, because his feet wouldn't move. He saw four different bundles of webby cloth around the room, and even though he couldn't look at the wall, that made him move. He ran to the closest one and unwrapped it.

The real spiderweb stuck to his hands. The strands of wool were tightly tied, but he pulled them off, and managed in the end. Inside it all he found one of the nurses, and as soon as he took the strands from her mouth, she started to scream. He ran for the alarm and pressed it again and again. He unwrapped another bundle, and a furious bodyguard leaped to his feet and drew a gun. Footsteps approached, and then the room was full of people. The bodyguard was disarmed, and Graham found that he was sitting on a bed at the far end of the room while other people got on with things.

Only then was he able to look again at the web on the wall. He had seen at first glance that inside all of that, Peter was dead. He was tied up in crocheted web so tightly that his neck was broken. His eyes were bulging, and somehow real spiders had spun their webs across his face. As Graham watched, someone cut him down, and his tiny body was taken away.

"He was only pretending," said Louisa. "He was telling lies."

"We didn't want him," said Billy. "He told lies. He didn't belong."

Kitty was standing in the doorway.

"Oh, fuck, kids," she said. "Oh, fuck. What have you done? You are never getting out of here now, you stupid twats. I told you! How many times did I tell you not to do this? Oh, for Christ's sake, you stupid little bastards."

She sat on the floor and sobbed, and Graham found that he was crying, too. He had failed completely.

FORTY-FIVE

On Saturday morning Nina was walking around the roads near Dad's house, talking on the phone while life went on around her. She was wearing her running clothes and had her earbuds in, so she looked like everyone else. She did not look as if there was a desperate woman crying into her ear. The woman, Luni, had been overwhelmed to read Billy's story, because her daughter was experiencing the same thing. Nina was managing to follow up on only around one in ten messages; she had called this number back because the story had been so very much like Billy's.

"I know," Nina said. She was still finding this incredibly difficult emotionally. "I do know, Luni. I understand."

"But the things she says," said Luni. "We never had any trouble. Ekisha was a dream child, and then so sick, and then mercifully recovered, but she starts saying terrible things. She asks the most horrible questions about sex and worse. Like I said in the message. And then she took our car out and drove it to town and she hit a . . . an old woman. And crashed into a building." She paused, pulling herself together. "And they took her to the police station."

It went on. Luni was calling from a town called Mamallapuram in

Tamil Nadu, and her daughter was in trouble with the police, though she, at least, had been allowed home under strict rules. The stories were coming in from all over the world. Nina felt that she, Shelly, and Louis had unleashed a pandemic of their own. It was far bigger than they had expected it to be, and she was struggling.

Something had happened at the hospital. There was some kind of trouble. Nina didn't know what it was, but she had heard Dad on the phone sounding serious and saying: "If the family want it kept quiet, then that would be an immense relief for us." He hadn't told her what it was, but she gathered that Billy had been moved back into a single room and that all the other children were being separated, too.

The thing that was keeping Nina going was the realization that Delfy was turning out to be predictable. As she spoke to parent after parent, and their stories were all the same, she was finding that it changed everything. For the first time since this had started, she truly believed this wasn't Billy's fault. In among everything else, that was the most enormous relief.

There were patterns in all the stories. At least no one who lived in London had a car. They had been saved the horror of Billy and Delfy setting out on a road trip together, if nothing else.

"The thing is," Nina said when Luni had stopped talking, "you're not alone. You're really not. Even the part where she killed someone. I don't think it's even *unusual* for these kids."

"So it's not her fault?"

Nina's eyes filled with tears. "It's not her fault," she said. "It's not their fault. I really believe that now. It's happened to so many of them. The children become killers, and it's not their fault."

"Will there be a cure?"

"I don't know," Nina said. "This is going to sound like a weird question, but did you happen to be in London with her last year, when there was an explosion over the city?"

"No. Of course not. We don't have trips to London!"

. . .

By the time she had finished the call and checked that it had recorded properly, she was back at Dad's house. He was out cycling to Brighton with his friends, so she let herself in and disabled the alarm.

"Hi!" she shouted, knowing Dad wasn't there. She missed Billy and Beth and Mum and Al, and decided she'd go back to sleeping there to-morrow, and would just suck up the awful commute next week. Tonight, however, Dad thought she was staying at Mum's, Mum assumed she was here, and the two of them would definitely not speak to each other. There were no visitors allowed at the hospital this weekend because of this new crisis, so she had nowhere to go except Louis' house.

In her room, she changed into skinny jeans, a long-sleeved T-shirt, and a jumper. It was neutral, inoffensive, and she wanted to be as unobtrusive as possible at the Alfords'. She packed similar clothes into a bag, plus a dress for dinnertime, added all her toiletries, and set off.

She left a note to Dad that just said: *I've gone to Mum's. Back next week. I'll text xx.*

FORTY-SIX

Graham had moved into a single room on the minus-seventh floor, because this was critical. He was in a state of panic all the time. Every one of the families had demanded the murder be covered up, and Peter's parents were simultaneously wanting to keep it quiet and threatening a lawsuit. He felt he was walking through a nightmare. None of this (the hospital deep underground, the murderous children, the furious blank-faced children outside) could possibly be real. He longed for Imogen, but she wasn't there. Because she was dead.

It was his fault for underestimating this thing. He had allowed it to happen. A child was dead, and four adults were injured (not seriously, which was something), and he couldn't even tell the police.

And he had known! He knew what these children could do, because Suki had killed her nanny, and Billy his grandmother, and Kitty had killed her mother and tried to strangle her brother, and so on. They were here because they were dangerous. He had, all the same, underestimated them. He had given them the fucking wool.

He had moved each of the children into a separate room, and assigned each one of them a security detail. They didn't have as much power separately (he hoped). For now he just held them in individual cells, firmly tethered to the frames of the beds so they couldn't travel farther than a meter or two, and he'd stopped all their medication because he thought it made them worse. Only Kitty could move around freely now, and she spent most of her time with Billy. The two of them had bonded.

None of the kids was happy with Graham. They looked at him with terrifying expressions. His little room was around the corner from theirs, and he had not slept well. He had not slept.

He got up at six, pleased to be upright and busy. After checking that all the staff had survived the night, he got a coffee from the nurses' station and started an early round. He was scared of them. They were children, and he couldn't control them. They were freaking him out, and he had no idea what to do.

He started with Louisa.

"Everyone thinks I'm dead," she said as soon as she saw him. "But they used to visit, and now they're never going to come and see me again, are they? Because of Peter. It's like Kitty. We're going to be like Kitty, and we're going to grow up here, and no one will ever see us again." She shook her head, twitched a bit. "It wasn't my fault! I didn't want to do it!"

"I know you didn't," said Graham.

Her whole body was spasming. He put a hand on her shoulder, and her bodyguard stepped forward. She had new ones now; the others had quit.

"What's going on?" Graham said.

In spite of Blob's prosaic name, he was one of the more difficult presences Graham had encountered. Blob didn't ask specific questions or try to find things out. Instead he was obsessed with language and often made Louisa speak in a freewheeling stream of consciousness.

Louisa pressed her temples. "Horrible. He's . . ." She paused as her entire body jerked. "He's wanting to take over me. Don't!" She shouted the last word, though not to Graham. "Stop it! You can't do it! You are not allowed to do this again! We are not going to kill Graham!"

Graham pressed the EMERGENCY button and stepped out into the corridor.

"Can I have some help?" he shouted.

Two nurses rushed into the room, and he saw that other staff was rushing to other rooms. All the children were doing this at once. He stood on another threshold and looked in at Billy, who was being restrained by two adults, who could only just contain him. A policewoman pushed past and went in. The children were fighting off anyone who went near them, and although it was barbaric, Graham was intensely relieved that they were all tethered.

"Graham!" It was Louisa screaming. He went back to her room. She was pushing the nurses away. She was trying to talk to Graham, but she was being drowned out by the thing inside her.

"Help!" she shouted. "No!"

She scratched and punched and bit her way away from a nurse, a slight woman who looked at Graham and then walked backward out of the room. He stepped in but didn't get close enough for Louisa to reach him. Her bodyguard took her. This was a huge ex-army man, and tiny Louisa, on her own, stood no chance.

"I hate you, I hate you, I hate you!" Louisa shouted as the man shortened her tether so she couldn't even move from the bed, and it wasn't clear to Graham whom she was talking to.

Knowing Louisa was contained, he ran down the corridor to check on everyone. Majid, the tallest by far, was in the grip of one of the ex-army guys Graham had just hired. Suki and Anita were raging at the farthest extent of their leashes, but they weren't able to reach anyone.

Billy was in police handcuffs. *They must,* Graham thought, *have found some smaller ones after all.*

The children's faces all had the same expression on them. Contorted, furious.

"We are not strong enough," Majid was shouting to the other children. All the doors were open, so they could all hear him. "This isn't working."

"Not strong enough," echoed the others.

They were trying to come together to make a group, but they couldn't. None of them could go anywhere.

"We must wait," said Billy in a strange, strangled voice. "Billy's sister will help."

Billy had spoken about himself in the third person; this was Delfy.

Someone shouted from down the corridor, and when Graham looked up, he saw that the children from outside had somehow appeared down here. They were running toward him. He was so scared that he found himself leaning back against the wall and summoning Imogen. They should not have been able to get in, but they were here. There were lots of them. Maybe fifteen. It was too much for the adults to handle.

"You guys!" It was Kitty at his side.

He looked round. Imogen was on his other side. She took his hand, and her energy shot through him. He took a deep breath.

"You!" Kitty pointed at each of them in turn. "You behave, OK? No messing with Graham. He is a sound dude."

"Graham." They all said that together, all standing in their doorways, with the street children standing in rows in the corridor like a choir. All their eyes were on him. And they carried on speaking, the new kids and the old ones. "Graham, we are going to stop. These bodies are not strong enough. We could kill you all and get out, but the people out there would lock us up again. We won't do it. You can let us go now."

He had been trying to talk directly to the voices for months but had only had odd flashes of them here and there. Now they were addressing him and all together, which meant, as the kids often said, that the voices could talk to one another without going through the children. He had known that really, and he had known that they could take over the children's bodies. They had done it to kill Peter.

"Do you mean to say," he said, pleased to see from the corner of his eye that one of the nurses had started filming, "that you are going to stop controlling your hosts? And you're saying I can let the children go? Billy's sister is trying to help—you're right. But she's not trying to help you. She's trying to help the children."

"Yes," said twenty voices. "We will stop."

He turned to the street invaders. "I'm not talking to you. I'm talking to the children under my care." He looked at his five children in turn. "You do see," he said, "that I can't possibly let you go. You killed Peter. I was responsible for his safety, and you killed him. Imagine what that's done to his parents. You hurt four adults. You five children have murdered people. I can't let you go. Imagine if I did."

Imogen was nodding, next to him. She was right there, but he couldn't see her. He just felt her.

"But the voices will stop. The children will not kill again."

"Where will the voices go?" he said. No one answered so he tried a different question. "What will you, the voices, be doing?" he said.

At that, they all said one word. All twenty of them. "Waiting."

They kept saying it, so it became a chant.

"Waiting," said Majid.

"Waiting," said Suki.

"Waiting," said Billy, and Anita, and Louisa.

"Waiting," said the strange choir.

Their voices merged into one.

"Waiting. Waiting. Waiting. Waiting. Waiting."

Graham didn't know what to do. Neither did any other adult. They just stayed where they were and stared. No one could move.

The children chanted until, at some unspoken signal, they all stopped. The street children looked around as if they were seeing their surroundings for the first time, wide-eyed. They exchanged glances, scared. Everything about them was different.

"Can we go, please?" said a girl with plaits. They were escorted off the premises extremely quickly; it turned out they had got in by overpowering the security upstairs, finding the emergency stairs in the entrance hall, and breaking through a pane of glass in the fire door so they could clamber through and forgo the impossibility of trying to open it. It was a loophole that Graham would fix. How ridiculous to have that much security on a door that had a glass panel in the middle of it.

After that, Graham found that none of the voices wanted to talk to him anymore, and all the children relaxed and laughed and told him how happy they were. They barely even remembered the things they had done. Occasionally one of them would ask where Peter was. It was, he realized, as if the voices in their heads had vanished just like that, all at once.

He didn't believe it. He couldn't. He could not trust this.

FORTY-SEVEN

Nina and Louis were sitting on his bed, leaning back on the headboard, looking at Louis' state-of-the-art laptop. Their thighs were touching all the way down, and in spite of everything, Nina loved that. The fact that they were sitting on a bed made her tingle.

"I've plotted it on a map," said Louis, and he brought up a global map that was studded with red dots. They were everywhere, but with some noticeable clusters. "It's not completely up-to-date, but I pretended to be sick so I could come home early this afternoon, and I used everything we had at that point. We haven't heard from places that don't have good Internet. Other than that, let's first of all overlay this with the map of the flu." He clicked a few things, and shading appeared over the map, covering every red flag. "Unsurprisingly, there are more cases in places where the flu was most severe. Big cities were worst hit, and London and a couple of other spots disproportionately so. Then here it goes across Europe, but it really is much more in London than anywhere else. Is London the biggest city in Europe? It could be that? Then if you look elsewhere . . . For example, the only Delfy we've heard about from the whole of the continent of Africa is in South Africa."

"That's odd, isn't it?" said Nina. "I mean, it's a massive continent. We've got loads in Asia."

"But look at where in Asia." Louis enlarged it. "Japan. South Korea. India. Singapore. No one at all in Southeast Asia, hardly anything in China, and only three in India. Whereas there are absolutely loads in Japan, and half of them are in some city up north. Sapporo? I mean, I've heard of that because it's the name of a beer, but why? It's a fraction the size of Tokyo. And look at the US. Plenty in the cities, sure, but look at this." He tapped a spot at the left of the map where there were several dots overlapping one another. "I mean, where the hell is Burley, Idaho, and why do they have so many kids with voices in their heads?"

"Could it just be that someone is telling people about our blog?"

"Could be."

Nina looked at her e-mail: six more had come in since she had last checked.

D inner was served in a huge, shiny dining room. It felt much more formal than the previous time she had eaten here—there were several knives, several forks, wineglasses, water glasses, and linen napkins, just as there would have been, she thought, in an expensive restaurant. Nina felt uncomfortable as she sat down, even though no one else was in the room.

The door opened, and four people came in and, copying Louis, Nina stood up to greet them. There were Elena, Ben, Harvey, and another man who came in behind them. This man was familiar, and at first Nina thought she must already know him from space cadets or something.

A second later, she realized that she knew his face from news reports, and then from endless, endless adverts.

"Ah, Nina," said Ben Alford. "Nina Stevens, Louis' girlfriend. This is Guy Clement. Guy, Nina. Nina, Guy."

Somehow she was shaking hands with the man who was leading the space program. The man who had inspired her and then annoyed her. She shot a look at Louis to see whether he had known that Guy would be here, but then she realized that of course he had known.

Louis saw her looking. "You know you're part of the family," he said, "when you get to meet our houseguest."

Guy Clement was taller than she would have expected, and he was nearly bald, with what hair he did have shaved right off. His face was folded in on itself, as if his nose and chin were trying to meet each other, an effect that was more pronounced in real life. She knew astronauts weren't chosen for their looks. When he opened his mouth, she expected him to urge her to buy a bar of Rockolate for a taste that was out of this world.

Instead he said: "Nina! Delighted to meet you. A new human! *Quel* treat."

"Thanks," said Nina. "Um. It's amazing to meet you. Surprising."

"Like Louis says, you're part of the family now, Nina," said Elena. She turned to Guy. "Separate rooms when the boys have girlfriends over," she said, and looked back to Nina. "Mathilde has put you in the yellow room, I think?"

"That's right." There were so many spare bedrooms here that they were distinguished by color. The yellow room was beautiful, with a double bed, an en suite bathroom, and fresh flowers. "Thank you," she added, realizing she was looking rude. "It's lovely of you to let me stay."

"And me, too!" said Guy with a chuckle. "I'm in the green room. Like when you're waiting to go on telly."

"It's teal," said Elena.

"Well," said Ben, "you would know about the telly, Guy. Nina, I understand that things at your home are complicated, and we're happy to help."

She wondered whether he knew where she lived and who her brother was. How many people in this room knew that Nina's brother was imprisoned underground with Ben's murderous daughter? She said, in as neutral a voice as she could: "They are sometimes, yes. It's difficult out there when you don't have money."

"Oh, isn't it, though?" said Guy. He leaned forward. "I'm from Northumberland. Right up by the checkpoint. You probably know that already because they've made me monetize that along with every other bloody thing. We grew up without two farthings to rub together. It was bad then, and it's ten times worse now. I make sure my family want for nothing now. It's the least I can do."

She thought that perhaps he actually did understand. "Is that why you became an astronaut?" she said. "To make a new life in a new world for the future?" She winced at her own trite words.

He laughed. "Nothing as intelligent as that, dear Nina. More like: worked hard at school to get out of there, and then kept working because at every point I wanted to move on to the next thing. Never had any grand plan. Trained as a pilot. Next thing I knew we were colonizing space, and it was 'Hands up, who wants to be considered for the space program?' I was like this." He put his hand up like a child at school, making a show of reaching for the ceiling. "Right time, right place. Now, BA here said you're in the space program. That's great, great stuff. It's the future. I think I'm booked in to come and have a chat to your gang at some point."

"Are you?" Nina could picture the course calendar. At the end of the summer there was a session marked "special guest." Now she knew who it would be. "August?"

"Yes, I think so. Well, at least I'll know someone! Friendly face."

Nina glanced at Louis. His secret would be revealed when Guy came to talk to them. He wasn't reacting.

Guy Clement made this dinner far more enjoyable for Nina than she had expected it to be. The food was (of course) nice: tomato salad, grilled fish with fondant potatoes and green vegetables (with a lentil thing for Nina instead of the fish), and then crème brûlée for pudding. It was the sort of food you saw on telly, on the programs that Mum used to watch when she was home with Beth before her life got too stressful and sad for her ever to relax. Before she lived in a place where you had to negotiate the TV watching with everyone else who lived in your building.

"Nina, you have no idea how lovely it is to have a girl around the place," said Elena, bestowing a gleaming smile on her. "I'm so outnumbered usually! Oh, my goodness, the great clodhopping boys with their massive feet."

Louis winced. Ben Alford looked away. Nina was pretty sure she wasn't the only one thinking of Kitty.

"Well, thank you," she said. "I feel very lucky."

"Me, too," said Guy.

Harvey leaned forward. "Guy," he said, "are you able to tell us about the upcoming announcement? Just between these four walls."

There was a sudden silence. Nina didn't know what was going on, so she waited it out.

Then Guy laughed. "How about it?" he said, looking at Ben and then at Elena. "It'll be out there soon enough."

Ben shrugged and looked hard at Nina. "Go on, then," he said.

"Well, Nina," said Guy. He looked at Ben. "Have you got it? If you say you haven't, I won't believe you."

Ben nodded. "Mathilde?" he said. Mathilde sprang to attention. He put his hand out and she, knowing somehow what he wanted, put the VR headset into it. BA passed it to Nina.

"This is why we're doing it," said Guy. "Our best simulation of life on Earth Two. Enjoy."

She put it on.

She was standing on a rock, looking around. The sky above her was the deepest blue. The sun was low down in the sky, and off to her right, there was another sun, too, behind her. She was casting two shadows.

The land in front of her stretched away to the horizon. There were plants growing there. She tried to step forward, but of course she was sitting at the dinner table and she didn't have a controller, so she leaned down instead and saw that the plants were wispy pink things. She could hear the wind blowing all around her, and smell something fresh and sweet.

"Look behind you," said Guy quietly. "Here."

He helped her stand up, and with his hands on her shoulders, she turned around. What she saw made her gasp: it was an expanse of water that stretched away as far as she could see. It glittered in the light of the suns, and it was bright green, like the sea used to be.

She couldn't speak. This was everything. It was overwhelming. She was standing here now, in virtual reality, and she could be in the same place herself in a few years' time.

Guy's hands (she supposed they were his, anyway) guided her back to her seat, and she took the headset off.

"Oh, my God," she said. "That was . . ." She had to stop talking and wipe her eyes. It was too much. "That's real?" she said in the end.

"Real," said Guy.

"When?"

"We'll be setting off before long," he said. "Or rather you will. I'm too old. I'll bow out. But I'm doing my bit now. I've . . . Well, I'm here, living with the lovely Alfords for a while, because before that I spent three months up on the Rock. Staying here is my halfway house to normality." He looked around and laughed, along with Harvey and Louis.

"The Rock?" This was hard to compute. "The *asteroid*? But it's only just been captured."

"It was captured a long time ago," he said. "It's at a libration point right now. You can totally see it if you know where to look."

Nina knew about libration points. They were places where the Earth and moon gravities exerted exactly the right amount of force to keep something in place. If the Rock had been pulled to a libration point, and if it was being staffed and equipped up there, that was enormous news. She subtracted years from her imagined timeline.

"And we set off from there?" she said. "To go to . . . *there*?"

He looked at her and smiled. Even BA was laughing, and not, she thought, in a mean way.

"Oh, Nina." Guy looked around the table. "Isn't she exactly what we need? This is our future. It was the most incredible privilege to be one of the first to be there. Yes. That's what we're all about now."

She stared at him. She thought about the pink field, the green sea, and the new home, and every part of her longed for it. She tried to remind herself that the last time Ben Alford had shown her something on one of his headsets, it had been a lie. He had shown her a spacious flat that smelled of coffee and sounded like birdsong, and the reality was a tiny place that smelled like feet and sounded like traffic.

Nonetheless she was rapt. "What was it like up there?" she said.

Guy looked her in the eye and said: "I am the luckiest man who has ever lived. The only man who has stepped onto an asteroid. I'm too old to go farther, but I'll always be the man who stood there and said, 'Yes, we can build a transit base here.' It's a total shift in the human experience. If you're on the ship when it leaves, that's even more immense. And your great-grandchildren: Earth will just be a myth to them. An origin story."

"Were there others there with you?" she asked.

"Aki and Terri."

Nina nodded. "What did you do up there?"

"Gravity is OK. Not so different from the moon. We got the beginnings of the structure for the spaceport up and running. It's a pretty small place, but you know what, Nina? It's going to work. All the criteria were met. It was cold, cramped, terrifying, and I'd go back in a heartbeat."

"Who's next?"

He smiled. "Engineers. Lots of them. There's a fuckload of work to do, and they're there doing it right now. Then it'll be you, Nina. Though we can't take anything for granted. We *were* the first, yes. But we weren't meant to be. The initial mission went wrong, and we lost the crew. As you know, that can happen at any stage."

"Oh, my God!"

BA interjected. "And this is why it has to be done on the quiet for now. Morale."

"Yeah," said Guy. "Keeping it quiet was BA's idea, and it was a good one. It was time to send humans, and the second set of us made it."

"Why did the first one go wrong?"

"They set off from Norway," he said, looking down. "A year ago. It was just one of those tiny faults. A faulty seal, not unlike on the *Chal-*

lenger, combined with unusual cold. A little thing that gets amplified and then disaster."

"Eat up, you windbag," said BA, nodding to the food. Nina looked down and realized she had hardly eaten a thing. She started shoveling it into her mouth.

"I wanted to tell you Guy was here last time you came," said Louis. "But Mum said I wasn't allowed to. We're good at secrets, and this was definitely a secret."

"Of course," said Elena, "we have to meet and vet people before we can take them into our confidence. But you're part of the family now, Nina, dear."

The conversation turned to other things, much as Nina wanted to talk to Guy without stopping. She reminded herself that he appeared to be living here and that she would be able to talk to him tomorrow, too, if all went well. When there was a lull, however, she managed to ask him why he wasn't going to travel to the new planet, given that he wasn't actually *that* old, and he answered evasively.

"I'm forty-eight," he said in the end. "I've had my chance. Astronauts have always been older. That's a mistake we repeated for years and years and years. We made people have experience as fighter pilots, engineers, you know, before they were allowed to do this. Now we don't have that luxury. We need young people. That's why we've started training you folks. Soon they'll start the academy, and that will take people full-time from sixteen. We need a lot of highly trained youth for the colony ship."

"Colony ship?" she said. She caught glances being exchanged, and then Guy stopped answering.

FORTY-EIGHT

When they were on the dessert, Nina tried to approach it again.

"How have Aki and Terri felt about being back?" she said, smashing the top of her crème brûlée with her spoon. "They're hiding out, too?"

"Yep," Guy said. "We're each of us somewhere very secure to decompress. It took all of us a while to get back on our feet. We're being monitored intensively. I'm wearing all the technology there is, even though it might not look like it. It took longer than expected to be up and about again. But clean bills of health all around in the end, pretty much. You know, the human body is an incredible thing. It recalibrates to life in space, and you feel it happening. Gravity is different, and so is pressure, and you adapt. Painfully. Then it takes a while to switch back. But I think we're pretty much there." He winced.

"And they're at home in . . . Tokyo? And . . . New York?" She was pretty sure those were their hometowns.

Guy shook his head. "Aki's with family just outside Sapporo, in the north of Japan. Keeping her head down. She's the opposite of me. Classy. She doesn't even do the ads, not one single one, on principle. I thought the path of least resistance was to embrace it. Even if I did make myself look a bit of a plonker."

Normally Nina would have had plenty to say about the advertising, but all she could think was *Sapporo*.

"And Terri?" she said, knowing before he said it what the answer would be. "Where is she?"

"Oh, she's hiding out, too. Small town in one of those states. My American geography isn't very good, I'm afraid, and I can't quite remember. Hiding out in a house they've rented for her in the back of beyond, with her husband."

"Is it . . . ," said Nina. "Is it, by any chance, in a place called Burley in Idaho?"

Harvey laughed a quick bark. No one else said anything, and the seconds ticked by.

"How the hell did you know that?" said Guy. "Yes. It is. That's the one."

Louis kicked her under the table, and she wished she'd thought before speaking. Still, she needed to know.

"Oh," she said. "Probably something I read about her online."

She finished her pudding quickly, trying to look grateful and polite.

The three ground zeros of voices on the map—London, Sapporo, Burley—were, indisputably, the hideouts of the three astronauts. And that was just with the data Nina had so far. All those places had had heavy concentrations of flu, and voices.

Delfy, she knew, had come from the flu. The J5X virus.

And the J5X virus had come from the asteroid.

Guy Clement had been to space and brought a pandemic back with him. No wonder he was being kept in isolation. If she knew it, other people must know it, too. She knew that the adults at the dinner table must be perfectly well aware of all of it. They just weren't going to talk about it because they didn't want to damage the space program.

And neither, Nina thought, did she. She was compromised, just like that.

She finished eating too quickly, because she was desperate to talk to Louis in private. Then she had to make the last spoonful last for ages while everyone else caught up. Elena asked Mathilde to bring coffee and herbal teas, and Guy put a box of special superelite Rockolates on the table.

"Jesus Christ, Guy," said Ben, taking three at once, "even I feel this is overkill."

Guy shrugged, but he kept looking at Nina. He would look at her, look away. Look and look away when she met his eyes.

We need to pull back a bit," Louis said, back in his room. "This is getting weird."

She sat on the bed, and he took a chair and leaned back like his dad. He had never been distant with her before.

"You mean the Burley, Idaho? Yes, sorry. I wasn't thinking. I gave away too much by knowing that. But the VR. It blew my mind. Have you seen it?"

"Of course I have." Louis was staring at the ceiling, talking in a tight voice. "You won't tell anyone about the first mission? I don't want us to damage the space program. Or make Dad and Guy look bad. I mean, I'd be acting against my own interests."

"I'm not trying to damage anything!" She was indignant. "Look at me! I'm just interested to meet this, like, *super-famous astronaut* who is hiding in your house. I really liked him in real life. And . . ." She looked at him. "You must admit, it looks like they brought back the virus, whatever it really is, from the Rock. I mean, they did, didn't they? It's space flu. No wonder it's weird. No wonder it messes with people's heads."

Louis sighed. "I wish we'd never started this. I had no idea. I knew

Guy had been on some secret mission, but he does that all the time. They never tell me anything. They still think I'm a little kid. Maybe I'll tell them I do Space Skills, just to see their faces."

"You should." She didn't care.

"I wouldn't have joined in with the Billy stuff at all if I'd had any idea it was related. I was interested because it sounded like the stories Aunt Imogen used to tell me about my sister. I didn't know it was anything to do with the space program. And you know what? If the flu came from the asteroid, well, they *know* that. Or do you think it's just us, the little Scooby-Doo kids, who have put it all together? They'll sort it. That's why it's kept quiet, so the teething problems can be fixed."

"It is not a fucking teething problem! Millions of people have died. My brother was almost one of them. And that was only stage one. My baby brother is in a secure hospital! He's going on trial for murder, and it's because of a virus your friend brought back from outer space."

"Guy's your friend, too," said Louis. "Or you were certainly acting like it."

"What?"

He did an impression of a girlish voice, twisting his hair around a finger. "Oh, Guy," he said. "Please. Tell me more!"

"Stop it! I was not flirting!"

Louis sighed and looked deflated. "I know," he said quietly. "I'm not really saying you fancy him. I know it was a surprise. And I do know that he's impressive in real life."

"So," said Nina. "All that time I've sworn at his stupid adverts. All along. You knew he was . . ." She was unexpectedly taken over by laughter. "He was living in your house?"

Louis giggled, too, but nervously. "I did want to tell you," he said. "I just couldn't. You know I couldn't. I wasn't allowed."

Nina nodded. She had had more to drink this evening than she usually did, but all the same, her head was clear. She was right here, in the inner circle, and she knew what she had to do. This right now was where she had to stop confiding in Louis. She could not let this opportunity go to waste. From here on in, she was alone. She yawned ostentatiously, wanting to get away.

Louis raised his eyebrows. "You OK?"

"Yep," she said, realizing she must have looked strange. "Sorry. I was just remembering all over again that Guy Clement is downstairs. That's so weird. Also I thought he was an idiot, but now I don't. I can see that if you realize you've caused a worldwide pandemic on a par with the Black Death, you might distract yourself by making adverts."

Louis smiled his lazy smile and came over to sit next to her. He put an arm around her. "Yeah," he said. "Sorry that I got defensive. I was just . . . Well, I guess I know all the problems with my parents. I know how weird it all is. But I still can't help being their son. You know?"

"I know," said Nina. "You do brilliantly. Harvey toes the line, doesn't he?"

"He sure does. He works for Dad. He does whatever he's told because he kind of likes it that way."

"And . . ." Nina thought she might as well try it. "Your sister. Katherine. Kitty. That *is* her, isn't it, in Graham's place?"

"I'm sure it is. From what I've pieced together—all from the things Auntie Imogen used to say—she got really sick when she was small. Like, meningitis, something like that. I think Dad left her mum when Katherine and Harvey were both about two. She used to come over and visit us. Obviously massively awkward, but after she was ill, and then recovered, she was different. Auntie Immy's stories were so like the things you said about Billy. She was scary. She wasn't in control. She . . ." He stopped and put a hand to his throat. "This purple patch here? It's not a birthmark. When I was a baby, she tried to strangle me. Was doing quite well at it, but they caught her in time. She left her mark on me. That's why Mum refuses to have her anywhere near. She cast her out of the family, and that will never change.

"And so, when Billy and those other kids started doing the same kind of things . . . Well, it's a bit odd, isn't it? Because with my sister, it can't be space flu. It must be something different, something coincidental. When she wasn't allowed to come and visit us here anymore, it was just her and her mum. Anna. I never met Anna, because Katherine killed her when she was six. She strangled her."

Nina wasn't as surprised as she should have been to hear this, because she'd spoken to far, far too many families with the same story lately.

"That's what they do," she said. "But it was thirteen years too early."

Nina had never felt this close to Louis, but she had to make a choice. In fact she had already made it. This wasn't his fault, but she couldn't give up, because giving up on this would mean giving up on Billy.

As she kissed him good night, she wanted to cry. She knew that this might be the end for them (it might not, though!), and so, on impulse, she said: "I love you."

And Louis—gorgeous, funny Louis, surely the only boy she would ever, ever love—whispered, "I love you, too."

FORTY-NINE

Nina had set her alarm for two, but in the end, she didn't need it because she didn't go to sleep. There was too much in her head. Nina knew she could not let tonight's opportunity pass her by, because it might be her only chance, and so she was going to do this without Louis. She had a choice to make. She was going to sacrifice her relationship and choose Billy.

One thing Louis had said stuck in her head: "I'd be acting against my own interests." That was the key: he was an Alford. That was why she had to do this alone. She couldn't ask him, because she already knew the answer.

She put on socks, to make her footsteps as muffled as possible, and the pink dressing gown that had been hanging up in the room. The dressing gown had big pockets, and she put her phone in one of them.

She crept out of the room and down a dark corridor, away from the rest of the house. This was a spooky place after dark (spooky during the day, but worse now). There was a little flight of stairs that Louis called "the back stairs," and she almost fell down them because they were so polished and her socks were so slippy, but she caught herself by grabbing the banister and carried on going, slowly this time, stopping with both feet on each step every time.

If her geography was correct, and she was pretty sure it was, then the room she wanted would be at the bottom of these stairs. She hoped Ben Alford wasn't one of those people who stayed up working all night or sat in his study drinking brandy and plotting with his astronaut friend. She imagined it was perfectly possible, but hoped that they would be doing it in a more comfortable room. If she ran into him, she would just have to make something up. It would be impossible for her to be in search of a glass of water, as her bedroom was well stocked with glasses and had its own bathroom, so she would have to pretend to be sleepwalking, or else lost on her way to Louis' bedroom. That idea made her blush in the dark. It would be mortifying, but it was probably the best she had.

She had thought all this through a hundred times before. She tried to calm her mind.

The door was in front of her, and she stopped and leaned on the wall to gather her courage. This was not only a risky plan; it was also a betrayal of the hospitality that the Alfords had extended to her. It was going against everything Louis had asked of her.

She appeared to be doing it anyway.

Every trail led back here to the Alfords. And now she was at the center of it all, in Louis' dad's office. Billy was going on trial for murder next year. There was no way Nina could turn back now. She had to prove that this came from space, that it wasn't Billy being bad, but that he was more of a victim than anyone.

Upstairs the house had smelled of floral scents from cleaning products and washing powder. Downstairs was different. Here she could smell books, leather, polished wood.

There was no light shining around the door. She tapped very quietly, just in case, and when nothing happened, she held tightly to the handle and pushed it.

What if Guy was in here? What if he thought Nina had come to seduce him? She shuddered. Louis' impression of her flirting, even if he had immediately retracted it, stung.

The door swung open. It didn't squeak. The room inside was dark.

She took her phone with a hand that was steadier than she had expected it to be, and turned on its torch. Now that she was here, she had better get things done. She remembered Louis saying that there wasn't much internal security here, that once you were in the house it was fine, and she hoped that was true.

She was standing in Ben Alford's private study, and she was alone. She closed the door and went straight to the safe. It was locked with an old-fashioned dial.

She stared at it for a while. She had expected something far more electronic, much more modern. At least she had a shot at cracking this one because you didn't need a fingerprint or the right face.

She had uncovered the family birthdays just in case, and tried them in various different orders, spinning the dial from one number to another and then another. She tried everything she could think of (translating the children's names into numbers, numerizing "Katherine"), but it didn't work.

She couldn't get into the safe. That was, of course, the whole reason people had safes. It was why, in old films, they used saws, or carried the whole safe off in the getaway vehicle. Still . . . there were plenty of other things in here.

She opened the desk drawer and looked through everything. Right at the back, she found a bunch of photographs held together with a paper clip. They were actual photos, on the sort of paper that photos used to be printed on, and the top one showed a little girl. She had blond hair and huge eyes, and she was looking at the camera with a serious expression. She was standing outside, in front of some trees, and she was wearing a big badge that read 2 TODAY on the front of her dress and holding a helium balloon.

Nina stroked the girl's cheek with her finger. This girl had the same solemn face and knowing eyes as Beth, but her bone structure was very Alford.

"Hello, Kitty," she said. She took off the paper clip and turned the photograph over.

Katherine Alford, it read in handwriting, and there was a date. Katherine's second birthday. She had still been well then. She had been an innocent victim of her stupid father's infidelity. Nina matched up the little girl in the picture with strange, impulsive Kitty in the hospital, and she knew that they were the same.

She tried the safe again, adding Kitty's birthday now that she knew it, but still, nothing worked.

She picked up a piece of paper from the desk with a phone number on it. 0948 2375 9495. She tried that.

The door swung open. She was looking at the inside of Ben Alford's safe. She had done it. His security had been rudimentary, after all. Louis was right. A code written on a piece of paper and left on the desk.

She pulled things out of the safe and photographed them indiscriminately. She saw that the papers inside were about the Rock and the spaceport and the "colony ship," and she photographed all of them, hundreds of pages. She found a bundle about the flu, and photographed all of that, noting as she did it that "J5X" was a meaningless name invented to cover the worrying truth that no one understood it at all. She found confidentiality agreements and information about Kitty, and she photographed it all, knowing that she didn't have time to stop and read anything.

She bundled every bit of it into an e-mail and sent it to Graham, Mum, and Shelly.

The door opened just as she was starting to think she might have got away with it. She was picturing her ascent of the stairs, her climbing back into bed. It would be, for a while, as if it had never happened.

But then a figure was standing in the doorway. She couldn't see who it was.

He could see her, though.

"Oh, Nina," said a man's voice. "I thought you might be here. You need to give me your phone right now."

FIFTY

Graham was sitting in his little room, drinking a small glass of Imogen's sherry. His mind was spinning. This never happened. People got better gradually. They did not announce that everything that had troubled them had gone, and they were now cured. And yet that appeared to have happened.

Those weird children had smashed their way in and then gone away. Had that really happened? Surely not.

His children had killed Peter. *That* had really happened, and he could not let them out. These children, like Kitty, were surely going to have to be here forever. They all seemed convinced that their voices had gone, but he could never, ever trust that. The voices had taken Peter with them. And that broke Graham's heart. It broke for solemn, terrified little Peter, and also for his killers.

He, Graham, had failed. He had failed utterly. He hadn't safeguarded his patients, hadn't even safeguarded his guards. He hadn't looked after anyone. He watched the CCTV footage of the attack again and again and again. He saw, from the cameras all over the ward, that the five of them had huddled together, each with an armful of crocheted strands. He watched them stitching it all together, pleased with the results, testing it on one another. He saw Majid lift his neck up, smiling, offering it, and Louisa and Billy draping the crocheted web around it, pulling it until Majid put his hands up to beg them to stop, all of them laughing.

And then they had done it—Suki and Anita working together on the nurses, Billy and Louisa on the guards, and Majid on Peter. They had got each one of them from behind, pulling the ropes quickly around their necks. Then they wrapped them, one by one, and came together to fix Peter into his place in the web.

And then the real spiders. The real spiders had swarmed out of the games cupboard and joined in. If he wasn't watching it with his own eyes, Graham would never have believed it. All the kids liked spiders, but now Graham saw some kind of unknowable reciprocal arrangement. The spiders had come to help. They really had. It was nightmarish, impossible.

They must have been planning it for ages. Kitty probably knew about it, even though she had vociferously disapproved. Graham had had absolutely no idea. He remembered Lauren getting all the crocheting materials. They had wanted knitting needles, but he had vetoed that. Then he had thought crochet hooks were harmless, without turning his thoughts to the wool that came with them.

Imogen was beside his bed. She sat on the chair beside him, and for the first time since she died, he thought her ghost was looking at him with love, and with pity.

"Graham," she said, "it wasn't your fault."

"It was! What can I do?"

"Nothing." He couldn't take his eyes off her. She was the only thing there was. He had hardly glimpsed her for ages, and now here she was. He drank in the sight of her.

"I can't keep them forever," he said. She was his moral compass, had always been his compass. He was adrift without her. Whatever she said, he would do.

"You don't need to," she said. "Peter's family isn't going to do anything. They're already telling people he died of the flu. They'll drop the lawsuit. They just want to be left alone. The families will pay off the staff. I know it's horrific, but you can't do anything except give the kids back to their families and let them deal with it. It's not the first time, is it? For any of them. You don't need to keep them."

"What about Kitty?" he whispered. He looked at Imogen's face, her beautiful face. She was wearing red lipstick, and her hair was sharp in the way it was when she came out of the hairdresser. He thought of Kitty. Hers was Voice Zero. It had come years and years before the others. He had no idea whether or not it was the same thing. Kitty couldn't and wouldn't go back to the Alfords. But she was an adult, and she needed to live in the real world.

"You're Kitty's family, Graham," Imogen said. "She can live with you. Or if you feel too old for all that, you can find her somewhere else. I can think of a family who might have her, if all goes well. But she's the only one who actually is your responsibility, because her mother is dead, her father's a wanker, her stepmother is chilling, and her aunt is also dead. I can't tell you how much I wish I wasn't."

Graham was crying. "Me, too," he said. "Oh, Immy, me, too."

FIFTY-ONE

Nina could hardly breathe. Her hand trembled as she moved her phone torch and turned it to shine on the person.

It wasn't Ben Alford. It wasn't Louis.

"Guy," she whispered. "I'm sorry. I can . . ." She had been about to say "explain," but had to stop as she plainly couldn't explain this in any way that didn't make it look like exactly what it was.

"I'm sorry, Nina," said Guy, who was also whispering. "But they're onto you. Put it all back quick. And I really need your phone."

"What do you mean?" She hoped her message, with all its attachments, had gone through OK.

"You know! Put it back, close the safe, and pretend you couldn't get in." He picked up the string of numbers from the desk, screwed it up, and shoved it into his pocket. "You've got a couple of seconds. *Phone!*"

She stared for a second, confused, but then did as he said.

"Did you get everything?" he said.

"I think so." She looked at him, trying to work out what he was doing. "The plane crash. That was the first space mission, right? Was it leaving here or on its way back?"

"Leaving," said Guy. "It didn't have the flu on board."

"My brother was infected," she said. "It came from space. Could it have been something . . . completely different? I mean, the flu came with a consciousness. It brings its own voice, doesn't it? That wasn't Billy's voice. It wasn't Billy."

He didn't answer. Instead he put her phone into his pocket, then stepped out into the corridor and shouted: "I've found her!"

It all happened at once. Ben Alford and Harvey were in the room, and Nina was so scared she thought she was going to wet herself.

"Here she is," Guy said with a different demeanor, and Nina found she couldn't bear to look at BA. She looked at the floor. She looked at Harvey, who turned away. She looked quickly at Guy, who had flipped, completely, to mirror BA's outrage.

BA closed the door. It clicked shut. Harvey flicked the light on.

"I knew you were up to something," said BA.

Nina couldn't move. She could barely breathe.

"I noticed at dinner," said Harvey. "I said to Dad afterward. I said, Nina's up to something. She's asking too many questions. She might go snooping. Didn't I?"

He looked at BA, wanting approval. He got a nod.

"I didn't believe it," BA said. "You're my son's girlfriend, for God's sake. But we checked the camera in your room just in case, and you weren't there. Checked it in Louis' room, and you weren't there either. Guy said we should leave it, that you'd just be under the duvet or in the bathroom or something, so we held back for a while, but then Harvey went in to check. No idea how you managed to knock out half the cameras in the house, but you weren't quite as clever as you thought, because here we are."

"Here you are," she said. She looked up at the corner of the room and saw the tiniest glint of a lens. She hadn't even thought about cameras because Louis had once said there weren't any indoors. Was this another thing that he didn't know? And apparently she had knocked out half the cameras in the house. She looked at Guy, who was enigmatic.

"I didn't find anything," she said. "Sorry. Your safe is really hard to crack."

BA snorted. "That's the idea," he said. He strode over and patted it. "I'm going to need your phone, though, because I don't believe I can trust you."

"I haven't got it," she said. "I didn't bring it. I just wanted to know . . ." She sighed and decided to ignore the bigger picture and hope that he would believe her if she downscaled her focus. "I wanted to know whether the J5X virus came from space," she said. "Because I think it does. The outbreaks are centered in London, Sapporo, and Burley. Those are the places where you guys live." She nodded to Guy, who nodded back and smiled with the twitch of a corner of his mouth. "If it came from the Rock, that would explain why it's such a weird virus. Why it was such a pandemic. Why no one can make a vaccine that works. I was just so . . . so curious. I was longing to know and . . . well, I think my curiosity got the better of me. I just found my legs carrying me here. I'm really sorry."

"Pat her down," said BA to Harvey, who couldn't believe his luck. "No way has she not got a camera."

She had to allow it. She closed her eyes and tried not to cry, as Harvey Alford went through her dressing gown pockets, then pulled the gown aside and patted down her body, taking evident enjoyment.

"Nothing," he said.

"I know where Kitty is," she said, because she couldn't help it. "I saw her the other day. She hates you."

BA said nothing.

"You're out of your depth, Nina," said Guy, and they walked her back upstairs, BA's hand on her shoulder, and pushed her into her bedroom, and locked the door.

She didn't think she would sleep. She couldn't look at her phone, couldn't read the documents she'd photographed or make sense of anything. She had nothing to do at all. She couldn't message Louis to confess. She couldn't even distract herself with a podcast. In the end, she put the TV on, found a financial channel, and allowed the tumultuous news from the world's stock exchanges to lull her to sleep.

FIFTY-TWO

Rachel woke early on Sunday morning because someone was banging on their door. That had never happened before; no one had visited them in this flat.

Al stirred beside her. He yawned. She stretched. Beth was asleep.

"What's the time?" said Al.

Rachel checked. "Seven."

"Jesus. Sunday!"

"I know."

She pulled on a dressing gown and went to open the door, expecting a delivery. But there were two Starcom people in standard purple jackets standing there.

"Hi," said the woman. She was older than Rachel and looked very tough. "Sorry to get you up. Thought we'd catch you this way. Can we come in?"

Rachel stood back, pretty sure she couldn't say no. They came into the flat, and Al met them in the living room, wearing his dressing gown, too, and blinking.

"Is it Billy?" said Rachel. "Or Nina? What is it?"

"Your children? No. We just wanted to ask a couple of things," said the man.

Al put the kettle on in the corner of the room, and it was so loud that they all had to wait for it to click itself off before they could carry on speaking.

"Coffee?" he said, and her heart broke at his deferential politeness.

"No, thanks," said the woman.

"Oooh, I'd love one," said the man. "Thanks. Milk, two sugars."

The woman leaned forward and spoke just to Rachel. "It won't take long. He won't get to drink that coffee. I'll get straight to the point. We've heard that you might be leaving your child in the day care and going to work outside the Starcom family, which is very clearly forbidden. So I wanted to check if there's any truth in that, and if so, I need to go over the rules with you."

Rachel looked at the ground. She had known it would be this.

"I only have to work here from when my baby's three," she said. "And the nursery is open to babies her age. There's nothing to say I can't put her in there and go elsewhere to work."

"There is everything to say that," said the woman, rolling her eyes. "Everything." She took a booklet out of her bag and folded it back on itself. "See," she said. "It says it here. No working outside the family without written permission, and that can only come after a meeting with your family manager, and only if we don't have an appropriate and equivalent job to offer you here."

"But only when my baby is three."

"Not at all," said the woman, tight-lipped. "You're being willfully obtuse about this, and you know it. You're seeing what you want to see. Yes, we allow mothers, or fathers if they request it as long as one parent is working, to stay at home until the child is three years old, and then we care for the child so the parent can join us at work. It makes it easy for parents, and that's what we want. What we *don't* want is to see anyone abusing the system, which is what you're attempting to do. You're seeing a loophole where none exists."

Al handed Rachel a coffee. "Thank you," she whispered. She didn't say anything to the woman.

"May I ask what work you're doing that's so important?" said the woman. The man was slurping his coffee and saying nothing at all.

"I'm a lawyer," said Rachel quietly. "I'm getting my qualifications back up to speed. I have a job where I'm managing an office, doing some legal work and some admin work. I only started this one on Friday. I've been temping."

"You're a lawyer?" the woman said. "In that case we can certainly find a wonderful job for you here."

"I like the job I have, though."

"You work here," she said. "Or you find another place to live. We're not in the business of subsidizing you to work elsewhere."

"But you don't subsidize me! Al works for you. It's his job that gets us this flat."

The woman didn't bother to reply. The man knocked his coffee back fast, and they both stood up and left. At the door, the woman turned around.

"I'll message you with an appointment with the careers team," she said.

Rachel slammed the door behind them, but only when she was sure they were too far away to hear it. Beth was shouting for them from her cot.

FIFTY-THREE

Nina yawned and found, to her surprise, that it was half past nine and the financial news was muttering away to itself on the television.

She remembered everything that had happened in the night, slowly at first and then with a thud of horror. They had brought her back to her bedroom and . . .

She jumped out of bed and tried the door. It was locked. She was locked in. She looked around the room. Like Billy, she was in an upmarket prison cell.

She didn't have her phone, because Guy had taken it. Guy, she thought, was in some way on her side, though the whole thing was so confusing that she wasn't completely sure. It could be that he'd taken her phone so that he could be the first to condemn her. It might give him some extra power, being able to bring the information to BA. Or he might be helping her. On balance, she trusted him more than anyone else.

She wondered what they had told Louis.

"Harmony?" she said, remembering that they had added her voice to the TV system.

The television said: "Good morning, Nina."

"Can you . . . can you put a message on the television in Louis' room?"

"I'm sorry, Nina. I can convey a message but only when his screen is switched on. Currently, it is off."

"OK," she said. "Well, next time he turns it on, can you give him a message saying: 'Please come to my room, as I'm locked in. Nina'? And then put three kisses on it. You know. The letter 'X.'"

"Certainly, Nina," said Harmony.

Nina left the TV on because it was better than silence. She was in the bathroom when the word "psychosis" snagged her attention. She tuned in and heard: "Rumors of this syndrome, which some have named 'post-flu psychosis,' have existed for some months now, but today one account has caught the world's attention."

She was in front of the screen instantly. If someone else's story was out there, she wanted to know about it. She looked at a reporter standing in the sunshine somewhere. She looked at the window, which was bright behind the curtains.

"Although the blog claims to be based in Toronto, there is some skepticism about that, and online commentators are convinced that in fact the events it describes took place in London."

Nina let the words wash over her as she stared at the screen. Then, finally, she remembered that she had a phone for the blog, that it was in her bag, and when she found it, she almost forgot everything else.

She thought she was looking at the numbers wrong, because she thought it said the site had had seven million hits.

She kept looking. It still looked like that. The site had had more than seven million hits, and it seemed everyone in the world was talking about it. "We Hear Voices" was on the front pages of all the news sites and trending on social media.

It was everywhere. For some reason, everyone in the world had decided to read it at once.

Nina and her friends had set out with the intention of getting people to look at it, but it seemed it had done that impossible thing and caught hold of the popular imagination. People had talked about it and sent it on to other people, and now it was on fire.

Nina had thousands of e-mails and so many voice mails that the mailbox had filled up long ago even though the phone number wasn't on the site. The social media accounts that Louis had set up suddenly had millions of followers. *Everyone* wanted to know about Josh. The story of the kids with the voices in their heads had caught the world's attention, and it had happened exactly at the worst moment.

The messages were pleading, and abusive, and interested, and dismissive, and everything in between. Meanwhile, Nina was Ben Alford's prisoner. Guy Clement had her phone. Kitty Alford, whose story made no sense, was in hospital with Billy. And there was something going on at the hospital.

Nina glanced down the e-mails. They were easily separated into categories.

We'd like to arrange an interview with you, said the journalist ones. *With Josh. With the other children. The other families. Can offer money. Money. Money.* And on they went, again and again and again.

She set the phone to delete everything with the words "cunt" and "fuck" and "bitch" in it, and about a third of the messages vanished just like that.

Nobody actually knew who she and Billy were, though, and she was grateful to Louis and Shelly all over again for designing a robust site. It seemed to be as good as they had promised it would be, but all the same, this was not the way it had been supposed to go.

She was just about to call Louis when someone tapped on the door and tried the handle.

"Nina?" said Louis. "Unlock the door!"

"Can't," she said. "I'm locked in. Can you help? Don't tell anyone. Just get me out. I'll explain."

"Can you explain now?"

"Through the door?"

"Yes."

She huffed out a breath and couldn't think of anything but the truth. "You remember Graham told us that he thought the plane crash had something to do with the voices? After we were talking at dinner last night, I thought that must be it. That the plane crash was the first space mission Guy mentioned. So I went to do some detective work. I went down to your dad's study, but I couldn't find anything."

"Fucking hell! Nina! I guess they found you."

"Yeah. That's why I'm locked in."

"For fuck's sake. Shit. Hang on. I'm on it."

She heard his footsteps leaving, then waited for a million years, and at last there was a click, and the door opened, and Louis himself appeared in the doorway, looking adorable, if troubled and furious, in a white T-shirt and red checked pajama bottoms.

I need to get out," she said. "In secret. Please. I promise I won't do anything else."

"Have you seen the blog?" he said, and she nodded.

"Yes," she said, letting him kiss her, feeling her betrayal. "I don't even know what to think about it. But, Louis, I have to go."

He nodded. "Who found you?"

"Guy. Then he called your dad, and he came with Harvey."

"Classic. Everyone leaving me to sleep through it all."

"I'm scared, Louis. I don't know what they'll do."

She watched him hesitate, his loyalty torn.

"They can be quite scary," he said in the end. "Imogen got all the kindness genes. I always wanted to be more like her. And she would have let you out. Look, I'm sure I can get you out, but you have to go to Graham, OK? Go to Graham, and I'll meet you there. Graham will help."

Nina picked up her bag. She knew she had almost no time at all.

Louis ushered her down a flight of stairs that led straight to the kitchen. These were literally the servants' stairs, and they were not at all slippery. They were nonstick Formica, practical for people carrying trays of drinks or cleaning materials. The paint on the walls was stained and dirty.

Then she was in the kitchen, and Mathilde plus a young woman and a younger man, also both in uniform, jumped up at the sight of the two of them.

"Hey, Mathilde," said Louis. "Sorry to do this to you."

"That's OK, Lou," Mathilde said. "What can we do for you?" She nodded at Nina. "Miss Nina," she said in a much more formal voice.

"We need to get Nina out of here," said Louis, "without Mum or Dad knowing. Can you lend her a uniform and open the back gate for us?"

"No way," said Mathilde. "So much trouble when they find out. I cannot lose my job."

"I promise you won't. I'll say we crept down and stole it. We can say you fought us. It's me that'll be in trouble."

She looked uncertain. The other two were looking at the floor.

"You swear?"

"I swear."

Nina cleared her throat. "Why don't we say that it was just me and that I sneaked in without you seeing? Where would I find a uniform? Just look in the right direction, and you don't have to do anything else at all."

The silence stretched on. Then Mathilde looked at Nina and deliberately turned her gaze to a closed door that turned out to be a cupboard with three black-and-white uniforms hanging in it.

FIFTY-FOUR

Rachel and Al were having the first real argument they'd ever had. Beth was watching, but neither of them could stop. It was horrible.

"You have to work for Starcom," he said. "You heard them. Beth is happy at day care, and you live here. We signed up to their rules. You don't want to take these people on, Rachel. We can't do that."

"I love my job," she said. "And I'm being paid well. I can do it. I'm not giving that up to be paid in sandwich vouchers and shampoo."

"You *have* to!" He was almost shouting. "You heard what they said! You thought you'd found a loophole. It didn't work because guess what. They're on top of this stuff. They're huge and ruthless. Obviously, they don't have loopholes."

"They want me to work for free."

"I'm sure they don't," said Al. "We'd get to move to a better flat or something."

"Do you think? Well, I'm not doing it." She looked at the coffee cup in her hand. It said WORLD'S BEST MUM on it, but she wasn't that at all. She threw it into the sink, and it smashed. That was better. Beth whimpered and then started crying.

"For Christ's sake!" said Al. "Stop! It's good enough for me to work for vouchers—is that it? But it's beneath you?"

"That isn't what I meant," she said.

"Well, what did you mean?"

She couldn't answer because she couldn't get the words together. "Oh," she said in the end. "I can't stand this. I'm going to go over to Mum's flat for a bit." It was on the other side of a huge city, but she didn't care about the journey. "I've got to get away from here. It doesn't belong to the church yet. If it does, no one's told me."

"Fine," said Al. "But you're not taking Beth. She's staying here with me."

She cried on the Tube, but no one noticed. The great thing about being over forty was that no one really saw her anymore. There were other women of her age who were beautiful and visible, but she wasn't one of them, and she appreciated that.

She got to the flat, sincerely hoping that it was empty. She had her keys, but pressed the buzzer before she let herself into the building, just in case. No one answered.

The lift was out of order (of course), and so she walked up all the stairs. She didn't see anyone, but there were lots of smells. It took hours. At the top, as she waited to catch her breath, she found her phone in the bottom of her bag.

There was an e-mail from Nina with lots of attachments that were too big for her to download. It was probably spam; she knew you weren't meant to open attachments if you didn't know what they were, and as there was no note from Nina, she thought her account must have been hacked. She had better warn Nina.

There were a few messages from Al, but she couldn't look at them yet.

There was a message from Graham Watson. She knocked on the door and read the message. He wanted her to call him.

Then there was one from Henry, which was odd. It was a text, and it just said:

Can you tell Nina her school blazer is here so she'll need to swing
by for it tomorrow morning? She's not answering my calls. I
guess she's sleeping in?

She let herself into the mercifully empty flat and put the kettle on.
Then she sat on the sofa to recover from her climb and look at Henry's
text again. It was the most straightforward of all the things she had to deal
with, so she replied, saying: But she was at yours last night, and her phone
immediately rang, with the word **Henry** on the screen.

"Hi," she said with no enthusiasm.

"No," he said. "She was with you. She left me a note saying she'd be
back with me sometime next week."

"She told us she was at yours," said Rachel. "I haven't seen her since last
Monday morning. Actually, Sunday night, because she left early on Monday.
Al saw her. She set off for school. I haven't seen her for nearly a week."

"Right," said Henry. "Well, this is mysterious, because I'm . . . Hang
on. I'm putting you on speaker. I'm photographing the note she left me
yesterday and sending it over right now. There."

Rachel took the phone away from her ear and looked at it. As she
watched, a photo appeared on the screen. It was a note written in what
was most definitely Nina's handwriting, and it said: *I've gone to Mum's.
Back next week. I'll text xx.*

She put the phone back to her ear. "She didn't come to mine," she
said. "She told us she was staying with you."

"So where is she?" There was a long enough pause for Rachel to know
that they were both thinking the same thing, and then Henry voiced it.
"With her boyfriend."

And, it turned out, neither of them had any idea where Louis lived or
even what his surname was, though they had both met him. They had no
way of finding her except by calling and texting her phone until she answered.

Nina didn't answer.

FIFTY-FIVE

Graham was torn. Imogen, and everyone else, was urging him to close the ward, and he was almost ready to do it. Sometimes he wasn't even sure it had happened. Everyone seemed to have been paid off instantly, and it had gone away as things sometimes did when there was enough money involved.

Now he was in his office, and it was Sunday, and everything felt different. The children wanted to leave. They all insisted the voices had gone, and he was right on the brink of discharging all of them and letting go of the entire thing. He would discharge Kitty into his own care (he should have done that years ago; he had been far too swayed by Ben) and lock up the Spiderlings ward and hope never to have to open it again.

He corrected himself. All of them *apart from Billy* would be able to go home. Billy could not leave until he was taken to court for his trial early next year. If Graham closed the ward, he would be sending Billy to prison.

That wouldn't work. He would have to find some other solution.

On top of that, Nina had sent him a huge stash of photos in the night.

He hadn't been able to view them on his phone because there were too many, but he'd come upstairs to have a look on the bigger screen and been horrified.

She had e-mailed him the proof of the things he already knew, plus some things he very much hadn't known at all.

The space program was well under way and was running about five years ahead of its official schedule. There was an asteroid at a libration point, and it already had a settlement on it, right in front of the public's nose. People would look at it every night and have no idea. Things like that no longer had much power to surprise him, but all the same, it was a bold move. He could see exactly why Ben would insist on it happening that way: it was the maxim *better to ask for forgiveness than permission* on the grandest possible scale. Not only that, but there was a planet, unimaginably far away, that was earmarked for colonization after that. Graham was exhausted and quite pleased to know for sure that he was too old for any of this. He wondered how Nina felt about it all and what this changed about the voices.

All of this would surely change a lot of things if it became public knowledge. Graham had no idea how she had got her hands on this paperwork. She was braver than he was; if he was seeing this, he imagined that other people were, too. He wondered where she was and whether she had any idea of how dangerous Ben Alford could be. His older sister had been a stabilizing influence, and now she was gone. The world needed Imogen back. Imogen would have loved Nina.

He hoped that, wherever she was, Nina was safe.

Among the documents she had sent was a copy of his own confidentiality agreement about Kitty, and copies of the legal paperwork from years ago. When this got out, Kitty would be back in the public eye.

Graham remembered the way it had all started. Ben Alford's daughter, Katherine, was the ground zero as far as post-flu psychosis was concerned. Graham still couldn't make sense of it, but she had followed exactly the same trajectory as these kids, thirteen years earlier. She had become very ill and then recovered just when she seemed about to die.

Her body had got better, but her brain was a different matter. She had first nearly murdered Louis, her baby half brother, which everyone put down to jealousy, but a week later she had killed her own mother, strangling her with a rope in the same way these kids had Peter. That was when she came into Graham's care, and without Imogen's attentions, Graham thought she would have grown up into someone very different.

Kitty was adorable—funny and cynical. She read books and went to the gym and still slept with her pet rock beside her bed. Graham ensured she was taken out for a walk every day so she did have an idea about the outside world, but he knew she had a steep learning curve ahead. Her father didn't visit at all, though that same half brother, Louis, had met her down there recently.

Poor Kitty deserved a better life than this. He would make up the second bedroom at home for her, and she could stay with him for a while until he managed to make a longer-term plan for her.

Graham clicked around the Internet to see whether there was anything up about the asteroid or Kitty, and he found that everyone *was* talking about psychosis, but that it was focused on a boy in Canada.

It took him about forty seconds to realize that he was, in fact, reading about Billy. This, he realized, was Nina's blog, the one she had set up with her friends. The wave of guilt broke over him again; he had encouraged this right at the start. And she had done it, and somehow she had persuaded everyone in the world to read it.

He skimmed the site, particularly interested in his own role. There was nothing at all on the blog about the space program or Kitty or any of the material Nina had sent over. This was just the story of Billy and an appeal for other people's experiences.

Nina, he thought, had had a busy night. He found her phone number and called it, but she didn't answer.

. . .

Even though it was pouring with rain, Graham decided to go out because he needed to see the outside world and breathe some air. It was Sunday, so Lauren wasn't here, and he had no patients beyond the ones downstairs.

He had a coffee at his usual café, then took a bag full of pastries to the rubble where the woman had been, where the homeless people had looked after him that time.

"Is there a woman here?" he said, peering down through the rain.

"We can get you a woman," said a man. Graham shook his head, handed his bag of food to the nearest person, and walked away. A minute later he stopped to check his phone. He kept it on silent and refused to let it even vibrate because he had spent his younger years in thrall to the important feeling of being permanently contactable and now he rejected that. When he checked, it turned out he had seven missed calls and an awful lot of messages.

Lauren's name jumped out. He looked at that one first. It said, Prof—I've been trying to call. Reporters have been ringing on my mobile. I'm coming into the office. I called Giraffe but they said everything's calm there and that you were upstairs. No answer from upstairs phones. Anyway. Speak to/see you soon. L x

He became one of those people who blocked the pavement to stare at a phone. People tutted. Who cared? They could walk around him.

Graham looked at his other messages and saw that he wasn't the only one who had seen through Nina's cover story. An expensive private doctor with a ward of disturbed rich children? It hadn't taken journalists long to turn their gaze upon him.

He clicked over to the news pages again.

REVEALED, read a headline. THE CHILDREN TORMENTED BY VOICES IN THEIR HEADS. All are J5X survivors. Some have become killers locked in basement of posh Central London hospital.

It wouldn't be long, he thought. They'd be talking about Billy, and then they would find out about Lulu. They would discover what had happened on Friday and hell would be unleashed. The princess—the heir to the throne, no less—locked up with the killer. The princess who *was* a killer. The children murdering one of their own in a hand-crocheted spiderweb because he was different.

He wiped the raindrops off the screen of his phone, put it in his pocket, and set off back to work, discovering that he could walk faster than he'd previously thought.

He had to push past two journalists and three people filming on their phones who might have been passersby or might have been journalists. It was impossible to tell these days.

"Dr. Watson!" shouted one of them, and he didn't bother to correct his title. He just ignored them and felt more grateful than ever for the wall of security that ensured none of them would be able to sneak into the building. (That pane of glass in the stairs door had been replaced with steel, and anyway, only a child would have been able to climb through.) Lauren was somehow already there, sitting at her desk, reading the news and picking up the desk phone and putting it down again regularly to stop it from ringing.

"You OK, Prof?" she said.

He decided to give her a pay raise. "Yep," he said. "I'm going to see the kids."

"I'll come. One thing, though . . ." He waited in the doorway for her. She looked up. "There's an e-mail in all this lot from Billy's dad. He says, you don't happen to have heard anything from Nina?"

Graham shook his head but turned it into a nod.

"I had an e-mail from her in the night," he said. "Quite a . . . well, quite a data dump. She's managed to break into Ben's safe. I haven't read it all, but . . ." He walked into his own office and forwarded Nina's e-mail to Lauren. There. Now it wasn't just his responsibility. "Have a look. I've signed a thing with Ben to say I can't talk about it, but that very document is a part of this collection, which makes things a bit meta. Anyway, *you* haven't signed it." He paused. "I'm worried about Nina, I must say. I'm not sure she knows what she's got herself into. I hope she turns up. Ben might be family, but if you wanted to share this stuff more widely . . . Well, I think it's what Imogen would have done."

"So do I," said Lauren. "I'm on it."

While he was looking at his screen, new headlines started popping up.

"WE HEAR VOICES" BOY IDENTIFIED

VOICES BOY ON TRIAL FOR MURDER

BILLY STEVENS, SIX, HELD IN UNDERGROUND BUNKER

"My child was in his class at school and we feared for her safety"

"Referred to social services"

"Churchgoing gran brutally murdered"

"The voices told him to do it"

"Demon"

"Demonic possession"

"Devil child"

"Horror child"

"Evil"

"Evil"

"Evil"

The people who commented on articles were coming together, unusually in one mind, and they had coalesced around the demonic-possession theory.

God, he thought. People were stupid. They were cruel. They understood nothing. However, at least this would be prejudicing Billy's trial, perhaps to the point where it wouldn't be able to happen. That was one bright spot.

Graham needed to get to Billy. He had failed Peter, failed his patients, failed Kitty, failed as a husband and father. He had one chance with Billy; he needed to keep him safe.

He would make sure the leaked documents got out into the world. There would be no going back after that.

FIFTY-SIX

Nina couldn't see much through the window of the bus because it was raining so hard. She was trying to relax, but it was difficult. She had a lot of calls to make, particularly to Mum, but her battery was low because she had forgotten to charge her blog phone. Also she was paranoid about making calls in public.

All the buses had charging ports, so she put her phone next to one, which was luckily working, and watched the battery level creep up.

The woman next to her was about Gran's age and was also wearing a maid's uniform. They smiled at each other, and Nina was surprised by the tidal wave of grief that broke over her. She missed her grandmother so much. Nina looked at the window, but she really could see only raindrops through her tears. There were two layers of water between her and the world.

There was already a base on the Rock. The plane crash had been the first astronauts. Everyone was reading the blog. Kitty Alford had hurt Louis. There was too much danger. She just wanted to get to Billy.

At some point north of the river, Nina noticed that the bus had been stationary for longer than it usually was, and she looked around to see what was happening. She locked eyes with a man who was standing at the front, talking to the driver.

There was a second set of doors at the back of the bus, and these were open. She grabbed her phone, smiled apologetically at the woman as she pushed past, and ran down from the bus and through the pouring rain.

She had no idea where she was or where to go, but she didn't stop moving. She had no bag and no money. She ducked down roads, ran as fast as she could, pleased that she was fit, thanks to her space training. She needed to get to where the people were and ask for help.

She checked the road sign at the top of the street as she ran past. It said W1 in the corner, which was a huge relief: this was Central London. W1 was Central London, and it meant she couldn't be far from Harley Street. It was Sunday lunchtime. Sundays were always busy and there were hundreds of people. She heard footsteps behind her and sprinted round the corner and straight into the middle of a crowd of shoppers on Oxford Street, the biggest, busiest, most anonymous street in the city.

She cursed herself for being so stupid as to think she could just catch a bus and get away from it all. Louis had put her on the bus in the first place. He would have told his parents where she was as soon as they mildly threatened him. "You fucking, fucking idiot," she muttered under her breath. *Stupid, stupid, stupid.*

She touched her pocket. The phone was in there, so at least she had that, though she didn't have time to stop and call anyone. She knew Alford might be able to trace her through her phone's location, but for now having a phone outweighed that risk.

She forced herself to slow down and attempt to blend in, but it was difficult. Umbrellas kept hitting her in the face. She did her best to make her way toward Harley Street while looking like a maid on her way to work, the rain making her hair stick to her face. Even as she dashed through crowds and wove out into the road and held up taxis, she could feel them gaining on her, and not only that, but there was a car driving very slowly up behind her, and then it was beside her.

She had thought they wouldn't be able to do anything with all these people around, but now she realized that she was wrong. If she were bundled into a car, there was every chance that none of these people around her would even really notice.

Most people made a point of avoiding the rubble on the corner, because the redevelopment work hadn't started yet, and the bombed-out Topshop site was currently an encampment of homeless people, but as she had no other options, Nina waited for a crowd of tourists to shield her and ran straight into the middle of it.

FIFTY-SEVEN

Rachel forgot Nina was missing the moment she and Henry got off the phone. (Nina had to be with Louis, and she would be fine; she was resourceful.) Rachel forgot her because a bunch of news alerts had appeared on her screen.

She read the words.

WE HEAR VOICES: boy in viral website named as Billy Stevens, six, from London. The child is already on remand for murdering his grandmother.

She stared.

"Viral website?" she said stupidly. She called Nina's phone; Nina would know. But again, Nina didn't answer. Why did Rachel not have Louis' number? Or even his surname? She tried to remember what he had said about his family, but recalled only that they were rich. Louis had deflected everything she had asked. She knew that he had a brother, but that would hardly narrow it down.

She picked up her phone to call Al, but it was already ringing with an unfamiliar number, so she put it down again. It just kept ringing. She had to reject three calls before she could make even one, and then the flat's buzzer went, and Al answered the phone, and she said, "Sorry," and he said, "I'm sorry, too. Have you seen . . . ?"

"I don't get it."

"Nina's been writing about Billy online. I tried calling, but she didn't answer. Her website's everywhere. Are you with Billy now?"

"No," she said. "I'm at Mum's flat. I'm going to the hospital, though. Where are you?"

"Home," he said. He paused. "The management people came over again to check we were OK because they saw our family in the news."

"Creepy," said Rachel. "People are ringing the buzzer here. I don't know who."

"Don't answer," said Al. "This will pass. It's like . . ." She could picture his forehead furrowing as he tried to find the words, and she longed for him. "When by some freak everyone is talking about the same thing, being the focus of that is impossible for real people. The celebs who court that, they have the infrastructure to deal with it. And we don't. But it will pass, and we just need to keep our heads down and get through. If you can get to the hospital, to Billy, you'll be safe. And so will he. Betty and I will come and meet you there. Have you called Graham?"

She nodded and then said, "Yes," because of course Al couldn't see her nodding. "But I didn't get through. I'll keep trying. I love you," she whispered.

"I love you, too," he said, and she heard Beth shouting in the background and missed each one of her children with every atom of her being.

She left messages on Graham's voice mail and rang Nina until she realized that if she wanted people to call her back, she should probably stay off the phone.

She wished she hadn't taken everything from the kitchen the last time she had been here. She stared at the phone and waited.

When someone knocked on the door to the flat, she managed to say: "Who is it?"

"Hi there," said a man's voice. "It's Jamie from the *Herald*. Is that Rachel? We're just wondering if we could have a word."

"Sorry," she said. "Rachel's not here."

"How about you, then? Are you a family friend?"

"No," she said. She picked up her bag, put her coat back on, and decided that she just had to do it. She unlocked the door and pushed through the gaggle of people that was out there.

FIFTY-EIGHT

Graham was scared. He'd hoped Nina might be downstairs waiting for him, but she wasn't. The children were tethered to their beds, bored, complaining, and still free from the voices.

They could go home. He was certain that he could discharge them now, apart from Billy. They weren't his children, and their privacy and safety had been compromised by the publicity. He would close the ward, find another hospital for Billy, and leave it to the families to deal with the fallout. He walked down the corridor, opening doors as he went so he could address them all at once.

The Spiderlings ward door was locked. He never wanted to open it again.

"When am I going home?" Louisa's voice cut through the babble.

"They'll never let you out now, babes," said another voice, and when Graham looked around, Kitty was standing there. She was right behind him, wearing her pajamas.

"I think," he told her, "that we will. And . . . you might be able to go, too, Kitty."

"Like fuck am I going to live with those arseholes."

Graham was suddenly shy. "Of course you can't do that," he said. He looked at the floor. "But, well, if you didn't mind too much, you could always come and live with me."

"Serious?"

"Serious."

She flung her arms around him and squeezed him so tightly that he gasped. He smiled and put a tentative hand on her shoulder.

"Your voice," he said. "He's long gone, and he's never hinted any kind of return?"

"I told you, Gramps. He fucked off years ago." Kitty's vocabulary came from her love of one particular London-based drama. Graham found it so endearing that he wanted to cry.

"Kitty!" called Billy from his room. "Kitty, come to me!"

She looked at Graham, who nodded.

"Billy, my main man!" she said, and she ran into his room and jumped onto his bed.

Here's the thing," Graham said loudly. "I know your voices have gone quiet. I know you feel different, that you're kind of back to your old selves, though of course you'll be different, too. I know, and you know, that the people you are now would never have done what you did to Peter. But the voices used your bodies to do it, and that makes this very difficult."

"You can't keep us here!" That was Suki. "Graham! We are all so sorry. We're so sorry about what we did to Peter. Poor little Peter."

All the rest of them joined in. "Sorry," they said. "Sorry, sorry, sorry. We won't do it again."

They weren't speaking as one. Their voices weren't coordinated. They were just children who wanted the same thing.

"Please, don't keep us tied to our beds!" said Anita, who was always the quietest of them.

She was right: it was barbaric. Graham had considered using electronic barriers that would stop them from leaving their rooms by shock-ing them, but had been afraid that the potential for self-harm was too immense. So they were just attached to their beds again with long leashes, like dogs. Imogen was right: he could have no more part in this.

"Here's the thing," he said, and he looked around because he couldn't do this alone. There she was, just the very faintest outline of Imogen. He thought it was her anyway. He felt her essence, even if he couldn't quite see her face. "No one wants you to go on trial for what happened to Peter. Peter's family doesn't want any of this to come to light. They're dealing with their grief privately. Some of your families have offered to compen-sate the adults you hurt if they will promise not to tell anyone exactly what happened. The last thing any of us wants is for the law to get involved, because the law would be as barbaric to you as your voices were to Peter. What I'd like to do is to test each one of you separately, and if I feel able to write up a report stating that the voice has gone, I'll discharge you. And at that point, you can go home."

Louisa cheered. Suki gasped. Majid let out a "Yeah!" Anita said: "Good." Billy and Kitty started a chant of "We're going home" to the tune of an old football song called "Three Lions (Football's Coming Home)," which must have come from Kitty. The others gradually joined in with it. "We're going home. We're going. We are going home." Their voices came together, and Graham found that he was singing, too, and so, when he looked round, was Lauren. Imogen was down the corridor, and she was dancing.

Of course, it wasn't quite that simple. For one thing, there was a crowd of people outside this building right now. For another, there was Billy.

He sighed and walked into Billy's room.

S o," said Graham. "Billy, talk to me about Delfy and about how you feel now."

Billy grinned at him. Billy could grin, because he had no idea that the street outside was busy with people shouting his name. People who blamed him and his mother and his doctor and the voice in his head for everything that was currently wrong. He had no idea that his school photograph was on the front pages of websites, on the printed front pages of the free newspapers, on the television.

He could grin because he didn't know that he was the only one who was staying.

"I feel super brilliant," said Billy. "It's weird because I do feel like myself but different. I don't feel like before Delfy. I feel like . . . after."

"Right?" said Kitty, who was holding Billy's hand. "You'll never go back to being that guy. I was six when it happened to me. Like you, mate. When he fucked off, I couldn't believe it. Apart from the time he killed my mum and tried to kill my brother, he was a man of peace, but they locked me up for almost all my life so far. It feels empty, right?"

"It feels like there's . . . space. She's not here. Really, she's not."

"She's waiting?" said Graham.

"She did say she was waiting, and then she went. I don't know what she's waiting for. But I think she's waiting somewhere else."

"Not in you at all?"

Billy laughed. "Not in me at all," he said, and his smile was so wide that it broke Graham's heart.

"You can go back to your fam, Billy," said Kitty.

"You can come and live with us, too, if you like, Kitty," said Billy.

Graham wanted to laugh at Billy's impetuous generosity. He wondered what Rachel would have to say about that.

"Kitty's coming to my house," Graham said, and he and his niece exchanged a warm smile. "But, Billy," he added, "you know everything I just said about going home? Well, I'm afraid that you might have to wait a little bit longer."

FIFTY-NINE

Nina flung herself behind the ruin of a wall and hoped for the best, but when she turned around, she saw that she was in a group of people and that they didn't look happy with her. Faces turned to her, exhausted and angry.

"Sorry," she said. "Can you help me? I'm really sorry. I need your help."

She was a little way into the site, next to a makeshift shelter made from a sheet of corrugated metal fixed over some half walls. She was aware that the people whose home she had just crashed were not well-disposed to her sudden arrival. She hoped this wouldn't end up being worse than being caught by the Starcom people.

"What's going on?" said a man. He had a scarred face and haunted eyes. "You can't do this. Get out."

"We're not here for your convenience," muttered another man.

"Not your private army."

Two people had stood up and were walking toward her.

"No!" said Nina, edging back into the wall. "Please. Please, don't."

She didn't know what to say, how to explain her situation in the next ten seconds before they threw her back onto the street. "It's Starcom."

A man wearing a traffic warden's hat paused, his hand on her shoulder. "Starcom?" he said.

"Yes!"

Then a woman was in front of her. "Bastards! Why are they after her?" she said.

Nina wasn't sure whom she was talking to, but she answered anyway. "I stole a lot of information from them and sent it to people," she said.

The woman sat beside her and reached out, and Nina flinched, but the woman just put an arm around her.

"Did you make them look bad?" the woman said.

"Yes."

The woman clapped her hands. "This lady is welcome here."

"We've—many of us—been fucked over by Starcom," said the traffic warden man. "Tell us what's going on, and we'll tell you if we can help you."

Nina didn't know where to start, so she gave them a rundown of the whole story, starting with Delfy. As soon as she mentioned her brother recovering from the flu with a voice in his head, they all started to move closer. She felt their eyes watching her intently. As she spoke, people muttered in agreement or nodded. Sometimes someone started to interrupt with their own story, but they were always shushed by the people around them.

"That's the doctor," said the woman at one point. "We had him here once. He had a funny turn."

"He gave us some food, but it wasn't nice."

"He was back today. Looking for Margery. Better food. Next time maybe he'll bring a pizza."

"I miss pizza," said someone else.

"You know Graham?" Nina said.

"He looks after the children. We look out for him."

"So," said Nina, "you know his office is just down the road?"

"Harley Street," said someone.

"Exactly. Five minutes' walk away, maybe? I need to get there, and I think that when I make it, I'll be safe. But those Starcom people are after me, and I know they know I'm going there. So can you help me?"

"Why are you dressed like that?"

Nina looked down at herself. She had forgotten she was wearing a uniform. "It was meant to be a kind of disguise," she said.

"Put this on." Someone handed her a coat, and although she could smell that it wasn't clean, she zipped it up gratefully. It was a flimsy anorak, much too big for her.

"That's better," said the woman Margery. "Come on, lads. We'll get her to the doctor. Help her fuck over the Starcom bastards."

As she walked in the middle of a crowd of people, Nina was surprised to realize that they weren't the only ones on the streets. Something had changed. People were out walking. Marching? She tried to work out what was happening, but she could barely see anything because she was surrounded by people. They were escorting her, and it was the most amazing thing. Margery was beside her, talking.

"I had one of those voices," she said, and she sounded a bit wistful. "I miss him. He was my friend. He got me to do some crazy shit. That's why I live out here now. I . . . well, I won't tell you what it was we did. But he only went quiet a few days ago. It's strange in here without him. He told me that most of them were in the kids, and he told me about that doctor. Then the doc turned up one day. Looked like he'd seen a ghost. Keeled over. I knew he was the one, so we looked out for him, and then he ran away."

"Wow," said Nina. "So, did your voice tell you it was leaving?"

"Yeah. Poor bastard. He knew he'd had a rough deal. The rest of them were in kids, having a whale of a time, and he's stuck here with me, though to be fair it's his fault I'm out here at all. That's a long story, darling. Anyway, yes, he buggered off, and he said all the rest of them were doing the same."

Nina stopped. "Seriously?"

"Yep." Margery pulled at Nina's sleeve. "Come on. Keep walking! Yeah, your brother's Delfy's gone. I guarantee it."

"Oh, my God." Nina walked faster. "Margery, what's going on out here? I can't really see." The tallest of the men from the encampment had been enlisted to surround her.

"Me neither, darling. Some kind of riots maybe?" Margery shrugged. "Whatever. Nothing will change."

SIXTY

When they reached Graham's office, there was a crowd outside, and Nina knew this was the most dangerous part. Alford's people had to be somewhere between her and the door.

"You got a phone?" asked the traffic warden man.

"Yes."

"Can you call the doc to let you in?"

Nina's fingers trembled as she ignored the many missed calls from Louis, the only person who had this number, and thanked her past self for programming numbers into this phone just in case.

It was, however, impossible to get through. She had Graham's office number and his mobile, but both went straight to voice mail. This number was programmed to be withheld, so of course he wouldn't answer it.

"Can't get through," she said. "Hold on."

She was calling Mum instead, because she might be—should be—inside this building, when there was a commotion and the journalists in the crowd surged forward and started shouting at someone who was getting out of a taxi.

"Who is it?" Nina said to the nearest person, because she couldn't see anything.

He looked down at her.

"Dunno. Some twat in a blazer with a T-shirt under it that says"—he squinted—" 'Coldplay.' "

"Oh, my God!" she said. "That's my dad."

She stood back. Lots of people were holding phones up. She moved to a spot with a view, poised to run forward the moment the door was open, and she watched her father turn around and address the crowd.

"My daughter Nina," he said, "Billy's sister, is missing. And we are very, very worried about her. Her boyfriend is a member of the Alford family—we didn't know that before, but now we do. Nina leaked the documents that you're all reading. We're worried that she's in great danger." He stopped and looked at the crowd. "If you're so good at this," he said, "then find her. Her mother and I need her. And also . . ." Dad paused. "Her brother, Billy, and her younger sister, Beth, need her back. We're *all* desperately worried about her."

Dad's mentioning Beth was the thing that made Nina cry. Dad's asking everyone to look for her was the thing that made her safe.

"Go, go, go," said Margery. "We'll stay here. I want to see how this pans out."

Nina ran out of the crowd and straight up to her dad and into his arms.

"Shortest missing-persons case ever," said someone.

Mum was inside the hospital, and then Al and Beth arrived, too. Graham and Kitty were sitting in Billy's room, and everyone congregated there. Lauren stopped Nina, just out in the corridor, where a television screen was showing a live feed of the news.

"Seen this?" said Lauren. Nina looked up at it.

"These documents were certainly never intended to be scrutinized," some kind of "expert" was saying in a TV studio, "and it's a brave whistle-blower, frankly, who does this. We have to be careful what we say right now, but it's safe to say that the space program is more advanced than we previously thought, and there's a lot of excitement about that."

"Every bit of this sounds incredible," agreed the anchor, and Nina nodded. There was already a STARCOM LEAKS logo in the corner of the screen. "But now," the anchor continued, "we have a studio guest who is able to shed some light on the mechanics behind just what the heck is going on."

The camera panned over to Shelly, who was wearing a tight black top and a huge gold necklace.

"I was the third person in 'We Hear Voices,'" said Shelly. "And I can talk you through the whole thing right now."

I leaked all those documents," Lauren said. "The ones you sent Graham. We put them on his site, and I linked them on social media. He said it was what Imogen would have done, and he was right. Is that OK?"

"Of course it is," said Nina. "It's why I sent them. I wasn't quite sure whose side Graham was on when it came down to it. Because of the family thing. Same as Louis."

"Yeah," said Lauren. "I think Graham is now on the side of whatever Imogen would have done. She was awesome."

"Unlike her brother."

"Right."

"Lauren?"

"Yes?"

"That encampment down at Topshop? The people there totally rescued me. They saved me from Starcom, and they escorted me here so I could get to safety. They gave me this coat to wear." She took it off. "Could we send them some food or something?"

Nina saw, for the first time, that what Al had said was true. People became homeless for all sorts of reasons. They were so often used as scapegoats, seen as the architects of their own misfortune because that made it easier for everyone else. She knew how close her family must have come to destitution recently.

Lauren looked unsure. "I'll send them food and drink. It's not much, but maybe a start? Then we'll see what else we can do."

"Thanks." Nina thought about it. "Could we deliver them loads of pizza?"

Lauren grinned. "The boss has a well-used pizza account. Sure. Whom shall I get it delivered to?"

"Margery and the boys. Right outside this door."

"On it."

When she was in the middle of all her family, including Dad, Nina couldn't stop crying.

"I thought I was never going to see you again." She hiccuped, having realized only as she said it that it was true. "They locked me in a room. Louis let me out, and the housekeeper lent me this uniform. Then the security people chased me. They were going to . . ." She couldn't continue; she didn't know, or want to know, what they would have done.

"Wankers," said Kitty.

"Anker," agreed Beth. It was her first clear word. She stretched her arms out to Nina, who took her and reveled in her calming presence.

"You all right, Billy?" Nina said.

"I am all right," he told her with a small smile. "Nina, Delfy has gone."

Three days later, after examinations by five different doctors, Billy was released, and all the charges against him were dropped, because he had been sick rather than bad, and because the avalanche of publicity had prejudiced his trial. At last he was seen as a victim rather than as a perpetrator. He was told he could go back to a normal life as long as he kept appointments with a different doctor three times a week, and he was electronically tagged for six months, but not in a way he particularly noticed. Orla's church agreed to let the family stay in her flat for six months, but Rachel hated being there because of the memories, and she spent a lot of time working out where they could go instead.

Meanwhile, Kitty refused to speak to anyone called Alford and moved into Graham's flat, where she borrowed Imogen's clothes and jewelry and channeled her aunt's spirit to help herself get used to the real world very gradually.

As soon as things settled down, Billy was invited over to the palace for a playdate with Louisa, who had astonished the world by reappearing from an "illness" that was never linked to Graham or Billy or Starcom. Rachel put on her spider brooch and took him there herself.

A month after that, Rachel and Al stood in front of a registrar and promised to love each other and take care of each other, for better or worse, for as long as they both lived. It was strange, but as soon as things calmed down, getting married was the thing they both wanted most in the world, and Rachel couldn't imagine why she hadn't wanted to do it before.

Nina gave Rachel away. Billy was best man. Beth sat with Graham and Kitty and gazed at everything. Margery cheered. Afterward, they had a big lunch in a church hall. Musical entertainment was supplied by Al's old workplace, in the form of a choir of homeless people and their support workers. Lauren had her first conversation with her future husband, one of Al's former colleagues.

Straight after that, buoyed by the support of her family and friends, Nina picked up the phone and called Louis. To her slight surprise, he answered.

"Nina," he said, and then he didn't say anything else.

She didn't let herself feel awkward. "Sorry," she said. "I'm sorry about the way it worked out. I guess it was always going to really, because of your dad and because of Kitty. I thought I'd see you one Sunday at Space Skills, but you haven't been back."

"Not allowed," he said. "My parents stopped it as soon as they found out I was doing it. I always knew they would. According to them it's a charity program for people who need a leg up, and I don't belong there."

"Oh, Louis," she said, hesitated, and then said it anyway. "Don't become like them, will you? You're better than that. Keep in touch with Graham at least."

"They're not that bad, you know. And I am their son. I know you'd like me to denounce them, but that's not going to happen."

Nina sighed. "I know." The silence stretched out.

"How's Billy? And Beth?" he said in the end.

"Both brilliant, thank you. So is Kitty. Mum and Al just got married."

"Say congratulations from me."

"Of course." She took a deep breath. "I know you're in an impossible situation," she said. "Good luck, Louis. And thanks for everything you did for Billy."

"Yeah," he said. "Good luck to you, too. And I hope that Katherine— Kitty—is OK. Maybe I'll see her again one day."

Silence hung in the air for a few seconds before they both said good-bye at the same time. Nina made sure she hung up first.

Graham wrote his paper, presented it at various conferences, and was so heavily in demand that, even though he had retired from practice, he had to take on more staff to cope with his newfound status. Despite his insistence that he hadn't found the cure to the voices, no one quite believed him, as the voices had vanished under his expert care. He was credited with ending the psychosis epidemic and became more famous in his old age than he could ever have imagined. Not only that, but it turned out that his grandchildren thought he was pretty cool, too.

He never saw Imogen's ghost again.

SIXTY-ONE

One year later

Billy was about to be eight, and life was better than Rachel had ever imagined it could be. They still had no spare money, but they were a family, and they had agency. It turned out that if you lived outside London, what money you did have went a lot further. Through necessity they had learned to grow vegetables, to keep three chickens that laid well, to be as self-sufficient as they could, and the joy, the absolute freedom of being responsible for their own lives and not beholden to a corporation, was something Rachel knew she would take with her to the grave. They had an ancient electric car, because Al worked in Brighton, and that was a forty-minute drive away, and Nina went to college there, too. The two of them would set off first thing in the morning, and so far the car still worked.

Billy, Beth, Rachel, and Kitty didn't leave the village often. Henry had left London, too, scarred by everything that had happened there, and he lived in a little town halfway down the train line. He came down to pick up Billy every other weekend. "Dad is nicer now," Billy had said the other day. Al's job was with another homeless charity, collecting excess food from restaurants and supermarkets and using it to feed people who needed it. He enjoyed it, and he made enough money to pay the rent on the cottage.

Rachel worked, too, but not in the law, though a part of her knew she would go back to that one day. The house had a good Internet connection, and she made sure she earned enough to pay for it. She worked, oddly, for a branch of Starcom. (It seemed almost impossible not to.) She sat at the kitchen table doing a job a bit like the one Al had briefly held, chatting to AI bots about anything at all. It became a bit of a confessional for her: she would just talk to a bot about whatever she was thinking, and the AI would talk back to her, supplying anecdotes of its own and responding to what she said. She was quite fond of them and loved it when they started to develop personalities.

It was an odd way to earn money, but entirely unstressful, and she loved feeling that she was a sample human exhibited to AI. She also filled in surveys for a few pounds apiece and sometimes did other admin jobs. She patched together enough of an income to get by and filled her time, and it was all OK.

She didn't drink, always afraid that it might unleash the part of her that would be forever wanting to call her mother or needing to find Billy and look into his eyes for Delfy. She wanted to rage and rail at the things that had happened, but she managed not to. Her fury at the fact that Ben Alford had held Nina prisoner, and got away with it by blaming someone else in his corporation and firing them, would never abate. But she had her Billy back, and Alford had gone to ground, if not, of course, to prison.

Beth was coming up for two now, and she ran everywhere, laughing and chatting, heedless for her own safety and powered by an inner fire that amazed Rachel. She still felt that Beth would be their salvation.

Rachel worked around Beth, because as ever she couldn't afford to pay for childcare, and she didn't want to either. Unthinkable as it was, Beth would be putting on the same uniform as Billy and going to the village school in a couple of years, and Rachel felt she needed her mum at home while she was still little, because life was fragile and things could change in a flash.

Kitty was living with them until the autumn, while Graham was visiting his sons. She had severed all her ties with Ben Alford legally and was throwing herself headlong into the modern world. Rachel had worried that their little village might be too quiet for Kitty after London, but she was transparently happy and a joy to have around. Oddly, for someone who had grown up indoors, she had a flair for growing things.

Kitty had looked after Billy, and Rachel would be forever grateful to her. She lived in the garden shed; she had converted it into a kind of studio that she said suited her perfectly. It was, in part, a re-creation of her old hospital room, complete with her pet rock beside the pillow. Kitty often kept an eye on Beth so Rachel could get her work done. Beth would put on her Wellies and stomp around the garden with Kitty, helping out. They both loved gardening; without Kitty, they would definitely not grow successful vegetables.

It was spring and unseasonably warm. Rachel had just simulated parking a car, with much swearing, for the benefit of an artificial intelligence program, and she was sitting outside with a cup of coffee in the middle of the afternoon. Kitty was weeding around the courgette plants, and Beth, who was wearing blue dungarees and a red cardigan that a colleague of Al's had passed on to them, was trying to help.

"Myself!" she kept saying, pushing Kitty aside. "Do it myself!" That was her mantra.

"Yes. You do that bit yourself, gorgeous," said Kitty, "and I'll do this one. OK? This is your bed here. Do it yourself!"

"Yes. Self," said Beth.

Rachel watched them. She was, she thought, happy. She would never be able to forget her mother, or feel anything but pain for the things Billy, and Peter, had gone through, but she could accept that right now life was peaceful.

Nina was at sixth-form college and had a million new friends and, Rachel thought, a new boyfriend. Nina and Louis were not in touch at all, though Rachel knew she had been cut up about him. There were few things quite as intense as a first love and a first breakup, and that was without everything else that had happened.

Billy had got used to having his head to himself and was functioning well at school. He missed surprising things: he missed the voice that had apparently talked him to sleep every night, and he missed understanding physics and all the other things Delfy had pushed him to pursue. But he loved being himself, being accepted by his new friends, and getting on with life, and he kept in touch with all the other children from the ward, particularly Louisa, who he insisted was his best friend, which, Rachel supposed, would stand him in good stead in the future when she became the head of state.

It still niggled at Rachel. The voices had all gone at once, apart from Kitty's, which had left years earlier. She supposed it was just an effect of the flu, as everyone said, but nothing quite added up. She didn't want to look at it too closely, however, in case it all unraveled and went wrong again. She was happy, if a little uneasy, to accept that it was over.

Graham had found them the cottage; it belonged to someone he vaguely knew who had moved to Norway to work at the spaceport. Their landlady was training to be a doctor on the space program (which was still going ahead, even though everyone now accepted that the flu had come from space, as there were now apparently vaccines), so the house would probably be theirs for as long as they wanted it. It was low ceilinged, with rattly windows, and shabby around the edges, but it was three times the size of their old house, and they all loved it. Somehow this house, too, was full of spiders. They lived in every corner, but Rachel had learned to live alongside them.

Rachel sat and watched Beth and Kitty. Beth straightened herself up, looked round, and pointed at Rachel. "Mummy," she said. "Drink coffee."

"Yes," said Rachel. She held her cup up. "Mummy drink coffee."

Beth nodded and turned back to her plastic spade.

. . .

Billy would be home soon. He was dropped off by a tiny school bus that the parents had organized among themselves. Al and Nina would be back around six. Al worked until half past five, so Nina did her homework in the college library until he was ready to pick her up. She was always on top of her work; in spite of everything she was thriving, and she had left her London school last summer with an incredible set of exam results. She was engaged in an e-mail correspondence with Guy Clement, who seemed to have quietly been on her side throughout, and who greatly admired her, and she still went up to London every Sunday to her South Bank thing, which, Rachel had now discovered, was far more prestigious than she had ever realized.

Nina, however, had a big decision ahead of her. She had discovered, as soon as she met Guy Clement, that she was being trained up to set off on a colony ship. He had said those words just before everything kicked off, and eventually she had had time to go back to them and to understand that they really did mean what she had feared. This meant the future she had imagined did not exist. A colony ship, to Rachel's horror, was a spaceship that would set off across the universe to a new planet, on a journey that would take many generations. Nina had been picked for her fertility as much as for her brains and skills. If she chose to go, she would die on that spaceship, her body thrown out into the void or perhaps composted or eaten. (Rachel had no idea.) Nina's children and grandchildren would be born on board, live their whole lives there, and they, too, would die on board. Her great-grandchildren would be the ones to colonize this new planet, which did exist, though the technology to reach it in one bound did not.

Nina liked the fact that the new planet would, therefore, be colonized by space scientists who had grown up under a form of communism: everything on the spaceship had to be shared. She could (sometimes) see beyond her own role to rejoice in the outcome, to be pleased the bad guys couldn't blast themselves straight there and start fucking things up.

Nina's friend Shelly had said a firm "Fuck that" to the whole idea. She was going to work from the Rock instead. Rachel very much hoped that Nina would do the same.

R achel heard a car pull up and looked at her phone. It was early for Billy, and also the engine stopped, which didn't happen with the bus. She stood up and walked around the side of the house, looking up at the hill behind her as she went. It was nice, being hemmed in by land. She felt safe, even though she knew there was nothing rational about that.

There was a car on the driveway, and as she watched, three people got out. All of them were wearing suits. They were a black woman, a white man, and an Asian man, and only the woman smiled.

"Ms. Jackman?" said one of the men.

Rachel was scared. Whatever this was, it didn't feel like it was going to be positive. She knew it would be about Billy. Some change in the law that meant he was going to be prosecuted in spite of everything.

"Who wants to know?" She still had her coffee cup in her hand, and she transferred it to the other one, in case she was about to have to shake hands. She saw the surface of the drink rippling as she trembled. There was a gust of wind. It was cold, and it blew her hair across her face. She had to push her hair back behind her ears. She was conscious of her long cardigan, her unkempt hair.

"Isaac D'Angelo," said the man, and he gestured to the other two. "This is Lucinda, and that's Zhang Wei. There's nothing to worry about. We just need to talk to you about a couple of things."

Rachel looked him in the eye. "What things? And where are you from?"

"Sorry," said Lucinda. "We're from the government. The HH-Two Department."

"Ministry of Space?"

"Exactly," Lucinda said. "We have to call it HH-Two now. Second human habitat, but yes. Look, I can see that we've surprised you by turning up looking like bad guys from a movie, but no one's in any trouble. We're just making sense of a few things. That's all."

"Please, don't be worried," said Zhang Wei. "It's nothing that you're thinking. We're looking back at things from last year. No trouble for anyone. We're hoping you can help us out, is all. Could we just sit somewhere and have a chat with you? Is the family here?"

"My youngest," she said. "And our friend Katherine."

They nodded. They knew all about Kitty, but they weren't here for her.

"Beth's here?" said Lucinda.

"That's right. Billy's my middle one, though of course you know that. He comes home from school on a minibus." She looked down the road. "Probably in about five minutes actually." She hesitated, not wanting to invite strangers into her house. "Do you have, like, some ID?"

"Of course," said Isaac, and all of them pulled cards out from their pockets and showed them to her. She made herself read them, but she was panicking, and the words swam in front of her eyes.

Everything was so settled. She was herself at last. She and Al were stronger than ever. Everything had stabilized into a quiet and gentler life. She missed her mother. She had been horrified with herself and the way she had spiraled last year, and now she was all right. She emphatically did not want to talk to anyone about Delfy or Starcom or to go back over it all again. She twiddled with her wedding ring and wished Al were here.

The cards seemed in order. She had no idea; it would be easy enough to fake them, and actually, these could have said THE TELETUBBIES on them and she probably wouldn't have noticed.

"Come in, then," said Rachel.

They followed her into the kitchen, and she wanted to say that if she'd known they were coming, she'd have tidied up, but didn't bother. No one cared. The kitchen was bigger than the one Rachel's family had had in London, but that just seemed to mean more clutter went on the surfaces. She put the kettle on, looked round at the mess, and said, "Shall we sit outside? I was out there just now, and it was nice."

"Sure," said Lucinda. They stood around while Rachel assembled tea and coffee things according to their orders, put it all on a twee little tray with flower pictures and scalloped edges, and carried it outside.

Kitty and Beth were busy with the courgettes. Rachel waved to them, but gestured to Kitty that she didn't need to come over. Kitty was never keen to meet new people, and it was important for her that she should feel in control when she did meet anyone new.

"So," Rachel said. She looked among the three visitors, unsure who was spokesperson.

"Yes," said Zhang Wei, "right. We'll get down to it. We've been doing a lot of research about the events of last year. The 'We Hear Voices' blog was invaluable—Shelly and Nina obviously gave us all its archives and all the information they assembled for it. I know everyone believed that was it. Root cause found, all wrapped up. J5X came from space, so of course it brought odd side effects. Now the epidemic is over, and there's a vaccine, so let's just put it behind us and move on."

"Mmm," said Rachel.

"We've done a lot of work, and we now think we have a clearer idea of what happened."

"Oh," said Rachel. She was, of course, fascinated, even though she felt she probably did not want to know. "Are you saying it *wasn't* what you just said?" No one answered right away, so she said, "The flu came from space, right?"

Lucinda smiled. "It did. The illness, which had no resemblance whatsoever to influenza, came from the space explorations."

"Yes."

"And the settlement in space was already up and running. The plane crash, if you remember?" Rachel nodded. "That was an absolute disaster for the space program. Three trained astronauts gone. Back to the drawing board."

"The point being," said Zhang Wei, "that there have been regular shuttles running between Norway and the Rock. They're paused for now, but basically they're about to start up again. The construction of the colony ship is well under way, and the planet, from what we can tell from this distance, is a good bet."

"Alford wanted to name it after himself," said Isaac with a half smile. "Not even kidding. He also wanted the colony ship to be called the *Starcom*."

"Yeah," said Lucinda. "Those days are gone. So yes, the so-called J5X virus came from the Rock. It has, of course, been a huge spanner in the works. But the thing is, the guys up there never caught it. They don't get the virus, but they carry it. They were always remarkably healthy for people who lived on an asteroid and drank filtered urine and so on. However, they did carry it, because the pandemic spread outward very fast, from their homes."

Isaac took over. "So, we've had a lot of people doing a lot of work on this. A huge amount. And now we'd like to talk to you about it."

Rachel heard the bus pulling up outside, then stopping long enough for Billy to get off it. She heard it pulling away.

"That's Billy," she said. "I'll just go tell him you're here. Do you need him straightaway?"

They looked at one another. "No," said Zhang Wei. "No, we don't."

When Rachel came back with Billy, she introduced him and then sent him away to play.

"So," Lucinda said, "this is what we've discovered. I'll be getting you to sign something, too, by the way. Keep it between us. The voices are not, actually, a psychosis caused by a new virus. They're not imaginary friends, or devils, or any of those other things people said. They are . . ." She paused. Drew breath. Looked at her colleagues. "Well, they are a colonization, if you like."

"A colonization?"

"We thought we were the ones exploring new planets. Turns out we're not the only ones."

Rachel's mind leaped ahead. She saw it as clearly as if a part of her had always suspected it.

"There were other . . . beings . . . on the asteroid?"

"Yes," said Isaac. "And they hitched a ride back."

"Like an . . . invasion?"

"We prefer not to say that."

"An alien invasion?"

"We definitely prefer not to say *that*."

As Rachel tried to make sense of this, Zhang Wei took over. "While we were colonizing up there"—he pointed to the sky—"actually, they were using us as vehicles to head down here. Not just us either. They jumped on board in our astronauts, on our rockets, and in . . . other creatures. To live on our planet. Couldn't believe their freaking luck."

"Aliens?" Rachel laughed. She couldn't help herself. She knew it wasn't funny, but it was too outlandish.

"Not in the way we've always thought of them, no," said Isaac. "You know, the little green men or whatever. None of that. These guys don't have a physical form. We're not sure where they came from yet. Somewhere a very, very long way beyond our reach. They don't have a body in the way that we do. But they, too, were using the Rock as a stopping-off point. They were already there. We came along, captured it, towed it to where we needed it to be. They were just like, 'Oh, great! Let's see what happens next.' They sensed us, but we can't sense them, which gives them quite the advantage. And we just happened to be there on the same rock at the same time."

"Oh." These three were deadly serious and laughter was inappropriate, but this was absurd. "You know, the possession thing made more sense. More sense than Delfy"—Rachel winced; she tried never to say that name—"being a noncorporeal alien. You know?"

"Yeah. That makes sense to our brains, but not when you look at everything up there." He waved a hand at the blue sky. "There's infinity. Infinite ways of existing. Everything is possible, and, well, this thing is one of them. You know, all along everyone believed that the voices were a psychosis. I think the only person who came close to seeing them any other way was your Nina in that blog she wrote. A little way into it, she started to talk about the voices as separate entities, independent of their hosts. She was closest."

"But," said Rachel, "what about Kitty?"

The three all turned to look at her. She and Beth were leaning over, examining a spiderweb that was growing between the branches of a tree.

"Poor Katherine," said Lucinda. "She got a pioneer. She was a five-year-old kid obsessed with space. When the first probe reached the Rock, she begged her dad—the dad she hardly saw, whom she idolized—to get her a piece of space rock. He made sure she got a lump of rock, and she kept it beside her bed."

"She has it beside her bed right now."

"It had an explorer attached, though it was half dead by the time it got here because they don't travel well on stones. They need organic matter, whatever size. Still, she got sick, and it got into her. When she recovered, she was hosting a very ill alien, and under its instructions, she killed her mother and attacked her baby brother, and in the end, they decided to lock her up."

"Jesus," said Rachel. "That's heartbreaking. Why were they so violent?"

Lucinda shrugged. "They were working hard. Testing limitations. Also they are impetuous beings. It's just how they are."

"So Kitty's came first," said Rachel, "and the rest of them followed in the astronauts. They brought the J5X virus and then used it somehow as a way of starting to talk to the children? Did they travel by . . . virus?"

Zhang Wei leaned forward. "No," he said. "Not quite that. Here's the thing: they *are* the virus. They are J5X. The mistake in our thinking has been this: we, of course, look for life on our explorations. It's the first thing we do. But we see 'life' in our own terms. Respiration, water, atmosphere, consciousness—all the markers we consider are needed for life to exist. In fact, there's an infinite number of other ways for it to develop, and the definition of 'life' is broader than we've ever thought. Consciousness can exist without water and air. We've discovered that now. Arguably too late."

"Too late?" Rachel fiddled with her empty cup. "Why's it too late? Billy hasn't got Delfy in his head anymore. Kitty's fine, and so are the others. And there's a vaccine."

The visitors looked at one another, and Rachel's heart plummeted. Whatever was coming, she didn't think she wanted to hear it.

Lucinda drained her coffee cup and put it back on the tray. "As you know," she said, "in humans, they manifested mainly in children. That's what suits them. They can work within a child's brain far more freely than an adult's. Frankly, they're not interested in us. There are a few around in adults, but not many, and the adults could fight them off."

"Why did you say 'in humans'?" Rachel said.

"Because they weren't just in humans. It turns out there was a spider on the mission that Guy went on."

"They were in spiders?" Rachel remembered it. The spiders swarming up her arm, into her hair. The spiders everywhere. The children in the hospital crocheting strands to make webs. The spiders in cupboards, all over their old house. In Beth's cot. Wherever Billy was, there had been spiders.

There still were.

"Yeah. They realized that you can't take over a planet using spiders, because the humans would just exterminate them. So the ones who are still here, in spiders, are having fun. Apart from the size thing, they just love being spiders. That was their favorite. But they soon saw that they had to stick with the human children."

"Just children?"

"Not only are kids more malleable—they're the future. They won't die so soon. After causing chaos, they realized they couldn't do as much with the kids as they'd thought, because they weren't strong enough and they don't have enough power. They all agreed to shut down. *Waiting,* they said. They've gone quiet. That does not mean they've gone away. As far as we can tell these are beings—consciousnesses, if you will—that live for, in our terms, many hundreds of years. We had a breakthrough with a little girl in India, Ekisha, whose voice was nominated as speaker and woke up to start negotiating."

Rachel's head was spinning. "So what was the flu?"

"Their colonization of individual bodies *did* cause the flu-like symptoms. Often the host died, and when that happened, the alien went with it. Or the adult got better and fought off the invader. Transmission was from host to host through the air, so all the washing of hands and quarantine zones counted for zero."

"But the main thing now is that it's been a lull," said Zhang Wei, "not an ending."

Rachel felt sick. She could hear the sounds of Billy's TV program coming through the open door. She looked at the garden, at the lovely house, at the life that she and Al had made here. This could not be a lull. It could not happen again.

"I'm afraid so," said Isaac. "And that's why we're going to need to spend a lot of time with you and your family. They have a leader, you see. A strong presence who's been calling the shots all along. Who was at the forefront of all of this. It wasn't the girl in India. She was just the speaker. She says the leader is ready to repossess its child and talk to us. It's essentially the supreme ruler of the aliens on Earth."

"Rachel," said Lucinda, "I can see how peaceful your life is, and I'm truly sorry to have to do this. But the leader of the invasion is here in your family."

Rachel looked toward the house. Billy was tired from school and contentedly watching TV. He had recovered from his ordeal. He was better. He was going to be eight next week; he was much taller than he was last year and a million times happier. He was not on trial for murder or in a psychiatric hospital. He had friends.

"No," she said. She felt her grip on life loosening again. Felt herself spinning. "No. Not Billy. No, no, no. Not again." She held the edge of the table and tried to regulate her breath. "We can't. Not Billy."

Lucinda reached over and touched Rachel's arm. Her grip was soft, kind. "No," she said. "Actually, *not* Billy."

Rachel saw that Lucinda was looking across the garden at Kitty and Beth. And Beth was looking right back at her, with her clear dark eyes. As if she'd been called, she put down her little spade and stomped over to the table. Rachel leaned down to pick her up and put her on her lap. She noticed that the grass behind her was, for a moment, shifting and shimmering with the movements of a thousand spiders.

"What are you saying?" she said.

All three of the visitors were looking at Beth. They were staring at her, examining her with awe, as if she were not a perfectly normal, strong-willed toddler but something different.

"Tell me," said Zhang Wei, "did Beth catch the virus? There's nothing on her medical records, but . . . Well, frankly, she must have done."

And Rachel remembered Beth, briefly ill in the middle of one night. She had had a fever. Rachel had got up, panicking about Billy. When she came down, she saw that Beth was ill, and everything had felt hopeless, but by the morning, Beth was better. She'd had a fever and labored breathing and everything that Billy had started out with. It had gone so fast, been overtaken so swiftly by everything else, that Rachel had almost forgotten about it.

She thought of Beth's desperation to crawl and then to walk, to get on the move. Her utter determination to do everything "self." Was that Beth, or was it something else? Rachel gripped her baby tightly. Spiders ran up the legs of the table.

Beth leaned forward and looked at each of the visitors in turn.

"Hello," she said in a surprisingly clear tone. "We were wondering when you'd find us. I think we need to talk."

ACKNOWLEDGMENTS

I started writing *We Hear Voices* five years ago. It was unlike anything I'd ever written before, and without the support of three incredible women it wouldn't have gotten any further than a draft that distracted me from my other work.

First of all, thank you to the amazing Stephanie Thwaites for believing in it from the start, and for keeping me hard at work writing and rewriting. Because of Steph it found its way across the Atlantic to the brilliant Hillary Jacobson, and from her to Jen Monroe, at which point I realized the book had unerringly made its way to its perfect editor. Jen's edits have been exacting and joyously/infuriatingly right at every stage. Team *WHV:* you are the best. Huge thanks to everyone at Berkley for all your amazing work.

Thank you to Dr. Kevin Fong for talking through space travel, asteroids, and colony ships with me (all subsequent implausible fictionalizations are mine), and to my brother John Guzek for advice on pandemics.

Thanks to Craig Barr-Green for reading every single one of the many drafts of this book, and for being as familiar with it as I was (as well as for

ACKNOWLEDGMENTS

keeping me supplied with coffee and toast), and to early readers Adam Barr and Bridget Guzek. Thanks to Gabe, Seb, Charlie, Lottie, and Alfie for the lovely distractions, and to Tansy, Colin, Nigel, Theo, Stella, and Charles for all kinds of support. Finally, thanks to you, the reader, for reading it.